DIVINER'S BOW

BAEN BOOKS by SHARON LEE & STEVE MILLER

THE LIADEN UNIVERSE®
Fledgling
Saltation
Mouse and Dragon
Ghost Ship
Dragon Ship
Necessity's Child
Trade Secret
Dragon in Exile
Alliance of Equals
The Gathering Edge
Neogenesis
Accepting the Lance
Trader's Leap
Fair Trade
Salvage Right
Ribbon Dance
Diviner's Bow

ANNIVERSARY EDITIONS
Agent of Change
Conflict of Honors
Carpe Diem
Local Custom
Scout's Progress
Plan B

OMNIBUS VOLUMES
The Dragon Variation
The Agent Gambit
Korval's Game
The Crystal Variation

STORY COLLECTIONS
A Liaden Universe Constellation: Volume 1
A Liaden Universe Constellation: Volume 2
A Liaden Universe Constellation: Volume 3
A Liaden Universe Constellation: Volume 4
A Liaden Universe Constellation: Volume 5

BY SHARON LEE
Carousel Tides
Carousel Sun
Carousel Seas

To purchase any of these titles in e-book form,
please go to www.baen.com.

DIVINER'S BOW

A New
Liaden Universe®
Novel

SHARON LEE &
STEVE MILLER

DIVINER'S BOW

This is a work of fiction. All the characters and events portrayed in this book are fictional, and any resemblance to real people or incidents is purely coincidental.

Copyright © 2025 by Sharon Lee and Steve Miller

Liaden Universe® is a registered trademark.

All rights reserved, including the right to reproduce this book or portions thereof in any form.

A Baen Books Original

Baen Publishing Enterprises
P.O. Box 1403
Riverdale, NY 10471
www.baen.com

ISBN: 978-1-6680-7252-3

Cover art by David Mattingly

First printing, April 2025

Distributed by Simon & Schuster
1230 Avenue of the Americas
New York, NY 10020

Library of Congress Cataloging-in-Publication Data

Names: Lee, Sharon, 1952– author. | Miller, Steve, 1950 July 31– author.
Title: Diviner's bow / Sharon Lee, Steve Miller.
Identifiers: LCCN 2024056814 (print) | LCCN 2024056815 (ebook) | ISBN
    9781668072523 (hardcover) | ISBN 9781964856056 (ebook)
Subjects: LCGFT: Science fiction. | Novels.
Classification: LCC PS3562.E3629 D58 2025 (print) | LCC PS3562.E3629
    (ebook) | DDC 813/.54—dc23/eng/20241127
LC record available at https://lccn.loc.gov/2024056814
LC ebook record available at https://lccn.loc.gov/2024056815

Printed in the United States of America

10 9 8 7 6 5 4 3 2 1

For Steve—always.

ACKNOWLEDGMENTS

· ·

Thanks to . . .

Nalini Singh, for keeping the psy alive

Jennifer Crusie, for the Dempsey Method

Lyn Barnes, for "Dragonflight," watercolor on paper

Maurita Plouff, for the recipe for mushrooms on toast

Special thanks to the *Diviner's Bow* Beta Readers and Tyop Hunters:

Adam, Alma Alexander, Art Hodges, Bex O,
Marni Rachmiel, Kathryn Sullivan, Gayle Surrette,
Patricia Washburn, Anne Young

CONTENTS

· · · · · · · · · · ·

Prologue
Colemeno
Second Wave

. . . .

IT WAS BEAUTIFUL, IN THE WAY THAT ORDERLY THINGS ARE beautiful. More, it would save lives.

They had lost so many lives.

It had taken them too long to understand that the atmosphere of this planet, their new home, was active. It had taken even longer to realize that it acted upon everyone differently: Some were untroubled—those were the core of their colony, strong and steady. Others were illuminated, uplifted, perhaps confused, but amenable to direction.

Still others were ignited—they burned hot, fast—and died.

It was for those, their most vulnerable, that they had undertaken this work, directed by their strong, unwavering core, built by those emboldened and strengthened by the brilliant new conditions under which they labored, calibrated by those whose lives depended upon success.

The project had required them not only to work as a team, but to learn as a team, feeling out the strange energies, understanding both the properties and the limits of possibility. Linked heart-to-heart, they undertook to create a shield under which the vulnerable might take shelter.

The forces with which they interfaced specifically rejected that intention. It was then that they understood that the scintillating ambient was a partner in their labor, and negotiation as important as either tenacity or skill.

So it was not a shield that they finally wove, but a latticework, that did not impede the energizing ambient, but slowed the rate of its benediction, from a downpour to a gentle drizzle.

1

There had been some doubt among them, that this open-work would suffice, yet they withdrew, knowing it the best—and the most—they could do, and the gods alone knew what they might try next, if it proved insufficient.

Improbably, it was enough. Those who had been stricken, their Gifts burning them to ash, recovered. Better, they thrived. Some of the stronger were able to join the subsequent work teams, that expanded the reach of the life-saving weaving.

At last the work was declared done; the Grid complete.

Those who required intervention began to build. Those who found that the Grid annoyed went out from under it, to make their own peace with ambient conditions.

Those who were affected by neither Grid nor the ambient conditions lived and worked and loved where they pleased.

And so, the world was brought into harmony.

Off-Grid
The Tree House

. . . .

IT WAS ASTONISHING HOW RELAXING IT WAS TO CHOP VEGETABLES.

Padi could cook, of course—scrambled eggs and toasted cheese sandwiches were specialties—but she was seldom called upon to demonstrate her culinary skills.

As a trader, her ability to order meals, correctly paired with beverages, sorbets, and side delicacies, where the courses flowed properly from first through last, was more important than her ability to stir a particular pot.

Aboard ship, of course, one depended on the kitchen. Padi had done her time there as an apprentice, stirring pots, learning basic tasks, safety procedures, and how to prepare such simple dishes as the cook deemed within her scope.

At home, there was also a kitchen and staff to call upon. If she should happen to fall hungry at any *very* odd hour, well—that was where her two specialties stood as allies.

Tekelia, however, not only knew how to prepare food, but enjoyed it, and was more than willing to make all their meals, if Padi so wished.

Padi had found that being in the kitchen while Tekelia prepared a meal afforded her a great deal of satisfaction, even when conversation was at a minimum. And if she was going to be in the kitchen, it seemed churlish not to offer what assistance she might.

After all, she *could* chop vegetables, stir pots, and clean up behind the cook. Indeed, those tasks were so far removed from her usual daily activities as to hold the charm of novelty.

To be in Tekelia's kitchen at the end of the day, contributing to the making of their meal, was therefore not only a privilege, but a relaxation.

She sighed lightly as she scraped chopped vegetables from the board into the bowl with the back of the blade.

"Is that sorrow?" Tekelia asked, looking around from the stove.

"Regret," Padi said, bringing the bowl over and setting it among the other prep dishes. "I have cut up all the vegetables."

"There will be more vegetables tomorrow," Tekelia offered consolingly.

"And I will be privileged to address them in their hour," Padi said. "For now, however, I move on to secondary tasks."

She leaned over to kiss Tekelia's cheek, gathered up the used bowls, and carried them to the sink.

When she had first found that Tekelia cooked most meals by hand, she had wondered why, which had earned her a sharp glance from eyes that had been in that moment one brown and one blue.

"Because I am such an immensely powerful Talent, you mean? Shall I conjure my meals from the ambient?"

Padi tipped her head, intrigued.

"Is that possible?" she asked, and Tekelia laughed.

"I can pull energy from the ambient, if I have need. But nothing so satisfying as a meal. Or even cake."

"So food must be prepared," Padi said, nodding wisely. "I offer information: equipment exists that would release you from the greater part of the labor."

"I've seen such equipment," Tekelia said. "Be warned that we're now approaching philosophy."

"I love to discuss philosophy," Padi said earnestly, and Tekelia laughed again.

"You'll find the Haosa do many things by hand that might be accomplished by equipment, or by Talent. The reason is to remind ourselves that we are not only our Gifts; that we have other talents, and relationships beyond the bond we share with the ambient."

"It keeps you grounded," Padi said. "I understand, I think. After all, one of the attractions of coming to you here—aside your company, of course!—is that I may set aside Trader yos'Galan, meet people as Padi, and attempt activities at which I might prove less than competent."

"I doubt I'll ever see you as anything less than competent," Tekelia said gallantly. Padi laughed, then, and the talk turned to other things.

"How was your day?" Tekelia asked, after they had carried their plates out to the porch and settled at the table overlooking the trees.

"Not so busy as they have been," Padi said. She used her sticks to guide crisp, spicy vegetables to her mouth, and sighed in satisfaction.

"Jes tells me that the whole port inventory is almost complete. She expects to have the final report for the master trader by the end of the week," she continued. "I just this morning finished the coursework to become certified as a route auditor, and sent the final test to be scored."

She paused for a sip of wine.

"In that regard, my timing is apt. I learned from the master trader this afternoon that the *qe'andra* who will accompany me on the audit of the Iverson Loop is also expected to arrive by the end of the week."

Tekelia sipped wine and looked at her over the rim of the glass.

"You'll be leaving soon, then?"

"I expect so, yes. Unless there is other work for me here. When it was decided that I would be the one to take the route audit, the master trader assumed that he would be on the port, rather than supervising from the *Passage*."

Thinking back to that conversation, she frowned.

"Also, I believe there's something else, though he hasn't said what it is."

"I believe I've learned there's often something he hasn't said," Tekelia commented.

Padi grinned.

"Now you see what it is to be a master trader."

"Well, he'll tell you when you have a need to know."

"Oh, no doubt there."

Tekelia laughed softly and slanted a glance in her direction.

"How long will you be traveling, when you go?"

"I'll be auditing the Long Loop. Trader Isfelm assures me that it's not nearly so extensive as the name suggests."

"Of course," Tekelia murmured.

Padi ate another bite of her meal, which really was very good, and considered the direction of the conversation. The fact that she would be leaving Colemeno had never been a secret. Still, she found herself somewhat wistful when she thought of leaving Tekelia, even as her eagerness to meet this next challenge buoyed her.

It was nothing less than the truth, that she had been born to trade. For as long as she could remember, she had wanted to be a trader, and in due course a master, one in a long line of yos'Galans traveling the stars for the betterment of commerce, and the profit of Clan Korval.

Indeed, she had so much wanted to be a trader, that she had very nearly done herself irreparable harm by locking away Talents that she had seen as endangering her preferred future.

Well, and she *had* proved herself, earning the garnet ring that marked her a full trader—not so very long ago—and coming to Colemeno as part of a team intending to open markets long made inaccessible by Rostov's Dust, and to build new routes in an expanding section of space.

She had not expected to find heart-ties here, nor this sudden alignment with her Gift. If she was honest, she scarcely knew how to properly honor everything she was becoming. The only thing she was certain of was that it would not do to lock *this* complication away, and pretend it did not exist.

She would, she thought, speak to Father. His *melant'i* was so very complex, surely he would be able to offer her insight.

It occurred to her just then that she had been wholly wrapped in her thoughts for some time, and that the silence between herself and Tekelia was not as easy as it often was.

She looked up to find that Tekelia had finished the meal, and was watching her.

"Your pardon," she murmured. "I am remiss in asking after your day."

Tekelia smiled.

"Well played, Padi yos'Galan. *My* day was tedious. I spoke to my seconds at Visalee, Deen's Fallow, and The Vinery, who have asked the Haosa at those locations if they would like to have a voice on the Council of the Civilized, and a part in ruling the planet."

A droll look followed this.

"I know you'll be surprised to learn that this is a contentious topic."

Padi laughed, and put her empty bowl on the table.

"You are of two minds yourself, as you told me," she pointed out.

"And I remain of two minds—or possibly three. The sheer amount of work that will be necessary to create a Council of the Whole—Civilized, Deaf, and Haosa together—is enough to daunt even Bentamin."

Bentamin was Bentamin chastaMeir, the Warden of Civilization, Tekelia's cousin, a Civilized Talent, as they had it on Colemeno, where the Haosa were dignified as Wild. Tekelia was Speaker for the Haosa because, as Padi had gathered, no one else had wished to take up the role of intermediary with Civilization.

"The second question—ought the Haosa voice at the council table be mine—is not nearly so contentious," Tekelia continued. "If I'm mad enough to undertake such a thing, no one will stop me."

"Then it seems the first question is resolved by the answer to the second," Padi said.

"Not quite. I may go to the table with the goodwill of my cousins everywhere. What remains at question is—will I represent them, or only myself?"

Padi frowned.

"Why would the Haosa choose to withhold themselves, now that opportunity has been offered?"

Tekelia sighed.

"For a very long time, Civilization has scorned—and feared—the Haosa. Not only that, but the manner in which many of us arrive off-Grid—cast out, and in most cases, cut off from family and friends—teaches a profound distrust."

"I can see that," Padi said, reaching for her wine glass. She sipped, and looked out over the trees.

"Do you know Majel ziaGorn?" she asked eventually.

"I know *of* him—the Deaf Councilor."

"And the trade mission's liaison," Padi added, bringing her gaze from the trees to Tekelia's face. "I don't pretend to know Colemeno history, and I am aware that your cousin is the Warden of Civilization, who very likely can advise you, but—"

She paused, frowning.

Tekelia sipped wine, and when she did not speak again, prompted, "But?"

She half-laughed.

"It's the trade, you see. So much of what I do is making connections, building networks..." She shook her head. "I'm meddling."

"Not in the least," Tekelia assured her. "I gather you think Councilor ziaGorn might be able to advise me?"

"Possibly. Despite not knowing Colemeno history, I do know—from Councilor ziaGorn—that the Deaf have not always had a voice in Civilization's deliberations. He may have a perspective that is closer to the current situation with the Haosa."

"A perspective that's not available to Bentamin. I see. Should I just—call him, do you think?"

"It would be my very great pleasure to introduce you, and I do mean that precisely," Padi said. "I fear I am a hopeless case."

Tekelia considered her from eyes that were grey and amber.

"You're a trader, surely?"

She laughed. "That, too. I made no secret of it."

"True." Tekelia sat back and raised the wine glass.

"Our next lesson with Dyoli is tomorrow night, I think?"

"It is. Will you join us for the evening meal, before?"

"I'd like that, but I'm afraid there's a complication. Eet would like to deepen his acquaintance with Lady Selph."

Padi raised her eyebrows.

"That's hardly a complication. I will of course consult the lady's preference, but assuming that she is willing to entertain Eet, you merely need to bring him. They can visit in her residence, and you may join us at the table."

"Eet," Tekelia continued, "wishes to introduce his children to Lady Selph, since they had, so I gather, figured largely in their first discussion."

"I see." Padi drank the rest of her wine, and put the glass on the table. Eet's children were Torin and Vaiza xinRood—twins—who had in the course of their eight Standards lost not only their mother, and their mother's partner, to violence, but had lately faced violence themselves, as one of their own cousins had attempted to murder them. They were not so much shy as wary, and who, thought Padi, could blame them?

"We might arrange a tray for norbears and twins to share," she said. "Or the visit might take two parts, with Eet and Lady Selph visiting privately while Torin and Vaiza eat with us. After the meal, they might be presented, and the conversation go forward."

She paused to again consider the trees, before looking back to Tekelia.

"Unless the children will be made uncomfortable eating with strangers, and outworlders, too?"

"I'll ask them what they'd rather," Tekelia said.

"A marvelous plan! You may let me know what they say when I give you Lady Selph's answer to Eet."

"More wine?" Tekelia asked.

"That would be pleasant," Padi said, rising. "Let me clear the table."

"Let me," Tekelia murmured. Bowls and sticks were gone in an instant, and were stacked, as Padi knew by now, neatly in the kitchen sink.

She would not have attempted such a 'port, out of concern for the dishes, but Tekelia not only possessed a strong Gift, but had extremely fine control.

Crossing to the rail, she looked up into the dusky sky, where the Ribbons were just rising.

"Your wine, trader," Tekelia murmured.

She turned to take the glass.

"Thank you."

"It's my pleasure," Tekelia said, leaning beside her and looking up in turn.

"I'll miss this," Padi said softly, pressing her shoulder against Tekelia's.

"The Ribbons?"

"Oh, certainly, the Ribbons!" she said. "As well as the trees, and the breeze; the village, your very audacious cousins—all of them!—Aunt Asta—"

She turned to look into eyes blue and green, before leaning forward to kiss a brown cheek.

"And you. Most of all, Tekelia."

On-Grid
The Wardian

. . . .

"YOU'RE GOING TO LIKE THIS, BENTAMIN!" MARLIN KELBIMYST predicted as she entered his office.

Bentamin chastaMeir, Warden of Civilization, looked at her over the top of his screen. Marlin was the Wardian's chief *qe'andra*, and it was rare enough to see her in his office at all, much less actually bustling.

"You're in spirits," he observed. "Will you have tea? Cookies? Wine will take a little longer, but if your news is startling enough to bring you down here to me, I think I might contrive."

She waved a dismissive hand, coming around to the side of his desk and flopping into the chair there.

"I was going to send a memo," she said. "But then I knew I had to see your face when you heard. It's not worthy of wine." She laughed, and waved her hand again. "Perhaps after all's set to rights."

"Worse and worse," he said, closing his screen and spinning the chair to face her.

"Tell me."

"I have received a petition from *Qe'andra* termaVarst, representing the kezlBlythe Family, in particular Luzant Zandir kezlBlythe, even now heroically suffering a wrongful imprisonment in the belly of the Wardian."

Bentamin snorted, then frowned.

"Wrongful? Luzant kezlBlythe was apprehended by no one less than the Chair of the Council of the Civilized, while in the act of Influencing With Intent To Gain."

Marlin raised a finger, and shook it at him.

"That is a self-serving and inaccurate description of events put forward by an overreaching government."

Bentamin raised his eyebrows.

10

"*Qe'andra* termaVarst, I take it, has an objective and accurate version of what happened?"

"Indeed. *Qe'andra* termaVarst informs us that his client, Zandir kezlBlythe, an upstanding and prominent member of Civilization, was not done the honor of being put under restraint by an equal, but was forced to suffer the indignity of—and possible contamination from—a Haosa's barbarous touch upon her person and her Talent. Said barbarian being in violation of the law that forbids Haosa to be on Colemenoport."

There was such a law, as Bentamin knew well, however—

"Councilor gorminAstir requested the Haosa's assistance in the matter, which conforms to Invitation Right," he pointed out. "The honorable *qe'andra*, and his influential client, are wasting your time."

"Yes," Marlin agreed, wilting slightly in the chair. "Yes, they are, because the damned thing will have to be answered, with statute and precedent. I'll put one of the 'prentices on it. But I thought you would be diverted by the quality of the straws being grasped for."

Bentamin rose and crossed the room to pour two cups of tea. He opened the drawer, took out the tin of Entilly's special cookies and carried it all back to the desk.

Marlin took her cup with a tip of her head.

"Not even a smile for the desperation of the kezlBlythe?"

"Well," Bentamin said apologetically, "it *is* the kezlBlythe. While I can understand that wasting your time with nonsense might be a goal, I can't think it's their *only* goal. So I wonder what else they mean to accomplish."

"There's that," Marlin said, reaching into the tin for a cookie iced in yellow.

Bentamin sipped his tea, and chose a cookie with violet icing.

"While you're here," he said, "may I ask if there's been any progress on locating Pel's files?"

Marlin sighed, as well she might. Pel chastaMeir had been a brilliant and tenacious investigator. And he had died under the wheels of a train during his investigation of the kezlBlythe Syndicate. That he had kept files—meticulous files—was not in doubt. The problem was finding them.

"The last report I have from Neeoni, just this afternoon, is that Pel's records are—dense. His partner, *Qe'andra* urbinGrant, knows that he kept deep files, and she knows he had extensive material on the kezlBlythe. Sadly, he did not share those files with her.

"Pel's assistant Osha, who has been working with Neeoni, does not have access to the deepest files, but believes there must be a key to them in the so-called second-tier files. They're searching, but—it's slow work."

"Yes, of course. Please tell *Qe'andra* Neeoni, and Osha, that I appreciate their efforts and ingenuity."

"I'll do that."

Marlin drank off the last of her tea and put the cup on the desk.

"I heard this morning from Forensics that the examination of those identified by the trade team's *qe'andra* has found some cases of possible Influence, but nothing yet to identify the actor." She sighed. "Who seems to have been very careful, indeed."

"Unlike Zandir kezlBlythe."

"Zandir kezlBlythe," Marlin said, with asperity, "has *always* believed that she was the cleverest person in the room."

Bentamin laughed. "Now, *there's* an indictment!"

"Was I too strong?" Marlin asked, with thoroughly bogus innocence. She stood. "Thank you for seeing me, Bentamin."

"Thank you for coming. I only wish it *wasn't* the kezlBlythe."

Marlin laughed, and turned toward the door.

"Now, Warden, I know you're shamming me! You've been after the kezlBlythe for years—you and Pel, both."

"And only see what happened to Pel," Bentamin said gloomily, walking with her.

He caught the edge of her concern, and the sharp glance she sent him.

"Good-night, Bentamin. Be careful."

"Good-night, Marlin. And you."

He closed the door and leaned against it, staring fixedly at nothing.

The kezlBlythe did nothing without a reason. Were they going to attempt to topple Invitation Right?

He huffed a laugh.

Toppling the whole of Civilization was not too much, if it returned to Zandir kezlBlythe the means to do harm. Also, now that he thought of it, Marlin hadn't mentioned Jorey kezlBlythe, also held in the Wardian on two charges of violent assault with intent to murder. Had the petition excluded him, as well?

If so, then it looked as if the kezlBlythe were washing their hands of a liability, kin be damned. And wasn't that true to form?

Dutiful Passage
Colemeno Orbit

. . . .

IT WAS NOTHING SHORT OF MARVELOUS, SHAN YOS'GALAN THOUGHT, surveying his inbox, how much one could accomplish, merely by writing letters.

He had written a number over the last several days, choosing his correspondents with care, and was gratified to see that two had already garnered replies.

The first was from Master Trader Til Den ven'Deelin, who stood as junior partner in the venture to reopen the Redlands system, and in particular Colemeno, to trade.

Master Til Den professed himself honored by Master Trader yos'Galan's confidence, and pleased to offer a solution to the conundrum put forth that he trusted would benefit all.

It happened that Namid ven'Deelin, Master Til Den's first tutor in the art of trade, discovered herself unsuited to a quiet retirement upon the homeworld. There was no place for her in clan administration, Ixin being fortunate in its numbers, and her proposal that she open and manage an exchange shop at Solcintra Port had not found favor with her delm.

In fact, she had recently written to Master Til Den, wondering if there was some use to which she might be put, and it struck him that Colemeno might suit her and her considerable talents well.

He trusted Master Trader yos'Galan was familiar with Trader ven'Deelin's record. Master Til Den, understanding that time was a factor, had made so bold as to bid her board ship at once. She had complied with notable alacrity, calling upon an associate who kept a courier fleet, and expected to reach Colemeno within the next week, Standard.

"Bold indeed," Shan murmured, leaning back in his chair and taking counsel of the ceiling.

As Master Til Den had supposed, he was familiar with Namid ven'Deelin's record—and with the trader herself. He knew her to be experienced, of strong character, good understanding, and tied into a contact-net worthy of a master—witness the associate with the courier fleet. Her methods were not his, but she *was* effective, and perfectly competent to handle either the details of establishing a permanent trade office at Colemenoport, or auditing the Iverson Loop.

He reached for the keyboard and composed a reply to Master Til Den, declaring himself delighted with the dispatch shown in producing so apt a solution.

You will be pleased to learn that the whole port inventory is all but completed. Preliminary reports are encouraging, and I trust that the next time I write to you, it will be with the news that we are opening Colemeno as a hub.

He signed himself as Master Til Den's partner in profit, sent the letter to the outgoing queue, and tapped up the next.

This was from Janifer Carresens-Denobli, another business partner, though of a different order altogether from Master Til Den.

Denobli was not a master trader. He was a senior commissioner of the Terran Trade Association, and the first of three ranking traders in the Carresens-Denobli Trade Syndicate.

He was clever, devious, honest, very probably dangerous—and Shan liked him extremely.

They had recently written contract together, forming a partnership on certain interesting fronts, which would possibly begin to bear fruit in two Standards. Or three.

Shan had also shared with Denobli the tale of Korval's acquisition of Tinsori Light. He had hoped this confidence would produce introductions to repair and rehabilitation enterprises that might be hired to undertake the considerable renovations needed to bring the old light station into usefulness. More, he had dared to hope for the Syndicate's support in the matter of establishing lines of credit with various of the Carresens yards.

What had materialized instead had been *Traveler's Aid*, a Terran Looper social artifact designed to provide immediate assistance to an emergency situation. Unstable systems would be stabilized, and the most necessary repairs made, while more comprehensive help was being organized.

It had been...rather startling...to find Korval the recipient of such immediate and decisive action, Korval being...rather unused to being rescued. Shan was still deciding what his feelings were on the matter, aside from a sense of mingled relief and gratitude.

He opened Denobli's letter.

Good greetings and fair profit to you, Shan yos'Galan.

I am firstly delighted with your report of progress at Colemeno, and expect hourly to hear that the inventory has proved your instincts.

Secondly, I share with you the news that Vanz Carresens-Denobli is apprentice no longer, but fully a trader. The Captains have put him to work reviving a Loop but lately relinquished by the Dust, which may prove to be mutually profitable.

Thirdly, I give you an accounting of the Family's actions on your behalf at Tinsori Light Station. The first wave of volunteers, experts, and persons of general usefulness have arrived to assist the light keepers in repair and renovation. In addition, the Captains have instructed a team specializing in Old Tech architecture to make Tinsori Light a priority. These experts will be traveling some distance, but should not be many weeks behind the second wave of volunteers, already on its way to the station.

Shan blinked. He had not expected a *second* wave, nor experts. Delm Korval had connections with Scouts experienced in the treacheries of Old Tech, and had surely already set them in motion.

On the other hand, one could scarcely have *too many* experts, given Tinsori Light's history.

So. Matters were in hand for Tinsori Light. That was well. However, there had been something else...

Shan scrolled back. Ah, yes. Denobli's nephew.

Lately, Shan had gained more information regarding this emerging route young Vanz had been set to rebuild. Interestingly, it had once linked The Redlands and the space near Tinsori Light. As he said, Denobli had his eye on profit, as what trader did not?

But there was possibly more here than mere profit, and pleasant dealings between business associates.

Vanz and Padi were of an age, of similar experience, and,

furthermore, business partners through their own devising. Denobli was audacious, as well as ambitious. The question was whether he was audacious enough to think of a marriage. Vanz was heart-struck, so far as Shan knew, and he had his uncle's support. Padi—well.

He moved his shoulders in a Terran shrug, and returned to Denobli's letter.

> *Lastly, I bring to you news that Reyshel Carresens, second administrator at Tradedesk, is agreeable to meeting you at Tinsori Light for a tour and a consultation. She asks me to inform you that she is soon to retire from her post. Because of this, she is open to a contract, if it is found that having a person experienced in modern station administration in residence would be useful to your purposes.*
>
> *I append her beam-code to this letter.*
>
> *It might be that I will join you at Tinsori Station if the timing can be made to work. I have been speaking with others of our traders, who have shared thoughts with me, which I am interested to share with you, in person by preference. Also, I have long been curious regarding that station.*
>
> *I leave you now to pursue work and happiness. Please present Trader Padi with my sincere good wishes for success in all her endeavors.*
>
> *Janifer*

Shan read the letter again. He leaned back in his chair and tapped his finger against the desk—once...twice...three times.

Administrator aside, there was nothing in Denobli's letter that required immediate action. Eventually, Traveler's Aid would come to Balancing, but that was for later. For now, let Vanz reopen the old Loop; let Colemeno be proved; and by all means let matters of the heart take their own course. Denobli was interested in strengthening his Syndicate's ties with Tree-and-Dragon. That was good. A closer alignment could only benefit both—the very definition of a successful trade.

He reached for the keyboard—and the screen pinged.

He glanced at the queue to see what had just come in, finding two messages from Colemenoport Yard. Third Mate Dil Nem Tiazan, who had for a time, some Standards in the past, been yard master at Lytaxin, had undertaken to inspect Colemenoport's equipment and give his opinion as to what would be necessary to modernize operations.

Curious to see what Dil Nem had recommended, Shan opened the message.

It was a comprehensive list—equipment and labor, all of which, Shan thought, running his eye down the screen, he could easily broker, and which would provide an influx of much-needed cash.

He smiled, opened the second message from Colemenoport Yard—and laughed aloud.

"You spoke to Dil Nem, of course," Priscilla said as he brought her a glass of cold mint tea and settled onto the couch beside her.

"I did. He allows me to know that he is willing to take the contract. Yard Master tineMena is too aware of her inexperience, and has a distrust of outworlders."

"Dil Nem," Priscilla pointed out, "is an outworlder."

"Yes, but he's a *known* outworlder," Shan said earnestly. "They've worked together; he has shown her his character and his expertise, and she feels she has his measure. She wants him there to ensure she isn't cheated, that the work is done to modern-day specifications, and also, to teach her how the new systems operate."

"I hope he negotiated a good price for all of that," Priscilla murmured.

"That falls to the master trader," Shan said, sipping his wine. "Yard Boss tineMena has provided a list and an upper limit. However, before I begin filling in fees, I must consult with you, in your capacity as captain. Dil Nem is third mate on this vessel. While the contract is lucrative and advances the master trader's plans, the ordering of ship and crew falls to the captain. Can the ship spare its third mate?"

Priscilla tipped her head, eyes slightly narrowed in thought.

"Toria Valdez is on the officer track. Whether she's ready to step up—I don't know. I'll consult with Danae—" She gave him a droll look, "with First Mate Tiazan, that is—and find what she thinks. When does the master trader need the captain's answer?"

"Tomorrow is soon enough, I think."

Priscilla nodded. "I'll talk with Danae. Is there anything else?"

Shan half-laughed.

"You are speaking to a master trader. Of course, there's 'else.' For one, Master Trader ven'Deelin has risen to the challenge cast to him, and is sending the trade mission his mother, Namid, a trader of many talents, who has found retirement to the home-world to be less enjoyable than she might have supposed."

"Trader ven'Deelin's mother," Priscilla murmured. "Is she Dyoli's mother, too?"

"She is, yes. In addition to this news, I hear from Denobli that he has found a Tradedesk administrator who will soon be retiring, and is eager to serve at Tinsori Light." He paused, brows drawn.

"It seems that retirement is not the gift that many suppose it to be, Priscilla. Shall you like to be captain when you see your hundredth Standard?"

"Will you still be a working master trader?"

"Absolutely. Nothing could induce me to retire."

"Then, yes, I'll be your captain."

He smiled, and leaned over to kiss her cheek.

"We have an accord," he murmured. "Thank you, Priscilla."

Colemenoport
Wayfarer

. . . .

IT WAS A COMFORTABLE ROOM, LARGE ENOUGH TO ACCOMMODATE a desk, screen, comm, and other accouterments of business on one side; bed, wardrobe, and reading chair on the other.

Between those two zones was a window to the outside. Before the window was a table. On it was a . . . construct of a slightly fanciful design. The front walls and the crenelated rooftop were transparent at the front, shading to opaque at the back, giving the impression of public rooms and private.

To call this construction a cage would be to do it, and its inhabitant, a severe disservice. Certainly, it was meant to guard its resident from the outside world, but equally it was meant to protect the outside world.

Locally, it was known as "Lady Selph's Residence," and this evening the lady herself was visible just inside the front wall, sitting dignified and tall, ears perked in an attitude of attention.

Mist swirled at the center of the room.

Lady Selph sat taller, front paws folded over the furry mound of her belly.

The mist swirled more tightly, thickened—and dissipated, leaving behind four persons. Two were tall—one dark, one fair—and two were small, very similar in shape and face.

"Here we are," Padi said, releasing Tekelia's hand before freeing Vaiza.

Tekelia slid a bag from one shoulder and offered it to Torin, who accepted it with a smile before looking inside.

"Eet," she said, "we're here."

Vaiza spun on his heel, and stopped, facing the residence and the dignified lady there.

"Is that her—Lady Selph? She's *beautiful*," he whispered loudly.

"Oh." Torin came to his side, and made a little bow. "Lady Selph, hello." She glanced down at the bag, from which a furry striped head was now protruding. "Eet told us about you."

Lady Selph trilled, and Eet answered, scrabbling a little against the bag.

"It seems that Eet and Lady Selph would like to speak together privately, while we share a meal with others of your team," Tekelia said, and looked to Padi. "Do I have that correctly?"

"You do. I'll call down for a fresh tray, if you'll help Eet get settled."

She went to the comm. Tekelia ushered the children and Eet to the residence.

By the time the tray had arrived, Eet and Lady Selph had gone deeper into the residence. Padi placed the tray at the food station inside, made sure the fountain was flowing freely, and that the water in the pool was clean and plentiful.

When she was done, she locked the door to the residence, and sat back on her heels to look at the twins.

"Do you have any questions, before we go to the other room?" she asked.

"No, thank you," Torin said politely.

"Will Warden Bentamin be there?" Vaiza asked.

"No, only members of the Tree-and-Dragon Trade Team, and not all of us. This evening, I believe we will have, in addition to ourselves, Dil Nem Tiazan, Dyoli ven'Deelin, and Mar Tyn pai'Fortana."

The twins exchanged a glance.

Padi met Tekelia's eyes over their heads. The twins had previously agreed to share the meal, but if there was a failure of courage now, the four of them could certainly picnic in the garden on the Wayfarer's roof.

She felt Tekelia agree with this alternate plan, and had just drawn breath to suggest it aloud, when Vaiza took Torin's hand.

"We *said* that we would," he said. "And I'm sure they're *nice* people. They won't let Cousin Jorey in."

"Indeed, we will not!" Padi said with feeling. "My best knowledge is that Jorey kezlBlythe is restrained in the Wardian. In addition, he is absolutely *not* invited to share *any*thing with us, and I will personally show him the door, should he arrive."

Vaiza leaned closer to his sister.

"She can do that," he whispered loudly. "We saw her."

Torin laughed, which was not so usual a thing for Torin, and looked up at Padi.

"In that case," she said, sounding considerably older than her eight Standards, "my brother and I will be glad to share a meal with the Tree-and-Dragon Trade Team."

Padi had previously given the team notice that there would be guests, so there was no surprise when she brought Tekelia and the children into the common room.

Tekelia was well-known to everyone present, and had even managed to inveigle Dil Nem into informality, which was proved now, as that gentleman inclined his head with evident delight.

"Tekelia," he said, "well-met."

"Dil Nem, it's good to see you," Tekelia answered.

"And these are?" Dil Nem inquired, looking at the twins.

"These," Tekelia said obligingly, "are Torin xinRood and Vaiza xinRood. They escorted Eet to his meeting with Lady Selph, and will be speaking with her themselves a little later.

"Torin, Vaiza—here is Dil Nem Tiazan, a member of the Tree-and-Dragon Trade Team."

"Dil Nem is third mate on our ship, *Dutiful Passage*," Padi added.

Dil Nem bowed with grave formality. "I am pleased to make the acquaintance of Torin and Vaiza xinRood."

The twins bowed in their turn—and Vaiza said, "Good meeting, sir."

Padi turned as Dyoli and Mar Tyn approached.

"Here are Dyoli ven'Deelin and Mar Tyn pai'Fortana. Dyoli and Mar Tyn, I bring Torin and Vaiza xinRood to your attention."

Mar Tyn smiled. "Good meeting," he said.

Dyoli took a step forward, and bowed lightly, in the Colemeno style.

"Good meeting, Torin and Vaiza xinRood," she said, straightening with a smile. "We are cousins, you know."

The twins exchanged a glance, not entirely unworried. Given the class of cousins they had been accustomed to, Padi allowed that a certain wariness was merely prudent.

"Cousins?" asked Torin. "But you're not from Colemeno."

"I am from Liad," Dyoli admitted. "Some of the ancestors of the people who now live on Colemeno came from Liad."

"We learned that in school," Torin admitted, though she was still frowning.

"I admit that it is a distant connection, but I would not be averse to pursuing it, if you would like it, as well."

"I would like to hear more," Torin said, and looked to Vaiza. "Brother?"

"I think it would be *interesting* to be cousins with someone from another world," Vaiza said, and looked past Dyoli to Mar Tyn.

"Are you our cousin, too, sir?"

"I very much doubt it," he answered. "However, I stand on no ceremony with friends. I wonder if you would call me Mar Tyn, as my other friends do."

Padi stood quietly, watching. Dyoli was a Healer, after all. The twins were orphans; their mother and her partner murdered by the same cousin Jorey who had recently tried to kill them. She must have Seen the children's distress. And while the care of the Haosa was not to be discounted, to have kin—or at least someone standing as kin—might go somewhat toward easing them.

"I'll call you Mar Tyn," Vaiza stated, "and you'll call me Vaiza."

"Done!" Mar Tyn said. "Shall we drink on it?"

Vaiza hesitated, glancing at Torin. Something passed between them, though Padi could not have said what, and Vaiza stepped toward Mar Tyn.

"Yes, let's! Do you have lemonade?"

"The kitchen just now sent up a fresh bottle. It's over here on the tray," Mar Tyn said, leading the way.

Torin looked at Dyoli.

"You're a Healer, Tekelia told us."

"That is correct," Dyoli said. "Do you require Healing?"

"I don't know," Torin said, and turned to look at Tekelia, who was in close conversation with Dil Nem. "The Haosa treat us well. They protect us and—and Vaiza likes it very much, off-Grid. Only, it's—I'm so tired. I don't think I was, before. Even when I was helping Vaiza. Can you Heal me of being tired?"

"Perhaps," Dyoli said seriously. "First, you and I will need to discover *why* you are tired. I can Scan you briefly, with your permission, to find if there is anything obvious."

Torin straightened. "Yes, please. I give my permission."

Padi stepped back to Tekelia's side to give Dyoli and Torin at least the illusion of privacy.

"Wine, Padi?" Dil Nem asked.

"Thank you. The white, if you please."

He moved in the direction of the tray, and Padi turned to Tekelia, who had already been supplied with a glass of the red.

"Will the Haosa object to Dyoli Scanning Torin?" she murmured.

"No, how could we? Torin asked for herself; there was no coercion. And we both know Dyoli for a deft and patient practitioner."

"Being our teacher, as she is," Padi said, and turned with a smile as Dil Nem arrived with her glass.

"We seldom see Dil Nem at Prime," she said, for Tekelia's benefit. "Are you in disgrace, Cousin?"

"In fact, my task is complete," Dil Nem said. He glanced at Tekelia. "It's been my part to study the shipyard and its systems and give advice on how to bring it into the modern era."

"Was that interesting?" Tekelia asked, perhaps lightly.

"In fact, it was," Dil Nem answered seriously. "It's no ordinary thing to tour a working yard brought intact out of the past. Also, it was a challenge, to find what can be retrofitted, what must be replaced with new, and how to bring it all online to work together. Colemeno Yard has been keeping those ships that come in up to spec and holding air since before the Dust enfolded this section of space—all honor to Yard Master tineMena and her predecessors. The last parts ship was stripped of its final gear cog a decade ago. Now they machine their own."

"I'd like a tour," Padi said suddenly.

Dil Nem bowed slightly.

"I can arrange that, but—why?"

"I'm to audit the Iverson Loop, and I suspect that all the yards and repair stations along the route are in similar straits. I ought to know what such a yard looks like when it is working and in good order."

"That's not a bad notion," Dil Nem acknowledged, and looked to Tekelia. "Shall I include you?"

"Yes," Tekelia said, after a pause. "Ship yards are utterly outside of my experience, so you'll have much to explain."

"I am always pleased to amend ignorance," Dil Nem said,

which was what passed for his humor. He sipped his wine, and looked to Padi. "Will tomorrow morning suit you, Trader?"

"It will," Padi said, "and Jes will thank you, because you know I will only be in her way if I stay at the office."

"Good to have a *qe'andra* grateful," Dil Nem said, and looked to Tekelia. "Is tomorrow morning convenient for you, Speaker?"

"Why, yes, since you're so good as to invite me."

A chime sounded from the kitchen area, signaling the arrival of the food lift.

"I will serve," Padi said. "Tekelia, will you gather the children?"

"I think the twins are in good hands," Tekelia said, nodding toward the sofa. Dyoli and Torin sat on one end, in close conversation, while Mar Tyn and Vaiza sat on the other, similarly engaged.

"I'll put our glasses on the table," Tekelia said, "and help you serve."

The meal had been pleasant, the conversation driven by Vaiza's wish to know what it was like to live on a ship in space, and was it lonely, without gardens or the wind or the sky?

Third Mate Tiazan was able to assure the young gentleman that *Dutiful Passage* was large enough to accommodate an atrium, where there were flowers and trees. Padi spoke of the hydroponics section, which provided the ship with fresh fruits and vegetables.

"Is the ship its own Grid?" That was Torin's question, and Padi looked at her thoughtfully.

"In a way, perhaps it is. It may seem very strange to you, but, in most of the places I've been—other worlds and other ships—the ambient has been...much less apparent than it is here on Colemeno."

Torin looked at Tekelia, who turned palms up with a laugh.

"It sounds strange to me, too."

"And, yet, it's exactly the case," Dyoli said. "It's been quite a challenge for us to learn how to go on under the Grid. I should like one day to go outside, to find what that is like."

"Easily arranged," Tekelia said. "Only tell me when you would like to make a visit."

"I will, thank you." She looked down-table. "Mar Tyn? Shall you wish to go off the Grid?"

Mar Tyn glanced at Tekelia.

"I wonder what would be the effects," he said slowly. "I

noticed a . . . difference in my Gift the moment we arrived on Colemeno's dock."

"To stand under the free ambient is a risk for all of us who are Gifted," Tekelia said. "Some find it so noisy that they're not able to access their own Talent. Others find that the ambient buoys them. If you would like to experience a lack of filter, I would take you to Pacazahno. It's off-Grid, but the ambient is less boisterous than we have it at Ribbon Dance Village."

Mar Tyn frowned. "I wonder if you could help me understand something."

"I'll try."

"On Liad, I'm known as a Luck."

"I See it in you," Tekelia assured him, and smiled. "The wildest Talent of all."

Mar Tyn raised his eyes, surprised, Padi thought.

"Under the Grid, I am dignified as a Serendipitist, and the documents I've read make the assumption that I am able to . . . exercise control over my Gift and moderate its action. Lifelong, my experience has been that my Gift overrides my own will and preferences, even to putting my life in danger."

"But since we've been here, on Colemeno," Dyoli said, "you *have* been able to foresee the outcome of ceding to your Gift, and moderate its effect."

Mar Tyn turned his gaze to hers, his face displaying shock.

"*That* is the difference," Dyoli said, positively. "You are no longer wholly at the beck of your Talent."

"The Grid might be working for you in that way," Tekelia said. "Serendipity isn't common. To your other point—Civilization insists that every practitioner be in control of their Gift."

Mar Tyn inclined his head.

"I would like to experience the ambient when it is not filtered," he said.

"I'll be happy to be your guide, at a mutually convenient time," Tekelia said.

"As to that, it will be after the inventory is done—" Mar Tyn started, and turned in his chair to look at the big clock in the foyer. "I regret," he said, turning back to the table, "I am on-shift with Jes this evening. The last data packets will be coming in."

He turned to Vaiza. "Duty calls me, but I hope you won't allow our friendship to languish." He reached into his sleeve pocket and withdrew a card. "Here is my comm code and my address. I would very much like to hear from you."

"Thank you," Vaiza said softly, taking the card and holding it tightly in his hand. "I don't have a card, and I don't remember the comm code at Rose Cottage."

"That's all right," Mar Tyn said, "you'll send it to me in your first letter."

He got to his feet, bowed to the table, and took Dyoli's hand in his.

"I have no idea—"

"Of course you don't," she interrupted. "I am promised to Padi and Tekelia for the next hour, but after—tell Jes she may call on me at need."

"I will," Mar Tyn promised, and left them.

"Does anyone wish more or something in addition?" Padi asked the table. "A sweet, perhaps?"

Vaiza and Torin looked at each other, apparently considering the sweet, but Dil Nem spoke before they did.

"The youngers and I will clear the table, then I'll take them in to see her ladyship, if that will suit you, Padi?"

"Thank you, Dil Nem," she said, and looked to Dyoli.

"I think we've been sent to our lessons."

Dyoli smiled. "I think so, too."

"That was an interesting question Torin had," Padi said.

"If the ship is its own Grid?" Dyoli nodded. "I thought so as well."

"She's quick, our Torin," Tekelia said. "And I'll own that her question—and your answers—waked in me a very strong desire to visit *Dutiful Passage*. I've never experienced a location that is utterly free of the ambient."

"As to that..."

Padi frowned at Dyoli.

"I wonder—is...Healspace not the ambient?"

Dyoli turned her hands palms up.

"I was taught that we each carry Healspace within us," she said slowly. "That said, I may bring a client with me into my Healspace for therapy. Also, I may meet other Healers in a shared environment that we *call* Healspace, which is, so I had always thought, a merging of separate internal spaces for a unique purpose. Now, I wonder if that...is not quite the operation we are seeing. If perhaps between myself and my colleagues, we create a space unique to *us*."

Tekelia stirred.

"When Padi and I first met, she was looking for Healspace."

"And found you, instead, waiting to serve me tea and cookies," Padi said.

Dyoli tipped her head. "So you allowed Padi into your own space, Tekelia?"

Tekelia sighed.

"Understand that 'Healspace' isn't a concept that readily translates to Colemeno. If I wish to create an isolated area for thinking or for working, my need is to shut the ambient *out*. The ambient is of course *ambient*. It flows through, and informs, me. If I've blocked its influence in order to do fine work, then I need to draw on the energy resident in myself."

Tekelia threw a glance at Padi.

"And I had best have set out cake and sweet tea for when I'm done."

She laughed, and Tekelia turned back to Dyoli.

"I Saw Padi's father enter Healspace, when we were together on Ribbon Dance Hill. It seemed to me that he merely...*stepped aside*, as one does in order to examine one's inner condition."

Dyoli raised her eyebrows, and Tekelia grinned.

"I agree—not the most helpful description. It was the first time I had Seen that particular combined use of the ambient and a personal link to establish contact, heart-to-heart."

Dyoli sat back in her chair.

"Since I was not present, I will ask that we put this discussion aside until we have Padi's father with us, and may ask him to demonstrate his technique.

"Before we commence our lesson, I have a question for Tekelia."

Tekelia smiled. "Ask."

"Who are the guardians of Torin and Vaiza?"

"The Haosa of Ribbon Dance Village acknowledge the twins as our children," Tekelia said promptly. "Just now, they are living with Geritsi slentAlin and Dosent. Geritsi is...a peaceweaver, we say. Dosent is a *sokyum*—a native feline, very protective. She and Geritsi are bonded."

Padi blinked, and Tekelia turned to her.

"Yes?"

"I saw Geritsi hit a man in the head with a shovel."

"She was very angry," Tekelia said gravely.

"And justly so," Padi said, with equal gravity. "I admire her restraint now, as then. But—why is a *peaceweaver*...Haosa?"

"Because her mere presence in a room is sufficient to cool high feelings and soothe agitated nerves. This isn't something that she can *not do*, you understand; it's at her core. The Civilized, who have appointed themselves the sole arbiters in these matters, decreed that she is an Influencer. Since she is unable to control her Talent, she is Haosa."

Padi closed her eyes.

"Yes," Tekelia said. "Exactly."

"Is Geritsi slentAlin the person I would ask if I might see Torin and Vaiza in my capacity as a Healer?" Dyoli asked into the silence that followed.

Tekelia turned to her. "You may ask me. I take it that you've Seen their connection?"

Dyoli sighed sharply. "I've Seen something very odd, which I don't quite understand. My Scan this evening suggests that it was...imposed. Manufactured." She looked sharply at Tekelia. "Understand that I am speaking of something other than their heart-link."

"I do understand," Tekelia assured her. "And it happens that the village has already agreed that this construct, which bewilders us as much as it does you, needs to be dealt with by a trained Healer. Which on Colemeno means a Civilized Healer. We of the Haosa who may have the Gift don't have the training, which makes us—"

"Hammers," Padi murmured.

Tekelia grinned at her. "You have a retentive memory. But Dyoli already knows I'm unsubtle."

"True, but I don't despair of teaching you a softer touch," Dyoli said. "Have the Haosa commissioned a Healer?"

"On the advice of our medic, and with the agreement of the village, I petitioned my cousin Bentamin to find us an appropriate Healer. The last time we spoke, he hadn't yet been able to locate a practitioner who will consent to examine a Haosa child."

Tekelia paused. Dyoli said nothing, though there was a certain...warmth in the ambient.

"As to the construct itself," Tekelia continued, "it's the opinion of our medic that, while it might once have been benign, it will inevitably become a danger to both. Already, there's some stretching apparent in their patterns. While we don't think there's immediate danger, it seems best to deal with the situation as soon as possible."

Dyoli's eyes had narrowed.

"Is that it? One is Civilized, and the other Haosa? And someone wove their patterns together. But—why?"

"We believe the weaver to have been their mother, now deceased. We also believe that it was a form of protection. It's probable that she meant to undo the work when their situation was...less dire, and before harm was done."

"I...see." Dyoli sighed. "Please tell me the proper way to bring myself to the Warden's attention. I am a classically trained Healer who has no objection to Haosa children. I would first wish to examine them both in as quiet an environment as can be managed, in order to understand what has been done. I cannot promise that I will be able to undo the weaving entirely, but it might be possible to mitigate it."

Tekelia inclined slightly from the waist in a seated bow.

"On behalf of Ribbon Dance Village, I accept your offer to assist our children. We can provide a shielded environment in which you may work, and will accommodate ourselves to your schedule."

"That's all?" Dyoli said.

Tekelia smiled. "One more thing. I'll tell Bentamin that we've located a qualified Healer. May I tell him who it is, if he asks?"

"Certainly. As to timing—it will be after the final report has gone to the master trader. May I call you—or Geritsi?"

"Here." A business card appeared in Tekelia's right hand, a pen in the left. Tekelia wrote, and held the card out to Dyoli. "My comm code, and Geritsi's, too."

"Thank you." Dyoli glanced over Padi's shoulder to the clock.

"This evening's lesson will be brief," she said. "Padi, if you please, extend a line of calmness to me."

The session *had* been brief, but intense. They had scarcely finished when the comm chimed in a particular sequence.

"That will be Jes," Dyoli said, and rose to answer the call.

Padi sighed, closed her eyes, and sank back against the sofa cushions. Healer training with Dyoli always left her adrift in her emotions, and aching in muscles she did not physically possess.

Carefully, she reviewed a mental exercise taught to pilots, centering herself.

She heard Dyoli say, "Yes, of course. I am on my way," and opened her eyes.

"Am I wanted as well?"

"Jes did not ask for you, Trader. In fact, she said she hoped you would enjoy your evening off."

Padi laughed.

"A threat, in fact!"

"Only a warning, I'm sure," Dyoli said, and was gone, the door closing behind her.

Padi looked to Tekelia.

"Should we find the children?" she asked.

"They are still with Lady Selph and Eet. Dil Nem is with them. We possibly have time to sit and rest before we must gather us all up and go home."

Padi smiled. "You are persuasive."

"Of course I am. Stay, and I'll bring the wine."

Tekelia rose and went to the buffet. Padi settled more closely against the cushions.

Home, she thought, and it was the house overlooking the trees, with the glint of the river below, and the glory of the Ribbons above, that came first to mind, rather than her quarters on the *Passage*, or her suite at Jelaza Kazone, Korval's clanhouse on Surebleak.

"Have I made a misstep?" Tekelia asked, placing the glasses on the table and sinking onto the couch at her side.

Padi shook her head.

"Not at all. I was merely reflecting on the fact that my suite at our house—the yos'Galan Line-house, I mean—had used to be *home*."

"Is it no longer?" Tekelia asked.

"It no longer exists," Padi said, reaching for her glass and raising it in a small salute. "Trealla Fantrol—our house, you understand—was...unmade before we left Liad. Father is building a new house, on Surebleak..."

"But it is not built yet, and *your* rooms are still gone," Tekelia finished for her. "I offer my house as your home for as long as you have need."

Padi laughed.

"It is precisely your house that—"

The door to Padi's suite opened, and Dil Nem stepped out.

"Your pardon, Trader. The master trader is on-comm for you."

Padi turned.

"Are the children still speaking with Lady Selph?"

"They are."

"Then please transfer the master trader's call to the common room unit," Padi said.

"Yes, Trader."

Padi rose and crossed to the comm. "Excuse me. I must take this."

"Of course you must," Tekelia said, rising in turn. "While you're busy, I'll pay my respects to Lady Selph."

"Good evening, Trader Padi. Forgive me for interrupting your reception."

"Hardly a reception, sir. Tekelia and I had brought Torin and Vaiza xinRood and their norbear, Eet, to visit Lady Selph. It transpired that Eet's topic was personal, so the children and Tekelia joined those of us who were in-house for the meal."

"It sounds a pleasant evening. I will attempt to be brief so that you may return to your guests.

"I have received the preliminary data from *Qe'andra* dea'Tolin, who tells me that the final report will be complete and ready for the master trader's review within the next day or two. Have you seen the preliminary report, Trader?"

"Yes, sir, I have. *Qe'andra* dea'Tolin has included me in her work, and has been so good as to illuminate those points that I found obscure. I understand that the data trends in favor of establishing Colemeno as a trade hub."

"Absent last-minute catastrophes, discovered in the final stages, which none of us expects—yes. This means that I will be required down-world, to plead the trade mission's case with the port, and with the Council for the Civilized. Should I win permission to proceed in developing a hub, I will file with the Guild, and make whatever adjustments are necessary to the team-in-place. Then, I will be on my way."

Padi took a breath.

On his way. Of course, she had *known* that he would be leaving Colemeno. A master trader could scarcely afford to sit 'round one world indefinitely. Indeed, purely from the standpoint of profit-and-loss, Master Trader yos'Galan, and *Dutiful Passage*, had already spent more time than was profitable on Colemeno.

Still, to hear it *said* brought a sudden shortness of breath, and a sting to the eye—

"Trader Padi?"

"Here, sir. I was—taking a moment to adjust my thinking."

"I understand. There are personnel developments of which you should be aware. As you know, we shortly expect the arrival of our *qe'andras*. We are also expecting the arrival of Trader Namid ven'Deelin, who will assist in the work going forward."

Padi blinked.

"In what capacity, sir?"

"A sapient question! Trader ven'Deelin is widely experienced. She might just as easily remain on Colemeno as our trade face, or undertake an audit of the Iverson Loop."

But that scarcely explained anything, Padi thought.

"I am—confused," she said slowly. "Does Trader ven'Deelin arrive without knowing her role?"

"She comes to us ready to serve in whatever capacity may be required. I hope to be able to clarify necessity for her when she arrives."

There was a pause, very slight.

"Padi yos'Galan, your thodelm has a question. May you answer him?"

"Indeed, I may answer Lord yos'Galan," Padi said, pushing away the whirl of her own questions. Thodelm yos'Galan was very seldom brought forth. On the route, the master trader was the ultimate authority. The thodelm's care was limited to kin, Line and Clan.

"Very good. Your thodelm asks, young Padi, after your relationship with Tekelia vesterGranz. I am informed that you 'dance together.' My duty to Line and Clan requires that I understand the breadth and depth of that dance; what is owed, and what is owing. These things must be regularized before the master trader departs Colemeno orbit."

Oh. Oh, *dear.*

Padi felt a flutter of dismay, and took a breath, holding herself calm so that Tekelia would not be distracted by her distress.

After a moment, she addressed herself to her thodelm.

"I have spoken to Tekelia, sir, and have learned that we share a bond that is unique to ourselves. Local custom celebrates this bond as 'dancing together.' Tekelia sees no need to define the relationship more closely, and nor do I." She bit her lip. "I remind the thodelm that Tekelia vesterGranz is not Liaden."

"Nor was your grandmother," the thodelm said, and Padi heard him sigh.

"Duty and the delm require a more regular answer. I therefore ask you to assist me."

"I will do my best, sir."

"Very good. I will wish to meet with yourself and your dancing partner during the master trader's upcoming visit to Colemeno. Such a meeting must of course be held on neutral ground. Please locate an appropriate venue and see it secured for our use."

Padi felt a hand on her shoulder, and sat back in her chair. Tekelia *had* heard her dismay, and had arrived to take part in this conversation, which, to be fair, was as much about Tekelia as it was about Padi.

And that, she realized, her stomach sinking, handily carried the thodelm's point for him.

"I advise the thodelm that Tekelia vesterGranz has joined me at the comm. The question of a neutral venue ought best, I think, to be put there."

"I agree. Tekelia vesterGranz, this is Thodelm yos'Galan. Do you understand?"

"Somewhat, sir. I fear my facility with *melant'i* is less than expert, though Padi has been teaching me. I believe I understand that you wish to meet with us to discuss . . . formalities of Liaden Code?"

"Admirably phrased. Yes, precisely. *Melant'i* dictates that the venue neither favor nor disadvantage any of the participants unequally. Is there such a place on Colemeno?"

"We might use the shielded rooms above Peck's Market," Tekelia said. "However, I wonder if it wouldn't be better if Padi and I came to you."

Padi laughed.

"Coming to me would require you to board *Dutiful Passage.*

Forgive me if I overstep, but that seems to hold the potential to disadvantage you—greatly," the master trader said.

"With respect, sir, we don't know that. I'm willing to waive my right to perfect equality for a chance to experience an environment which is, as Padi tells me, ambient-free. If I'm disadvantaged, I trust Padi to guard my interests."

There was silence, much longer than lag could account for, before the master trader spoke again.

"Has no one from Colemeno ever boarded a spaceship? Ships *do* come to you—the Iverson Loop, and others."

"Yes, sir, they do, and it's possible that some one or other of the Civilized *has* been aboard a ship—even traveled. If they did, they didn't speak publicly about their experience. Civilized law forbids Haosa the port, unless invited, as I think you know. If I understand the purpose of the trade mission correctly, we'll be seeing more ships at Colemeno, and the Haosa...It would be helpful to know if we can profit from the changes that are about to occur."

"Ah."

Another long pause. Padi turned to look up at Tekelia, who met her eyes with a smile.

"The master trader advises me that he is willing to bring Trader yos'Galan and Speaker vesterGranz aboard the *Dutiful Passage* so that Trader yos'Galan may attend to necessary business, and Speaker vesterGranz may gather data of import to the Haosa," Thodelm yos'Galan stated. "If conditions allow, and all parties agree, it is possible that the thodelm's purpose may also be accomplished during this visit. If conditions do not allow, the meeting will be postponed until it may take place in the shielded rooms above Peck's Market. Be advised, both, that this is *not* optional."

"Yes, sir," Padi said.

"Yes, sir," Tekelia said.

"Trader Padi," the master trader said, "I will expect you immediately after *Qe'andra* dea'Tolin has filed the final report. You will please find from Lady Selph if she is ready to rejoin her cuddle. If she is, please bring her with you."

"Yes, sir. Is there anything else?"

"Do you know?" Father said, "I think not, at this present. Go back to your guests, child. Sleep well."

"Sleep well, Father. Give my love to Priscilla."

"Of course. Tekelia-*dramliza*, a good evening to you."

"Good evening, sir," Tekelia said.

Padi ended the call, and turned in her chair to meet Tekelia's eyes.

"Why—" Tekelia began—and stopped as the door to Padi's room opened, admitting Torin, Vaiza, Eet in his carry bag, and, somewhat less exuberantly, Dil Nem.

Tekelia stepped back and Padi rose.

"Has Lady Selph dismissed you from her presence?" she asked.

"She said she needed to dream on us," Torin said, "and told Eet to take us home."

"Dismissed, indeed," Padi said, meeting Dil Nem's eyes over Vaiza's head. He moved a shoulder. Nothing untoward, then. She looked back to the twins.

"Would you like some cake before we go?"

Wildege
Kelim Station

. . . .

THEY FINISHED PACKING THE WAGON JUST BEFORE RIBBON-RISE.
Vyr went back to the domi to start the meal, leaving Kel to tighten
the tarp and check the balance one more time. It was an old wagon;
the spin-lifts tended to get cranky with an unbalanced load, and
walking into Visalee to barter for a repair wasn't in Kel's plans.

So, one more check, a tug on the ropes, and back to the
domi for dinner.

Kel paused at the center of the clearing to look up past the
highest branches of the highest trees, into the bowl of a sky
flushed with dancing colors. She could feel the Ribbons at the
core of her, and raised her arms as if she were a tree herself,
reaching for the sky, drinking in the ambient. Kel danced—six
steps—then another six, before she remembered Vyr, the domi,
and the promise of supper waiting.

Maybe she'd come out later, she thought, after the meal, when
Vyr was asleep. Come out and dance for true.

Maybe she'd do that.

Sure.

"So," Kel said, after they'd tasted the dinner—which was
wonderful as always; Vyr had a Talent for cooking. That was
Kel's opinion. Vyr said there was no such thing as a Talent for
cooking, as if that settled anything. You might as well say that
there was no such thing as having a Talent for wood.

"So," Kel said again, and waited until Vyr looked up, green
eyes like glass in a wary brown face. "You'll be coming with me."

She put it like it was a certainty, having learned that asking
was a certain loser, while assumption sometimes took the trick.

But not this time.

"No," Vyr said, his voice brittle, "I'll overload the wagon."

"Won't," Kel said. "I left off one of the burled slabs. You don't weigh near, so there'll be room for extra food."

"Take the burl," Vyr said. "I'll stay here."

Normal times, that would be the end of it, Vyr not having a particularly changeable nature, and Kel not wanting a fight. Tomorrow, though, that was something a little out of the way. Midsummer Market at Visalee, which Kel had certainly been to, on no set schedule, for trade or supplies. But this was the first time she was going on purpose to one particular Market, and for the whole week, too.

Kel was inclined to wonder at herself, now she was on the edge of leaving, but, there. Nimbel had Seen it, as many as six Wild wagons at Midsummer Market, and the Seeing had moved him to take the unprecedented step of visiting his neighbors to share it.

"Something dark riding the Ribbons," is what he'd said, sitting at Kel's kitchen table, and having a sip of cider. "Whatever it is, it ain't gonna miss us, no matter how deep we go into the trees. Best we find what the village-bound know." He'd finished the cider and thumped the mug to the table, giving Kel a look that was equal parts dread and glee.

"Aside all that, Midsummer Market's a party bar none."

Nimbel's Sight, so far as Kel knew, was as erratic as any Seer's. But this was the first time in all the years she could remember that he'd cared to leave his station, and travel the not-inconsiderable distances to tell his neighbors what he'd Seen.

It wouldn't be the first time trouble had ridden the Ribbons, Kel knew; and it wouldn't be the last, trouble being the natural condition of humankind. She'd found herself agreeing to go, and besides—she hadn't been to a proper party in too, too long.

So, Kel's reasoning went now, if Nimbel could leave his station, to share his Seeing, the least she could do in the here-and-now was to try one more time with Vyr, though she didn't expect his answer to change.

And, unless an increase of irritation counted for change, she wasn't wrong.

"I said I'll stay here," Vyr snapped. "Leave it alone, Kelim."

Her whole name. Well, *that* was never good. Kel dug back into her dinner.

"Good meal tonight," she murmured, by way of a peace-gift.

In the normal way of things, Vyr would answer that hunger was a better spice than anything he could put into dinner, and they'd be back on their usual footing.

Only this time, Vyr didn't answer—at all.

Kel looked up. He had pushed the plate aside, with half the meal uneaten, and was staring down at the wooden table inset with river pebbles Kel had made long ago, when she'd just been feeling out her Gift. His shoulders were tight and his pattern... crumpled, like it was a sheet of paper he had balled up in his fist.

"You all right?" Kel asked. She reached across the table, and touched his hand where it was curled on the tabletop. "Vyr?"

He swallowed, and raised his head. He smiled, faintly, but with good intent, and put his other hand over hers.

"I'm fine," he said.

And that was a lie. Kel Knew it.

Off-Grid
The Tree House

. . . .

PADI STOOD ON THE PORCH, HER HEAD TIPPED BACK, WATCHING the Ribbons dance.

They were beautiful. Possibly, they were the most beautiful thing she had seen in her life, absent her father's face, after the liberation from Runig's Rock. Even tonight, when they were not yet fully risen, Padi felt a connection—an affinity with the ambient and its chaotic energies.

Standing there, bathed in Ribbon-light, it occurred to her for the first time that this affinity that gave her such joy might also be the source of great sorrow.

"What disturbs you?" Tekelia asked, arriving at her side.

Padi looked away from the Ribbons to the face that had become very dear, so very quickly.

"I was only just realizing that I can feel the Ribbons dancing at the core of me."

Tekelia smiled.

"Then you are Haosa, indeed."

The smile faded, and she felt a *click* inside her head, as if a connection had been made.

"You're concerned that you won't be able to leave; to trade," Tekelia said. A warm hand caught hers. "I didn't think of that."

"Nor did I until this very moment," Padi said, and laughed, rueful. "Truly, I am a daughter of dragons."

"Padi—"

"No," she said, placing a finger across Tekelia's lips. "We will not entertain tragedy before its time! Now, tell me if you've found someone to stand in your place while you're in orbit!" She lifted her finger away. "You may speak."

"Thank you," Tekelia said gravely. "Blays has risen to the challenge. She'll be staying here in order to be immediately available in case of need." Tekelia looked wry. "Which means she will have to be fetched, tomorrow, so that I can introduce her to the Warden day after. Will you make my excuses to Dil Nem?"

"I will, though I mention that Blays would be welcome to tour the shipyard, too. The opportunity to relieve *three* minds of the burden of their ignorance must weigh with Dil Nem, you know."

"I'm sure, but Blays is at Visalee, on Wildege."

Padi tipped her head. "You will of course tell me what that means."

Tekelia laughed.

"It means it will take me the better part of a day to fetch her."

"Ah, I see! I will make your excuses to Dil Nem."

"Thank you, and now turnabout— Tell me why your father must speak with us about our relationship."

"No, that was Thodelm yos'Galan," Padi said. "Thodelms are the keepers of the Line's integrity. He *must* account our relationship, else yos'Galan might fall into error."

"Errors happen. I understand that."

"Yes, but—forgive me—you are not yos'Galan. It matters very much to the thodelm, whose error might result in something as minor as missing a meeting, or as great as failing to extend protection when lives were the stake."

Tekelia stared at her.

Padi sighed.

"It really is very important. I realize that it will be a disruption of your life, but if you could do me the—"

Tekelia put a finger over her lips.

"Do not ask me to do you either a favor or the honor. We are in this muddle together, and we will work our way out together. I suggest that what we should do, first, is sit together, while you explain who said what to whom, and the consequences of those things, so far as you know them. I hope to have us both on the same ground, so that we can usefully reason together."

One well-marked eyebrow lifted.

"Is that a sound procedure?"

Padi grinned.

"Very sound. I do believe, Tekelia vesterGranz, that you were born to be a councilor."

"You're forgetting that I have Bentamin as a model, and a great deal of practice. The office of Speaker for the Haosa is ridiculous on its face, as each individual Haosa is more than willing to speak for herself. What little skill I have, I've learned through lengthy bouts of trial and error."

"A quibble," Padi declared. "If we are to proceed with due deliberation, we ought to take this indoors, so that I'm not distracted from my explanations by the Ribbons. It would also be helpful to have wine at hand."

She felt Tekelia's amusement ripple along their link.

"As dreadful as that?"

"Such explanations do sometimes become—intense," Padi said, as one being fair.

"Wine we will have, then. Green or red?"

"Oh, green! I don't expect anything worthy of the red."

They were settled on the sofa, the wine poured and waiting on the table before them. Padi turned to face Tekelia.

"The first thing you need to understand, though I make no doubt it will hurt your head, is that Shan yos'Galan's *melant'i* is varied and complex."

She paused, but Tekelia said nothing.

"So," Padi said, folding her fingers into her palm with only the thumb showing, "the first tier is kin-ties. He is Priscilla's lifemate, elder brother to three siblings, father, and foster-father. He is also variously uncle, cousin, and brother-by-Code to the lifemates of his siblings."

She paused again. Tekelia said nothing. Padi unfolded her index finger.

"The second tier is life-work, and there he is master pilot, master trader, and Healer."

Tekelia was watching her attentively, but offered no comment or question. Padi unfolded her middle finger.

"In the third tier, standing within the clan, he is Thodelm yos'Galan, keeper of the Line, its debts, and its credits. In this role, he is also advisor to the delm."

She folded her hands primly onto her knee, and Tekelia at last spoke.

"That seems like rather a lot."

"In fact, it is. The Code suggests that thodelm and master trader are each sufficient unto themselves. If Korval were not so thin, Father would not list thodelm among his honors.

"As it is, he has managed to sort the thodelm into an extremely precise box. We very rarely see him, the master trader being more than sufficient to most situations that might arise."

"Does this make . . . Shan yos'Galan's head hurt?" Tekelia asked carefully.

Padi frowned slightly.

"In the present instance, it may, though generally, I don't believe so. The thodelm is willing to be advised by the master trader—indeed, that would be the case if—if Aunt Nova were thodelm."

"Why isn't Aunt Nova thodelm?"

"That had been intended, I think. Then, Uncle Val Con fell into his scrape and Aunt Nova was Korval-*pernard'i* until he returned to us, with his lifemate. Uncle Val Con and Aunt Miri are now Korval, which freed Aunt Nova to rise as Thodelm yos'Galan, but the clan removed to Surebleak, and Aunt Nova became Boss Conrad's—that's Cousin Pat Rin's—administrator. Father calls her Boss Nova, and from what I hear from Quin—Cousin Pat Rin's heir—that is at least as complex as standing thodelm—and Surebleak has no Code to guide them."

"You said your family was thin," Tekelia protested, holding up a hand. "This seems quite a crowd, to me."

"We are much reduced in numbers," Padi said.

Tekelia raised an eyebrow.

"There was a war," she said repressively. "Shall I send you a condensed history?"

"That might be helpful, thank you," Tekelia said politely.

"When it arrives, recall that you asked for it," Padi said. "In any case, since the master trader and Thodelm yos'Galan had long ago perfected their arrangement, and Aunt Anthora does not at all have the proper skill set to stand up as either Boss or thodelm, matters continued as they were."

"Could *you* be thodelm?" Tekelia asked.

Padi felt a jolt, and raised her head to stare into one black eye and one grey.

"Have I been an idiot again?" Tekelia put a hand on her knee.

"Never an idiot, I insist," Padi said, and took a breath. "I—I am too young to accommodate Thodelm yos'Galan, though, as Shan yos'Galan's heir, that may be required of me, in the future."

"Does that disturb you?"

"I scarcely know," Padi said flatly. "There's training for it, of course, though I've had—nothing."

"Because of the arrangement between the master trader and the present thodelm?"

"Quite possibly. Not to mention the profound disorder of the clan's arrangements while the *stupid* Department of the Interior was pursuing us."

She paused, frowning in the general direction of the floor. Suddenly, she shook herself and looked up.

"I will," she said to Tekelia's speculative gaze, "speak to the master trader about it. However! For us here this evening, *that* is a side issue. We are discussing Thodelm yos'Galan's necessities with regard to ourselves."

"We were, yes."

Padi glanced down at her fingers, laced together on her knee, then into Tekelia's face.

"You and I dance together. The Code, so far as I am aware, does not acknowledge such a relationship. It is therefore Thodelm yos'Galan's duty to find what Line yos'Galan owes you."

"Line yos'Galan *owes me* nothing," Tekelia said firmly.

"Not true. As I think about it, the Line at least owes you protection," Padi said. "However much the Haosa may love danger, Clan Korval—which encloses Line yos'Galan—has enemies. You heard the name of one just now."

"The Department of the Interior."

Padi inclined her head.

"They have lately been much constrained, but one dares not believe that their malice has come to an end. We ought not to leave you exposed."

Tekelia frowned.

"Is that all?"

"Well, that is what Thodelm yos'Galan seeks to establish," Padi began—and stopped, blinking.

"What?"

"I only just—what you said to the master trader. Would you care *very* much if we were found to be lifemates?"

Tekelia stared at her.

"I would—have to know more."

Padi laughed. "Of course you would."

"You had better tell me what I said," Tekelia prodded, when she did not continue.

Padi took Tekelia's hand.

"You said, 'If I am disadvantaged, I trust Padi to guard my interests.' And *that* will be heard as an avowal, my friend. According to the Code, one puts perfect trust only in one's delm, one's kin—and one's lifemate."

Tekelia's blink was a flash of amber and blue.

"The Code is in error."

"Yes, it's been said. However, unless the delm means to break entirely with Liaden culture and form Korval anew—which, as Uncle Val Con is Scout-trained, isn't *wholly* impossible—it is the Code that must guide the thodelm's thinking."

She squeezed Tekelia's hand, and released it.

"To answer your question—lifemates share one *melant'i*. That means either partner is understood to speak, and act, for both."

"No, *that* won't do," Tekelia protested. "I dance with others, as you know—"

"Yes," Padi said. In fact, she had met those others with whom Tekelia shared heart-ties: Geritsi, Kencia, and Vayeen, all persons of impeccable *melant'i*, their affection for Tekelia, as Padi was able to See now that her Inner Eyes were fully open, profound and true. They had each made Padi welcome, but—

"No, it would be entirely ineligible," she said now, half-laughing. "Only think of me, daring to speak for you! Geritsi would hit me with a shovel!"

"Nothing so violent, I think," Tekelia said, squeezing her fingers. "But she certainly wouldn't think that she had been bound by anything I had agreed to."

Tekelia paused, head tipped.

"It goes just as ill in the other direction. How could I begin to speak for you? I'm neither a trader nor Liaden."

"No, you are quite right. As pleasant as it would be to accommodate the Code and offer Thodelm yos'Galan a convenable solution, it cannot be done. We shall think of something else."

Tekelia laughed. Padi smiled.

"Come, let us recruit ourselves with a sip." She took up the glasses and handed one to Tekelia. They savored the wine in silence. Tekelia's eyes closed, and Padi watched the play of shadow along cheek and brow.

"What if we come at this from another angle?" Tekelia murmured.

"Such as?"

Tekelia opened eyes that were both by chance blue.

"What if I outline my necessities and expectations?"

"That is well-thought; I will need to know those precisely. Tell me."

Tekelia took Padi's glass, and put both on the table before taking her hand between two warm palms and leaning forward to look directly into her eyes.

"I will accept *nothing* that results in limiting your goals or impinging your joy. I will not be a rock tied 'round your neck, or a shackle, holding you against your will."

Tekelia's expression was quite savage, brows pulled tight.

"Nor do I relinquish those others with whom I dance."

Padi waited. Tekelia said nothing else, fairly vibrating with a tension that she scarcely understood, even linked as they were.

When it seemed clear that Tekelia was not going to speak further, Padi inclined her head.

"Very good," she said calmly. "These are very clear conditions. If it does fall out that I stand as your negotiator, you may depend upon me to see that your necessities are honored."

Of a sudden, all the tension left Tekelia.

"Thank you."

"It is no more than we have agreed to do," she said, and flung forward to hug Tekelia tight. Strong arms came around her in response, and she sighed.

"Between us, we have made a most *spectacular* muddle," she murmured. "It bodes well for our collaboration, going forward."

Tekelia gave a shout of laughter.

"To the astonishment and peril of the universe!"

"Well, yes," Padi said, settling her head comfortably on Tekelia's shoulder. "After all, it *is* Korval."

Dutiful Passage
Colemeno Orbit

. . . .

"MAY I BRING YOU REFRESHMENT, PRISCILLA?" SHAN ASKED.

"Please," she said, and watched him cross to the buffet.

He brought two glasses of cold tea to the chair where she reclined, handed one to her and kept the other as he perched on the edge of the couch. With a wry smile, he lifted the glass in a toast.

"To a fortunate outcome."

Priscilla raised her eyebrows.

"Is that wise," she asked, "at this stage in the proceedings?"

"First, we must ask ourselves *which proceedings*," Shan said sagely.

Priscilla frowned at the carpet for a long few seconds. Shan brought his glass to rest against his knee and waited, head tipped to one side. Something flickered against his Healer senses—a sensation he had felt before, when Priscilla was using her Long Sight. His breath caught, then. It was never wise to make light of Korval's luck, and in the vicinity of Colemeno even less so.

"No," Priscilla said finally, looking up and catching his gaze firmly. "I think it's best not to be too particular."

"I agree," Shan said, "and I repent my attempt at humor."

She smiled and raised her glass. Shan met it with his.

"To the very best of all possible outcomes," she said, and Shan had the sense that the words had . . . weight.

"Are you," he said carefully, "attempting to influence the Luck?"

Priscilla met his eyes. "Merely praying," she said.

Shan took a careful breath. Priscilla was devout, once a priestess, and vessel, of a goddess, recently deceased. In her own parlance, she was a Witch, or, as they had it on Colemeno, a very strong multi-Talent.

"Who could object to prayer?" he asked lightly, and drank some of his tea before putting the glass down.

"How was your day?" Priscilla asked, by way, perhaps, of changing the subject.

"Not particularly arduous. The master trader has decided that he can ignore the Delm's Word no longer, and will therefore be asking the captain to lay a course for Tinsori Light Station. There is remarkably little in the way of established trade routes between here and there—which we knew, of course. Much of the work was therefore researching routes that were in use before Rostov's Dust arrived, obscuring everything in its path."

"That actually sounds pleasant," Priscilla said.

"There is something restful about poking around in records so old that they're dusty themselves," Shan admitted.

"Does the master trader intend to test a new route?"

Shan shook his head. "That had been the first notion—tradeships are, as you may have noticed, expensive to keep, and we've lost both potential opportunity and profit while we surveyed Colemeno. The work we've done here will eventually return both, but the operative word is *eventually*."

"So, we'll be going directly to Tinsori Light?"

"That seems prudent. The master trader has been directed by his delm to open a trade office there. Also, there's Denobli's idea that he and I and Administrator Carresens meet on-station to consult—which has worth. And I confess that I would like to observe Traveler's Aid in practice."

"That *does* sound like a direct route," Priscilla said with a smile. "When do we leave?"

"As soon as all personnel have arrived and roles are sorted going forward," Shan said. "No more than twelve ship days; possibly sooner."

"That will please Danae," Priscilla said. "She believes the crew is tired of leisure."

"As who would not be?" Shan asked with an extravagant wave of his hand.

"Padi and Tekelia will be arriving—soon, then," Priscilla murmured.

"Indeed."

Priscilla took a breath, and had recourse to her glass.

"No, that won't do," Shan said. "What did you not say, just then?"

She shook her head, mouth wry.

"*Can't* they just be friends?"

"If they were *only* friends, the thodelm would not have concerned himself," Shan said. As his lifemate, Priscilla shared the burden of clan administration that fell to Thodelm yos'Galan, though she rarely involved herself in those duties. Her position was that Shan had long ago achieved a working understanding with the thodelm. She stood ready as backup, and as sounding board, but left policy to him.

That she involved herself now, in this matter, was—notable. Shan sipped his tea and reviewed the thodelm's necessities once more.

"One's friends are not the proper concern of the thodelm," he said. "Unless, of course, one's friends lead one into error."

"We haven't seen that Tekelia has led Padi into error," Priscilla pointed out. "In fact, Tekelia did what we couldn't. Padi now accepts her Gift, and she's eager to learn more."

"Tekelia was able to show her unlimited power."

"Tekelia," Priscilla said, her voice so stern that Shan looked at her in surprise, "was able to show her joy in a Gift she had previously understood only as a burden."

She paused, then asked, still stern.

"Will you separate them?"

Shan considered her with interest. "I look forward to learning how you think I would enforce that."

"Honor would enforce it," Priscilla said, piously. "Honor and obedience to the thodelm."

"Ah. While I am the first to acknowledge that Padi is a woman of honor," Shan said, "I must also note, as her fond parent, that she is not a dolt."

Priscilla laughed. "All right then, what can you—what can the *thodelm*—do? She's of age; the heart-tie is strong, even if it's not a lifemating—"

"The single point on which all of us agree," Shan murmured, and Priscilla laughed again.

"It's a start."

"So it is. If I were clever, I would find some way to build from it. Well. Leaving the thodelm entirely aside, and standing as a mere parent, I will tell you that I fear Padi might be in a scrape. Yes, she's of age, but she's *young*—more naive than she might otherwise be, all thanks to the Department of the Interior. Instead of going about the world, roistering with one's friends, falling into and out of adventures, learning who were true companions, and who were simply out for their own advantage, she was hidden away with her clanmates, living isolated, and in fear of her life, not to mention what she might have been required to do in order to preserve it."

He took a hard breath. Priscilla extended a hand and he gratefully laced his fingers with hers.

"In short, Padi had not found a like-minded companion until now—on Colemeno, with its vexed ambient—and Tekelia vesterGranz."

"If," Priscilla said softly into the silence that followed this, "Thodelm yos'Galan wishes to assign Balance correctly, he might find that Tekelia is owed."

"Yes!" Shan said, leaning forward. "That is *precisely* why Thodelm yos'Galan must be involved, dreadful bore that he is. Tekelia has acted in a manner that benefits—that *materially benefits*—yos'Galan. There is very little doubt that Tekelia *is* owed, and the thodelm has no desire to stint the payment. Unfortunately, it appears that the matter is more complicated than that."

"Because of the heart-link," Priscilla murmured.

"It is a profound attachment: a bond so strong *you* needed to examine it closely to determine that it was *not* a lifemate link. And that is where Thodelm yos'Galan comes into the matter."

Priscilla's eyebrows rose.

"I see. Thodelm yos'Galan needs to know if the link makes Tekelia kin."

"He needs to know precisely that, and, once he is satisfied, he will need to tell the delm what call Tekelia vesterGranz has upon Clan Korval. What protections are we obligated to extend? In what circumstances and to what degree can Tekelia be understood to be speaking for Padi, and through her, for yos'Galan and Korval? Shall we dock a ship here, for Tekelia's use?"

Priscilla took a breath, and he felt a sweet draft of calmness flow through him.

"You'll figure something out," she said.

"Your faith in me, Priscilla, is humbling."

She laughed.

"And Padi?" she asked.

Shan moved his shoulders. "Clearly, Padi is—attached. I don't wish to hurt her. Especially, I don't want her angry with me."

"I can see that must be a frightening prospect."

"Absolutely terrifying, even in the normal way of things. As matters stand now, with our departure so soon..."

"I see," Priscilla said gently. "Best not to part on a quarrel."

"Yes."

He finished his tea and smiled at her.

"Let us have another topic. What did Keriana have to say to you today?"

Priscilla sighed. "She hasn't changed her mind. I'm to stay on the *Passage*, where I'm likely to be under less stress than I would experience on Colemeno, until our child is born."

Shan said nothing. Priscilla leaned over to touch his hand.

"It troubles you. I'm in no danger—even Keriana admits that! It's only that this is my first child, and our medic, who is intimately familiar with me, wants me under her care, rather than the care of a medic chance-met, as it were, on Colemeno. It seems best to humor her in this, unless the master trader—"

"The master trader knows far better than to contend with a medic on the topic of her patient's health." Shan said. "The master trader is also required to descend to Colemeno, which means—" He turned to look at her. "Our child may be born while I'm gone."

"If that's the case, I'll be sure to introduce you to her when you return," Priscilla said tranquilly.

Shan took a careful breath.

"Your lifemate would not leave you without support, love."

Priscilla laughed, and put her hand on his knee.

"My lifemate has provided first-rate support! Unless you doubt Lina and Keriana?"

"Of course not, but—"

"But you would rather be present, so we can welcome our child together. I understand. Depending on her timing, it may be that you can be present."

Shan raised an eyebrow. "Teleportation?"

"I don't think even Padi can manage the distance from the surface to orbit. No, I only meant that we *are* lifemates. Of course, you'll be present."

He blinked.

"Priscilla."

"Yes?"

"I'm a fool."

"I'd say distracted," Priscilla said, as one giving due consideration.

"Hardly the frame of mind one might look for in a master trader hovering on the edge of success."

"Or failure," Priscilla said. "After all, Colemeno might decide that it doesn't wish to be a trade hub after all."

Shan laughed.

"Everything that is supportive!" He took her hand. "Will you sleep with me tonight, Priscilla?"

"That sounds pleasant," she answered.

Wildege
Kelim Station

. . . .

THE RIBBONS WERE STILL VISIBLE WHEN KEL WENT OUT TO THE wagon. Vyr had packed her a basket—actually, he'd packed two, but she'd laughed, and handed the second back.

"Ribbons, boy! Visalee's practically Civilization, and beside—it's Midsummer Market! There'll be plenty to eat."

The second basket . . . Vyr felt his stomach cramp, and, despite the state of the sky, followed her out to the wagon.

"*In case*, Kel," Vyr said, pushing the basket at her, and heard the urgency in his own voice.

She tipped her head, eyes narrowed.

"Seen something?" she asked, then moved her shoulders, as if she'd just remembered there were questions that were better not to ask, and took the second basket.

"Sure. *In case*, hey? Never know what Chaos might get up to."

"Thank you, Kel," he said, with more fervor than was surely called for.

She smiled and patted his cheek, then jumped lightly into the wagon, stowed the second basket, and got herself settled on the bench.

Vyr stepped back, watching as she engaged the power, and eased the bar back.

The wagon rose smooth, sweetly balanced over the spinners, showing nary a wobble nor a list. Vyr let out the breath he'd been holding. The track to Kelim Station was rugged by design—no sense giving folks the impression you wanted visitors, was what Kel said—but Main Path was good hovering all the way to Visalee.

Kel pushed the left stick. The wagon moved. She raised a hand, without looking back, and Vyr raised his, too.

"Travel safe," he said, though she couldn't hear him.

Off-Grid
The Vinery

. . . .

ROUGH BARK WAS UNDER TEKELIA'S PALM, AND THE NEWS TREE'S welcome warming the ambient, even as glad voices rent the morning air.

"Tekelia! Good morning! Tekelia!"

Tekelia smiled, patted the Tree, and stepped away. It was scarcely past dawn; dew was still sparkling on grass and leaf.

"What are you three doing up so early?"

Manci, the eldest of the Ribbon Dance children currently being fostered by The Vinery, rolled her eyes. "I hope you know better than to think *Howe* was going to meet you at this hour."

Tekelia laughed.

"I did think it was possible, if he'd still been dancing."

"That's fair," said Gust, the next eldest. "But he went to bed early."

"I hope he's not ill. He seemed well when we spoke yesterday."

"He's courting Timit, and promised to be up in time to help him fix the frost-crew's breakfast," Gust said, and grinned. "But not *this* early."

"Tekelia!" Spryte called from the table at the square's center. "Come and eat! We brought cake, and juice, and cheese!"

"That," Manci said with a sigh, "is also fair." She pointed to where the youngest waited, arms crossed over her chest.

"Thank you," Tekelia said, taking a cup of juice. As expected, it was tart. The Vinery depended on grapes for its livelihood— wines, juices, and jams that were prized in Haven City.

"How goes the crush?" Tekelia asked, reaching for a piece of cake.

"Well enough," Manci said. "We expect to be finished today."

"But it's the *small* crush!" Spryte added. "On the inside of the hill. The frost-crew is on the outside."

"Protecting the next," Tekelia said. "I remember fighting the frost."

"It's fun," Spryte said. "I was on-crew for the down-close trellis."

Tekelia reached for a wedge of cheese.

"Are you really going to Visalee and back, *today*?" Manci asked, low-voiced. "Why not spend the night, and come back tomorrow?"

"Time's short, or I'd do just that," Tekelia said.

"Howe said that you were going to be—gone?" Gust put in.

"That's right. Blays agreed to stand in my place while I go to the master trader's ship, in orbit around Colemeno."

Gust squinted, and Manci said, "Why?"

"Well, surely it's an adventure," Tekelia said, with broad surprise. "That should be enough for any Haosa."

"Yes, but that's not why you're doing it," Manci said shrewdly.

Tekelia finished the cheese wedge and poured another cup of juice.

"No, it's not. The ship and the trade team may be of use to the Haosa, and, as Speaker for the Haosa, it's my duty—no, *don't* wrinkle your nose, Gust!—it's my duty to explore this opportunity." Tekelia put the empty cup down. "*And* because it will be an adventure—that does figure somewhat." Tekelia stepped back from the table. "Thank you for your care. Tell Howe I expect to see him this evening."

"You're not leaving already!" cried Spryte.

"I must, dear heart," Tekelia said, smiling down at her. "Visalee is a long way, even for me."

"Well, be careful," Manci said.

"Adventure will wait," Gust added, sounding so like a stern elder that Tekelia laughed.

"Adventure never waits; it only changes shape! Until this evening!"

Mist swirled, and Tekelia was gone.

Colemenoport Shipyard

. . . .

"TEKELIA NOT WITH YOU?" DIL NEM ASKED AS PADI ENTERED THE office that had been assigned to his use.

"Tekelia sends abject apologies, and hopes that you will be able to provide a tour to amend their ignorance at some future date. Today, with the lift to the *Passage* coming so soon, it is important for Blays to be fetched from Visalee Village, so that she may be formally introduced to the Warden of Civilization as Speaker for the Haosa in Tekelia's absence."

Dil Nem tipped his head, eyes narrowed. "Takes it that seriously?"

Padi frowned.

"Tekelia is not always playing," she said.

"I had noticed that," Dil Nem assured her, rising from behind his desk. "Though I receive the impression that the rest may be—playing, that is."

"The rest are—mistrustful," Padi said. "Which is easy to understand once you know that most are born Civilized and cast out—of Civilization, and often from their families—when it is discovered that they are Haosa."

"Which means what, exactly?"

Padi produced an owlish look. "Have you not been paying attention, Cousin? Haosa are not Civilized."

Dil Nem actually laughed. "Well. That's for them to sort out. Speaking of raising the *Passage*—I'll be going with you." He held up a hand. "I have no need of flight time, Pilot; the lift is yours."

"Everything that is gracious. You did say your work here at the yard is done—but that will mean you won't be able to give Tekelia a tour, after all."

"It means nothing of the kind," Dil Nem said. "I'm under contract to Colemeno Yard to supervise the upgrades."

Padi fairly stared.

"You won't be going on with the *Passage*?"

"Not at this time. Truth told, the contract presents a welcome change."

"Who will be third mate?"

"Captain Mendoza wants to see what Toria Valdez can do." He moved his shoulders. "I think she'll show well—she has the basics; and *I've* never seen her at a stand."

"She may put you out of a job," Padi said, watching his face. Dil Nem threw her a quick glance, as if he had felt the weight of her speculation.

"I might not regret that," he said, and produced a glare. "Do not *meddle*, Trader."

Padi showed him two empty palms. "Meddle?"

"No, that won't fadge. I know you—your father's daughter, and all too willing to do *some*thing. In this case, you need do *nothing*."

"I understand," Padi assured him earnestly. "Only tell me when I am to wish you happy."

Dil Nem looked sour. "Do you want a tour of the facility or don't you?"

"I absolutely want a tour, and I hope that you will be unstinting in lightening the burden of my ignorance. Please, lead on."

Off-Grid
Deen's Fallow

· · · · · · · · · · · · · · ·

THE SKY WAS BRIGHT, THE SUN WELL-RISEN, AND THE BREEZE
had an edge like a knife.

Firgus held out a steaming mug of morning wake-up, which
Tekelia took gratefully, and drank while leaning against the
News Tree.

"*Thank* you, Cousin!"

"No trouble to me," Firgus said. "Thought you might be chilled."

"Well, if you didn't keep it so cold here," Tekelia murmured,
and the other laughed.

"That's the Fallow's business! I only live here."

Tekelia sighed and straightened away from the tree.

"Tired already?" Firgus asked, taking the empty mug. "Visalee's not next door, you know."

"In fact, I do know," Tekelia said, somewhat sharply—and
instantly flung out an apologetic hand. "Your pardon, Cousin.
Obviously, I'm in need of cake."

"Right over here," Firgus said, leading the way to a table
bearing a plate of sandwiches, another of cake, a bowl of nuts,
and a hot-bottle.

Tekelia took a slice of cake while Firgus refilled the mug, and
filled another, for himself.

"Sit a moment and go over this nonsense with me again," he
said, settling onto the bench.

Tekelia raised an eyebrow.

"We spoke last night."

"We did. Let it be known that I'm slow, and haven't quite
caught up. Why must Blays be brought to Ribbon Dance with
no delay?"

"Because Blays is the only one of the three of you mad enough to agree to stand as Speaker for the Haosa while I'm gone."

"Right," Firgus sipped his drink, and pointed at the plates. "Eat."

"Eating," Tekelia said, choosing a sandwich.

"Why does anyone have to stand as Speaker for the Haosa while you're—gone?"

"So that the Warden of Civilization has someone to contact, should the need arise," Tekelia said promptly.

"*Will* the need arise?"

Tekelia half-laughed, and took another sandwich. "You know I'm not Sighted."

"True." Firgus reached for the hot-bottle and refreshed his cup. "So you're of a mind to play Civilization's game?"

Tekelia sighed.

"Chaos is in it, Cousin—I don't think it's a game. I think the Warden and at least some of the councilors grasp the need for—change."

"The Oracle's last Seeing frightened them, you mean?"

"Well, it might have," Tekelia conceded. "The end of Civilization and the Haosa? It serves warning that *something* needs to change. The offered chair at the council table isn't a hoax, though I'm of two minds whether it ought to be me who sits in it."

"And our cousins haven't been helpful in that regard." Firgus waved a hand. "Haven City is far away."

"It's on the same planet," Tekelia countered.

"So it is. Well. While you're gone and Blays is standing firm, I'll make one more push for a consensus. May I use the file we built for our planning?"

"What, facts and projections?" Tekelia laughed and snatched a handful of nuts.

"Well, why not?" Firgus said. "Facts are interesting things, after all. Here's one: The annual Census of Gifts reveals that fewer Talents were registered under the Grid last year, that number being significantly down from the previous year's census."

Tekelia considered him.

"Significantly."

Firgus waved a hand. "I'll send the reports to you, with my notes. But I haven't told you the joke yet."

Tekelia dusted cake crumbs from fingertips. "Better hurry."

"Oh, it's simple: The number of Deaf living under the Grid has grown..."

"Significantly?" guessed Tekelia, reaching for the mug.

Firgus gave it consideration. "I think that can be fairly said."

Tekelia sighed. "You realize you've just given me another reason to take the damned chair?"

"Have I? Well. Maybe it will have the same effect on our cousins."

Tekelia laughed and put the empty mug on the table.

"I'm away. Look for Blays and me this evening."

Mist swirled.

Colemenoport Shipyard

. . . .

"NOW, THIS IS THE MACHINING SECTION," DIL NEM SAID, TRIG-gering the door, and stepping through ahead of Padi.

It was a large bay with three work stations: two idle, and the third undergoing either repair or maintenance.

At the back of the bay was a large unit, also idle, though every so often a light flickered along its surface.

"This is what we'll be upgrading first," Dil Nem said, waving Padi toward one of the idle work stations.

As they passed the machine being worked on, the tech looked up with a tired grin. "They've held together for two hundred Standards," she said. "It's a lot to ask of anything, and the devil's in it that you can't fabricate a fabrication unit."

"Two hundred Standards of increasingly hard use," Dil Nem said, nodding at the tech. "At first, there was an inventory of parts, but as they were used, and no new ones being delivered—"

"The yard started machining everything from paper clips to Struvens," the tech said, standing away from the unit she was working on. "Now, we're running out of raw material, not to mention that the extruder over there's getting very temperamental." She sighed, and wiped her hands on a rag. "We test everything that comes out of it, and we don't let anything go that's under the ninety-seventh percentile, but you have to take into account that the test equipment is two hundred Standards old, too."

She bowed then, taking off her cap to reveal short grey hair fairly standing up straight on her head.

"I'm Moji tineMena," she said. "I'm pleased to meet you, Trader yos'Galan."

"Yard Master." Padi bowed. "It's an honor." She straightened. "Thank you for allowing me to tour your facility."

"Why wouldn't I, when Tree-and-Dragon already has our signed contract?" the yard master said practically, putting her cap back on. "And, you know, when Dil Nem told me the reason you wanted to tour—that you're going on the Iverson Loop, and want to have some idea of what you're looking at when you visit the yards further in—that was so commonsensical, who could say no?"

Padi smiled. "I wonder if I might ask you a question."

"Anything you like, Trader."

"As we were coming in, Dil Nem said that this room would be the first to be upgraded, and I wonder why that would be. Surely, with new pre-made parts on order, the demand for machining parts will fall off."

"The new parts inventory is an investment in Colemeno's future," the yard master said. "Those parts will be needed by the ships coming in from Dust-free space, as you did. Most of our customers—our base, if you will—are ships from inside the cloud—ships that are two hundred Standard years old, and more. *Those* parts will still have to be machined."

Padi shot a glance to Dil Nem, who met it blandly.

"There are," she said slowly, "junk yards in the Dust-free zones."

"I don't doubt there are," said the yard master, "but those parts will be—if you'll excuse me, Trader—*junk*, or at least used. With an up-to-date fabrication room, we can produce brand-new parts, within, so Dil Nem assures me, the ninety-ninth percentile."

"I am instructed," Padi said, "and I will bear the lesson in mind."

She glanced at Dil Nem again.

"I wonder if you would share your upgrade proposal with me."

"Certainly, Trader," Dil Nem said. "I'll send it to you when we're done touring."

Off-Grid
Visalee

· · · · · · · ·

IT WAS WARM, AND THE SUN RIDING HIGH IN THE SKY. THE NEWS Tree announced Tekelia's arrival loudly, which waked a chorus of shouts, stamps, and whistles from nearby.

Looking over the square, Tekelia saw tables and hover-wagons; the warm wind bore the scent of baked goods and roasting vegetables, as well as the sound of a mandola and tintringo being played with ... enthusiasm.

Tekelia pushed away from the tree as a slender figure alighted on the grass, holding a tall mug between her palms, a bag slung over one shoulder.

"Hello, Blays."

"Tekelia," she answered. "Have some good Wildege cider."

The mug wafted forward, and Tekelia caught it with a smile.

"With great pleasure."

"You don't half look rugged," Blays observed, as Tekelia took a long swallow.

Tekelia sighed.

"I started early."

"You started *far*," Blays corrected, and pointed a finger. "Are you still for going back tonight?"

"Have to, we've a meeting with the Warden of Civilization tomorrow morning at Peck's Market."

Blays tipped her head, hair swirling around her face.

"As quick as that?"

"I explained that the timeline was short, and the Warden was able to make an accommodation," Tekelia said, finishing the cider. "It would be rude to disappoint him."

"I suppose." Blays touched the bag. "I've got food. Are you eating here, or should I take you to the way-lodge?"

"The way-lodge, if you please."

"This way, then."

Blays turned, waving Tekelia to follow her as she skimmed over the grass, her hair eddying like storm clouds. From some-where in the crowd a timpani began to thrum as people shouted and clapped.

"What's the reason for the party?" Tekelia asked.

"Besides being Haosa?" Blays threw a look over one shoulder. "It's Midsummer Market. First day, and we've already got six wagons in from Wildege, which is something worth dancing for."

"It is," Tekelia agreed, glancing speculatively at the crowds and the line of wagons piled with produce and goods.

"No," Blays said sternly, "you won't go down *just for a moment* to chat. I'll do the needful, like I was planning to do, while *you*, Cousin, will enter the way-lodge—" She pointed ahead of them, where a low hut sat peacefully beneath the flowering branches of a tree. "You'll eat, and you'll sleep until this evening. When you wake up, you'll eat again."

Tekelia grinned. "Thank you for your care of me, Cousin."

"Say rather my care of me," Blays said, with a droll look. "I have an interest in the trip to Ribbon Dance being flawless and smooth."

She descended to the grass once more, pushed open the lodge's door, and stood back so Tekelia could go inside.

"As it happens, I have a similar interest," Tekelia said, taking the bag she offered. "Until this evening."

"Sleep well," Blays said.

Colemenoport
Offices of
Tree-and-Dragon Trade Mission

. . . .

PADI CHECKED HER MAIL QUEUE ONE MORE TIME, FINDING NO new messages.

Before returning to the office, she had spoken with Jes dea'Tolin, and been told that everything was well in hand. A glance at the calendar showed her next appointment as tomorrow mid-morning.

"I do believe you're free to go, Padi yos'Galan," she told herself, and sighed. She had become accustomed to spending her free hours with Tekelia—a pleasant habit, and one that she would not be able to indulge once she had departed on the route audit.

"Practice, then," she told herself. She shut down the screen, and reached for her case, recalling that she had a project in hand for the evening. She thought that she might have worked out the route to Healspace. An unencumbered evening was just what she needed for experimentation. And, if she was right, then—

A tone sounded and the blue light over the door flashed, twice.

Padi gave a wry grin, and crossed the room to open the door.

"Thought I might've missed you," Trader Isfelm said. She was carrying a bag over one shoulder, and to Padi's eye seemed rather . . . less buoyant than usual.

"Had you been six minutes slower, you would have," Padi told her, stepping back, and moving her hand to invite the trader in. "What may I be pleased to do for you?"

"Got a couple things—won't take long," Trader Isfelm said, walking to the table and putting her bag down. "Comes to me you'll want to inspect *Ember* before you stand up as her trader. Talk on the port is that the survey your team's been working on is finding its end. I'm thinking you won't want to dawdle on Colemeno too long after the results are in."

Padi stared at her in some dismay. Of course, she ought to do an inspection of the ship, introduce herself to crew, and familiarize herself with on-board routines. She should have thought of that. Only—

"First time for both of us," Trader Isfelm said in her matter-of-fact way. "Bound to be mistakes and missteps on both sides." She grinned. "We'll learn, Trader. We'll learn."

Padi laughed.

"Yes, I suppose we must! But I wish that I at least had learned sooner, because now the case is that I will have to put this off for some number of days. The data-gathering is, as you say, nearing its end, and the master trader has let me know that I will be wanted aboard *Dutiful Passage* upon its completion, in order to be part of the planning, going forward."

She went to her desk and tapped the screen on.

"He'll be moving on pretty quick after that, won't he?" Trader Isfelm asked, her voice betraying tension.

Padi looked up.

"There is still some work to do," she said. "If the Whole Port Inventory shows that Colemeno may support a trade hub, the master trader will file an Intent to Open with the Guild. He must then present the trade mission's findings to the port administrators and the planetary government, and formally seek their permission to establish a hub. Assuming those permissions are forthcoming, the master trader will forward them to the Guild, which may not unreasonably withhold its approval."

Padi stopped and drew a breath.

"The master trader's work here is done as soon as the proper permissions are secured. The ongoing preparations for opening the Hub will be handled by the administrative team on Colemeno."

Trader Isfelm drew a breath.

"So it's down to days, then," she breathed, and shook herself with a laugh. "If you're wanted on the ship as soon as that," she said, "let's look at your time when you come back. I'll take you aboard, o'course, and introduce you around."

"Yes," Padi said. "And you know, we should have the *qe'andra* who will be accompanying me in hand by that point, so you may introduce both of us."

"That's the dandy," Trader Isfelm said, though Padi thought it was with a little less than her usual enthusiasm.

"Will you be going with the *Passage* when the master trader leaves Colemeno?" she asked carefully.

Trader Isfelm sighed.

"Hasn't been finalized yet—which is more to my side of the ledger than his. Guess I'd better make my mind up, eh? In the meantime, when do you suppose you'll be back and able to inspect?"

On-Grid
Ganelets on the Quiet

. . . .

"THE END OF CIVILIZATION?" BALWERZ SNORTED. "THE COUNCIL was right to retire her; the old woman's senile."

"As may be," kirshLightir said from the buffet where he was refreshing his glass. "The rumor is that the Council takes the Seeing seriously, and is forming a committee."

"Well," ramKushin said, returning to her seat. "Maybe the Seeing is accurate, after all. Surely, the Haosa would do their most to destroy Civilization. If Civilization hands them the means to succeed, why shouldn't they take it?"

"Is there a reliable reading as to how accurate the Oracle's Seeing *is*?" asked imbyValt. She turned from the window and stalked into the room.

"Cousin Jenfyr kindly let me know that the Warden felt the Seeing had merit," trolBoi said. "It may be worth noting that the Oracle has chosen to retire to her kin, the Haosa, rather than remain coddled in the Wardian."

"Yes, I heard that, too," imbyValt said. "And I wonder if that isn't an indication of how certain the *Oracle* is of this Seeing."

kirshLightir put his drink down. "That's—disturbing," he said.

"Say instead, *interesting*." balWerz was frowning. "We've had the Haosa on our agenda for some time, after all."

"On that topic," imbyValt murmured, "has anyone spoken to dimaLee lately?"

"We were both at the most recent Protectors meeting," ramKushin said. "I spoke with him for a few minutes, after. He's done workshops at the central security station, and the north substation, as well as the central port guardhouse. There, he was given leave to tune the high security rooms."

imbyValt raised her eyebrows. "That's impressive."

"Apparently there were willing ears present," ramKushin said.

"In light of that progress, shall we still file the petition?" balWerz asked.

imbyValt glanced around the room. "Does anyone have an objection to filing the petition?" she asked.

Silence, before trolBoi spoke. "I say present it. It will give us a reading of the table."

imbyValt nodded. "How informative is your cousin?" she asked him.

"Jenfyr? She takes her obligations seriously. I've been able to convince her that she's not betraying her sworn trust by discussing any rumor I bring to her, but she keeps herself close otherwise."

"We could use another friendly ear on the Council," balWerz murmured. "What with seelyFaire withdrawn."

"We could use several," kirshLightir said, "if not the whole table."

"It ought to be easy enough to Influence the Deaf councilor," said trolBoi.

"If that simpleton firnPeltir hadn't attacked him and put him in the news—" balWerz began.

imbyValt waved her drink, cutting him off. "Precisely. The present Deaf councilor has lost his value to us. Better to arrange for another. ramKushin, see to that."

"A new councilor puts us back," balWerz objected. "The value in the incumbent is that he *is* in place; he has his network; he's on several potentially valuable committees—"

"Yes, and people will notice, if he begins to alter his policies."

"Only if we're clumsy," balWerz said. "Do we intend to be clumsy?"

imbyValt considered him. "Are you volunteering to feel him out?"

"Yes."

She moved her shoulders. "Do it, and report back."

Another glance around the room.

"Are there more projects to discuss?"

"Actually..." ramKushin said. "There's the kezlBlythe situation."

"Zandir expects assistance in leaving present lodgings," said imbyValt. "I've been getting letters."

balWerz sighed. "I'll warrant we've all been getting letters."

"Letters? I had a *personal visit* from the redoubtable terma-Varst," ramKushin said.

trolBoi grimaced. "I suppose we'll have to do something."

imbyValt raised her glass and looked at him over the rim. "Why?"

There was a moment of silence, before ramKushin said, somewhat uncertainly, "We've been partners."

"We have," imbyValt said serenely, "and it was a mutually profitable partnership. Neither the kezlBlythe Syndicate nor we lost by our association. However." She looked around the room. "However. We have more important matters than Zandir kezl-Blythe before us."

"For instance," kirshLightir said, "the outworlders. How will they impact our plans?"

"What should the outworlders care about our plans, even if they were known? They're here because there's money to be made," trolBoi said forcefully.

"Precisely," said imbyValt. "The outworlders are traders. Their motive is profit. There's no reason for them to meddle in planetary government, so long as their commercial efforts are amply rewarded."

She sipped wine, and looked 'round the room.

"Have we other business?"

There was none.

Colemenoport
Wayfarer

· · · · · · · · · ·

MIST FROTHED AROUND HER—LAVENDER MIST, LACED WITH TEN-drils of indigo blue, bright yellow, and mahogany—streaming, surging, and dreadfully busy.

For a moment, Padi wondered if she had achieved Healspace, or had again bumbled into some other place altogether, only this time, there was no Tekelia to meet her.

"Healspace," she said aloud, "comes from within."

Father's Healspace, that she had entered at his invitation, to assist in Healing Vanz, had been filled with mists of varying shades of pink. There had been motion, but nothing so energetic as what she was seeing—no. Father's mist had *boiled*, flaring silver as it dissolved the terrible working that would have made Vanz nothing but the extension of a villain's will.

In fact, Healspace had acted as an extension of *Father's* will. Which meant that—*this*...

Padi eyed the cheerful, energetic chaos surrounding her with fond dismay.

Which meant that this display was a reflection of *her* will and intent.

"Really, Padi, you might try for a *little* order," she murmured, and closed her eyes. Carefully, she reviewed a pilot's calming exercise, and felt serenity flow into her.

When she opened her eyes again, the fog was still largely laven-der, shot with bright ribbons and dark, but its movement was less frenetic, a slow swirling that was at once soothing and exuberant.

She laughed suddenly and rose up on her toes, spreading her arms wide, as if she would take flight, while the mist caressed her cheeks, and swirled 'round her waist.

Briefly, she wondered if she *could* fly here, as well as under the Ribbons, but the moment passed, and she settled back into center, suddenly sober.

It appeared that she had found Healspace—or, if Dyoli was to be believed, *her* Healspace. But that had been only the first step in her plan.

Now that she was here, however, she found she had... qualms regarding the second step. It came to her that she did not know the protocols. Did one ask permission before one called? How precisely *did* one call? Was it a whisper, a yearning, or—

To her right, the mist became slightly agitated, flowing from lavender to silver-spangled pink.

A figure formed within the agitation, and took one step forward, the mist falling behind.

"Hello, Padi."

"Father!"

She threw herself forward, and it seemed that the mist did support her, so that she flew into his arms, hugging him as tightly as he hugged her.

"Did I—did I wake you?"

"Not quite," he murmured, and she felt a light pressure, as if he rested his cheek against her hair.

They stood so for a moment—or a year. Padi felt the slight easing of his embrace, and the absence of that light pressure. She sighed, and released him, stepping back until Father caught her hands, and they stood among the dancing mists, facing each other.

"I see that you found Healspace," he said, gently. "My congratulations." He turned his head, surveying the area; she saw his gaze settle on the dancing colors.

"Ribbons?" he asked.

Padi sighed. "I think so? But, truly, Father, I've only just arrived, myself."

He laughed.

"Well, then. You will have to tell me, when you know."

"Yes, I will," she said, her voice going to a whisper. She had wanted him, wanted to talk to him, yet, now that he was here, she scarcely knew what to say.

"May I Look at you, child?" Father asked softly.

Padi raised her chin.

"Yes, please. May I—may I See, too?"

"Certainly," he said, and stepped back, his hands slipping out of hers.

Between them, the mist boiled lavender, pink, and silver. *Working energy*, Padi thought, taking note of how the colors changed and flowed.

A tapestry formed against silvery fog, a weaving of bright threads and dark—not so steadfast as Vanz's pattern, nor anything so intricate as Father's.

"I am much older than you are," Father murmured, as if he had heard her thought, and in this place, Padi realized, he may well have done.

She brought her attention to the tapestry that was her own inner self, finding that she could name the threads now; there was Quin, Aunt Anthora, Priscilla, Father himself, and the many others of her kin; valued associates—Jes, Mar Tyn, Dyoli, Dil Nem. One broad thread was a rich, deep brown. Padi Looked closer, and felt a sense of *Vanz* informing it.

And then there was the wide, bold thread that tied her to Tekelia.

Padi felt Father's attention touch it; felt, rather than heard, him sigh.

"Tekelia says that it can be undone," she said.

Father blew out a breath, setting silver mist spiraling into lavender.

"That might be," he said, "but I am not the Healer to attempt it." She felt his attention rest on her.

"Do you *wish* it undone, Daughter?"

"No," Padi said, and felt the echo of her certainty roll through the foggy landscape.

"Then there's nothing more to be said." Father paused. "I offer information."

"I am *more* than willing to receive information," she assured him fervently, and this time she felt his laughter at her core.

"Tekelia is correct: Heart-links may be cut. I myself cut the links I share with Priscilla. Mind you, I was of the opinion that I was going to die very soon, which was an important factor in my reasoning.

"It meant I could make the cut close to myself, thus sparing Priscilla most of the pain of separation."

Breath-caught, Padi asked, "Was . . . dying . . . important to your plan?"

"Well, yes. If I failed to die, the link would grow back, exposing Priscilla to our enemy. As you can see, I did fail to die, so it was fortunate our enemy found other business to occupy her."

"I wonder if Tekelia knows about the links growing back."

"Possibly not. Heart-links are not lightly severed. There may exist a reason less dire than mine to do so, but to separate those who are so intimately bonded, knowing that such links regrow—it could only be done to inflict pain, or perhaps to disorder someone in order to gain an advantage."

Padi drew breath, meaning to ask—and turned her head, drawn by a change in the quality of the mists.

"Ah," Father said softly, "we are approaching time, I fear. Even Healspace is not forever. Have we accomplished what you wished for in this meeting?"

"Yes," Padi said slowly. "Only—I wanted you to know, Father, that I will miss you!"

He extended a hand, fingertips caressing her cheek.

"And I will miss you, Daughter. It's not a clean break, you know. We will certainly still be in communication, and if nothing but a face-to-face meeting will do—well, you *are* a pilot, and my routes are filed with the Guild."

Padi laughed. "Yes, of course."

Father smiled, took one step backward into a bank of silver-shot pink—and was gone.

Off-Grid
Peck's Market

. . . .

TEKELIA AND BLAYS ARRIVED AT PECK'S MARKET EARLY. THEY opened the basket Tanin had provided, and snacked on savory pie with cold, sweet tea, sitting at one of the tables between the pavilion and the trees, enjoying the warm breeze and the flow of the ambient.

Suddenly, despite the breeze and the sun, Tekelia shivered.

"Cold, Cousin?" asked Blays.

"Trying to imagine what it might be like not to...*feel* the day."

Blays stared—then blinked.

"It's probable that you won't be able to sense the ambient on the ship," she said, and raised a hand. "I know you told me that, but it's so strange that I keep forgetting."

She drank tea and put the bottle on the table.

"Do you think the Haosa will *want* to go on the ships?" she asked. "To leave the Ribbons, and the ambient—to become something other than Haosa?"

Tekelia raised an eyebrow.

"Are the Haosa nothing but our Gifts?"

"No, Cousin, that won't do! The Haosa are much more than our Gifts, but without the ambient, there can be no Haosa!"

"You sound so certain of this," Tekelia said. "Have you seen proof?"

"The merest exercise of logic—"

"But we can't exercise logic against unknown conditions. We don't *know* what the effects of being separated from the ambient will be. The Talents who came down with the trade team were Talents when they arrived. Colemeno's ambient may have given them a boost, but they are very far from Deaf aboard their ship."

Blays blew out a hard breath.

"No, you're right; we have to *know*. But—does it have to be you who makes the test?"

Tekelia grinned. "Afraid of being left as Speaker for longer than a week?"

"That's not an unreasonable fear," Blays said primly.

"It's completely reasonable. I offer that I'm the...sturdiest specimen of Haosa available."

"That *might* be true," Blays said slowly. "Depending, again, on what we're measuring."

"We have to make a start somewhere," Tekelia said softly.

Blays bent her head in agreement—and looked sharply to the left. Tekelia heard it, too.

"That will be the Warden's car. Shall we go to meet him, Cousin?"

"I suppose it's only polite," Blays said, rising to walk with Tekelia across the grass to the drive. "Is it...protocol, the car? I thought the Warden is a teleporter."

"He is," Tekelia said. "He may have needed to carry something—or someone—more than just himself. Or, he might only have wanted to drive, it being an activity he enjoys, and which is not in the least like playing."

Blays laughed.

The sound of the engine grew louder, and a small yellow car swept into the drive, pulling to a stop at the edge of the grass.

There was a moment when nothing moved, then the driver's door opened and Bentamin chastaMeir emerged, impeccable as always in his city clothes. The passenger's door also opened, and another man debarked, dressed like a sober and serious on-Grid merchant.

"Oh, *pretty*," Blays breathed. "Who's *he*?"

Tekelia looked more closely at Bentamin's companion—neatly made, and certain in his movements, his cropped curls shining like spun copper in the clear morning light. His pattern was likewise neat, bright with connections, dense with purpose, honor, and not a little humor. There was no smallest glow of Gift or Talent, and that was the clue that established his identity.

"We haven't been introduced," Tekelia told Blays, and stepped forward.

Bentamin turned toward them and raised his hands, empty palms on display.

"I took a liberty," he said. "If I've presumed, Councilor ziaGorn has agreed to sit under the pavilion with his paperwork."

"It's surely too beautiful a morning for paperwork," Tekelia said, Feeling Blays's agreement in the ambient. "Though I should warn Councilor ziaGorn that he may disappoint Trader yos'Galan."

Copper brows rose over deep brown eyes.

"I would not willingly disappoint Trader yos'Galan," Councilor ziaGorn said, his voice calm, which was at variance with the surprise Tekelia Saw in him. "I wonder if you would illuminate my error."

Tekelia grinned.

"Actually, as I think more closely, I see that it's Bentamin's error."

"My relationship with Trader yos'Galan has not been straight-forward," the Warden of Civilization said gravely. "Still, I wouldn't want to disappoint her. What have I done, Tekelia?"

"Well, she had been looking forward to introducing me to Councilor ziaGorn herself." Tekelia glanced at the red-haired councilor, meeting a speculative gaze. "She thought we might do each other some good."

"In that case," Councilor ziaGorn said, turning toward Benta-min, "perhaps we should simply tell the trader the truth—that we had all three—" He glanced at Tekelia—"four?—had the same good and useful idea nearly simultaneously."

"I confess that I didn't think of it," Tekelia said, "but once she mentioned it to me, I could see that it was such a *very* good idea that the ambient must have delivered it to several minds, to insure that it wouldn't be lost. Perhaps that's the case to make to her."

Tekelia bowed, lightly.

"I'm pleased to meet you, Councilor ziaGorn. I am Tekelia vesterGranz, Speaker for the Haosa. My companion is Blays ess-Worthi, Counsel to Chaos."

Councilor ziaGorn bowed, also lightly, humor sparkling against the ambient.

"I'm pleased to meet Tekelia vesterGranz and Blays essWorthi," he said.

"I'm not sure what good I can do Councilor ziaGorn at the moment, Bentamin," Tekelia said, "since we were meeting to introduce you to Blays, who will be standing as Speaker while I'm gone."

"But you'll be coming back, won't you, Cousin? It's an easier matter to reopen an acquaintance than to make a new one."

"True. I've lately been given a lesson on neutral ground—which is to say that the location shouldn't favor one party over the rest. There are shielded rooms above the market, Councilor, if—"

"I'm content to be out in the free air," Councilor ziaGorn said easily. "It is, as you say, a beautiful day. Perhaps the Warden, though—"

"I believe I may tolerate an hour of mild exposure," Bentamin said, and waved a hand toward the pavilion. "That seems a likely spot."

"As you choose," Tekelia said, glancing to Blays.

"I'll bespeak a tray," she said, and jogged off toward the market.

Tekelia turned toward the pavilion, gesturing Majel ziaGorn and Bentamin to follow.

"I mention, as a point of information, that the ambient is playful today, Bentamin."

"Thank you," came the placid answer.

"Brave to the point of bravado," Tekelia murmured, and Bentamin laughed.

"That is, I believe, a defining trait of our family."

• • • ❄ • • •

Despite being family, Bentamin chastaMeir did not look a great deal like his cousin Tekelia vesterGranz, Majel thought. Both were dark-haired, and moderately tall, but there all similarity began and ended. The Warden was square in jaw and broad in shoulder, his complexion an even tan; his nose aquiline, his eyes a deep blue that seemed almost black beneath stern brows.

Speaker for the Haosa vesterGranz was more lightly built; round-faced, complexion decidedly brown, nose short and turned slightly up at the tip. Where the Warden's dark hair was crisp-cut and disciplined, Tekelia's was in a long braid, tied off with a bit of lavender ribbon.

And then there were the eyes.

Tekelia vesterGranz's eyes *changed*. When they had first introduced themselves, the right eye had been blue and the left, brown. The next time Majel had looked, the right eye had been brown and the left, grey. The third time, they were green and amber, and at that point, Majel had told himself sternly to stop staring at Tekelia vesterGranz's eyes.

Blays, on the other hand—Blays was near enough his own

height, her figure lithe; complexion rosy; her brow broad and her chin narrow. Her eyes were the same shade of lucent amber; eyebrows slightly slanted. Her hair was a light color between blond and silver, that tumbled carelessly to her shoulders, some strands floating about her head as if she were attended by a gentle, private breeze.

Like Tekelia, she had chosen to come to a formal meeting dressed in boots, tough pants, and a sweater.

And here she came back, bearing a tray that was clearly too large and too heavy for her, though she seemed to have no trouble carrying it as she walked briskly toward the pavilion.

Majel began to stand, meaning to help her with her burden, and turned his head when he heard Tekelia vesterGranz say, "Ah."

"Yes?" Majel said.

"Blays is entirely capable," Tekelia said. "Not a drop will be spilled, I guarantee it."

To Majel's mind, that was hardly the point, but if her intimate was unconcerned...

He resumed his seat, and Blays arrived, leaning to place the tray in the center of the table.

"There," she said, sliding onto the bench next to Tekelia, and smiling. "I think we're well-provisioned."

"Who was on kitchen?" Tekelia asked.

"Grazum—can't you tell?"

"I had a feeling," Tekelia admitted, and nodded to include Bentamin and Majel. "Let's do this Haosa-style—please, serve yourselves."

· · · ❖ · · ·

"I'll be pleased to see you at my office, Counselor essWorthi," Bentamin said. "Shall we make an appointment now?"

Blays eyed him.

"Is there a particular reason you and I must meet under the Grid? Do you anticipate a crisis?"

Bentamin smiled. "Merely, I thought you might like to see for yourself how we go on, so you know where our arguments and assumptions come from."

"Tekelia will be away no longer than a week—"

"And yet you are Counsel to Chaos," Majel ziaGorn said in his calm, reasonable voice. "Speaker vesterGranz may profit from your independent observations. In fact—" he leaned slightly forward. "Have you seen the Council at work?"

Blays didn't laugh—not quite. Tekelia gave her full points for that.

"Pardon me, sir, but I'm Haosa. The Council room isn't for the likes of me."

Majel glanced first to Bentamin then to Tekelia.

"I thought that was about to change."

"It's the wish of the Warden of Civilization and the Chair of the Council of the Civilized that the Haosa be given a seat at Civilization's table," Tekelia said. "You understand that this has to do with a foretelling given by the former Oracle?"

"Yes—that Civilization will fall, and the Haosa, too," Majel said crisply. "That has been shared with the Council of the Whole. If the Haosa are to share in Civilization's fall, then surely they ought to have a seat at *Colemeno's* table."

Tekelia feared that Blays had sighed. Surely, the intensity of her interest had sharpened, becoming so bright and particular Tekelia feared Bentamin would notice.

"There's the small difficulty of convincing the Haosa," Tekelia said, and paused, waiting for Majel ziaGorn to wonder why this would be a difficulty.

The Deaf Councilor, however, merely inclined his head.

"Naturally. They fear a trap, or at the very least a hoax. It was so when the Deaf came to the table, though we had fought to be there. Many are still wary, and—I beg your pardon, Warden—they are right to be. We took our seat, and we demonstrated what we could do from that vantage. Slowly—and it *is* a slow process—we build more trust among ourselves, and gain the respect of our fellow councilors."

Tekelia smiled.

"Trader yos'Galan was right to advise me to talk with you."

"Trader yos'Galan is a perceptive person," Majel ziaGorn murmured. "May I ask—a delicate question?"

"By all means!" Tekelia said. "It will be a novelty."

Blays laughed, and Majel ziaGorn smiled. Tekelia even felt a ripple of amusement from Bentamin, who was wearing his impassive Warden face.

"Well, then, delicately— Is there someone who is more favored than yourself to go into the Council Chamber?"

Tekelia laughed.

"No, you misunderstand the Haosa! My cousins are perfectly at peace with the notion that I accept the offered seat if it suits my whim. What they can't agree upon is whether *my* promises will bind *them*."

"I understand," Majel ziaGorn said, and Tekelia Saw that he did. "Have you only one Counsel to Chaos?"

"Three. Blays is merely the most forward."

"Utterly shameless," Blays admitted, smiling into the Deaf Councilor's pretty eyes. "I talk to everyone."

"A useful talent in an advisor," Majel ziaGorn said calmly, affecting not to understand Blays's flirtation, though Tekelia thought there had been a . . . flicker in the ambient, before the man turned to Tekelia.

"If you were to recruit aides to assist your counselors, whose tasks would include speaking to"—a sharp glance at Blays—"*everyone*, you might be able to win the interest of more of your cousins. I assume that you or your counselors report to the villages?"

"Occasionally, I visit and make a formal report at a village meeting," Tekelia said. "My counselors gather gossip and let me know what I should pay attention to."

"A reasonable system," Majel ziaGorn murmured, "but you won't have time to travel to all the villages yourself, should you take the offered chair."

Tekelia turned to Blays. "Well, Cousin? Are you willing to appoint two assistants, and stand up at Visalee's meeting as the Voice of Chaos?"

"It had better be three," Blays said thoughtfully. "If you won't have time to attend meetings yourself, you surely won't have time to chase down the Wild and coax them to talk with you."

"The Wild," Tekelia pointed out, "don't share your skill in speaking with everyone—or even *anyone*."

"True, but Ryanna's uncle lives Wild, and is very sociable of his kind. There might be a connection to be made there."

It was, Tekelia knew, one step closer to a commitment of time and effort that looked to overwhelm all the rest of life. And, yet—

"Change does need to happen," Majel ziaGorn murmured, as if he had read Tekelia's thoughts.

"And if not us, then who?" Tekelia turned both palms up. "I've been taking that lesson from Trader yos'Galan, as well, and no reflection on her, that I'm not an apt student."

Tekelia looked to Blays.

"Find what's possible. When I come back, the counselors will meet. Hopefully, we'll be able to determine what *we* think."

"That sounds like a reasonable way to go forward," said Bentamin, speaking for the first time since he had invited Blays to visit his office.

"It does," Majel ziaGorn agreed, and looked to Tekelia. "I'm at your service, if you find yourself with questions."

Tekelia laughed. "Oh, I don't doubt I'll have questions! You might come to regret that offer."

The Deaf Councilor smiled—truly smiled—and it was a thing of rare beauty reflected in the ambient.

"I think I'll find it one of the best offers I've ever made," he said. "Let's see who's right."

"Done! Now—Blays, will you or will you not visit Bentamin in his office while I'm away?"

"Given it all, I suppose I ought to," Blays said. She looked at Councilor ziaGorn. "I think you were about to invite me to watch the Council at work," she said.

"I'd be delighted to seat you as my guest. During the session, you'll be in a gallery with other observers—guests of councilors, and interested citizens. After, if you like, we can sit together to discuss what was done, and why. It might give you insight into the Council's mind, and illuminate what needs to be changed."

Blays raised her eyebrows. "I think you're a revolutionary," she said, sounding pensive.

Majel ziaGorn laughed.

"It's one of the many things I value in him," Bentamin said. "The Council knows its business too well, and Councilor ziaGorn keeps them on the off-foot."

"No, ivenAlyatta is in the fore there," Majel protested.

"Not so much as she had been," Bentamin told him. "Lately, she's been waiting to see how you'll play."

"Now, you've made him self-conscious," Tekelia said.

"My apologies, Councilor," Bentamin said, inclining his head.

"I," Blays said, voice raised, "accept both of your kind invitations." She produced a notepad from some pocket or another and flipped the cover open, tapping the screen to life.

"What days and times are best for you?"

Colemenoport
Offices of
Tree-and-Dragon Trade Mission

. . . .

"TRADER." JES DEA'TOLIN LOOKED UP FROM HER SCREEN WITH A smile. Dyoli and Mar Tyn were standing one on each side of her desk, faces serious, postures alert.

Padi paused to consider the picture thus made. "Virtue flanked by the guards to her honor," she said, as one making a call in a game of Tableau. "I hope I'm not to be cast as Wickedness."

"Far from it!" Jes cried. "You are Fortune Herself!"

This was an unusually gay mood, Padi thought, even as she bowed.

"A much more apt role. I allow it." She came closer to the desk, noting that the blue light indicating a transmission line to the *Passage* was open, was lit. She felt a spike of excitement.

"Is it ready?" she asked.

"Only this moment compiled and queued," Mar Tyn said. "We were about to call you."

"And here I am." She opened her arms and caught Jes's eye. "At will, *Qe'andra* dea'Tolin."

"Trader," Jes murmured, glancing down at her keyboard. She tapped in a rapid sequence.

The transmission light flickered, there was a breathless moment . . . two . . .

"We have an ack," Jes said, and sat back, grinning.

"The Colemeno Whole Port Inventory has been submitted to Master Trader yos'Galan for review. It is done, and, if I may say it, done well." She rose and bowed as to valued comrades.

"I could not have been more fortunate in my team or in my trade liaison. All of us know that the master trader's timetable was ambitious in the extreme, and we may take pride, that we met—no! we *exceeded*—the demands of that challenge. I stand in awe of us, and of our accomplishment."

"We could not have succeeded so well without your experience, courage, and guidance," Padi said, producing a bow of her own—honor to the team.

She straightened and considered them: Jes glowing; Dyoli radiating satisfaction; even Mar Tyn alight with pleasure.

"This," she said, flinging a hand toward the now-dark transmission light, "calls for wine! I invite you all to my office, that we may drink to a challenge well-met, and to our future profit."

Off-Grid

....

"WHAT DID YOU THINK OF OUR HAOSA?" BENTAMIN CHASTAMEIR
asked, as he guided the car down the road to Haven City. Unlike
the city streets, there was only the truck link on this road, which
meant all other drivers were required to navigate manually.

Majel glanced at him.

"I liked them," he said slowly. "As we all agreed, Trader
yos'Galan's instincts are sound. You know that I've long believed
the Deaf and the Haosa ought to make common cause."

"Yes, against Civilization!" Bentamin laughed, and glanced
at Majel before returning his attention to the road. "And you
refused the compliment of being recognized as a revolutionary!"

"I'm only trying to effect necessary change—"

"Which is, I believe, the precise definition of *revolutionary*."

"It sounds more violent than I intend," Majel protested.

"Yes, we would all like our opponents to be persuaded to a more
sensible course by the brilliance of our arguments. Unfortunately,
it rarely happens that way. Do I recall that you were attacked in
your own casino, and a school targeted in Pacazahno Village, by
people who believe the Deaf are unfit to govern—even themselves?"

"You do," Majel admitted. "Both incidents are proof that violence changes nothing."

"No?"

"No. I haven't resigned my seat, nor has Pacazahno Village
accepted an oversight board composed of Civilized experts, to
protect them and keep them from error."

There was a pause before the Warden said, "True. I hadn't
thought of it in those terms."

Ahead, the road curved, and it seemed that Bentamin had
put his whole attention into navigating the car.

When the road was straight again, he said, "My cousin Tekelia would rather not take the Haosa seat at Civilization's table."

"I thought I saw reluctance—or at least resignation. Do you think Speaker vesterGranz will come to the table, even lacking the approval of the rest of the Haosa?"

"Tekelia is certainly capable of doing just that. And reluctance aside, I believe my cousin does see the need."

"Well, the Oracle's Seeing—"

"That, I think, weighs less than the arrival of the trade mission," Bentamin said. "Tekelia sees the opening of Colemeno to more ships as an opportunity for the Haosa. That's why Blays essWorthi has been brought forth as Speaker pro tem—so Tekelia can visit the master trader on his ship."

Majel sighed. "Now *there* is a missed opportunity," he said ruefully. "Had I known it was possible—"

"There's still time, surely?" Bentamin sounded amused.

"Time, and more ships incoming," Majel agreed. "Still..."

"Still," Bentamin agreed. "Maybe we can make a delegation."

"That's not a bad notion. I'll put it to Trader yos'Galan."

"Let me know what she says."

"I will." Majel paused. "What do you think," he said slowly, "of Blays essWorthi?"

"I think she's well-chosen to hold the office of Counsel to Chaos. And you?"

"I found her . . . interesting," Majel said temperately, trying not to think of a pair of warm amber eyes, or light hair floating around a triangular face. "I'm looking forward to seeing her again."

"Ah," Bentamin said softly. "Yes, it will be interesting to see what she makes of the Wardian and the Council. Speaking of revolutionaries, I think you have an ally in her, as you do in me. Have I given you my emergency number?"

Majel turned his head to consider the Warden's profile.

"You haven't, no. Is there a reason that I ought to have it?"

"I like to keep my allies close. The number is seven."

"Seven?" Majel repeated. "That's the whole of it?"

"Who has time to recall and punch six digits in an emergency? The number seven entered into any comm unit will reach me directly."

Majel laughed, and spread his hands. "Thank you; I'll use it only at need."

"Which is exactly why you should have it."

Colemenoport
Offices of
Tree-and-Dragon Trade Mission

. . . .

THE WINE HAD BEEN TASTED AND PRONOUNCED FITTING. PADI brought out cheese, crackers, cake, and nuts. Eventually, the glasses were refreshed and Mar Tyn carried the empty plates into the kitchen.

"We must not give ourselves wholly over to pleasure," Jes said, smiling 'round the table. "It's true that we have completed our report, and made our recommendations. The master trader, however, may require clarity on some point or another. Therefore, we must hold ourselves ready."

Dyoli laughed.

"Holding ready is several levels down from where we have been operating these weeks," she pointed out. "I believe a nap may be called for, unless you think the master trader will need clarity within the next few hours?"

Jes tipped her head consideringly.

"I think we may dare a few hours of . . . light-time. I'm thinking along the lines of a walk through the Wayfarer's garden, and *then* a nap!"

"Always ambitious," Mar Tyn murmured surprisingly, and Jes turned her smile on him.

"Be grateful, Master pai'Fortana, that I do not in this instance require similar ambition from my 'prentice." She finished her wine and set the glass aside. "Though I do expect us to meet after Prime, on the topic of inventory and costs of merchandise."

"I look forward to our session," Mar Tyn said calmly, and Jes's smile this time was speculative.

"You have gotten bold since our first lesson."

He inclined his head.

"What can I say, but that accounting suits me?"

"Now, *that*," Dyoli announced, reaching for the bottle and dividing what was left between their four glasses, "is worthy of a toast, indeed!"

Padi had shown her guests to the door and was considering the wisdom of closing her office in solidarity. A glance at the calendar confirmed that she had no meetings until late the next day, which, she thought, would need to be canceled.

For it suddenly struck her, what it meant that the final Whole Port Inventory had been sent to the master trader. She and Tekelia were expected aboard the *Passage*.

Even as she turned toward the comm, it chimed, announcing an incoming call.

She tapped "receive."

"Tree-and-Dragon Trade Mission, Trader yos'Galan speaking. Service?"

"Hello, Padi," Tekelia said.

"I was just about to call you with the news," she said.

"What news?"

"Jes has only an hour ago released the final inventory to the master trader. You and I, therefore, must lift. That is, if you are still of a mind to experience ship life."

"I am! Are we lifting now?"

"We have twelve hours before the best window. I need to speak with Dil Nem, who will be accompanying us."

"Would it be wrong of me to ask you to come to the village potluck this evening?"

"I will be piloting tomorrow," Padi said.

"And it will be prudent for you to have slept before you do; I understand. I swear that I will extract us in good time. And, you know, my bag is already packed."

"And mine," Padi said. "Very well, the potluck it is! Will I meet you there?"

"Come to the Tree House. Blays is here and we can all three go together."

"All right. Let me make some calls, and change my clothes."

Wildege
Kelim Station

. . . .

VYR HAD FINISHED UP ALL THE LITTLE REPAIRS THAT ACCUMU-
lated, even in a stead as well-kept as Kelim Station. Then, he'd
cleaned the kitchen, scrubbed the foyer's stone floor, tidied the
parlor, aired his sleeping space, cleared leaves off the array, and
in an excess of zeal, walked up onto the roof to inspect the berm,
which was of course just fine.

In fact, the only thing he hadn't done since Kel had left for
Visalee was look to his shields.

Vyr went to the kitchen, poured himself a mug of cider, and
went outside to settle into a chair under the sunlit sky.

Now that it was days too late, he wondered if he shouldn't
have gone with Kel to Visalee.

Practically Civilization, he remembered Kel saying, the morning she'd left, and snorted. Visalee wasn't the farthest thing from
Civilization—that would be Kelim Station. Which made Visalee
the *second* farthest thing from Civilization.

Along Winterdark, when the Ribbons never left the sky, after
a long day with the wood, and a couple ciders in her, Kel could be
persuaded to speculate about the likelihood of more steads, beyond
them, in the Backaway. Kel had heard stories when she'd been a girl
in Visalee—longer ago than Vyr had been alive—stories of people
living solitary among the trees. Those stories had grabbed her by
the heart until one day she decided to find if they were true. And
that was how Kelim Station came to be the last stead off Main Path.

Or, at least, the last that anybody knew about, because finding
a Wilder who didn't want to be found was a fool's game, doomed
to failure.

Kel now...If his life had fallen out otherwise, Kelim of Wildege might well have been the most frightening person Vyr had ever met. It wasn't that she had so *much* of any specific Talent, but that her link with what she casually referred to as "the ambient" gave her access to what seemed to be a limitless *range* of Talent.

Kel was always and entirely open to the unfiltered Condition of Colemeno, as it was formalized in the technical books. Her pattern a spiderweb woven out of cloud and chaos, she should have been one of the monsters that had destroyed the first wave. Or—and more likely—she should have been an idiot—a savant, maybe; her body nothing but a vessel for random, deadly forces.

But Kel *wasn't* a monster, and Vyr hadn't met the knife that was sharper. She was an old woman with an affinity for wood, a fondness for cider, and a strange connection to chaos that he had reason to be grateful for, since she'd saved his life.

Truth told, he hadn't expected to survive the initial fall, much less the blare of confusing energies that had drawn his Gifts like metal shred to a lodestone.

But the impact with the ground hadn't killed him; and he'd fortunately broken an arm, not a leg. He'd lain, stunned, on the ground, staring up at the multitude of dancing lights above him, his mind insisting that he was somehow *upside down*, and the lights—the lights of the city—were properly below him. The draw on his core, terrifying in its strength, had finally roused him. It had been the basest instinct for survival that prompted him to reach out, clawing chunks of untamed energies to him, patching a shield together over his native shield until the draw lessened—and faded—enough.

Faint, head ringing, somehow he had gotten to his feet and staggered through a kaleidoscope of color until at last he found—a door.

He fell against it, that was his recollection, his broken arm screaming protest. The door wavered; it *changed*. It became an elder, her snowy hair in a braid, eyes reflecting the chaotic colors of forest and sky.

"They're trying to kill me," he gasped, and her face creased into a smile.

"Well, we can't have that, now can we?"

That was the first time Kel had saved him. She was a Wild Haosa, jealous of her solitude, yet she granted him room in her domi; work; a place to huddle—yes, *huddle*. Hiding from those who wanted him dead.

She'd asked him no questions, not about his past, not about those who had dropped him, a Civilized man, into the middle of the Wild. She didn't ask him to leave, though he had no doubt she'd be glad when he did go.

Which... maybe he should have left by now. He'd thought about it. But in the end, he stayed. He'd *waited*, though he didn't know what he was waiting for.

The Ribbons were rising. He could feel them at his core.

Vyr got up and went inside the domi.

Off-Grid
The Tree House

. . . .

"AND WHAT DID YOU THINK OF MAJEL ZIAGORN?" PADI ASKED, as Tekelia handed her a glass of the green wine.

"I liked him a great deal," Tekelia said, settling beside her on the couch. "He thinks we can do each other some good. I only see one side of that coin, frankly."

"Tekelia hardly does him justice," Blays said. She was sitting on the edge of Tekelia's desk, wine glass in hand. Her hair drifted and flowed around her face like a snow squall, and her amber eyes were bright.

Padi tipped her head.

"I take it you think well of him, too?"

"Think well of him!" Blays cried. "He was *magnificent*, sitting full under the ambient, as cool and ordered as you please, while the Warden of Civilization cowered behind his shields!"

Padi blinked, and heard Tekelia murmur inside her head, *Blays is smitten.*

So I apprehend, Padi answered. *Is she always this warm?*

Warm moreso than cool, though this seems rather warmer than usual. On the other hand, he is *pretty.*

Aloud, Tekelia said, "Not *cowering*, Blays."

"Well...perhaps not. His shields weren't entirely closed."

"You know," Padi said, suddenly struck. "I also value Majel ziaGorn. He has been a good and stalwart friend, and I would not like to see him come to harm. He is Civilized, is he not? Will he take any harm from his boldness, sitting out unprotected?"

"Councilor ziaGorn isn't Civilized, Padi; he's Deaf," Tekelia said. "The ambient isn't there for him. It's exactly as if his ears were stopped; music would be lost to him."

"That doesn't mean he's lesser," Blays put in strongly. "In fact, based on today's display, I would say he's of far more use than your typical Luzant. Neither the ambient *nor* the Grid acts on or distracts him, so he's able to keep his wits about him—always."

"Yes, exactly," Tekelia said. "He lives in Haven City, under the Grid—which is also invisible to him. Civilization calls him and his folk Surda, not Luzant—and they have only recently won the right to sit at the council table and speak with an equal voice. Not too many years ago, Deaf businesses were required to accept the oversight of Civilized boards, it being believed that, otherwise, the Deaf would fall victim to unscrupulous Citizens."

Padi stared.

"Why not control the unscrupulous, then?"

Blays laughed.

"Yes! I like her! Why not, indeed!" She pointed her wine glass at Tekelia.

"A question, Cousin."

"Ask."

"Will you want a report of my meeting with the Warden and my day observing the Council? In fact, how will I get in touch with you, if I need advice?"

"Suddenly," Tekelia said, wonderingly, "she's serious."

"I am taking my lesson from Majel ziaGorn," Blays said primly, "who would *surely* wish to know something similar, if he were left to speak with your voice."

"Would he?" Tekelia asked, apparently charmed by this assertion.

"Wouldn't he?"

"He did seem very organized, and quick to point out that the Counsels to Chaos will themselves require counselors, as—if—their role expands."

"That will be an agreement," Blays announced to the room at large.

"Yes, but as to your question—"

"As to your question," Padi interrupted, pulling a card from her sleeve-pocket, and offering it to Blays. "That is my comm code aboard *Dutiful Passage*. Call it and I will connect you to Tekelia."

Blays smiled.

"Thank you, Padi."

"Yes," Tekelia said. "Thank you, Padi. I should have been more forward-looking."

"It is," Padi murmured, "a new adventure for you."

Tekelia laughed and rose.

"I suggest we go to the potluck, if you're both ready?"

"Ready *and* hungry!" Blays said, sliding to the floor.

"Actually, I *am* hungry," Padi said, it being perfectly acceptable to discuss such things among the Haosa. She extended a hand. Tekelia took it and she rose, only then seeing that Blays was quite frozen, eyes wide.

"I *told* you," Tekelia said.

"Yes, Cousin; yes. You did tell me. But hearing it and seeing it are very different." She bowed. "Please forgive me; I'm only a Wild Haosa with no wits to support me."

"I should mention that Blays indulges from time to time in sarcasm," Tekelia said, leaning to kiss Padi's cheek. "Let me get the basket, and we can be on our way."

"Does one walk to a potluck?" Padi asked, and Tekelia smiled at her over one shoulder.

"If the evening is as fair as this one—yes."

Padi turned toward Blays.

"Have you ever seen Tekelia...discorporate someone?"

"Ribbons avert! I haven't. Tekelia is very careful of us."

Padi closed her eyes, trying to order her next question, only—

"Am I going by myself, then?" Tekelia called.

Off-Grid
Ribbon Dance Village

· · · · · · · · · · · · · · · · · · · ·

THERE WERE MUSICIANS IN THE VILLAGE GREEN, AND A FEW dancers, but more people with plates and cups sitting on benches or blankets. Someone began to sing. One of the musicians laughed, and shook the stick she was holding, waking a sound like pelting rain. Another brought his mandola to a knee and began to strum, as other voices took up the song.

Blays, who was slightly ahead of Padi and Tekelia, danced a few steps, and executed a spin that took her quite off the ground. Someone called her name and she turned in that direction, laughing.

"When's the next Ribbon Dance?" Padi asked, watching as Blays vanished into the crowd.

"Three months, local," Tekelia replied, pausing on the threshold of the meeting hall to bow her in.

"Tekelia— Padi!" Geritsi slentAlin joined them at the buffet. "I need to talk with you after you've had something to eat."

"We can eat and you can talk," Tekelia suggested. "Or we'll find you after—"

"Simultaneous talking and eating sounds perfect," Geritsi said. "I'm in the front corner."

"Not if you're here, you aren't," Tekelia said, eyeing the room, which was crowded, though it was still early, in village potluck terms.

"Dosent is asleep under the table," Geritsi said, and Padi laughed.

"Well-played," she said. She finished filling her plate, turned—

"You must have some of Vayeen's goulash!" Geritsi said. "If you wait until seconds, it will be gone. I'll bring you both a bowl."

Padi poured herself a glass of cider, and thought the question to Tekelia.

The front corner?

To your left as you put the buffet behind you, Tekelia answered. *Follow me.*

"So," Geritsi said, once they had all sat down, admired Dosent, and sampled the goulash—which really was, Padi noted, *very* good. Perhaps Vayeen could be persuaded to trade for the recipe.

"You said I might be hearing from Dyoli ven'Deelin—and I have, just an hour ago. She told me immediately that she had been given my comm code by Tekelia vesterGranz. She represents herself as a member of the Tree-and-Dragon Trade Mission, and also a—" Geritsi closed her eyes, as if she was lining the phrase up in her mind's eye—"*a classically trained Healer in the Liaden style.*"

"She is," Padi said, "all of those things."

"She's also tutoring Padi and me in the—more subtle arts of Healing," Tekelia said.

"Someone ought," Geritsi said, without visible irony.

Tekelia smiled. "Exactly."

Geritsi pushed her plate aside and leaned her elbows on the table.

"Healer ven'Deelin asked particularly after the twins. She said that you agreed to her examining them—*formally,* is the word she used—in hope of finding some method of disentangling them from each other before active harm is done."

"Yes," Tekelia said, putting the bowl aside, quite empty. "Do you think Vayeen can be persuaded to part with the recipe for that?"

Padi laughed. "I was just thinking the same thing."

"As was everyone in this room," Geritsi said. "No one's been quite brave enough to ask, yet."

"Maybe I'll try my luck," Tekelia said. "I need a word with him, in any case. But, first let's finish with Dyoli. I think she's absolutely trustworthy, and far better than we're likely to get from under-Grid."

"Which so far has been exactly nothing," Geritsi said, picking up her glass. "I wonder if you also know Mar Tyn pai'Fortana?"

"Mar Tyn is Dyoli's partner," Padi said. "He's quite gentle."

"I would add protective," Tekelia said. "It was wonderful to see him draw Vaiza out."

"Vaiza has written to him, apparently by prearrangement,

and was over the Ribbons when he received an answer. Torin, on the other hand, informs me that Healer ven'Deelin is a 'Liad cousin,' which she seems to think is...interesting."

"Healer ven'Deelin is a member of Clan Ixin," Padi said, "which, with my own clan, Korval, brought the Small Talents from Liad to Colemeno when they were being persecuted."

"The old records do indicate that the 'xin' prefix originally derives from Ixin," Tekelia said, giving Geritsi an earnest look. "I admit, after all this time the connection is...thin, but—"

"But it's far better than any other connection they have," Geritsi finished, "excepting Eet."

"And yourself," Padi said, "and Dosent, and the whole of the village—aren't they Ribbon Dance's children?"

"Yes, but you see, that was something decided by the village, and not by the twins," Geritsi said.

"Oh," Padi said. "I do see, yes."

"Healer ven'Deelin proposes tomorrow morning for a meeting and examination," Geritsi said. "Does that seem to you rather quick?"

The question was perhaps directed to Tekelia, but Padi put herself forward to answer.

"Dyoli has been part of the team most concerned with compiling the whole port inventory, which was sent to the master trader only today. Tomorrow, she can be certain that she will be free; after that"—she turned her palms up—"the master trader may have questions."

"Oh. It's good of her to come to us on what ought to be a day of rest," Geritsi said, and looked to Tekelia. "Will you be coming with us?"

"Padi and I will be lifting early tomorrow," Tekelia said.

Geritsi blinked.

"I hadn't realized it was *that* soon. And Blays will be standing up as Speaker?"

"She's agreed to a week. After that, who knows what might happen?"

Geritsi laughed.

Tekelia leaned forward.

"Geritsi. You need to know that—we *don't know* what will happen, once I'm inside the ship's field. It might feel as though I'm—absent."

Geritsi frowned, and looked at Padi. "Absent?"

"We *don't* know," Padi said. "Which is what Tekelia wants to establish. You may notice no change in your connection."

"After all, Padi and I first met when she was traveling on the ship," Tekelia said. "Only, if you should find me gone, don't despair."

The ambient reflected, if not despair, then something like distress. Dosent sat up and put a large paw on Geritsi's knee. She laughed softly, and rubbed the big cat's ears.

Padi smiled, retrieved a card from her sleeve and offered it.

"This is my comm code on-ship. If you need to speak with Tekelia—*about anything*—call me and I will make sure you are connected."

Geritsi blinked, looked at Tekelia, then took the card with a slight bow of her head. "Thank you, Padi."

"There's Vayeen and Kencia," Tekelia said, rising. "I need to talk with both of them. Padi, I swear I will be no longer than half an hour and then we will leave."

"I will hold you to that," Padi said. Tekelia laughed, and vanished into the crowd.

"Do you know why Tekelia needs to talk to Kencia and Vayeen?" Geritsi asked.

Padi raised a shoulder. "I assume to tell them about the possible change in their connection—they both dance with Tekelia." She smiled at Geritsi. "As you do."

"And you do," Geritsi said, putting the card into her pocket. "You must allow me to thank you, Padi yos'Galan."

"Thank me? The card is nothing. I—"

"Not for the card, though I'm grateful for it. No, I want particularly to thank you for being...a positive influence on Tekelia."

"I—" Padi began, but Geritsi held up a hand.

"Please, let me finish. There had been a...darkness in Tekelia. Not cruelty, or despondency. Maybe it was only loneliness, for a touch. Even linked to Tekelia, I can't quite imagine what it must be like, never to even press the hand of a friend. *Your* connection has cast that shadow out, and increased the joy in Tekelia's life. I'm grateful to you for the happiness you've brought to one who is very dear to me."

Padi inclined her head.

"I hear you and understand you," she said carefully. "But—you do know that all of this is the veriest accident?"

Geritsi grinned, and leaned forward to touch Padi's hand with light fingertips.

"There are no accidents," she whispered, "only gifts from the ambient."

Geritsi and Dosent left to pick the twins up from their time helping behind the buffet, and Padi began gathering together the dishes, thinking that she would clear the table, then step outside, where it would possibly be quieter.

She had everything in a pile and was about to rise when someone sat in the chair Geritsi had recently vacated.

"Padi yos'Galan!" exclaimed Tekelia's Aunt Asta. "*Just* the person I wanted to see. I hear that you and Tekelia are bound for the master trader's ship, beyond the Ribbons—in mere hours!"

"That is correct," Padi said, having some idea of what might be coming. "It's a very select group—myself, Tekelia, and Dil Nem, who is a member of the Tree-and-Dragon team."

"Isn't there room for one more?" Aunt Asta asked, not *quite* wheedling, for that would surely be unworthy of a woman of her years.

"Did you think Padi would give you a different answer?" Tekelia asked, arriving at the side of the table with two companions.

Aunt Asta lifted her chin.

"It does no harm to ask," she said.

"Indeed, it does not, but I'm afraid there is no room," Padi said. "And you know, it is a *little* risky to surprise the master trader. One never knows what he might do."

Aunt Asta laughed.

"Oh, I *must* meet him!"

"I did relay your invitation, ma'am," Padi said, and took out another card. "This is my direct comm-code on the ship. If you wish to reach me, or Tekelia, for any reason, please use it."

"Thank you, my dear," Aunt Asta said, and rose. Tekelia fell back to give her room to pass. "Do be careful, Tekelia, dear."

"As careful as may be, Aunt Asta," Tekelia said, and watched her slip away into the crowd.

"Padi, you recall Vayeen and Kencia."

"I do." She smiled at them, and produced two more cards. "As you heard me tell Aunt Asta—if you need to speak to Tekelia for any reason while we are with the ship, use that code and I will be sure to connect you."

They took the cards with murmured thanks, even as Kencia looked at Tekelia.

"Do you think the ambient will forget you?"

"I don't," Tekelia said firmly. "But a friend posits that the ship is its own Grid, and therefore the ambient may have trouble seeing me while I'm aboard."

Kencia looked at Vayeen; Vayeen looked at Tekelia, and turned his hands palm up.

"Aunt Asta is ahead of us. Be careful, Tekelia." He turned and bowed. "And you, too, Padi."

"We will do our best," Padi said.

"Exactly our best," Tekelia said, and looked at Padi. "I promised to remove you early so you can rest before tomorrow's labors. Shall we leave now?"

"Now does seems auspicious," Padi said.

Tekelia pointed at the dishes Padi had gathered. "Kenny, cope with these, will you?"

"Why me?" Kencia demanded.

"*You're* not leaving *now*," Tekelia said, and caught Padi's hand.

Mist swirled, brief and energetic. When it cleared Tekelia and Padi were gone.

Kencia and Vayeen exchanged a glance.

"You balance," Vayeen said. "I'll break trail."

Off-Grid
Peck's Market

. . . .

"HERE THEY COME!" VAIZA CRIED, LEAPING UP FROM THE BENCH. "Torin, come on!"

He turned as if to run down the slope from the pavilion to the driveway, only to find a large furry obstacle across his path.

"Dosent!"

"Why not let them arrive, and take a minute to orient?" Vayeen asked. "That would be the civilized thing. Am I right, Ritsi?"

"I was taught that it wasn't polite to rush visitors," Geritsi said solemnly.

"The car isn't even here yet, Vaiza," Torin added. She remained seated, Eet the norbear on the table before her.

"But I can hear it!" he answered, with only slightly diminished enthusiasm.

"I can't," Torin said.

He turned to look at her. "Truly? It's plain as plain."

"It's a whisper on the ambient," Vayeen said. "You're not hearing it with your ears, boy-child. Now, be glad I'm not Tekelia, who'd be asking how you'd go about knowing one from the other."

Vaiza spun toward him. "Well, how *do*—oh. Wait."

Vayeen exchanged a glance with Geritsi, then looked back to Vaiza, who was staring up into the Ribbon-laced sky.

"Well," said Torin, impatiently, "how *do* you tell the difference?"

"I—I just heard your voice with the *outside* of my ear," Vaiza said, turning to face her. "And I'm hearing the car with the *inside* of my ear."

Torin frowned. "The *inside* of your ear?"

"*You* know. Where we hear each other—and Eet."

"Oh." Torin transferred her frown to the tabletop. "I don't—no, there *is* a car coming! But Vaiza, I'm hearing it with my *ears*."

"And so am I," Vayeen said, standing and walking a few paces away from the table. Geritsi had asked him to attend this meeting because he was a teleporter. His Gift was nowhere near as strong as Tekelia's, of course, but he was more than able to snatch two small people to safety if it should happen that the outworlders weren't quite as benign as was thought.

Vayeen was of two minds regarding the outworlders. On the one hand, they seemed to be thriving under the Grid, and he had on principle no use for anyone who styled themselves Civilized.

On the other hand, Tekelia vouched for them, and it wasn't easy to fool Tekelia. The fact that the Healer was Tekelia's own tutor in the finer points of Healing would make it even more difficult to conceal a nefarious purpose.

And the Healer was partnered with a Serendipitist, a Gift that was not only rare, but ten times out of twelve found to be a Wild Talent by those whose business it was to make such determinations, because it required no tools to operate. The sole criteria for declaring a Serendipitist Civilized was the individual's ability to control their Gift.

Which, Vayeen thought sourly, was all you needed to know about Civilization, right there.

The whirring of a car's engine grew louder. Vayeen looked around to see that Geritsi had risen, and come forward, Dosent at her side, Vaiza on Dosent's other side. Torin remained at the table with the norbear.

The engine-purr increased, and the car came round the curve into the driveway—a bigger car than Vayeen had expected, bright blue and sleek. It pulled onto the grass at the side of the drive, out of the way of traffic. The engine cut, and the front door opened to release a person wearing the style of clothing favored by the outworlders. Vayeen felt himself tense, even as he asked the ambient for the driver's signature. He was obligingly shown a mellow inner tapestry informed by a firm core dedicated to protection and order, laced with mordant humor. There was no Talent evident, not even the most minor Gift.

The driver opened the back door and a woman emerged, dressed in the same style, her shields closed tight. That, Vayeen thought, would be the Healer. A man exited behind her, closing the door, and Vayeen felt the ambient... *shiver*.

If the newcomer had shields, he didn't care to use them. He

stood fully exposed, as if he were Haosa born. The ambient coiled and flowed around him in a lover's embrace, crooning softly.

"Well," Geritsi breathed, at the same moment that Vaiza let out a yell.

"Mar Tyn!"

The man turned, raised a hand, and started quickly up the slope, his companions coming behind.

Vayeen felt Geritsi's sigh in the ambient.

"Please, children, welcome our guests," she said.

Vaiza leapt into a run. Torin got up from the bench, took Eet into her arms, and followed her brother. Slowly.

Vayeen stepped closer to Geritsi.

"The driver—is Deaf."

"That seems to be so," she agreed. "We did hear that the trade mission's security officers were all of them Deaf."

"So we did," Vayeen murmured, as he watched Vaiza fairly throw himself into the arms of the ambient's sweetheart, who caught him, spun him around, and set him onto his feet again.

The Healer, in the meantime, had lengthened her stride, and met Torin higher up the slope, where she paused, apparently being made known to Eet, before the driver joined them and they all three came on together, the man slightly behind, Vaiza his satellite.

Arriving, the Healer was seen to be plump, with pale red hair pulled neatly back from a round, personable face. Her eyes, very blue, met Vayeen's for a moment before she bowed to Geritsi.

"I am Dyoli ven'Deelin Clan Ixin," she said, her voice strong and smooth. "Do I have the pleasure of addressing Geritsi slent-Alin?"

"You do, Healer," Geritsi said with a smile. She moved a hand in Vayeen's direction.

"I bring you my cousin, Vayeen cozaLima."

"And Dosent!" Vaiza called, arriving. "Don't forget Dosent!"

Geritsi laughed. "And Dosent, who is a *sokyum*, and my bonded companion."

Dyoli ven'Deelin inclined her head. "I am pleased to meet Vayeen cozaLima and Dosent. Allow me to bring to your attention Mar Tyn pai'Fortana, one's partner, and Tima Fagen, Tree-and-Dragon security."

Mar Tyn and Tima bowed.

"I wonder if there is a place where Tima could rest and

have something to eat while we tend to our business," Dyoli ven'Deelin said.

"There's a cafe inside the market," Vayeen said to Tima. "Or, if the atmosphere isn't a problem, they'll make a tray and you can sit out here."

"Outside," Tima said decisively. "It's been too long since I had a chance to sit and enjoy the free breeze."

"Then that's decided," Dyoli said. "I believe we are destined to be inside where there is a shielded space." She looked to Geritsi. "Or so I was led to understand."

"The upstairs back apartment is shielded," Geritsi said. "I can't say if it's shielded enough for you, Healer..."

"Dyoli, please. And there is only one way to know if it will do. Is now a convenient time to inspect it?"

"Yes, let's go inside," Geritsi said, and smiled at Tima. "We'll show you the cafe on our way through, and make sure the counter knows to put your meal on Ribbon Dance Village's account."

"Do we *have* to go inside?" Vaiza asked plaintively.

"Yes," said Mar Tyn pai'Fortana, firmly. "Dyoli needs a certain amount of quiet in order to See clearly."

"I would like to go inside, too, please," Torin said. She looked, Vayeen thought, a little pale, her pattern inclined to wobble against the ambient, as if the excitement of their guests' arrival had worn her out.

"Another piece of cake, hey, Torin?" he said. "There's plenty in the basket."

She smiled at him, wan. "No, thank you, Vayeen. I just want to go inside."

"Inside it is, then," Vayeen said, and nodded to Geritsi.

· · · ❄ · · ·

The sense of constant whispering movement—nothing so unsubtle as *pressure*—that Dyoli had felt growing beyond her shields since they had crossed into the countryside, lessened appreciably as she followed Geritsi across the threshold of the back apartment.

She was still aware of a faint sense of—curiosity—which she hoped would be resolved once she opened her shields.

"Here," Geritsi said, from beside a wooden table and four chairs standing on an oval rag rug. "This is the center of the shielding."

Dyoli stepped to her side, aware of Mar Tyn and the twins entering the room, followed by the alert, untrusting shadow that was Vayeen, who closed the door behind him.

"Will it do for you, Healer?" Geritsi asked.

"In a moment, we will both know the answer to that question," Dyoli said. She closed her eyes, centered herself—and opened her shields.

Color flowed before her Inner Eyes, and she felt a quick tug at her core, as if a question had been asked—and answered.

The mild sense of curiosity faded into a sense of warm welcome, that itself spread out into a general feeling of goodwill.

She stood there, open, holding herself quite still for a slow count of twenty-four, then deliberately opened her Inner Eyes.

Geritsi's pattern was sweetly balanced around a core of vast calm; the bond with Dosent a pure and shimmering green. The big cat herself was self-satisfied, as every cat Dyoli had ever met, with an underlayment of ferocity that the bond with Geritsi mitigated, softening it into a desire to protect.

Vayeen was less structured, and rather darker—vigilant, suspicious, protective. Both patterns included a bright red thread that to Dyoli's senses tasted of Tekelia.

"Yes," she murmured, "this will do very well."

She did not seek out the twins—not yet—but she did Look for Mar Tyn—and very nearly gasped.

She was by this point in their partnership very familiar with Mar Tyn's pattern—a lacy affair that one might expect to unravel under the mildest stress. Yet it did nothing of the kind. It shifted, it rewove itself, it *made accommodation*, but it never wholly unraveled, while his core remained straight, and true; taut and unassailable.

Only, the lacy confection had acquired...depth, and a certain carefree fluency, as if it were tying and retying itself into new patterns for the sheer joy of experimentation. His core had also altered. Straight, true, and taut, but now showing swirls of color, as if interacting with the dancing lace.

"Dyoli?" he said, coming to her side. "Is the room well?"

Luck was a Wild Talent, Dyoli told herself. And Mar Tyn's Gift had been changing since they arrived on Colemenoport, under the Grid. Why shouldn't it change again, when the Grid was left behind? Luck was, above all else, adaptable. There was the question of what this change might do to their shared Gift, where Dyoli's Short Sight...possibly...guided the flow of Mar Tyn's Luck. But that was for later.

"The room will answer," she said. "How are you, my Mar Tyn?"

He smiled at her. "Very well. The air is exceptionally fresh here."

"Is it?"

"Well, we had no basis for comparison before, having come on-planet under the Grid, but it seems to me now, as we're out from under, that the air was a little—stale."

Vayeen laughed.

"There's a truth, Cousin! Stale is the hallmark of Civilization."

Dyoli turned to Geritsi.

"My purpose is to examine Torin and Vaiza, with particular attention to the artifact that has been identified," she said. "As I told you when we spoke, I received a sense of the working the other day, but was not able to make a detailed study. With the children's permission, I will do that now."

"On behalf of Ribbon Dance Village, I agree to this," Geritsi said.

"So noted; thank you."

Dyoli approached the back window, where the twins had taken over the cushioned bench. Vaiza was kneeling, gazing down at the lawn. Torin was wilted, her back against the wall, norbear on her knee. Dyoli paused, considering the norbear, waiting for a face to be proposed. But the norbear was—remarkably, in Dyoli's experience of norbears—reticent.

She took a deep, quiet breath.

"Torin. Vaiza. May I speak with you?" she asked.

"Of course," Torin said. "Vaiza, come listen."

Her brother twisted and collapsed cross-legged onto the cushion, face turned up to Dyoli.

"I am here today in my capacity as a Healer," Dyoli said.

"Yes!" Vaiza said. "Geritsi told us. There's a kink in our patterns."

"Not a kink," Torin corrected. "A tangle."

Dyoli smiled.

"And that is why I *particularly* want to examine you—to find first if it is a kink, a tangle, or something entirely else. This is important because Torin had said she was tired, and I wonder if this...irregularity may be the reason."

Vaiza looked at his sister.

"*Still* tired?" he asked. "Even after—"

"I told you that it didn't seem to help," Torin said, and looked to Dyoli. "Our mother had taught us a—*balancement*. That's what she called it, though Pel said that wasn't really a word. If Vaiza was falling behind in his studies, or his headaches were coming back—then we would dream together—us and Eet—and balance the flow so Vaiza's head didn't hurt anymore."

"We did it a couple times after we came to the Haosa," Vaiza added, "when Torin got tired, and it worked—*didn't* it, Torin?" He turned to her, brows pulled.

"It *did* work, before," Torin said. "But not this last time." She paused, frowning, then said quietly, "I think I might be feeling *more* tired now."

Dyoli felt a thrill, not entirely pleasant, and resisted the urge to focus immediately on Torin.

"I will Look very carefully," she promised. "Will you come with me to the table?"

"All right." Vaiza rose, and bent to pick the norbear up. Dyoli held a hand down to Torin, who took it with a pale smile, and came to her feet.

Vayeen, Geritsi, and Dosent had withdrawn to the window seat, where they could observe and yet not intrude on the process. Mar Tyn sat beside Dyoli, with the twins side-by-side in the chairs across the table. Eet sat upright on the table before them, radiating interest, and a certain amount of wariness.

"You have done this before, I think," Dyoli said. "I will ask you both to consider a blank white wall. As well as you can, empty your mind of all thought. If a thought should intrude, merely bring the wall once more before your mind's eye."

"Yes," Torin said. "Eet, do you hear? You must be very quiet and let Dyoli See."

A picture formed inside of Dyoli's head—a dark-haired woman, rather too thin, with a look of sorrowful desperation around her blue eyes. She looked too much like the twins for there to be any doubt of who she must be.

"Yes," Vaiza said. "Mother would have wanted us to find out why Torin's so tired, and to fix it."

There was a moment when Dyoli thought the norbear might lodge a protest; there was that sense in the aether.

"Eet," Torin said sternly, "you need to help us with this."

The moment passed; Eet subsided, and the children settled into themselves, obediently stilling their thoughts.

When they had achieved as much stillness as seemed reasonable to expect from two bright children, Dyoli extended lines of peace to ease them into a light sleep. Then, she brought her attention fully to their patterns.

At first glance, they were perfectly ordinary, their heart-link strong and vital. Vaiza was slightly brighter than Torin and showed the hazy border Dyoli had previously noticed in Tekelia's pattern, and today in Geritsi and Vayeen. She filed it as a marker for Haosa.

Torin's pattern was the more ordered, the border more pronounced. Dyoli marked that, and Looked more closely still, finding the bruising of broken connections, as well as the spark of new growth. Dyoli Saw a heart-link forming with Geritsi, another with Dosent, a thin sturdy thread that was Tekelia; and a lacy, flat connection that stretched and vanished into the flare and confusion that was all her Sight could make of the norbear's pattern. The whole was symmetrical and—

No.

There—*just* there—a thread quivered with strain, pulling others out of true, altering the pure boundary line.

Dyoli put her attention on the strained thread, following until it looped into the indistinct edge of Vaiza's pattern, and looped again, back over the distorted boundary and into a dense portion of Torin's pattern. Dyoli Felt more tension, and discovered one whole section quivering with distress.

Dyoli paused, thinking she had seen a thread that she might with care loosen, and followed it back—only to find it tightly knotted inside Vaiza's pattern.

Carefully, she relocated the original thread, followed it inward, then out, then—

Into a hopeless knot that gave off hints of norbear empathy, sparking with Vaiza's unrestrained energy. With difficulty, Dyoli followed Torin's thread into the center of the tangle, and marked the place where it was choked and grey.

Dyoli withdrew as quickly as she dared, knowing that she was trembling.

"Geritsi," she murmured, pushing her chair back. She got to her feet, aware of Mar Tyn's hand under her elbow, and paused a moment to be certain that the children were still asleep.

Geritsi rose. "Vayeen—cake," she said, and came forward to take Dyoli's hand.

"What's amiss?"

"Torin was right," Dyoli said. "It *is* a knot—and a dangerous one. Vaiza, Eet, and Torin are entangled in a spontaneous weaving, and Torin's essence is burning up."

Geritsi frowned.

"I don't understand," she said, as Vayeen arrived with a slice of cake on a napkin and a bottle of cold tea.

Dyoli took the cake with a nod of thanks. Mar Tyn received the bottle, and cracked the seal.

"If I were to guess, I would say that they—the three of them, working together—attempted something that was beyond their combined abilities—or perhaps the energy outlay was unequal. Again—how and why scarcely matter. We are left with a desperate snarl, which is draining Torin's core energy."

Geritsi took a breath.

"Maradel—our medic—said the threads binding the twins together might contract if there was a growth spurt—"

"Or a threat!" Vayeen snapped. "That damned madman with his gun—"

"Yes, but they protected themselves!" Geritsi said, turning to him. "They caught the bullets and sent them back—Tekelia told me. They said that Eet had—" She stopped and looked at Dyoli, who was dusting cake crumbs off her fingers.

"They said that Eet had helped them," Geritsi finished slowly. "Could that—"

"Very possibly," Dyoli said, accepting the tea bottle from Mar Tyn, "but that is, if you'll forgive me, of secondary importance. What must be done, and at once, is to release that knot before Torin weakens any further."

Geritsi pulled herself up. "Are you competent to do this work, Healer?"

Dyoli looked grim.

"I am," she said, "and necessity is. However, I cannot guarantee that I won't do damage—even mortal damage."

The color drained out of Geritsi's face.

"Mortal damage, Healer?" Vayeen growled. "Would you murder one of our children?"

Dyoli moved her hand in a sharp gesture. "I hope I am

more skilled than that. However, the possibility exists that the process will damage the norbear. I can hold the children inside Healspace while I make repairs, but the norbear—the points of connection are not congruent. I cannot say what will happen. You understand that I may have to cut certain threads. Happily, the original weavings were done in such a way as to avoid critical systems. The children may be bruised, a little, but they will recover entirely."

"Having only lost their final link to their mother," Geritsi said, "and their constant companion."

Dyoli spread her hands.

"I will do what I can to keep them all safe. In my capacity as a Healer, I recommend an immediate intervention, before Torin becomes any weaker, and Healing becomes both more difficult, and more dangerous."

Geritsi looked to Vayeen. Vayeen drew a deep breath and turned his palms up.

Geritsi inclined her head.

"We agree to an immediate intervention. However, I insist that all of us be fortified before work goes forth. Vayeen, please bespeak a tray from the cafe. Dyoli, will you wake the children?"

· · · ✳ · · ·

They had all eaten a very substantial snack, whereupon Vaiza asked if their trouble was a kink or a tangle.

"It is past any tangle I have ever seen," Dyoli told him, truthfully. "It Looks to me like a terrific snarl. If you would like to think of your patterns as woven from slightly stretchy threads, it is as if something stretched certain of your, Torin, and Eet's threads much too far, and when they rebounded, they did not tidily return to their proper places, but tangled around each other, as if trying to make a new pattern. If it had been dealt with immediately, it would not have been difficult to set right. But it has had some time to continue to grow, and now it is dangerous, especially to Torin."

Vaiza looked at Torin.

"We made it worse," he said, "with the balancement."

"That is an open question," Dyoli said. "You may instead have slowed its growth. We cannot know that."

Mar Tyn, sitting next to Dyoli, felt a shiver along the inner pathway his Gift traveled upon. He sat up a little straighter, breathed in, and waited, not without some trepidation. It was true that his relationship with his Gift had changed dramatically since they had arrived on Colemeno. For most of his life, he had been Luck's puppet, and he was on his guard, lest the old order seek to reestablish itself.

His Luck did not seek to move him, however. The feeling faded and he brought his attention back to the table.

"I do not hide from you that what we will be undertaking between us is risky," Dyoli was saying. "Torin is more at risk than you, Vaiza, because she is being drained by the action of the knot. Eet is more at risk than either of you, because he is a norbear. It's possible that I will not even be able to bring him into Healspace, in which case, he may not survive the Healing."

Torin gave a cry, her hand going to her throat.

"No!" she said. "I won't have Eet harmed!"

"Torin—" Vaiza spun in his chair and caught Torin's free hand. "If we don't have the Healing, you won't get better." He turned his head and caught Mar Tyn's eye. "That's right, isn't it Mar Tyn?"

"As I understand the situation," Mar Tyn said gravely, "if Dyoli does not repair this now—or very soon—Torin will get weaker, until she becomes too weak to wake."

There came a flicker in the space behind his eyes, where Lady Selph had more than once shown him faces, and offered reassurance. This touch was different, though, definitely not Lady Selph; someone less polished, though no less assured.

The first face that formed was of a woman with the same dark hair and blue eyes as the twins, followed hard by a man's clever face, sharp black eyes, and determined chin.

"Yes, but Mother and Pel are dead," Torin said straitly, apparently in answer to those comments. Eet the norbear sat on his haunches and stared at her. Again, the woman's face, from a different angle, as she sat on the edge of a bed, gazing down at two young sleeping children. Mar Tyn had the impression of concentration, of infinite care; almost he saw the flicker of the threads as she wove—

"Yes—" began Torin, but Eet was not to be interrupted. The woman continued weaving, and her focus was terrible to observe. Finally, she paused, and raised a hand. Mar Tyn felt as if she were pressing the top of his head, realized it must have been Eet she was touching, even as he felt a question asked, a promise made—and a compact sealed.

"Mother made Eet promise to protect us," Vaiza said solemnly. Torin spun to face him.

"But she didn't make him promise to die!"

"Pel promised to protect us," Vaiza said. "And he died. Mother protected us—"

"And she died!" Torin cried, tears running her cheeks.

"I don't want *you* to die," Vaiza said simply.

In the space behind Mar Tyn's eyes, another picture formed, this of Eet, standing tall between the twins, all three of them facing Dyoli. The image was saturated with strength.

It was an impressively complex sending, Mar Tyn thought, and after a moment, Torin wilted.

"No one wants anyone to be hurt," Geritsi said quietly.

"I will be as careful as I may be," Dyoli added. "Eet is very brave and he has so far upheld his oath with strength and with honor. I have no doubt that he will continue to do so."

There was silence around the table. Dyoli drank what was left of her tea, and put the cup on the table.

"I will need permission to continue," she said gently. "Torin? Vaiza? Eet?"

Eet's agreement came first, firm and loud.

"Yes," Vaiza said, and took his sister's hand. "Torin?"

She hiccuped and raised her head to look Dyoli directly in the eye.

"Yes," she whispered.

· · · ❋ · · ·

Dyoli closed her eyes, centered herself, and stepped into Healspace.

Orange and cream mist wafted about her, cool, comforting, and vital. She breathed that vitality into her core, breathed it out and said, "Torin. Vaiza. Eet."

Two tapestries immediately formed in the mist before her—Vaiza and Torin. A moment later, a third tapestry arose, slowly, as if learning its shape even as it formed. It was smaller than the other two; there were gaps, and a tendency to fade. But it was connected to Torin and Vaiza. Connected by strong threads of love, accommodation, and duty.

Dyoli waited, and it was well she did so, because a fourth pattern abruptly snapped into existence—a twisted, spinning snarl of energies, distorted and hungry, with thin threads binding it to Vaiza, to Eet—and one thick cable anchored in Torin.

Dyoli brought her attention to that malicious knot, extending her senses, *willing* there to be a loose end. Their mother—so skilled a weaver!—surely she would have left a loose end, something harmless and quick, that would undo what she had wrought, painlessly, as soon as danger was past?

But there was nothing to be found; the snarl was too tight. She was going to have to cut threads...

She hesitated. The knife was not her first, or even her second, tool. Mitigation, ease, gentle regrowth—those were her preferred methods. In this case, a cut *should not* be necessary. All that was needed was a simple release.

Why, she thought desperately, was there no release?

Isn't there? Mar Tyn asked, just inside her ear.

Safe inside Healspace, Dyoli shivered, and felt the electric tingle that meant the Gift she shared with Mar Tyn was—active.

Do you See it, my Mar Tyn? she dared to ask, and felt the ripple of his amusement.

No—you're our Eyes in this. I only ask: Couldn't *there be a release?*

She took a breath as before her Eyes, the patterns shifted, the snarl fading to the background, the sparse alien pattern that was Eet coming to the fore.

And there—yes, *there!*—was a simple black thread, homey and ordinary, with a loop tied in its end.

Dyoli took hold—

And pulled.

· · · ✳ · · ·

The Healer had once again entranced the children, this time including the norbear in her web of peaceful drowsing.

Vayeen, Watching from the window seat with Geritsi and Dosent, allowed that the Healer knew her work. Gentle she was, and specifically unthreatening, easing the children, and Eet, too, into a state of warm vulnerability.

He Saw the moment she *stepped aside* into a pocket of the

ambient, and Felt the action of her will as she drew her subjects to her.

Beside him, Geritsi drew a hard breath, and put a hand on his knee. He shifted so that she could lean closer against him, sharing comfort.

Long minutes passed, the ambient reflecting fierce fires of concentration, and dogged care, amidst twisted shadows of hungry malice.

There came a glimmer, as if the Healer had found her answer. Vayeen caught his breath, feeling Geritsi start forward even as the shadow loomed, and the glimmer died aborning.

Vayeen Felt the ambient tighten with the Healer's despair, and looked to the table, where all sat motionless, his Eye drawn to Mar Tyn pai'Fortana, at the Healer's right, his hand pressing hers, surrounded by the colorful nimbus of the ambient's regard—which should not be possible, Vayeen thought, in a shielded room.

Even as he Watched, the nimbus grew brighter, until the entire table took fire. The ambient was crooning, close and dear, and Vayeen heard dice rattling inside his ear.

In that moment, there came a lurch, a lunge, a leap; the ambient's song became a shout! For a moment Vayeen's Vision doubled, so that he saw two tables, both equally possible, stretching away into the realms of what might be—

Something *snapped.*

Everything was still and calm at the only table that was possible—the only table that had *ever* been possible—in this time and place.

The nimbus faded; the ambient's song was a pleased and loving trill.

At the table, Dyoli ven'Deelin opened her eyes, took a breath, and said to the room at large—

"It is done."

In Transit

. . . .

NO MATTER WHAT ELSE CAME OUT OF THIS TRIP FROM THE SUR-
face of the planet into the space where the Ribbons danced, being
allowed to observe Padi yos'Galan as she piloted their small vessel
was a privilege Tekelia would never forget.

As brilliant and as bold as her pattern was, it sharpened into
something Tekelia could only call ordered chaos the moment she
took her place at the control board.

In a word, she was riveting. Tekelia occupied the small seat
behind and between the pilots—Dil Nem sitting co-pilot—and
Watched the process of her art, ignoring the screens that displayed
the dwindling homeworld, until there was a moment—a cusp—
when every thread and thought aligned, her fingers moved—and
stopped.

"Check, please, Co-pilot," she murmured.

"Check, Pilot. All numbers align."

"Now," she said, "we wait."

"For what?" Tekelia asked.

"For the *Passage* to be in position for an approach. Here."

She nodded at the screen before her—one large, with four
smaller images tiled down the right side.

"In the upper right tile—that's the *Passage*, do you see?"

Tekelia leaned to look—blinked and looked again.

Tekelia had only before seen ships at dock—ships like this
shuttle.

Dutiful Passage, however—was difficult to make out against
a background that provided no scale. Surely, though, Tekelia
thought, it was larger—in every way—than the Wardian, the
largest building in Haven City. It seemed ... somewhat ... like
a tree, though nothing could have been further from a tree in

shape and complexity. But there was an...organic feel to it, as if there were no other possible way for it to have taken form.

"That's why the *Passage* can't come to dock at Colemeno," Tekelia said softly.

"Which reminds me," Dil Nem said suddenly, "that I'll be wanting to talk with Moji—Yard Master tineMena—about mooring capacities. We ought to add some big ship docking."

Padi glanced at him.

"Oughtn't that go to the portmaster?"

Dil Nem moved a shoulder. "Surely. But the yard master has to bring it, not the contractor."

"Yes, of course."

Dil Nem turned his head to give Tekelia a nod.

"Well-observed."

"One could scarcely *not* observe," Tekelia protested, and Dil Nem laughed.

"Accustomed eyes see *home*," he said. "New eyes see what's there."

"*Passage* Control to approaching shuttle." A firm voice issued from the board. "ID?"

"*Dutiful Passage* shuttle number three. Padi yos'Galan pilot-in-charge; Dil Nem Tiazan second. Arriving on the word of the master trader."

"Very good, Pilot. You are cleared for the reception dock."

Tekelia felt Padi's surprise flicker through their link.

"The reception dock?" she repeated.

"Yes, Pilot. I was to say that the Speaker for the Haosa will be fitly received."

Another jolt of surprise, closely followed by irritation.

"Thank you, Control," Padi said, her voice cooler than her pattern. "Shuttle number three for the reception dock."

She and Dil Nem were busy at their boards for some few minutes. Eventually, there came a sensation of...gripping, as if the vessel they were on had been a thrown ball, arrested in flight.

"Fairly caught," Dil Nem murmured, taking his hands from the board. Padi nodded, and leaned back in her chair with a sigh.

When it seemed certain that the pilots were for the moment at rest, Tekelia put the question, "What is the reception dock?"

"The formal entry, that opens into the salon where important visitors are received," Padi said slowly. "We occasionally host leaders of planetary governments, ambassadors, heads of trade missions . . ."

"And Speakers for the Haosa?"

"Indeed," she said, still uneasy in her pattern.

"Am I to be schooled?" That did not match what Tekelia knew of Master Trader yos'Galan, but—

Padi threw a smile over her shoulder.

"No," she said, slowly. "The master trader might wish to honor your *melant'i* as a leader of your people. You had, after all, spoken to him about the possibility of the Haosa seeking work among the ships."

Tekelia waited, feeling her dismay deepen. When she said nothing more, Tekelia murmured.

"Something else worries you."

Padi took a sharp breath.

"*Melant'i* knots," she murmured. "The master trader loses nothing by allowing a quiet arrival and time for a guest to adjust to strange conditions. In fact, he might come out a little to the good in such a transaction. The thodelm, however, may require a *display* . . ."

She was becoming agitated. Tekelia offered a line of calmness, and marked the flare of gratitude as she accepted it.

"Apparently," Padi said, more moderately, "Thodelm yos'Galan wishes to impress the Speaker for the Haosa with yos'Galan's luster, and our *worth*."

Dil Nem was heard to laugh, very quietly.

"It is *not* funny," Padi said severely.

"Yes, Pilot," he replied.

"So I *am* to be schooled," Tekelia said. "Or at least put in awe. Will there be a great many people present?"

"Gods. I hope not. No, *surely* not a full reception."

Her thoughts were heavy enough to weigh on their link, so perhaps a full reception was still a possibility. Tekelia thought about formal receptions, and *worth*. Business attire was what Tekelia had chosen to wear; that had seemed respectful for a meeting with the master trader.

For a full formal reception, however, perhaps something . . . *more* would be appropriate.

Tekelia reached for the ambient—

And found—nothing.

There was no sparkle in the blood as the ambient rose to one's thought, no flow from thought to reality, and especially, no change in the garments one wore.

Padi glanced over her shoulder again, apparently having felt... *some*thing through their link.

"Your dress is unexceptional. You would wear that to—to call upon the Warden in the city, would you not?"

"Yes."

"Then it will do. It is honest and does not seek to establish you in an unaccustomed mode. If the thodelm wishes to give himself airs, that is of course his privilege."

"Are you angry with your father?" Tekelia asked, to keep from thinking about that lack of response, of the stillness—of the *silence*—outside one's own core.

"At Father? No, of course not. Nor at the master trader. The thodelm is another matter entirely, though I suppose he must— and as I said, we very rarely see him."

"So you don't know what it's possible for him to do."

"It is possible for Thodelm yos'Galan to do *any*thing," Padi said with feeling. "It's parsing which limits he will choose to honor that vexes me. Ah."

Drawn by her thought, Tekelia looked up at the screens, seeing a door rolling aside as they approached, and their little ship slipped inside the belly of the giant.

Dutiful Passage
Colemeno Orbit

. . . .

TEKELIA HAD SEEN IMAGES OF THE COUNCIL'S FORMAL RECEPTION area in the Sakuriji: mosaic walls, vaulted ceiling, ornate furnishings, and floors that had been cut from living rock.

The room they entered from the shuttle bay was a variation of the type. There was plush carpet underfoot, rather than stone, but the ceiling did, indeed, vault, showing a glittering pattern of dots against a deep blue ground.

To the left, the wall displayed a large and detailed rendering of the badge the trade mission wore on their jackets, and Tekelia gave a smile for the familiar tree-and-dragon. In this room, the tree was mighty, branches strong, leaves glistening green. Above, the guardian dragon hovered, emerald eyes reflecting the leaves, bronze wings extended protectively.

"Has the dragon a name?" Tekelia asked.

"Megelaar, so we have it," answered a voice that was familiar for all it was not Padi who replied.

Tekelia turned to face the person who was Padi's father, Master Trader yos'Galan, and, rarely, Thodelm yos'Galan. There was, so far as Tekelia could see, no visible hint as to this gentleman's current *melant'i*. As always, the white hair was crisp, eyebrows thin and slightly slanted over eyes of so light a blue they seemed silver; strong nose, wide mouth. True, he was not on this occasion wearing the usual uniform—what Padi called "trade clothes"— which included the jacket with the tree-and-dragon badge on the breast. Instead, he wore a deep red shirt with a collar that rose to frame his face, wide sleeves buttoned tight at the wrist, and a pair of soft grey trousers. His hands were positioned in a formal-seeming manner, and he was not, Tekelia noted, wearing his ring set with the purple stone, but another, on the second finger of his right hand—a wide band rich with enamel work. And that was perhaps a hint, after all.

The face was another, Tekelia thought. The master trader's habitual expression was one of gentle good nature, while Padi's father allowed a range of expression to be seen.

At the moment, however, there was no expression at all on the austere brown face; and the light eyes might have been mirrors.

"The name of the Tree is Jelaza Kazone," Padi added from Tekelia's side. "Father, it's good to see you."

The straight mouth twitched toward a smile, and one stern eyebrow lifted slightly.

"An admirable attempt, Daughter. However, we must allow the thodelm his moment."

"Must we?" Padi murmured, and without waiting for an answer folded into a bow as intricate as a courting dance.

"Thodelm yos'Galan, I bring to your attention Tekelia vester-Granz, Speaker for the Haosa of Colemeno and the Redlands System."

She turned to face Tekelia and moved her hands in a soft, deliberate pattern apparently meant to direct attention to the thodelm's person.

"Speaker vesterGranz, I bring before you Thodelm yos'Galan, Head of my Line, standing staunch in support of the delm and Korval."

Thodelm yos'Galan inclined his head, his gaze skimming past Tekelia's right ear.

"Speaker vesterGranz," he said, his voice cool, but not . . . *specifically* unwelcoming.

Tekelia took a breath.

There was no chance of reproducing the bow Padi had performed. Still, respect was owed, if not to Thodelm yos'Galan, then surely to the master trader and Padi's father, both of whom Tekelia liked and admired.

So, then, a bow of respect for the office, such as the Warden of Civilization ought to command, if the Speaker for the Haosa were not of the opinion that the current holder of that office needed to be pricked in the self-importance, often.

"Thodelm yos'Galan," Tekelia said, straightening. "I am honored."

"Gently said, and cannily navigated, Tekelia-*dramliza*. If it does not offend, I congratulate you."

Tekelia met the master trader's eyes, and smiled.

"No offense, sir. Only, I feel you should know that I can't go on in that style for very long."

"Nor can I, so we're well-matched." The master trader turned to Padi.

"Well, Trader Padi?"

"Well enough, Master Trader," she answered, dryly.

"You relieve me, but I wonder—wasn't Dil Nem to accompany you?"

"He did. However, as we were making ready to debark, he announced his intention to stay with the shuttle and move her to a more appropriate mooring."

"Surely someone else could have done so."

"I suggested it, sir, but he said that *he* had no reason to speak with Thodelm yos'Galan."

The master trader laughed.

"Valor, of its kind. And now I may ask it—Tekelia-*dramliza*, how do you go on?"

It was kindly meant, but it did rather focus one on those things that one was trying to—ignore.

The *absence* of things...

"It is," Tekelia said to the Master Trader, "very *quiet* here."

"Is it so noisy off-Grid?"

Padi stirred, but said nothing, so Tekelia made answer.

"The ambient sings, sir, beyond being ever-present—like a friend at one's elbow, that you might lean on at need—"

Meaning to illustrate the point, Tekelia leaned, exactly as one might do after a particularly trying encounter, taking a moment's rest by leaning into the ambient—

Which *wasn't there*.

Boots tangling in the unaccustomed nap of the rug, Tekelia staggered, reaching *again* for that absent support. The master trader flowed forward, hand extended—

Tekelia flung backward, *into* the dis-balance, and was abruptly and ignominiously sprawled on the rug.

Padi dropped to her knees.

"Are you hurt?" she asked, hands on Tekelia's shoulders.

"Merely wounded in my pride," Tekelia said, equally wry and

foolish. Dismay washed across—*not* across the ambient, though the source was perfectly discernible: The master trader was distressed that his help had been refused.

Tekelia looked up and met serious silver eyes.

"You might have taken my hand," the master trader said, gently. "There would have been no—offense against protocol."

"No, sir," Tekelia said, "only think how ill it would look if I discorporated you within the first five minutes of being on-board."

"We don't know if that effect is in force," Padi said.

"That's correct, and I don't care to risk your father!" Tekelia replied, with some heat. "You're fond of him, I think?"

"Yes, very," Padi said gently. "Thank you for thinking of that. Here."

She stood, holding her hands down. Tekelia took the offered aid, and rose.

"Padi doesn't seem to have discorporated," the master trader said, as one noting an interesting fact.

"Yes, sir. That's the action of Padi's Gift on mine. My Aunt Asta has proved that I am not a danger while Padi is touching me, but, that not having been the case—"

"I recall you said something similar, the first time we met," the master trader murmured. "I thought that the location was the danger, not yourself."

"The location made me more dangerous," Tekelia said. "I am never *not* dangerous, sir."

"I see. Well. Thank you for your vigilance, Tekelia-*dramliza*. I feel that I would not have cared in the least for discorporation.

"Now, if you will both come with me, we may retire to my office, where Captain Mendoza will be joining us. I've arranged for refreshments."

Off-Grid
Peck's Market

. . . .

"BUT, *I*'M NOT TIRED!" VAIZA PROTESTED.

Mar Tyn glanced to the window seat, where Torin and Eet were frankly asleep, the norbear tucked against the girl's shoulder.

Between the window and the table, Dyoli was speaking with Geritsi slentAlin, and Mar Tyn could Feel the ache of weariness in her bones.

He rose from his chair.

"Do you know?" he said to Vaiza. "I'm not tired either. Why don't we go outside and see if Tima wants to go for a walk with us?"

"Yes!" said Vaiza, fairly bouncing to his feet.

Vayeen glanced at Geritsi, got her nod, and also rose.

"I'm feeling restless myself," he said. "Might I bear you company?"

"Certainly," Mar Tyn said. Vaiza was already at the door, jigging from one foot to the other.

"Vaiza? May Vayeen join us?"

"Yes! If Tima likes it, we could play skip-ball—it's best with four."

"Alas, I haven't a ball," Mar Tyn said.

"We can borrow one from the market," Vayeen said, reaching beyond Vaiza to open the door, and waving the boy on ahead. "I should warn you, though, that this lad is a demon for the—"

The door shut, cutting off the rest of Vayeen's warning.

Dyoli took a breath and turned back to Geritsi.

"Now what?" she asked.

Geritsi smiled. "Now, you may also rest—there's a bedroom behind that door." She used her chin to point. "While you're recovering your resources, I will call our village administrator, and our medic. They should be here by the time you wake up and skip-ball has taken the edge off of Vaiza's energy."

Dyoli breathed a laugh. "By which time, he'll want a nap?"

"Possibly," Geritsi said. "But it's more likely he'll want something to eat." She crossed the room and opened the door to the bedroom.

"If you please," she said.

"Thank you," Dyoli said, and entered the bedroom, closing the door behind her.

Geritsi crossed the room to the comm and punched in Arbour's code.

Dutiful Passage
Colemeno Orbit

. . . .

CAPTAIN MENDOZA SMILED AS THEY ENTERED, THOUGH SHE MADE no move to leave the chair where she reclined.

"I see you rescued them," she said, apparently to the master trader, who had preceded them into the room.

"Korval's *melant'i* was properly displayed, Tekelia-*dramliza* was seen to be suitably awed by yos'Galan's splendor; recognized as well as a person of wit and courtesy—and, thus, the field was mine."

Were *you awed*? Padi whispered inside Tekelia's head.

Say chagrined, Tekelia answered.

Padi's laughter rippled along their link, brightening Tekelia's whole being. *That will do, I think.*

"Tekelia-*dramliza*." The master trader beckoned and Tekelia stepped to his side, facing the reclining captain.

"Captain Mendoza, you will of course recall Tekelia vesterGranz, Speaker for *the Haosa of Colemeno and the Redlands System*—do I have that correctly, Trader Padi?"

"Yes, sir," Padi answered calmly.

Captain Mendoza smiled from the depths of her chair.

"Hello, Tekelia. It's good to see you again. Please forgive me for not rising. The ship's medic allowed me to attend a formal meeting only if I swore that I would sit with my feet up, entertain no excitement, and be as decorous as pregnancy allows."

"It's good to see you again, Captain Mendoza," Tekelia said, honestly. "I'll try not to be exciting."

She laughed as Padi came to Tekelia's side.

"Hello, Priscilla. Keriana is being strict with you. Are you perfectly well?"

124

"Hello, Padi. I'm more than perfectly well, and Keriana is operating from an over-abundance of caution."

"Which is precisely what you would expect her to say," the master trader interjected.

"Well—yes," Padi acknowledged.

A chime sounded and the master trader went to the door.

"Refreshments arrive," he said, standing aside to allow a man to wheel a table bearing numerous covered plates into the center of the room.

"Will there be anything else, sir?" the man asked, after he had locked the wheels and removed the covers.

"No, I believe we are well-supplied," the master trader said. "Thank you, Kolin."

"Yes, sir." The man bowed slightly from the waist—respectful, without being at all ornate—and exited, the door sliding closed behind him.

"I suggest that we serve ourselves," the master trader said. "Saving Captain Mendoza, who will tell me what I may be honored to bring to her."

He turned, and raised a hand, as if he had suddenly remembered something.

"Before we begin, I would like to make clear that Thodelm yos'Galan has been persuaded to allow the master trader to continue negotiations with regard to yos'Galan's alliance with vesterGranz, which I believe even Trader Padi will allow to be a concession."

Tekelia felt Padi's start of surprise, followed by the sudden, melting warmth of complete relief.

"A coup, indeed, Master Trader," she said smiling. "I thank you."

"No, I won't have that. Only think how tedious it would have been to stand on ceremony for everything. Why, we would have had to have poor Kolin stay and serve us our snack, and I am persuaded that he has other, more important, matters to tend to."

"Very true," Padi said, and Tekelia felt the quiver of her laughter through their link.

Off-Grid
Peck's Market

· · · · · · · · · · · · · ·

"I DON'T WANT TO GIVE OFFENSE," VAYEEN SAID, SETTLING ON TO the bench next to Mar Tyn pai'Fortana. After an energetic round of skip-ball, Tima had wondered aloud if there were any boys nearby who might like to explore the operating system of the tour car. Vaiza had volunteered, and they were both at the moment leaning over the engine box in the back of the vehicle, hatch raised.

Mar Tyn glanced at him. "All right."

"Well. I only wonder how—or *what*—you did upstairs, just before the Healer separated our children and their norbear from that dire tangle."

"What do you think I did?"

Vayeen laughed. "You must know Tekelia. What I believe *I Saw* was a future chosen, and another—tossed aside."

Mar Tyn tipped his head, as if considering.

"For my part, much too active. I only suggested to what I think you call the ambient that the possibility of a satisfactory outcome existed. Once that had been suggested, Dyoli chose it, which negated the other possibility, and it ceased to exist."

He paused.

"Dyoli has Short Sight and in certain conditions—which I don't myself understand—her Gift and mine act together."

"To choose a preferred future," Vayeen said, wanting to be certain that he had this correctly.

"*Another* future," Mar Tyn said.

Vayeen frowned.

"That," he said slowly, "is a Wild Talent, indeed."

"Yes," Mar Tyn said. "It is very dangerous. Happily, it happens neither instantaneously nor often."

"How—" Vayeen began, then turned at the whisper of disturbed leaves from the trees behind them.

"Geritsi must have called in some of our cousins," he said, rising as a hover-wagon sidled out of the trees and made for the pavilion.

Mar Tyn stood, and looked down to the car, where Tima had closed the hatch, and had an easy hand on Vaiza's shoulder. The boy was looking up at her, talking with his usual animation.

The wagon had come to a halt at the side of the pavilion and two figures jumped to the ground.

"Arbour and Maradel," Vayeen said, on a note of understanding. "Come and meet them, Cousin."

· · · ❋ · · ·

Dyoli sighed, and nestled under the blanket, both aware and not, residing in that state that was neither sleep nor wakefulness, but a melding of each.

She opened her eyes and gazed up at the ceiling, where an intricate pattern of thin wires crisscrossed, serving as a pathway for streamers of what seemed to be live fire that traversed the complicated lacework in ever-slowing ripples, until they rained slowly out of the pattern and sublimated.

It was a very pretty sculpture, with the bright lights dancing down the wires, and Dyoli was sleepily pleased that the color was not lost entirely, but joined with and informed the shared environment.

"Healer?" a soft voice said, interrupting these interesting observations. "Dyoli?"

She stirred, the last of her drowse slipping away.

"Yes."

"Arbour and Maradel are here," Geritsi said, "and a meal has been sent up."

Dutiful Passage
Colemeno Orbit

. . . .

SHAN SAT ON A CHAIR NEXT TO PRISCILLA, TEKELIA AND PADI side-by-side on the sofa. There was silence while the snacks were sampled—not only sweets, but a savory pie that was new, and quite tasty. He would have to talk to the kitchen about making it more often.

In the meantime, he owned himself content. Better, the *thodelm* was content, which bade well for a satisfactory outcome to negotiations.

And really, the children had shown to advantage, from Padi's attempt to turn the *melant'i* of the greeting into something less exalted, to Tekelia's demeanor—straightforward, thoughtful, and *not* overawed. Even the tumble to the rug fell onto the positive side of the ledger. Not only had the mishap been accepted with just slightly embarrassed grace, but it illuminated that—while certainly no pilot—Tekelia had quick reactions, and quicker wits.

"I don't wish to be inept, but I wonder if I might ask, Tekelia-*dramliza*, how you feel now?"

Velvet brown eyes lifted to his face.

"Am I disadvantaged? I think not, unless part of the negotiations will have me walk a tree limb."

"Nothing so strenuous, I assure you! I ought also to have said I was merely inquiring after the health of the guest. Negotiations will not begin until we have all rested from the travails of the day—unless there is some reason you must rush forward, of course."

"I have no reason to rush," Tekelia said. "Blays has agreed to stand in my place as Speaker for a week, and while I wouldn't like to try her patience for two—"

"I understand. Trader Padi, have you a need for speedy reso-
lution?"

"Indeed, no. I think we have all earned a period of rest before
we set to work."

"I," Priscilla said comfortably, "agree with all of this expressed
wisdom. Absolutely—rest before work."

"We have an accord!" the master trader said. "Trader yos'Galan
will be gratified to learn that the *qe'andra* have arrived. They,
too, are embracing wisdom. We have agreed to meet at second
hour tomorrow in order to review the whole port inventory and
consider our options, going forward. Will you join us, Trader?"

"Thank you, yes."

"Splendid. We three may therefore plan to meet at fourth
hour for our discussions, provided that there are no changes in
the condition of the principals. Does that suit?"

He did not miss the glance Tekelia shot Padi, nor the half-
smile and slightly lifted shoulder which was her reply.

"That timetable suits us."

"Splendid," Shan said again, and looked to Tekelia.

"It is possible that I will stop at Metlin as we leave the system. May I trouble you for an introduction to the Haosa there?"

Tekelia drew a sharp breath, and, significantly, did *not* look
at Padi.

"There are no Haosa on Metlin, sir."

"Aren't there?" Padi murmured, which was really too bad of
her, given that Tekelia's elevation to Speaker for all the Haosa of
the Redlands System had clearly been her invention.

Tekelia turned.

"Padi, there isn't a Grid on—"

Tekelia froze, lips parted, eyes focused on some startling
thought.

"There's no Grid on Metlin," Tekelia said after a long moment,
and very quietly. "Therefore, there are no Haosa."

"Is it the Grid that makes Haosa, then?" Padi asked.

"No," Tekelia said slowly, as if working carefully at a crusty
and long-tied knot. "The Grid makes *the Civilized*. Without it,
all are Haosa."

"Do you think the Council knows that?" Padi asked, breaking
a corner off of her piece of cake.

"I expect it's not the way the Council is accustomed to

thinking about the Grid, no," Tekelia answered, and sighed, deep and rueful. "It appears I'm going to have to take that seat at the table, if only to give them this new idea."

"That will be fun," Padi said blandly, and Tekelia laughed.

"Do you know? It might be."

"Have you been offered a Council seat, Tekelia-*dramliza*?" Shan asked, as he Watched the play of their patterns, Feeling the flow along their heart-link.

"I have, yes, sir. I'm . . . becoming inclined to accept it. As Padi points out, it will be a wonderful opportunity to sow chaos. However, the Haosa have not yet confirmed that my voice will be theirs."

Tekelia met Shan's eyes.

"May I ask you to do something for me, sir?"

Shan raised his eyebrows.

"You may ask."

"Thank you. I wonder if you would call me 'Tekelia.' Everyone does."

"Ah." Shan inclined his head. "I believe I might do that for you. Tekelia."

Tekelia smiled.

"Thank you, sir."

Off-Grid
Peck's Market

· · · · · · · · · · · · · ·

MARADEL HAD EXAMINED A PAIR OF VISIBLY PATIENT TWINS. SHE thanked them gravely for their forbearance, and everyone had something to eat.

Afterward, Arbour, Maradel, Geritsi, and Dyoli withdrew to the bedroom while Mar Tyn, Vayeen, and the children cleared the table and set up a board game, closely supervised by Eet.

"An effective and clean Healing," Maradel said, easing into a chair, and nodding at Dyoli. "My thanks to you, Heal— Dyoli. I could have hoped for nothing better."

"And now," said Geritsi, who was sitting on the floor, back against the wall, Dosent sprawled across her legs, "we have a new problem."

"Happily," Maradel added, "*this* problem isn't life-threatening, and it doesn't need to be solved at once."

"It will have to be solved soon," Geritsi said. "The children can stay here at Peck's for another day or two, if we bring in occupation, but sooner or later Vaiza will have to come back to the village—and Torin..."

"...can't," Arbour finished.

Dyoli, seated beside Arbour on the bed, shifted, drawing all eyes to her.

"Why can't Torin return to the village with her brother? I had understood from Tekelia that they are children of Ribbon Dance Village."

"So they are," Arbour said, "and Ribbon Dance doesn't relinquish them. But a Civilized child can't live off-Grid. Even shielded, the ambient is just—too much."

Dyoli frowned. "How if we teach her to make one of those?"

She pointed toward the ceiling, where she was pleased to note that she could still See the pretty lacework highlighted by the flashing colors, and the droplets melding with the common air of the room.

Arbour blinked and looked at Maradel.

Maradel looked at Dyoli.

"The shielding, you mean?"

"But it's *not* shielding," Dyoli said. "All it does is slow the arrival of—is that the ambient? The colors?"

Arbour raised her eyes slowly to the ceiling, took a deep breath, and seemed for a moment to be—absent.

Another deep breath, and she was fully present again, her attention on Dyoli.

"Yes. The colors are the ambient. The lattice is meant to slow its flow, so that it doesn't overwhelm those who are Civilized."

Dyoli glanced at the ceiling again.

"So, all we have to do is help Torin make a lattice small enough for her pattern to accommodate."

"A personal Grid?" Arbour murmured, looking to Maradel.

"Never been tried, in my knowledge," Maradel said.

"But it *ought* to work," Arbour said.

"Torin has a very strong Talent, and is extremely organized," Geritsi said from the floor. "If we can show her the path..."

Maradel lifted a shoulder.

"We cannot know until we try," Dyoli interpreted. "Very well. We ought at least find if Torin is willing to try."

Dutiful Passage
Colemeno Orbit

. . . .

"YOUR EYES ARE BROWN," PADI SAID, ONCE THEY HAD ACHIEVED the privacy of Tekelia's stateroom.

"Sometimes they're both the same color for a time," Tekelia said. "Chaos being chaos."

"Of course," Padi murmured. "I only mean to say that they have been brown since we met the thodelm in the reception hall."

Hours.

Tekelia shivered.

"So it would seem that the ship *is* its own Grid. That's useful to know—though it *doesn't* mean I'm going to be seizing the hands of people who are not you."

"No, I wouldn't expect so." Padi tipped her head. "Isn't there anything . . . less dire that your Gift works against? We could structure a test."

Tekelia showed empty palms.

"At home, I'd simply allow Chaos to rise. Let me think about it. In the meantime, I wonder if you'd be willing to help with another test."

"Is it dangerous?"

"It ought to either work or not," Tekelia said. "If you would stand out in the hallway? I'll come to you."

Padi frowned. "That *does* seem rather tame. Just outside the door?"

"If you please."

She hesitated, then leaned to kiss Tekelia's cheek.

"Don't be long," she murmured, and left.

Tekelia took a deep breath—and another. Teleportation was one of the few Gifts that operated in the same way for Civilized

and Haosa. One merely visualized the place, or person, one wished
to arrive at, engaged one's Gift, and—

There came a chill, a frisson, a long, slow smear of grey fog...

Then nothing.

· · · ❈ · · ·

The door closed, and Padi turned, half-expecting to see Tekelia
behind her, laughing.

Only, Tekelia did not appear.

A minute went by, slowly. Prompted by panic, perhaps, or some
new instinct associated with her Gift, Padi Looked within, and
nearly cried out. Tekelia's brash scarlet thread had faded to pink.

Tekelia? she asked, keeping panic out of her mental voice
with a stern application of will.

Padi?

A whisper inside her head. But there, just outside the closed
door, mist swirled, painfully slow, thickening, until it was Tekelia
standing, staggering—

Padi flung forward and caught Tekelia around the waist, triggered the door with a thought, and got them both inside.

She half-carried Tekelia to the bunk, looking down into a
face that was paler than usual, the skin stretched tight over
broad cheekbones, eyes closed. Instinctively, she caught one of
Tekelia's hands, feeling a soft glow at the base of her spine,
where Lina taught that her Gift resided, and a gentle flow,
upward, and out—

"No!" Tekelia snatched their hand away, lashes fluttering.

"Yes," Padi said firmly, recapturing the disputed member, and
holding it firmly between both of hers. Tekelia's skin was *cold*,
and she felt a shiver of fear.

"Unless you think you'll drain me, leaving nothing but an
ever-hungry ghost to roam the corridors, wailing?"

Tekelia's eyes opened. Brown eyes, perfectly matched.

"That's a very specific image. What have you been reading?"

"There's a serial Tima and Karna watch on their off-time.
Apparently, it's quite compelling. I overhead them talking about
the episode where the Haosa lover of a highly placed Council
member had been drinking of her Gift. Tragedy struck when she
drank too deep and her lover—"

"—was left a hungry ghost, wailing in the halls. They're

watching the *empatos*." Tekelia slid their hand free. "That's more than enough, thank you."

"You're welcome," she said, sitting on the edge of the bunk. Reaching into the pocket of her jacket, she pulled out a fruit and nut bar, which she dropped on Tekelia's stomach.

Tekelia laughed, a trifle ragged to Padi's ear, and twisted to sit up, back against the wall. Padi pulled a second bar out of her pocket, and opened it.

"I don't deserve you in my life, Padi yos'Galan," Tekelia said.

"No, I won't have that. I believe that we precisely deserve each other." Padi took a bite of nut bar, and chewed. Despite the substantial snack they had just eaten, she found she was a little peckish—and had another bite.

She looked up, finding that Tekelia had finished. "Do you need something more?" she asked. "Shall I call for a tray?"

"I believe I'm well enough for the moment," Tekelia said. "Though I will ask you to show me how to call, if I should be in need, later."

"I'll do that," Padi said. She finished her bar and dusted off her hands.

"Now," she said, looking into Tekelia's face, which was considerably less strained. "How foolish *was* that experiment?"

"It shouldn't have been foolish at all!" Tekelia protested. "Teleportation is done the same way, on-Grid or off. It's expensive of energy, but—I've never experienced anything like what just happened. I thought—"

Tekelia stopped, mouth tight. Horror reached Padi through their link and she shifted so that her hip was against Tekelia's knee.

"I thought I was lost," Tekelia said quietly. "The process was—too slow, as if there wasn't enough energy to . . . finish."

"So *you* would have become a hungry ghost, wailing in the halls?" She did not *quite* keep her voice steady.

"That might have been the happiest outcome," Tekelia said. "I—are you able to teleport in this environment?"

Padi raised her eyebrows.

"*You* taught *me*, recall it?"

Tekelia sighed sharply. "Yes, of course."

Padi got up and crossed the room. She drew two cups of water from the wall unit, and brought them back to the bunk.

"Thank you," Tekelia said.

"What is it that you wish to prove—or disprove? That the ship is its own Grid?"

"I want to find if the Haosa can work or take passage on the ships," Tekelia said. "Blays would have it that there are no Haosa without the ambient. Yet, the trade team included several Talents. The ambient didn't *give* them their Gifts—their Gifts that operate *in this environment*." Tekelia drew a hard breath to damp the sudden flare of frustration.

"Well—yes. But teleportation isn't very—common. The energy drain might be the reason for that." Padi sipped her water.

"I was taught that my Gift is *of me*, seated specifically at the root of my spine."

Tekelia looked dubious.

"Yes, I know, except that I do feel *some*thing, when I draw on my Gift, and it's not at all like what I feel when I engage with the ambient. The ambient is—outside of me."

"That's correct. The ambient *acts on* the Gifted."

Padi frowned, thinking.

"I wonder," she said slowly, and slanted a look at Tekelia.

"Tell me what you wonder."

"I wonder if it might be beneficial for you to speak to Lina Faaldom, who tutored me in how to use my Gift, thankless task that it was. She's a very experienced teacher, and may be able to . . . explain technique better than I am able to do."

"This is the person who taught you tool-building?"

"Say that she tried her best to teach me tool-building. It is no fault of hers that I largely failed to learn. I was neither the most apt, nor the most biddable, of students."

Tekelia drank the last of the water.

"Counsel me—would consulting the tutor be a conservative route?"

"It would," Padi said, seriously. "In fact, it might not emperil anyone. I know the Haosa love danger—"

"But this Haosa has no wish to become a wailing wraith. How would I meet Lina Faaldom?"

"I'll ask her if she would be able to see you tomorrow while I'm with the master trader and the *qe'andra*. Would that suit?"

"Yes, I think I had better have something other than my own thoughts to occupy me."

"I'll call her now," Padi said, rising.

Off-Grid
Peck's Market

. . . .

IT HAD COME NIGHT, THE DARK SKY A BACKDROP AGAINST WHICH a multitude of bright colors streamed and flowed.

Mar Tyn lay on his back on one of the tables, gazing at the sky, half-tranced. It seemed he could hear the music to which the streamers danced; that he could *feel* the dance at the core of him, as if his Gift had joined the streamers and become one with the sky.

Half-smiling, he took a deep breath of cool, fresh air, and wondered if he dared go upstairs again, and suggest to Dyoli that she might rest. A similar effort, made several hours previous, had not met with success—exactly the opposite, in fact. Still, if they were going to spend the night, they ought at least to let Jes—

Vaiza, who had been napping at Mar Tyn's side, suddenly stirred and sat up.

"Torin wants me," he said. "Will you come?"

"Yes," Mar Tyn answered, and rolled off the table.

Dyoli had fallen asleep with her head on Mar Tyn's shoulder before Tima had fairly gotten the car moving. He sighed comfortably and settled deeper into the back seat, which gave him a good angle to watch the ongoing dance of the streamers through the window.

"The sky is beautiful here," he said softly.

"I was thinking that myself," Tima said quietly from the driver's seat. "We don't see those in the city, not even from the roof."

"No. Vaiza says that the Grid specifically blocks the energies from which the colors are formed."

137

There was a small silence before Tima said, "Well, I guess they have their reasons."

"Indeed," Mar Tyn said, drowsily, "I suppose they do."

He woke some time later, Dyoli's head now on his lap, and looked out the window, to a sky faintly red, a street lined with shops, and a feeling that the air was, just a little, stale.

"Tima," he said softly.

"Yep."

"Might you bring us to the lobby door? I would like to get Dyoli upstairs as quickly as possible."

"I think I can make that work," she said. "Ysbel won't let anybody snatch you."

"Thank you," he said, and set himself to rousing Dyoli.

"Here you are," Tima said, opening the back door from her place in the driver's seat. "All out."

"Thank you, Tima," Dyoli murmured. "It was a longer day than we had promised you, I fear."

"Long, but largely restful, for me," the security guard said placidly. "Other people were doing the heavy work."

"They did, at that," Mar Tyn said, helping Dyoli out of the car, and sliding an arm around her waist. "Thank you, Tima."

"I'll wait here until Ysbel lets you in—there we go—"

The door to the Wayfarer's lobby swung open, and Mar Tyn guided Dyoli across the threshold. He looked back once they were inside, just in time to see the car pull away.

"Good evening, Ysbel," he said to the woman behind the security desk.

"Luzants," she answered with her usual calmness. "A good evening to you both." She tapped her control board and the lift behind her opened.

They entered, the door closed, and Dyoli sighed.

"Despite having eaten quite an amazing amount of food today," she said, "I fear I must confess to being hungry, my Mar Tyn."

That, he had no trouble believing. The Healing she had performed would have been enough to tax her resources, but the work she had done afterward in concert with the Haosa Healer had not only been groundbreaking, but expensive of energy.

Though he had done far less, he too was thinking favorably of a snack and a glass—or two—of wine.

"Once we're in our room," he said, "you may rest while I call down to the kitchen for anything you might like."

"Done," Dyoli said, and sighed again. "I may have overstretched myself," she admitted.

Mar Tyn snorted, that having been the suggestion that had seen him banished from the apartment in mid-afternoon.

"Poor Mar Tyn," Dyoli murmured. "Were we brutal to you?"

"Merely firm. Though I do want it noted that I took the hint well."

She laughed lightly.

The lift chimed, and the door opened onto their familiar hallway. Dyoli stirred, and Mar Tyn let her go ahead of him, alert for any unsteadiness or stumble.

He was by no means as tired as Dyoli, but there was a certain heaviness in his joints, and an ache behind his eyes. The air in the hallway struck him as too still, and a thought over-warm. Well, they'd soon be in their suite, and able to order things more to their liking.

Dyoli put her hand against the plate. The door slid aside, and she entered, Mar Tyn at her heels.

She passed into the common room and stopped so suddenly Mar Tyn had to dance a step to the left to avoid knocking into her. This new position afforded him a fine view of a plump woman in neat trade clothes, pinkish grey hair cut close around her ears. She rose from the couch, reader in hand.

"Dyoli ven'Deelin," she said, her voice firm and dry.

"Mother?" Dyoli's voice keyed upward in shock. "What are you doing here?"

"Master Trader yos'Galan found a need for an experienced trader able to cover multiple duties. He appealed to Master Trader ven'Deelin, his partner in the Colemeno venture. Knowing that I was at liberty, Master Trader ven'Deelin put the case to me, and I was able to come immediately."

Dyoli's mother was *angry*, Mar Tyn thought, but not at either of the master traders.

"When," she finished, her voice coming sharper, "were you going to write to me?"

Dyoli sighed.

"I wrote to the delm," she said. "And Til Den of course knew where I was."

"Of course," the other woman said with an icy politeness that bade fair for an extended, and acrimonious, discussion, which was not, Mar Tyn thought, what Dyoli needed at this moment.

He stepped forward.

"You will pardon me, Trader, but Healer ven'Deelin has been long at labor today, and requires nothing so much as a meal and some sleep. Surely your topic can wait until she has rested."

Aware of his lack of High House polish, he chose to speak in the Liaden mode of adult-to-adult, which was permissible between strangers.

Blue eyes speared him.

"Who are you?" she asked, and it was not adult-to-adult she chose, but some other mode far beyond him.

"Mother, this is Mar Tyn pai'Fortana, my partner," Dyoli said, her voice cool, but perhaps not entirely... calm. "Mar Tyn, this is Trader Namid ven'Deelin Clan Ixin, who has the honor to be my mother, and Til Den's."

Mar Tyn bowed in the Colemeno style, that seeming better than mistaking his mode in the Liaden, and murmured, "Trader."

It seemed to Mar Tyn that the trader's face tightened.

"pai'Fortana," she repeated. "A Low Port house, I believe."

"Yes," he said. Once, he thought, he would have cowered away from this High House lady's disdain, but at the moment he felt a certain—pride. True enough, he had been born in Liad's Low Port. He had survived to adulthood against heavy odds, and was now a valued member of a trade mission, studying to be a *qe'andra*, and partnered to Dyoli ven'Deelin.

There was shame, he thought, in none of that.

He met the lady's gaze and held it, calmly, for a long moment, before turning to Dyoli.

"You had overstretched yourself, you said," he reminded her.

"So, I did—and so I did," Dyoli said ruefully. She bowed to the woman before them.

"Truce, Mother, until tomorrow, when I will accept whatever scold you find fitting. Are we agreed?"

Trader ven'Deelin tipped her head, as if considering the merits of this proposal, then produced a bow that, to Mar Tyn's eye, matched Dyoli's.

"Agreed," she said. "Rest well, Daughter."

Her eyes moved and she bowed again, very close to the Cole-meno style. "Mar Tyn pai'Fortana. Thank you for your care of my kin," she said, and the mode was adult-to-adult.

"Come," Dyoli said, taking his hand and turning toward the door to their suite. "You offered to call the kitchen while I rested," she said. "I am going to hold you to that promise."

On-Grid
The Sakuriji
Council Chambers

· · · · · · · · · · · · · · · · ·

DESPITE BLAYS'S DOUBTS, IT HAD SO FAR PROVED TO BE AN interesting morning.

The Warden had sent a car to bring her from Peck's Market to the Wardian. He had himself given her a tour of the facilities, and introduced her to several people who worked for the benefit of Civilization, all of them cordial, and not in the least horrified to discover a Haosa in their midst.

Blays had particularly liked Luzant kelbiMyst, lead *qe'andra* of the justice and accountability department.

"Counsel to Chaos!" she exclaimed with a wide grin, her pattern glittering with glee. "Do you know, I've often felt that my own profession is something of the sort. I wonder if I might persuade the Warden to change my job title?" This with a mischievous glance at Tekelia's cousin, who was, surprisingly, amused.

"I have no control over what you put on your business card," he said.

"True!" Luzant kelbiMyst said, as one much-struck. "I believe I might order a new set."

She turned back to Blays then, extending a hand.

"Don't hesitate to call on me, for anything. I'm always pleased to expand my net of acquaintance. May I hope to be able to call upon you, should I have questions regarding Haosa law and business?"

"I'd be happy to hear from you," Blays said truthfully, "though I don't know how much help I might be." She sighed. "And I'm afraid I don't have a card."

"No, that won't do *at all*! Allow me to order a set for you, as a networking gift! Here—" She brought a notepad out of her pocket and flicked it on.

"Give me your name, and your comm code, so I'll not only have you in my contact list, but for ordering the cards—"

Blays hesitated, somewhat concerned, and sent a glance to Tekelia's cousin, hoping for a clue as to the propriety of allowing chance-met *qe'andra* to order cards for her.

To her surprise, Bentamin chastaMeir smiled.

"Let her have her fun; she gets so little chance to play," he said.

"As if I would *play* with something as important as a business card!" Luzant kelbiMyst said with utterly false indignation. "Blays—may I call you Blays? Because you *must* call me Marlin. We're colleagues, after all! In any case, ignore that man's insinuations. I will order you cards that are worthy of you and your office. I'll have the proof sent to you, for final corrections and approval!"

"That's—very generous," Blays said, slowly. "I regret that I have nothing of equal value to offer."

"No, no! We are colleagues, not sparring diplomats! We will each assist the other, many times, going forward. I'm certain of it."

"Thank you," Blays said. "I'll look forward to seeing the proofs. May I have *your* card?"

"I insist upon it!" Marlin announced, and produced one with a flourish.

The last stop on the tour was the Wardian Reading Room.

"Marvelous!" Blays cried, spinning on her toes in the center of the room. There were stained glass windows set in the ceiling, which gave a comforting illusion of having the Ribbons overhead, though the room was as tightly shielded as any other she'd visited that morning. "I would willingly come under Grid for this."

The Warden smiled. "You may wish to take one of the guided tours of the city. Haven Central Library casts the Wardian's holdings into the shade."

He took a timepiece from his pocket.

"I regret pulling you away, but we just have time for tea and cake in the cafeteria before I'm wanted at the Council meeting. Will you be going as well?"

"Yes, I'm to meet Councilor ziaGorn."

"Then we may go together, if that pleases you."

"Thank you," Blays said. "I accept your offer of transport."

· · · ❈ · · ·

Majel arrived in the lobby early. While it was only good manners not to keep a guest waiting, he did not have to be *quite* so early.

He had told himself that, but it had become entirely impossible to focus on his work, so much did he anticipate seeing Blays essWorthi again.

He wondered what she would make of the Council's business; in fact, he wondered what she would have to say concerning the Wardian. He had received the impression that she did not often come into the city, which made him wonder what she made of *it*—and at that point, he admitted defeat, turned off his screen, and left his office.

He did manage to muster enough self-control to take the long way 'round, stopping to chat with colleagues and visitors met on the way, and by such stratagems insured that his wait for her arrival was mere minutes, instead of an entire quarter-hour.

He smiled when the Warden's car pulled up, though he did not rush the door. He waited, and only stepped forward when they were in the lobby, feeling his entire body warm when she turned her amber gaze and frank smile on him.

"Councilor ziaGorn! I'm happy to see you."

"I'm happy to see you as well," Majel said, which was true to a rather astonishing degree.

She turned to address the Warden. "Thank you! The tour was interesting, and I was especially glad to meet Luzant kelbiMyst."

The Warden smiled. "She doesn't get to meet as many new people as she would like. I'm afraid I'm responsible; I keep her too busy on the Warden's business."

"Maybe she needs some time off," Blays said. "To play."

The Warden's answer was slightly too long in coming.

"Maybe she does," he said, and bowed. "I leave you in Councilor ziaGorn's very capable hands. Thank you for a pleasant morning."

With that, he moved off, leaving Majel with his guest.

She was dressed in Civilized fashion, long vest over silky shirt and soft trousers. Her hair, he noted, with a certain feeling of dismay, was confined in a knot at the back of her head, not a floating lock left free. Suddenly aware that he had spent too long in silence, he bowed and gestured toward the lift.

"If you will come with me, Counselor essWorthi, I will see you seated in the gallery."

Blays did not move.

"No," she said decisively. "That won't do."

He blinked. "Don't you want to observe the Council at work?"

"Oh, that! I did come to see that. No, what won't do is *Counselor essWorthi*." She frowned, and then asked, with a certain forcefulness, "Are we *colleagues*?"

"I would say so," Majel answered, slowly. "After all, I'm a councilor and you're a counselor."

Blays smiled, brilliant. "That's exactly what I was thinking! One of the things I learned this morning is that colleagues may dispense with a level of formality. I would like you to call me Blays. May I in turn call you Majel?"

"Yes, I would like that," he said, and added, "Colleague."

Blays laughed, and stepped to his side.

"Come, then, Majel; show me this gallery."

· · · ❄ · · ·

Majel ziaGorn was even more beautiful than she had recalled. He smiled with a sincerity that warmed her, head to toe, and good-naturedly accepted the fiction that they were colleagues.

He took her up to the gallery, saw her seated in an advantageous place, and brought her a bottle of tea and a packet of cake from the buffet at the side of the room.

"Are you perfectly comfortable?" he asked.

"The Grid's a bit of an itch," Blays said, truthfully, "but I find that as soon as something interesting happens, I can ignore it."

He smiled. "Then we'll do our best to be interesting."

A bell rang, brassy and stern. Majel straightened.

"That's my call to duty. After the session is done, it would be my pleasure to escort you to lunch, if you wish."

"That sounds—" *perfectly wonderful*, Blays thought, but remembered that Civilized people were often put off by Haosa enthusiasms, and moderated herself to "pleasant."

"Good. I'll come to you here, after."

The bell rang again.

"Don't be late on my account," Blays said.

"No, that would be too bad of me."

He bowed and left her, walking briskly toward the lift at the back of the gallery.

Blays settled into her chair, leaving the cake and the bottle of tea on the wide arm as she looked about her.

It was not over-crowded, and at least two of her fellow observers had settled deep into their chairs, as if preparing to nap.

Balancing them was a group of four, clustered together at the rail, their excitement sparking against the sluggish ambient. At some distance from them, sitting firm, straight, and severe, was a group of three, cases at their feet, shields closed, auras disciplined to the point of bleakness.

Blays shivered, aware of the itching of the Grid against her Gift, and glanced to the room below in time to see several persons clad in long robes the shade of moss arrive in the chamber. They each stood behind one of the chairs at the table, which left one empty—Blays thought it must be the chair that had belonged to Councilor seelyFaire, who had recently resigned in disgrace.

While the councilors stood waiting, another figure came into the room below, the black robes doing nothing to disguise the fact that this was Tekelia's cousin, the Warden. He went to a desk set to the right of the council table, and stood behind the chair there.

The brass bell sounded again, followed by the noise of chairs being drawn out, and the councilors settling themselves.

The identical robes ought to have made the eleven seated 'round the table seem all one and the same—Blays thought that was the intent. If so, it was a failure. Ten of the eleven displayed genteel shields to the public and each other. Only Majel ziaGorn was exposed, his bonny, ordered pattern on full display.

Someone, Blays thought, *needs to teach that man how to build shields.*

She wriggled in the chair as the Grid scraped along her nerves, and thought about pulling her own shields closed. Before she could decide if that would be an act of prudence or cowardice, another bell rang, this one silver bright, piercing every corner of the room, commanding attention.

"The Council of the Civilized is convened," a woman's voice said, as emotionless as words on a page. "All come to order."

Blays sat very still, senses a-tingle, expecting to feel the enforcement of that order. Surprisingly, imposed peace did not waft through the chamber, though those at the table settled into themselves, as if the ritual of the bell and the announcement focused them.

Blays leaned forward, Seeing that Majel ziaGorn's considerable attention was also focused, his pattern calm.

"Our first order of business is the progress report on the commercial rail line connecting Arthenton Vane and Peck's Market." The woman at the top of the table—who must, Blays thought, be the council chair—glanced 'round, as if expecting a comment. Nothing was said, though, and she inclined her head.

"The Council sees Nersing carnYllum, Project Manager."

A tall, skinny man stepped to the front of the room, and stood under the screen suspended there. Blays thought he might have been sitting in a chair around the edge of the council room and out of her sight. At his appearance, the group of four at the gallery rail jostled and shifted, as each sought the best place.

Below, the skinny man bowed and straightened, hands folded neatly together at his waist.

"I am pleased to report to the Council that Phase One Construction of the spur line which will connect the city warehouse district to Peck's Market is well underway. As I indicated in my last report, the Citizen Review polled a high level of approval for this project, and I am pleased to note that enthusiasm continues to grow. The owners of Peck's Market are finalizing plans for an additional warehouse installation which will double their current ability to receive and store goods."

He paused, as if expecting a question, but no one said anything. The four at the railing, Blays noted, were rapt, barely seeming to breathe, their auras bright and focused.

"Work on the terminal at Arthenton Vane proceeds on schedule, and we are looking forward to entering Phase Two both on-time and to-budget."

Again, he paused. Again, there were no questions.

"I should mention to the Council that Master Trader yos'Galan spoke with my staff and myself at length regarding the rail line and the timetables not only for this phase, but in future. He has an interest in trade accessibility and . . . *reach*, as he put it. If Colemenoport is to become a trade hub, then the ability to move goods quickly to and from all points, on-Grid and off, will be a necessity."

Now at last came a comment, from the person sitting two chairs to the left of Majel.

"We're to make ourselves entirely over to suit the master trader's whim, I collect?"

Project Manager carnYllum was visibly taken aback.

"Your pardon, Councilor, I doubt the master trader had any such thing in mind. Merely, his own project requires him to be aware of the port, and what changes may benefit it. The rail system—he felt that the spur was a good beginning, but—"

"But we must proceed one step at a time, even as we survey the path ahead of us," said the councilor directly on Majel's left, allowing amusement to be seen. "This is the case whether one is a project manager, a master trader, or a councilor. Don't you agree, Councilor tryaBent?"

"Bah," replied the first councilor.

"Indeed," said the council chair. "Have you more to report, Luzant carnYllum?"

"Councilor, I have not." He smiled tentatively.

"So! A short report and a satisfactory one. The Council thanks you for your efforts on behalf of Colemeno. We look forward to receiving you again when Phase One has been completed."

He bowed. "I will be honored, ma'am," he said, and exited the way he had entered, vanishing from Blays's ken.

There was a mild tussle at the railing as the four observers got themselves sorted out, and headed for the lift at the back of the gallery.

The silver bell rang, recalling Blays to the floor below, where the Council Chair had risen to speak.

"Our next piece of business, Councilors, concerns the mandate of this body. We are charged with upholding the planetary civilization, and all who partake of it. I was a councilor sitting at this table when the vote was called to add a seat for our voiceless under the Grid. It came at the end of a long and acrimonious debate, and I was never prouder of this council, and of Civilization, than when that seat was created.

"While the path has not been easy going forward, we are stronger for our diversity."

She paused, and looked around the table, deliberately meeting the eyes of each councilor in turn.

"Today, we are presented with a like challenge, and I have no doubt that we will rise to meet it as we did the first, years ago.

"The Grid does not encompass the entirety of Colemeno. We share the planet with those who are in every sense our kin, differently suited to meet the world's challenges, but no less worthy of the protection and support that this council is charged to provide. It is time, and in my opinion, past time, for a great and shameful wrong to be rectified."

She bowed to the table.

"I move that full membership be granted to, and a chair placed at this table for, those citizens of the planet who choose to live beyond the borders of the Grid—the Haosa of Colemeno."

"I second the motion," Majel said. Someone else said, "third," and the councilor on Majel's left said, "Call the vote."

"I have," said the grumpy councilor—tryaBent, Blays reminded herself—"an amendment to the motion."

The council chair sat down, folded her hands on the table before her and said, very calmly.

"The Chair sees Councilor tryaBent."

"Thank you, Chair gorminAstir." Councilor tryaBent rose and bowed to the table. "Colleagues.

"The last time a new place was made at Colemeno's table— the event so eloquently alluded to by Chair gorminAstir—the substance of the debate centered on whether the natural state of the person to be seated would impede their ability to properly reckon the weight of Gift and Talent in the many and diverse matters with which this body deals."

She bowed again, gently.

"That doubt need not be raised in connection with the proposed newest chair," she said.

Then why mention it? Blays thought, angry on Majel's behalf.

"What we must ask ourselves in the case before us," Councilor tryaBent continued, her voice reasonable and smooth, "is if the Haosa understand governance, and the necessity to sometimes impose limits on the many so that the few are not unjustly burdened."

Now Blays was angry on behalf of herself, and her cousins. Did that person think the Haosa had no understanding of *limits*? As to governance—

"So we come," Councilor tryaBent said, making a show of looking around the table, "to my amendment: That the Haosa chair be created, and that it be a limited—that is to say, a non-voting chair— for the thirty-six days following the seating of the Haosa councilor."

She bowed again and sat down.

Chair gorminAstir inclined her head.

"Thank you, Councilor. Discussion?"

"I wonder what this non-voting period is meant to achieve," said the councilor directly to Majel's left.

"To allow the new councilor to observe this body at our work, and to hear discussion of the issues, as well as the weight assigned to various considerations. This will all be beyond someone from a society that governs by—shall we say—committee?"

Blays gripped the arms of her chair to keep from rising. If the grumpy tryaBent thought governing "by committee" was easy—or was that *primitive*?—she'd be pleased to stand back and let her try *her* hand at getting cousins to agree.

"There are," Majel said, "newspapers, newscasts, libraries, books. The library matrix is free to anyone who has a screen or the means to access a public screen."

"Very true, Councilor," said tryaBent, with a chilly smile. "Is there a point to that observation?"

"Only that the work of this council is public, and that there's no reason to suppose that our new colleague will be utterly ignorant of Civilization and its workings." He raised a hand. "In fact, I believe it's human nature to closely study those things that oppress or belittle one's way of life."

"Indeed," said the councilor to his immediate left. "In order to understand, or, I think more frequently, to find where it might be vulnerable to change."

"The Haosa have *hardly* been oppressed!" Councilor tryaBent protested.

"That," said the Council Chair, "is another discussion for another day. We are at the moment debating the virtue of adding a waiting period to the creation of the new chair."

"Speaking from my own experience as the newest councilor at the table," said the councilor directly across from tryaBent, "I would like to point out that, the day I took my seat, I voted on two pieces of council business on which I felt myself reasonably informed. The conversation of my colleagues was very useful, and this entire table was patient with my questions."

She inclined her head. "That day, I also abstained from a vote, feeling that I did not have sufficient grasp of the issues involved. I would expect the Haosa Councilor will also be given the support of colleagues around the table, that they will ask questions, and not operate in a vacuum."

She looked across the table.

"It is why we are a *council*, isn't it, Councilor tryaBent? Because we support and inform each other and hold the benefit to Colemeno at center, even when we might disagree on how best to serve." She paused, and added diffidently, "That's what you told me, at the end of my first day, when you were good enough to sit with me in the cafeteria over cake and tea, and discuss the business that had gone forth, and what were the obligations of a councilor, aside voting and signing. I don't believe I told you how much your insights meant to me, and I do so now."

There was a moment of silence before the Council Chair spoke again.

"Is there more discussion of the amendment?"

Silence.

"I move that we vote," said the councilor to Majel's immediate left.

"Second," said the councilor two places to Majel's right.

"Those in favor of amending the motion to create a full chair after a non-voting period of thirty-six days, please raise your hands."

Councilor tryaBent and a councilor who had said nothing, raised their hands.

"Those against amending the motion to create a full chair to include a non-voting period of thirty-six days, please raise your hands."

Hands came up.

"The amendment fails," the chair said.

"Call the vote," someone—Blays missed who—said. "This is long overdue."

"All in favor of seating a representative of the Haosa as a full member of this council, please stand."

There was a rustle of robes, and a scrape of chairs.

Blays rose from her own chair, her heart thumping. The whole table was on its feet—no. No, Councilor tryaBent alone was still seated, abandoned even by her ally for the amendment. Blays felt a grudging admiration for her commitment to her principles.

"All be seated. The motion passes."

The motion passes, Blays thought, with something like amazement—and gasped. Tekelia was gone! *She* was Speaker! If she was called down from the gallery—

"Warden, will you extend the invitation of the Council to

Speaker vesterGranz, and ask that a fitting person be sent to represent the Haosa at the table of Colemeno?"

The Warden rose from his desk, and bowed to the room at large.

"I will be honored to do so," he said, and reseated himself.

There was a long moment of silence before the silver bell rang again.

"Our next piece of business, Councilors, is a citizen's petition, entitled 'Plan to Insure a Safe Port and Civilization.' You may see it on your screens, and also on the overhead."

Blays leaned forward, the better to read the big screen, half-aware of a tightening in the air, as if—she glanced to one side—yes. As if the grim threesome had gotten grimmer still. *So, this one is theirs*, she thought, and returned her attention to the screen.

"This plan mandates continuing service seminars for all port and city security personnel, to bring them current with modern procedure," Majel said. "Surely such a petition ought to be first directed to the portmaster and the Haven City manager."

"Quite right," said the councilor to his immediate left.

"Portmaster krogerSlyte," said the council chair, "do you have anything to report to the Council with regard to this petition?"

The large woman sitting beyond the councilor to Majel's left raised her hands to show empty palms.

"No, ma'am, I have not," she said. "This is the first time I've seen it. I can report that ongoing education is a requirement for continued employment and promotion at the port. Courses and credit accounting are handled through the Resource Office. If this petition is, as it seems to be, a move to add a course to the existing curriculum, there's a submission system in place." She moved her shoulders. "Your pardon, Council Chair. My answer is no, I have not previously seen this proposal."

"In fact, the petition is out of order," said the councilor who had offered the amendment. "I move that it be remanded to the Clerk of Council for proper handling."

"Second," said the councilor on Majel's immediate right.

"Call to vote. All in favor?"

Every hand went up.

"The motion passes. Petition is remanded to the Clerk of Council."

The group of three stood as if moved by one will, picked up

their cases and left the gallery, walking silently, grimness trailing them like a dank cloud.

Blays looked around—the gallery was now occupied by the two sitting deep in their seats—definitely napping—and herself.

She opened the bottle of tea and had a drink before returning her attention to the business below, which had moved on to budgetary matters.

Blays tried to pay close attention, but she was very swiftly left in the dust. She did manage to keep up when the Warden rose to make his report on the State of Civilization, but only because he had talked over some of its points with her as part of the Wardian tour.

When the silver bell rang again, and all those seated rose to file out, Blays flopped back in her chair, and closed her eyes.

There was something—*seductive*—in how smoothly the Council conducted itself, with a lack of high emotion that was completely different from a Haosa meeting of similar scope.

In fact, she thought, it was almost *too* smooth, as if all the answers were already known and the daily business done by rote.

The Grid *itched*. Blays wrinkled her nose, drank what was left of her tea and rose to put the empty bottle and the cake wrapper in the receptacles at the side of the gallery.

On-Grid
The Wardian

. . . .

MARLIN SENT OFF THE ORDER FOR BLAYS ESSWORTHI'S BUSINESS cards in a state of high good humor. *Counsel to Chaos*, indeed. It was enough to tempt a Civilized woman to leap off the Grid to see what adventures awaited her.

Aside from her title, Blays essWorthi had been . . . interesting. Humorous, intelligent, by turns naive and cynical—Marlin had liked her at once. Even a glimpse of a pattern that seemed to have no boundaries save a soft, colorful fog, had intrigued rather than horrified.

Marlin was well aware that her own tendency toward exuberance put off some of the most Civilized of her colleagues and acquaintances, and had long since decided that she could not be responsible for the discomfort of others. Her Gifts were firm; her education impeccable, her professional record sterling. She could not have risen to Chief *Qe'andra* of the Wardian's own Department of Accountability and Justice had she been anything other than superb at what she did.

And, truth told, she *liked* her job.

Only, it would be . . . agreeable, from time to time, to play, *truly* play to the limits of her energy and her Gifts.

She had sensed in Blays essWorthi a significant capacity for *play*. Even Bentamin had allowed himself to be amused—at the two of them, Marlin thought. Playing.

It was said among the Civilized, who did not know as much as they assumed they did, that Haosa were always at play, and never serious, but Marlin knew that for prejudice. It was likely that she had met more Haosa than the average Luzant underGrid, and while they had all been willing to join a frolic or participate

154

in a round of nonsense, they had possessed, every one, a center made of adamantine.

Well, by all measures, she had played enough this day. It was time to—

"Marlin?"

She looked up to see her aide in the doorway, pattern showing an interesting mix of victory and dread.

Marlin produced a smile.

"Neeoni," she said. "What can I do for you?"

The girl took a breath, stepped into the office, and leaned over to place a data stick on the desk by Marlin's hand.

She gave it a moment of serious consideration, then transferred her gaze to Neeoni's face, eyebrows up.

"And this is...?"

Neeoni gulped. "Pel's deep files," she said. "We found them."

Colemenoport
Wayfarer

. . . .

DYOLI DRIFTED TOWARD WAKEFULNESS FROM A DREAM OF SOFT colors flowing into, and melding with, the gentle mists of Healspace. There was from somewhere close by the soft sound of keys clicking—very nearly as comforting in its everydayness as Healspace itself.

The keys stopped clicking, and perversely Dyoli waked even further. She was curled on her side, snuggled into blankets, but—alone. That was sufficiently unsatisfactory to wake her fully, and she opened her eyes.

The door to their designated workroom was open and she could see Mar Tyn's back as the keys began to click again.

"Good morning, my Mar Tyn," she said, not very loudly. The keys clicked on briefly before he rose and came in to sit on the edge of the bed.

"Say rather, good afternoon," he said with a smile.

"Truly?"

"Truly."

"What can my excuse be, save that yesterday was quite the adventure? I do believe I may have done something that no Healer has done before—not, you understand, that there would have been need, in anyplace other than Colemeno."

"In the whole universe, there are no other despairing mothers seeking to protect their children by binding them in support of each other?"

"But you see," Dyoli said earnestly, "that is the function of heart-links. Torin and Vaiza share a very strong one. Even their rogue of a norbear is not stinted."

She sighed. "No, it was the mother's necessity to see that her

156

children not only supported each other, but that they *remained together*. *That* could only be accomplished if both were seen to be Civilized. Which is a situation, my love, that only could have arisen on Colemeno."

"If you say so."

"Well, I have said so, after all." She smiled. "Have you been up long?"

"Some hours," he said. "I finished the section self-test, and reviewed the first chapter of the new section. I'm just now answering a letter from Vaiza. He reports that Arbour and Vayeen returned to the village last night. Geritsi and Dosent stayed to bear them company, and saw him, Torin, Maradel, and Eet onto the early delivery van to Pacazahno Village. The twins are to spend the day at school, while Maradel takes care of 'some business,' as I'm told, for Arbour. They will possibly stay the night in Pacazahno. He wonders when we will invite them for dinner again."

Dyoli laughed. "That sounds promising. Maradel, Arbour, Geritsi, and I had talked about this trip to Pacazahno. It will give Torin another day and night in a less chaotic environment, where her micro-Grid will still need to function."

Mar Tyn tipped his head. "If it fails?"

"They will be with Maradel, who is a Healer in her own right. Also, there is a Healer in Pacazahno, and several rooms shielded like the apartment at Peck's Market. If the tool fails, Torin can quickly be moved to a less active environment."

Dyoli sighed, and stretched.

"And interacting with children their own age will be good for both of them. Geritsi tells me that there are no other children in Ribbon Dance Village at the moment. Negotiations had begun with the Pacazahno administrator to bring a small class to Ribbon Dance, which may be the business Maradel will be taking care of for Arbour."

She smiled at him. "Really, it's a very sound plan, and respectful of limits."

"As you all agreed between you."

"Exactly." She tipped her head. "Speaking of limits—have you any ill-effects from yesterday's adventures?"

"My arm may be a little sore from skip-ball, but I don't think it's serious," Mar Tyn said, with what Dyoli realized, was playfulness.

Mar Tyn was not often playful. It seemed the relationship with Vaiza was pushing him into bloom.

"I don't wish to rush you," he said, more seriously, "but I should mention that I've put your mother off twice with a promise that you will come to her in the common room as soon as you have waked, and eaten."

Dyoli stared.

"Good gods. My mother. I had completely forgotten." She took a breath. "Perhaps I'll go back to sleep."

"Are you sleepy?" Mar Tyn asked with interest.

"No, more's the pity." She closed her eyes, ran a calming exercise, and twisted into a sitting position, pushing the covers back.

"May I beg you to order whatever meal is appropriate to the hour while I shower and dress?"

"It will be my pleasure," Mar Tyn assured her, rising from the edge of the bed. He paused a moment, then leaned down and kissed her, sweet and warm.

When she was able, Dyoli laughed, rather breathlessly. "Will you make my mother call again?"

He tipped his head, as if considering.

"No, I don't think that would be...useful."

Dyoli sputtered a laugh. "Useful," she repeated, recalling choice lectures from her childhood. "No—not useful at all."

· · · ✳ · · ·

In the common room, Namid ven'Deelin had set her portable screen up at the small desk by the window overlooking the street.

Colemenoport was not given to tall buildings, the Wayfarer being the tallest in this vicinity. Namid could therefore see from her window the other tower of note—the Port Administration building. The low, spread-out port argued for an economy where land was cheap, or business sparse. The files the master trader had provided suggested that, in the case of Colemeno, it was both.

Locked away from the wider routes of commerce by Rostov's Dust, as it had been for so long, Colemenoport had held the line, but expansion was, Namid suspected, a concept foreign to current culture and thought.

That was going to change if Master Trader yos'Galan had his way, as it seemed he would. Once Colemenoport was officially a hub, it would be the job of the trader-on-port to work closely with administration on the topic of growth, the trader being ready to provide models from other successful transitions.

Namid opened a sub-screen. The master trader had of course been meticulous in his gathering of data, but it would do her no harm to build some searches of her own, if only to get a feel for the local information networks.

She had just finished loosing her third, and for the moment final, search when it came to her that she was not alone.

"Good afternoon, Mother. Forgive me, that I kept you waiting."

Namid took a careful breath. Years, it had been, when she had thought her daughter was dead; that voice forever silenced. To hear it again was a strike to the heart, if joy could be a dagger.

She came out of her chair, and turned to face the woman who stood there, pale red hair pulled back into a tail, blue eyes firm. She was dressed in trade clothes, as was Namid herself, and her hands were folded before her. She wore, Namid noticed, no rings.

"Your partner said that you had overreached yourself, and before all else required rest." Namid allowed herself a thin smile. "He is very protective."

"He is—yes. And if it had not been for him—his protectiveness and his love—I would not have survived to greet you today. I will not have him abused."

Namid raised her eyebrows.

"Have I abused him? That was far from my intent. Tell me how I may best make amends. We will be working together, after all, and I know nothing to his discredit."

Dyoli tipped her head slightly, and bowed.

"Forgive me yet again," she said mildly. "Indeed, Mar Tyn made no complaint. Merely, he felt that putting you off a third time would not be *useful*."

"Ah, was that it? I had no idea there was fine calculation involved."

Dyoli looked amused.

"Would you care for some wine, Mother?" she asked. "We may sit more comfortably and address your topic."

"Wine would be pleasant," Namid agreed. "Only let me close my screen, and I will meet you on the couch."

✳   ✳   ✳

Dyoli, Namid thought, had changed. Til Den's letter had hinted as much, laying the alteration at the feet of unspecified "ill treatment" by a cruel patron.

Til Den had also alluded briefly to "Dyoli's partner" who had been with her in peril and had saved her life. Til Den being Til Den, and Dyoli his favorite sister, he had added that the connection appeared to him both true and firm.

She had, of course, read Mar Tyn pai'Fortana's file, included in the master trader's information packet. As his name declared him, Master pai'Fortana had been a denizen of Liad's Low Port, one of those known as a "Luck." He had been canny enough—or lucky enough—to have survived to adulthood, gathered the means to buy into a Subscription House, and also to pay his quarterly membership fees.

In practical terms, she could have wished for no better partner—wily, tough, and lucky—to accompany her daughter into peril. However—

"Here." Dyoli placed a tray on the couch table. She poured a glass of pale green liquid, and handed it to Namid, who took it and waited until Dyoli had her own in hand. They tasted the wine together, and Namid murmured, "Very pleasant. Local?"

"In fact. The pale green is the lightest of the three local vintages we have in our cellar. There is also an emerald, which is dry and silken, fruity—and a red, which is *quite* stern and will, as Padi has it, *pucker your eyebrows.*"

Namid smiled and raised her glass while Dyoli sank onto the couch across from her.

There was silence while the wine was sampled again, and the glasses placed on the table.

"So," Namid said mildly. "When *were* you going to write to me?"

"Truly? After I had written to Ixin over a signed contract naming me port-side general manager of the combined Tree-and-Dragon and Ixin trade hub newly established on Colemeno."

Namid leaned back against the cushions and gave her a straight look.

"You didn't think I would wish to know that you were alive before that?"

"I thought that Til Den would write," Dyoli said.

"Which he did, of course." Namid sighed. "I understand that

you wished to present your uncle the delm with an accomplished fact. Certainly, that would make matters easier for you."

"Indeed. The clan would have no need to inquire into my personal arrangements, or the particulars of my household."

"Your brother," Namid said, reaching for her glass, "did mention a partnership with Master pai'Fortana—whose very name declares him, as I'm certain you're aware."

Dyoli sighed. "Yes—and he is also—"

"He is also," Namid took up, "'prenticed to *Qe'andra* dea'Tolin, whom I met at breakfast this morning. She speaks of him in the warmest terms possible, and has no doubt that he will pass his certifications within the Standard, fitting him to do the financial work of the trade office, while he continues his studies for the next level."

"I believe Mar Tyn has found his calling," Dyoli said. "Jes has not yet been able to push him too hard or too far."

Namid inclined her head.

"*Qe'andra* dea'Tolin also had gratifying things to say about you and your work as part of the team compiling the whole port inventory. I am of course pleased by this evidence that you did attend your lessons."

"Well, of course I did," Dyoli said, somewhat sharply. "After all, had I not come a Healer, I would have gotten my license to trade."

"As certain as that?" Namid asked interestedly. Dyoli laughed.

"Not at the time, no—and my trader took care to keep me in suspense." She lifted one shoulder in a shrug. "The cards were taken from both of us."

"So they were."

Namid leaned forward, picked up the bottle, and refreshed their glasses.

"Returning to our earlier line of discussion—your plan was to preserve your place in the clan, and your quartershare, while also pursuing this partnership that Ixin by policy cannot like. Do I have that correctly?"

"Yes."

"Allow me to praise it as an excellent plan of its kind." Namid sipped her wine. "Now, how if I should tell you that I have with me a letter to you from Ixin, desiring you to return home and marry to contract, as you have yet to present the clan with an heir?"

Dyoli sighed, picked up her glass, and sat holding it, meditatively.

"I fear," she said slowly, "that I would not be able to accede to my delm's Word. Ixin is rich in resource; my child will not be missed in the crowd of others. I might—" she paused, eyes narrowed as if in thought, "I might offer a counterproposal, to establish a Kin House on Colemeno. There is a viable Line here—xinRood—as well as others whose claim to kinship ought to be investigated."

Namid moved a hand in approval. "Clever. And if Ixin refuses both gambit and bait?"

Dyoli sighed. "Then I would regretfully withdraw from the clan, ceding my quartershare as a death-gift to my beloved brother Til Den."

"Who would of course pass it through to you! Well thought out, Dyoli ven'Deelin! And all for the sake of a clanless rogue out of Low Port?"

"Mar Tyn is not—" Dyoli began, when a door opened, and Mar Tyn himself came across the room, stopping at the couch and leaning his elbows on the cushion by Dyoli's shoulder.

"In Low Port," he said conversationally, "the prime goal is survival. Other goals are secondary. Also, beloved, you must remember that I was at the beck of my Gift, and *it* has no sense of right nor wrong."

"Very true," Dyoli said seriously. "Yet you are not at the beck of your Gift any longer, are you, my Mar Tyn?"

The smile he gave her struck Namid to the heart. Til Den had written nothing more than the truth, she thought. This *was* a true and firm connection.

"I think not," Dyoli's partner said in answer to her question. "May I bring you more wine?"

Namid stirred.

"It is very bad of us not to offer you a glass. Especially so since I have a question, Master pai'Fortana."

He looked to her. "Please—ask."

"Yes. I wonder what you felt was the *use* of denying me my daughter twice?"

"Aside from allowing Dyoli to reap her needed rest?" He moved his shoulders. "I thought perhaps you might meet others of the trade team and be interested in what they had to say. And, I thought that it might provide time and reason for your temper to cool, for truly, ma'am, you were far too angry last evening, which I think you knew. A quarrel is *never* a good way to begin a new venture."

Namid considered him.

"Are you a Healer, Master pai'Fortana?"

"No, ma'am," he said, gently. "But Dyoli is."

Dyoli turned her head. "Mar Tyn?"

He smiled at her. "Our trip off-Grid wrought changes, I fear."

"Well! You must tell me more. First, however, let Mother and I finish our business."

"I believe we are done for the moment," Namid said. "I will write to Ixin on your behalf, Daughter. This idea of a Kin House on an emerging world in which we have a trade interest may well beguile him. Perhaps you should begin gathering particulars."

Dyoli smiled. "I will, indeed. Thank you, Mother."

"Not at all. On another topic—I wonder if you are free to give me a port tour? I wish to find my feet."

"Certainly," Dyoli said. "Shall we leave now?"

"Yes, I thank you."

On-Grid
The Sakuriji
Council Chambers

. . . .

MAJEL ENTERED THE GALLERY TO FIND BLAYS LEANING SOMEWHAT alarmingly over the railing. He stopped, unwilling to startle her into a tumble—and heard her chuckle.

"No, I'm not going to fall," she said, reversing herself and turning to face him with a grin. "Just curious."

"About what?"

"Well, I'd been wondering what was protecting the councilors from Influencers and the like. I thought there might be a sub-gallery, you know, where Dampers were posted."

"Ah. I'm told the chamber is shielded," Majel said. "I'm afraid I don't know the mechanisms involved."

"No reason why you should. It was a thought—I'm prone. If it bothers me enough, I'll ask the Warden. He did say I was to consider him a resource."

"That sounds as if you had a productive morning."

"It was unexpectedly interesting," Blays said, and, caught by sudden recollection, blurted—"Have you *seen* the library in the Wardian?"

"The reading room? I have. It's especially well-appointed, I think."

"It's beautiful! We have *nothing* like it, off-Grid. The Warden says there's a grander library in the city."

"Haven Central," Majel said. "One of my favorite places, when I was growing up. I felt so much at home there that I thought I'd study to become a librarian."

"What changed your mind?"

It had been years since he'd thought of his youthful ambitions; he was surprised by the flicker of pain as he recalled them now.

"As it turned out," he told Blays evenly, "I was found ineligible for the curriculum."

Blays blinked, and for a moment he thought she might ask further, but she said nothing.

"We have a choice before us," he said, after the moment had passed. "Would you prefer to eat in the cafeteria here in the Sakuriji or would you like to go down to the port and eat at my favorite provianto?"

"The port!" Blays said with decision, and Majel smiled.

"In that case," he said, "we have a train to catch."

Dutiful Passage
Colemeno Orbit

. . . .

"LINA, HERE IS MY HEART-FRIEND, TEKELIA," PADI SAID, WITH very nearly Haosa-like informality.

"Tekelia, here is my teacher, Lina. Despite the results you see before you, she is a very fine teacher, an experienced Healer, and a good deal too patient."

She looked to Lina, moving a hand in a gesture that conveyed rueful regret.

"I cannot stay," she said. "Tekelia and I are to meet with the master trader at fourth hour in the contract room, if you—"

"I will be certain Tekelia arrives on time," Lina said calmly. "Go! We will do very well together."

And Padi was gone, as if she had indeed teleported, leaving Tekelia facing the teacher over the counter in the ship's library, for it came about that, in addition to being a teacher, Lina Faaldom was a librarian.

She was a small person, tidy and unassuming, with dark brown hair and honey-colored eyes. Her expression at the moment was cordial, but curious, which matched her pattern very well.

"Healer," Tekelia said, politely. "Thank you for the gift of your time."

"You are very welcome, though I confess I was hoping we would have a chance to meet. Now, tell me, how may I serve you?"

Tekelia sighed.

"I need tutoring in conservative approaches to one's Gifts."

Lina Faaldom laughed.

"And she brings you to me! I see it all! I wonder, would you like to visit the norbears?"

"Is that Lady Selph's cuddle? I'd be pleased to speak with them, and bear any messages they may have for her."

"Then we will go to the pet library," said Lina Faaldom, coming 'round the counter. "This way."

· · · ✳ · · ·

Despite being early, Padi was the last to arrive at the meeting. The master trader and the *qe'andras* were already seated 'round the table, files and screen at the ready.

The master trader greeted her with a smile.

"Welcome, Trader Padi! Have you seen to the guest's comfort?"

"Librarian Faaldom has agreed to assist Speaker vesterGranz with some research," Padi said, approaching the empty chair across from the master trader.

"Excellent! Allow me to make you known to our *qe'andras*—" the master trader said, and moved a hand on which his ring flashed purple lightnings, showing her the others—blond hair and grey—

Padi met the elder *qe'andra's* eyes, not quite believing it, even as he inclined his head.

"I believe you are acquainted with Mr. dea'Gauss," the master trader was saying.

"Yes, of course," Padi murmured, bowing. "Mr. dea'Gauss. I am—very pleased to see you, sir."

"As was I," said the master trader. "And no less pleased to see Elassa dea'Fein, who is a wizard with bringing archaic systems into the modern day."

"*Qe'andra* dea'Fein," Padi murmured, bowing. "I am pleased to meet you."

"Trader yos'Galan, I am honored."

"Come and sit with us, Trader Padi. We have much to discuss."

She took her seat, and disposed her case, folding her hands on the table before her.

The master trader looked 'round at them all, glanced down at the control pad by his hand, and looked up again.

"We have before us an opportunity to practice flexibility," he said. "I have spoken at length to Ship's *Qe'andra* dea'Tolin, who has asked leave to stay at Colemeno until the second stage is complete, and the office functioning. She is training a promising apprentice, who has not quite finished the mandated courses, and does not wish to subject him to the stress of changing masters. As her apprentice is destined to be part of the permanent Tree-and-Dragon hub office on Colemenoport, she wants him not only to be the equal of his duties, but to *know* himself their equal."

He looked around the table.

"I find her reasoning sound, and am inclined to grant her request, if we at this table can accommodate her."

He looked to Padi.

"Elassa is destined for Tinsori Light. As you know, Trader Arbuthnot will be setting up a Tree-and-Dragon office at the station. Also, the light keepers' systems are out of date and need to be modernized."

Padi inclined her head. "I understand."

"So." The master trader looked to the younger *qe'andra.*

"I wonder, Elassa, if you would take on the duties of Ship's *Qe'andra* until we raise Tinsori. Once we arrive, you will transfer as planned. I will be there some weeks, working with Trader Arbuthnot and the light keepers. *Qe'andra* dea'Tolin believes that her 'prentice is capable of accommodating an accelerated course, which means she will be in a position to board a courier and meet the *Passage* either at the Light, or at our following stop."

Elassa dea'Fein inclined her head.

"I am perfectly comfortable with this plan, Master Trader. If I am truthful, I was wondering how I would fill my hours, as a mere passenger. I would prefer to work."

The master trader smiled.

"I think we will be able to find something for you to do."

"Then I am content."

The master trader turned his head. "Mr. dea'Gauss, you will be assisting in the audit of the Iverson Loop."

"Indeed, I look forward to working with Trader yos'Galan."

"Ah, but you may be called upon to exercise flexibility, as well!" the master trader said. "Trader Padi's role in the route audit hangs on the outcome of several situations which are still fluid. If it comes about that she will serve best by standing as Tree-and-Dragon's face and voice at Colemeno, then you will still be needed for the audit, but you will be partnered with Trader Namid ven'Deelin, who awaits us on-world. Are you able to accommodate so much uncertainty?"

Mr. dea'Gauss inclined his head. "I believe so, Master Trader."

"Our next order of business is to review the final Whole Port Inventory prepared by *Qe'andra* dea'Tolin."

He tapped the pad by his hand and brought up the group screen.

· · · ✳ · · ·

Tiny and Delm Briat were keeping themselves aloof, pending the outcome of the ... discussion ... between Tekelia and Master Frodo.

If Master Frodo was adamant, Tekelia was equally so. Eventually, Lina felt obliged to step in.

"He really does wish you to take him up," she said. "I vouch for his good manners."

"He doesn't understand his peril," Tekelia said, rather sharply.

"Explain it, then," Lina said. "I also vouch for his understanding."

"I fear that I might frighten him—them."

"If his peril is as great as you believe, then a fright will be salutary." She tipped her head, reading Tekelia's doubt.

"They live protected here, but if I am to believe Delm Briat—who is very trustworthy!—they are descended of a warrior race and bold in the face of danger."

Tekelia sighed, reluctance plain, before dropping gracefully into a crouch that put Master Frodo at eye level.

"Attend me, for I am both your friend and a danger to you. My Gift is born of Chaos, and this is what it can do ..."

An image grew in the space where one interacted with norbears, showing two persons at a distance. One grasped the hand of the other, who bent back in seeming agony, a swirl of color escaping into the ether, while the form crumbled to the ground and lay still.

The image hung for a long moment before Lina felt Master Frodo accept it.

There was a sense of waiting.

Another image formed. This time, one of those present was recognizably Tekelia. Horror and rage colored this sending, and it was seen that the person being confronted held a gun.

Tekelia grabbed that one's hand, deliberately; power surged, black ribbons flowing—

And evaporating in a sudden blare of lavender, as Padi yos'Galan appeared from seeming nowhere, to grab Tekelia's hand in turn.

Anger and chaos alike died. The gun-person crumpled to the ground. There came an image of a hand, claw-shaped and wasted.

Once again, Master Frodo accepted the image, then offered one of his own.

Lady Selph, standing tall on her hind legs, ringed round with dignity, bathed in love.

"Yes," Tekelia said. "A grand and noble lady. I'm privileged to know her. We've dreamed together, and had many conversations. I've never held her, though of course I wished I might. Understanding who I am, she never asked it of me. We were wise together. And safe."

Another image formed—Padi yos'Galan, lavender eyes bright.

"That's correct. Padi anchors my Gift. But Padi is her own person. She can't always be at my side to make sure that I'm safe for others. I understand very well that I'm *not* safe, and I accept the constraints of my Gift."

There was a long pause, while Master Frodo absorbed this. Then, he turned to approach Delm Briat and Tiny.

Tekelia sighed.

"I've offended."

"No, that's not the sense I received. Merely, your information must be shared, and very probably dreamed upon. Which means we might have our own discussion, if you like. Will you allow me to—make an examination—of you and your Gift?"

Tekelia rose, half-smiling. "I think that might have been in Padi's mind."

"But as you pointed out, Padi is her own person, as you are your own person. May I?"

"Yes, please, Healer."

Lina inclined her head, and brought her attention specifically to Tekelia's pattern.

A vivid pattern it was, woven with strong color, displaying no clear boundaries. On first glance, one might think it the pattern of a child or of one not yet fully grown into themselves. It was only with concentration that subtleties and depth became apparent. Tekelia was no one's fool, and the links shared with others were firm and certain. The entire pattern was laced with humor. Though there were some darker weavings of melancholy, the whole was infused with a strong need to protect, and to nurture.

Viewed thus, it was the pattern of an adult who had come to

terms with themselves, who guarded their core, and who, once committed, stinted nothing.

Tekelia's Gifts were strong, and bright. Lina had Seen teleportation only once before, but its structure was unmistakable. More prosaically, she found empathy, and also the particular twist that was a marker for a life-worker.

Next, she considered the heart-links—not many, but so *very* strong.

And there was of course that *other* link, that fairly sparkled with acceptance and affection, strengthening the other ties by its mere presence, glowing with such joy that Lina felt tears rise to her outer eyes.

She did not need to touch that bond to know it for Padi.

Heart-friend, indeed, Lina thought, and brought her attention nearer still, Seeking...

"I See competence," she murmured, "I See a protective and unstinting nature. I See that your strongest Gift is the ability to jump from one point to another. Also, you have several Gifts on the Healer spectrum."

Lina allowed the pattern to fade from her Sight, and opened her eyes to look into Tekelia's face—round and tanned, with strong brows over deep brown eyes, a firm chin and a firmer mouth.

"Does your touch wither plants?" she asked.

Tekelia lifted a shoulder, smile glimmering.

"That would be useful, when it's my turn to weed, but—no. Plants are safe from me."

"What makes you particularly deadly to—blooded life? Because I will tell you that I See no such Gift in you."

Dark brows rose.

"I'm what's styled a Child of Chaos, which means I enjoy a closer relationship with Colemeno's ambient conditions than most of those who live unshielded. My teacher in these matters—who was himself a Child of Chaos—had it as an article of faith that it's our link to the ambient that makes us deadly."

"Does the ship shield you from the ambient?"

"That's the theory I was attempting to prove last night. I tried a simple 'port from one side of the door to the other, only to... lose my way. If Padi hadn't been by, I don't know that I would have found it again."

"Thus the call for tutoring in conservative methods. I wonder—"

An acrid taste at the front of the mind interrupted her. She turned toward the norbear's enclosure, and gazed down upon Delm Briat, who was standing tall on his hind feet.

"That was rude," Tekelia observed. "The Healer was about to ask me a question."

This objection was roundly ignored, as an image of Lady Selph formed.

"I'll happily take messages to Lady Selph," Tekelia said. "I know she misses her cuddle, but she's been mentoring one of our own norbears, who has children to care for in what have been very difficult circumstances."

There was a pause before the request came.

Tekelia smiled.

"Of course."

An image formed of a rather slender norbear, grey-striped and serious. The image was accepted with gentle respect, as were the next images: two children with dark hair and blue eyes, enough alike that they might be twins.

"I will tell Lady Selph that you honor her, and will welcome her gladly when her work is done," Tekelia said, apparently in answer to a private communication.

Satisfaction swept out from Delm Briat, even as an image built, unmistakably from Master Frodo, of Padi yos'Galan and Tekelia leaning close together, each holding a norbear.

"I will pass your request on," Tekelia said, gravely.

"Indeed," Lina murmured. "And now, I fear we must go, friends. Tekelia will be wanted soon by the master trader."

Farewells were exchanged, and they left the Pet Library.

"Am I wanted so soon?" Tekelia asked.

"The hour is approaching, but not quickly," Lina said. "There was something that I thought you might like to see— two things, as it happens. The first is just here in my office. I'll be a moment."

The object she sought was where she had left it, which, given its history, was something of a relief.

"I wish to put something in your hand," she said when she rejoined Tekelia at the library counter.

Tekelia raised an eyebrow, and took one step back.

"If you please, put it on the counter." A tip of the head and a winsome smile accompanied this. "I mean no disrespect, but

I do feel that Padi would not wish a teacher of whom she is so fond to be harmed in any way."

Lina frowned. "I almost think you expect me to try the proposition that the ambient does not reach you here," she said.

Tekelia outright laughed. "I'm scarred, I admit it. My favorite aunt performed a like experiment, and the moment of raw terror before it was proved that Padi's hold on my hand renders me harmless is something I never want to experience again."

And that, Lina Saw, was nothing more nor less than the truth.

"Very well," she said, and placed the item on the counter.

"A stylus?" Tekelia said, frowning. "But why is it burned?"

"It is burned," Lina said with spirit, "because Padi yos'Galan exerted what might be said to have been a little too much force."

"Haosa to the core." Tekelia laughed, and it was admiration and true affection that accompanied that statement.

"As you say. You may keep that, if you like."

"Thank you, I'll treasure it."

"Now, if you will come with me, I will take you to the second thing I would like you to see," Lina said. "It's somewhat distant from the contract room." She paused. "Unless you would rather not. It would be too bad of me to exhaust you before you sit down to negotiate with the master trader."

"A walk," Tekelia said, with what she read as amused relief, "would be welcome."

"Then a walk it will be. We may speak of prudence as we go, if that would be useful."

"Thank you, Healer. Though I warn that you may find me a less than apt pupil."

"Oh, I'm quite accustomed to that," Lina said.

It was a longer walk than Tekelia would have credited, taking them down gleaming corridors and up several lifts, until they turned into one particular hallway with a single door at the end.

"The observation deck," Lina said. "Our timing is good, but I regret that you will only have a few minutes before we must leave, if I am to bring you to your appointment on time."

She put her hand on the plate beside the door, which opened silently, and indicated that Tekelia should proceed her.

The room was dark, lit only by the images on the enormous screens that swept 'round the walls.

There was a field of black, and spinning masses, such as Tekelia had seen on Padi's screens when the shuttle had risen to the ship, only—

Tekelia stopped, wonder nailing boots to decking, and *looked* at the screens.

"These are windows? Open onto space?"

"Not open, I assure you!" Lina laughed. "But, yes, you are seeing Colemeno space. If you look down—"

But Tekelia had already seen it, and was moving forward, drawn by a dark curve crowned by dancing fires.

A railing caught Tekelia's hips, and they stood, eyes on the dancing fires, which—surely it was the Ribbons themselves, seen from above, as joyous and as awe-inspiring as ever they could be.

Tekelia felt tears rise, and whispered, "It's beautiful."

"Yes," Lina Faaldom said simply. "It is."

Colemenoport

. . . .

THE TRAIN RIDE FROM SAKURIJI STATION TO THE PORT WAS PAR-
tially underground, the lack of scenery doing nothing to dampen
Blays's enthusiasm. It transpired that she had never before been
on a train, and therefore found much to exclaim about, especially
after they came onto the surface track.

Majel had hoped to discuss the council meeting, a hope that
melted in the face of such exuberance. In fact, it seemed as if
Blays's interest sparked his own, so that he found himself looking
out at the mundane world with renewed interest.

They were on the outskirts of the port before she turned
from her observations to ask if he thought the rail line would
be completed.

"I see nothing to impede it," Majel said. "Luzant carnYllum
is administering the project responsibly, keeping to schedule and
to budget. We ought to see completion inside the Standard."

Blays said nothing.

"Do you think the rail ought not be built?" Majel asked
carefully.

"Not that. Not exactly," Blays said slowly. "We—by which I
mean the Speaker for the Haosa and the Counsels to Chaos—
followed the Citizen review process closely. We expected the
project to be stopped at any point, and you could have knocked
us over with your little finger when it was declared funded, and
bids went out for the work."

"Why?" Majel asked, and moved his hand. "I know there's a
long and fraught history. That was the reason the Rail Committee
implemented the community education and input sessions, and I
think they won the day. People were able to see that there was
no cause for concern, and—"

"But there *was* concern," Blays interrupted. "The train will bring the Haosa closer to Civilization. That point was raised several times."

"Yes!" Majel said. "It was that *unspoken* concern that stopped the previous projects before they were begun. This time, we provided a venue where the question could be raised openly, and fairly discussed. The benefits were brought forth, as well as the perceived disadvantages. People were able to see that the rail connection would in fact benefit everyone—Civilized, Haosa, and Deaf."

"More workers into the city," Blays murmured, gazing out the window again. "The ability to move more goods, and passengers, faster than the trucks do, now."

"All benefits," Majel answered, keeping his voice at the level of hers.

She turned to look directly into his face.

"But the Haosa are *not* a benefit, not to Civilization. Do you know of any Civilized businesses that will hire Haosa?"

"I employ one of your cousins who has only recently discovered himself," Majel said. "He's worked for me for several years, and I have no complaint. If there was reliable transport, more Haosa might seek work—or even seek to live—in the city. And, now, you know, the Haosa have a chair at the council table. That will alter matters, as it did for the Deaf."

Blays's lips parted, and Majel waited for what she might say—in vain, as it came about, because she turned once again to the window.

He had the sense that she was wrestling with herself, so he sat quietly, watching out the window, hands folded in his lap.

"This is our stop," he murmured, when the train began to slow.

He slipped out of his seat and waited until Blays joined him in the aisle before leading the way to the exit.

"Another question," she said, as they waited for the door to open.

"Certainly."

"What's going to happen to that petition?"

The door slid open and they stepped out onto the platform. Majel turned to the left, Blays at his side. There were only a handful of passengers debarking from the other doors, all of them in a rush, so they were essentially alone as they walked down the ramp to street level.

"The Clerk of Council will return the petition to the principals, explaining that it was out of order, and providing information on correct procedure." He glanced at her. "Which is, if you're interested, that any propositions to improve or regulate the port or the city ought first to be directed to the portmaster or to the city manager's office. If the proposal finds no satisfaction there, *then* a petition may be properly filed with the Council."

"But the portmaster hadn't been approached, and that was— improper procedure."

"Yes."

"I think the petitioners were in the gallery with me," Blays said slowly. "Three, with briefcases, very stern. They got up and left after the decision to send the petition to the clerk."

She paused, and added, with a grin, "You'd think people who had so *many* briefcases would've known the proper procedure."

Majel laughed—and abruptly sobered.

"Do you think it was an attempt to go around the portmaster?" he asked.

"It *looks* that way, doesn't it? But, then, the next question is *why*. They must've known what would happen."

"Maybe not," Majel said, around a faint feeling of disquiet. "Or else, they—"

"You, there! Stop and submit!"

City-dweller that he was, Majel glanced over his shoulder, seeing a uniformed port security officer moving energetically out of the box at the base of the ramp.

"You, there!" the officer repeated, louder. "Stop or be stopped!"

It came to Majel that the officer was on an intercept with *them*, and his feet did falter. Blays, however, continued onward— until she stopped, suddenly and unnaturally, as if she had been grabbed and held.

"I *said* stop or be stopped," the security officer snapped as he circled in front of her.

Majel stepped forward, putting himself between Blays and the officer.

"Security," he said, calmly, "what's the problem?"

"Haosa not permitted on port, sir," the security officer told him, crisply. He nodded past Majel's shoulder. "That person is Haosa."

"That is correct," Majel said, keeping his voice calm. "I invited her to accompany me to the Skywise Provianto."

The security officer sighed.

"With all respect, sir, you're Deaf."

Majel felt a flicker of irritation. "What has that to do with the matter?"

"Well, sir, she might be Influencing you, and you'd never know it."

The flicker of irritation became an actual flare of anger.

"Surely, you can See such things," Majel said sharply. "Release her, Security Officer, you have no reason to restrain her."

"Begging your pardon, sir, she didn't stop when ordered."

It wasn't often that Majel lost his temper, and he did not do so now, though it was a near thing. Instead, he turned his back on port security and looked at Blays.

Her face was set and pale. She met his eyes, but said nothing.

"Blays, can you speak?"

"No, sir, she can't," the security officer said from behind him. "She's fully restrained. Influencer, you know."

That did it. Majel spun on a heel to face the security officer, who retreated one step.

"What is your name?" he snapped.

The man actually blinked.

"nimOlad, Timin, Port Security," he said, "sir."

"Have you shields, Officer nimOlad?"

"Sir? Yes, sir!"

"Then engage them, if you are concerned that you will be Influenced. When you have done that, release my colleague, and—"

"No, sir," nimOlad said. "She's got to go to the port guard house, to be charged."

"Charged with what?"

"Being a Haosa on-port."

Majel closed his eyes and took three deep breaths, thinking of the card in his pocket, that identified him as a member of the Council for the Civilized—and did not reach for it. He opened his eyes and met the security officer's incurious gaze.

"Release my friend to her own will," he said.

"No, sir; can't do that. Have to keep her fully restrained. She's a Lifter."

"*And* an Influencer?" Majel asked caustically.

nimOlad inclined his head. "Yes, sir. I See Lifter, and Influencer—both strong. There's bits of other things, but the core of the matter is she's Haosa, and Haosa are specifically disallowed from the port."

A klaxon was suddenly heard, becoming rapidly louder, which

would, Majel thought, be the transport to the guard house. He looked at Blays, her expression as frozen as her stance, and back to the security guard.

The klaxon was louder, still.

"I will remove us both from the port," Majel said, because it had to be tried, and not because he expected to prevail. "You may escort us to the platform and wait with us until the next train to the city arrives."

"No, sir. The law's already been broken," nimOlad answered, which was, Majel had to admit, the proper answer.

A bright orange van careened around the corner, approached them and stopped, back hatch rising.

"Right," said the security officer. "Let's go, Haosa."

He turned toward the van, and Blays turned with him, moving with a heaviness entirely unlike her usual light stride.

Majel followed. When they reached the back of the van, nimOlad directed Blays to the bench seat on the right, reached in and twisted a security cord around her wrist.

He turned away, and blinked to see Majel standing there.

"There's nothing for you to do, sir," he said. "Unless you want to press charges?"

"No. I want to accompany my friend to the guard house and see that she is treated properly."

The security officer stared—not *at him*, Majel thought—but *around* him. It was a look he sometimes saw on the face of his own security chief at the casino, when she was cataloging things that he would never be able to see.

After a moment the guard shrugged, and nodded at the left-side bench.

"Suit yourself."

· · · ✲ · · ·

The restraints were clumsy, heavy, but not so well-crafted that she couldn't break them and be gone. That had in fact been her plan, as soon as Majel was well out of it, but—

Majel hadn't left. Not only had he stayed with her, when he should have walked away, he had tried to convince the stupid, Grid-bound lunk of a security officer to let her go.

It had been a noble, doomed, effort. The lunk had been salivating to arrest her, and even through the restraints Blays could feel his sense of triumph. Then the van arrived, and there was no more reason for Majel to stay. She'd readied herself for action—

But Majel remained with her, even to climbing into the van, and she couldn't risk him—his reputation—by behaving like a savage Haosa from Wildege.

And now they were *both* in the van, and she had no idea—

"As you heard," Majel said, his voice calm and reasonable, "we are bound for the port guard house. There we will be able to set this right. You will be brought to a Truthseer, who will quickly establish that you are not Influencing me." He took a deep breath, and leaned forward to touch her wrist, which warmed her despite the binding.

Had she been able to speak, she might have pointed out that she hadn't been restrained for Influencing, but for being "a Haosa on the port." There was no arguing the fact that she was Haosa, and most definitely on the port, though it begged the question of what the security lunk expected to accomplish by taking her to the port guard house. She wasn't likely to *stop* being Haosa, and she would still be on the port. The most practical solution was the one that Majel had proposed—that they go back to the city, therefore removing the Haosa from the port.

It was well-known that Haosa were not allowed on the port, except—and this was a very important loophole that Tekelia had made certain all of the counselors had by heart, so they could instruct any of their cousins who cared to listen—when the Right of Invitation was in force. That meant that any Haosa wanting to visit Colemenoport had to be *invited* by someone who was *not Haosa*.

Tekelia, for instance, had been invited to the port—to a Council function, no less!—by Padi yos'Galan, who had probably been operating in ignorance, but the fact remained that Tekelia had *not* been arrested for being a "Haosa on the port."

To arrest *her* while she was in Majel's company, his assertion of Invitation Right casually cast aside—Blays would have gasped, had she been able.

Was this a strike, not at a mere Haosa, but at *Majel*? There were those who felt that the Deaf stood somewhere between imbeciles and clever pets, not competent to order their own lives. He'd been attacked by that sort of person just recently, in his own casino; the same sort that had vandalized the school at Pacazahno Village—where the population was largely Deaf.

If this was a plan to harm the Deaf Councilor, Blays thought fiercely, *some*one had made a serious mistake, because no harm was going to befall Majel ziaGorn while she was alive to prevent it.

She felt warmth wash through her, as if the ambient had noted and approved of her determination.

The restraints itched abominably, but she would bear with them for now. She would be calm and biddable, unless someone tried to harm Majel. *Then* she would act. Even through the restraints she could See his beautiful, orderly pattern showing signs of stress—he wasn't as calm as his voice had made him seem. In fact, he was worried. That was good, Blays decided; he was aware of his danger.

The van came to a halt; the hatch rose, and there was the security lunk, blocking out the day's pleasant light, and offending the ambient by his lumpish existence.

He leaned in to remove the cord from her wrist while simultaneously tightening the restraints around her. It was only uncomfortable, Blays told herself, around a spurt of anger. It was not *actually* painful. Nor was it by any means unbreakable, if she didn't care who she hurt.

Blays considered her options. She could break free, grab Majel and Lift them both. The city was beyond her range, but the train station—she thought she could get them that far, and—

And, her good sense supplied, sounding suspiciously like Tekelia, Security would call in reinforcements to retake them, binding Blays so tightly they'd have to carry her to the guard house. Who knew what would happen to Majel, if they decided he was dangerous on account of being Influenced by a Haosa?

No, Blays thought regretfully. Best to go along for now, and trust the ambient to look out for its own.

The lunk tugged on the restraints, believing that he compelled her. Blays slid out of the van, and followed him up the ramp into the station house, Majel at her side.

· · · ※ · · ·

The van had stopped in the service way behind the station, not at the front door on the main thoroughfare. Officer nimOlad walked Blays—Majel very much feared that this was *exactly* what was happening, that Blays had been separated from her will, and was being moved forward, puppet-like, by the guard's greater Talent. The likelihood of that made him *angry*—surprisingly so—and he took a moment to breathe himself into a calmer state. Anger would not serve Blays, and in any case, the matter would be solved quickly; as soon as they were brought before the Truthseer.

The door at the top of the ramp opened into a receiving room, where a grey-haired security guard stood behind a counter, screen before her. Benches were set against the left wall. A door in the right wall had a yellow light glowing above it. The whole space was just too bright for comfort, and it was perhaps unworthy, Majel thought, to suspect that it was designed to keep people off-balance.

"This the call-in?" the intake officer asked, reaching to her screen.

"That's right. Haosa on the port."

"Haosa on the port *by invitation of a citizen*," Majel said, stepping up to Blays's side. Both of the security guards ignored him.

"Talents?" asked the intake officer.

"Lifter, Influencer."

"I See you've got her under tight control. Well done. Can't be too careful with Haosa."

She glanced down at her screen, tapped; looked up.

"High-risk room three's available—" She blinked as if she had just become aware of Majel.

"Who's this?"

He stepped forward.

"I am Majel ziaGorn, owner of the Cardfall Casino in Haven City." He moved a hand, showing them Blays, standing stiff and silent, so very different from her normal manner. "This is Blays essWorthi. I invited her to join me for lunch at the Skywise Provianto, here on port. She's done nothing to offend the law, and is on-Port by my explicit invitation."

The intake officer stared at him. Security Officer nimOlad sighed.

"He's Deaf as a post," he said.

His colleague frowned more deeply. "And she's an Influencer." She nodded to Majel.

"I'll get you a Healer, Surda. Just have a seat over there." She jerked her head toward the bench at the side of the room, and looked back to her mate.

"Get the Haosa locked in, then come back, and—"

"On behalf of Blays essWorthi, who is on-port as my guest," Majel said, firmly, "I demand that she be interviewed by a Truth-seer immediately."

"First," said Officer nimOlad. "we make sure she's under control. That's procedure. Confine Haosa first in maximum security."

"What," Majel asked, "is the penalty for being a Haosa on the port?"

Both guards looked at him as if he had run mad.

"Confinement," they said, as one.

"For how long?" demanded Majel.

The guards shared a glance. The intake officer tapped the counter; the door in the right wall swung open.

"Walk, Haosa," Officer nimOlad said, and Majel saw Blays stumble on her way to the door, as if she'd been pushed.

"Healer's on the way, Surda," the intake officer said, but Majel had already turned to follow Blays and her captor into the hall-way behind the door.

· · · ✳ · · ·

There was something . . . not quite right going on, Blays thought, observing the two guards. The damned restraints were getting in the way of understanding exactly *what* was wrong. If only she could *See*, she might be able—no, she would not break free; here and now it would be worse than useless, and Majel might get hurt.

Still, it very much seemed as if these two fine, upstanding security guards, so very worried about her Influence over a help-less Deaf citizen, were themselves operating under Influence. The guard behind the counter ought to have pulled her ID, but neither one of them had even asked her name. That *couldn't* be proper procedure; surely they had reports to fill out, listing who they had arrested and why?

All that was worrisome, but this high-risk room—this *third* high-risk room—sounded like nothing Blays wanted to experience in person. She'd made a mistake by not breaking away in the alley.

Too late to regret lost opportunity. The facts were that she was inside the guard house, being hauled toward the door that was opening into a bright-lit corridor. Well, maybe the lunk would remove the restraint once she was in this precious room of theirs, and she'd be able—

They were scarcely four steps into the hall, when Blays shivered inside her bonds.

Something was *very* wrong. The air was cold—heavy—almost too thick to breathe. Her ears rang with a vicious, twanging sing-song that was the polar opposite of the music produced by the ambient. She could *feel* her Gifts shrinking from the noise, the clamor making it hard to think.

Another step, the air heavier still, and they weren't *yet* arrived at this room of theirs. Looking ahead, she saw thick green mist swirling, sluggish, filling the hall from wall to wall.

High-risk room, she thought, panic boiling in her stomach. They meant her to be no risk at all, to be deaf and blind, crushed under the weight of the air; to be—

Her Gift lurched to the fore—the most minor of her Gifts, the least trustworthy, she knew that, only she Saw...she Saw...

A door opening into darkness, the lights slowly glowing to life, and—*herself*, huddled on the floor, eyes staring, pattern extinguished.

They meant to kill her.

Blays stopped walking. *Not another step*, she told herself. *Not one more step forward.*

"Move, Haosa!" the guard snapped, yanking on her restraints.

Blays breathed into her core, feeling her fires quicken—and took one, deliberate, step backward.

The guard yanked on the restraints again. Blays gathered herself, feeling her Gifts take fire from her core. *No more*, she thought, *and no quarter*. These people were intending to murder her, and possibly Majel, too, if they didn't just mean to turn him over to their Influencer and break his mind.

· · · ❈ · · ·

Majel stopped when Blays did, watching as she remained unmoving, despite the guard's obvious effort to assert control. She stepped backward, and Majel glanced to the left, verifying that, yes, there *was* a comm on the wall over a bench. He shifted in that direction—and stopped, staring.

The bench was...rising. And Blays, as he had not so very long ago been informed, was a Lifter.

Slow and steady, the bench continued to rise. nimOlad hadn't noticed, and Majel dared not speak, lest he call the guard's attention to the fact that Blays was not as much under control as he supposed.

"Haosa—" nimOlad growled. "This is your last warning."

Still the bench rose, implacable. Majel—

Majel took a breath, and—it was beyond foolish and yet seemed both reasonable and the only path he could possibly take—

Majel *thought* at Blays, as clearly as he was able.

Blays, if you can hear me, please. I will get you safely out of here. Trust me.

There was a moment when it seemed every breath stilled, the bench frozen two hands above the floor. Majel felt a rush of warmth, a snap of connection, and heard her, as if she whispered into—no, *inside of*—his ear.

I trust you.

The bench drifted downward. Majel leapt for the comm, slapped the connect, and punched the number seven.

"Yes," said Bentamin chastaMeir, Warden of Civilization.

"It's Majel," he gasped, turning to watch nimOlad, who was attempting to walk toward Blays and having no success at all.

"I'm at the Colemenoport Guard House. Blays has been taken up and restrained as a Haosa on-port. They intend to confine her in a high-risk room. She's—resisting, and I fear—"

The line went dead.

A *boom* of displaced air rolled down the corridor, and Bentamin chastaMeir was standing between Blays and Security Officer nimOlad.

"What," he asked, "is the meaning of this?"

· · · ☀ · · ·

It was unsubtle, throwing a bench. Tekelia wouldn't approve. But Tekelia would hardly approve of her failing to protect herself, not to mention those in her care.

So her plan—throw the bench, creating a diversion and an opportunity to break the restraints with the least harm done. If the lunk continued to prove troublesome, well—she could always Lift him—

And drop him.

That would leave the problem of getting *out*—

Blays, Majel said inside her head, *if you can hear me, please. I will get you safely out of here. Trust me.*

Trust him. Her heart pounded. *Trust him*—and asked in such a manner. How could she not?

I trust you, she sent back, and began to lower the bench.

Majel leapt for the wall comm.

The guard *reached*—and Blays staggered, knocked back by the shockwave of a teleporter's heedless, hasty arrival.

She kept herself upright, staring at the broad back before her, and hearing Tekelia's cousin snap, "What is the meaning of this?"

"Warden," Majel said. "Blays essWorthi has been wrongly restrained, and separated from her will."

"Security, explain yourself," the Warden said, and Blays was aware of Majel's presence at her side. He touched her arm, and she felt him wonder if she was in pain.

She tried to send him reassurance—not hurting, only itchy, and frightened, and *angry*. She couldn't tell if he heard; didn't know if he understood that *she* had heard, and what that . . . might . . . mean.

"Standard procedure for apprehended Haosa," the lunk was saying, sounding more and more to Blays's ear like he was reciting a script implanted by an Influencer. "First, confine Haosa in maximum security holding area. Do not risk officers, Healers, or Truthseers."

Blays tried to speak—and failed.

"He's not allowing her to talk," Majel said urgently. "I fear she did herself harm—"

"Security, release your prisoner," Bentamin said sternly.

nimOlad hesitated.

"I take full responsibility," Bentamin said, his will igniting the sluggish, Grid-bound ambient, and setting the sticky green mist roiling.

Blays felt the lunk's will fail.

Immediately, her body and her will were her own—and her voice, too, which she discovered when she heard herself shout, "Murderer!"

Dutiful Passage
Colemeno Orbit

. . . .

"NORBEARS ARE DIFFICULT," LINA SAID IN ANSWER TO TEKELIA'S question. "Lady Selph's cuddle travels with us willingly, and the crew benefits from their presence. However, it will not have escaped your notice that they are confined—and not only that, but they reside in what we are pleased to call the *Pet* Library."

She looked to Tekelia.

"Are norbears lawfully sentient on Colemeno?"

"Not at all. Colemeno has some difficulty understanding competence outside of . . . certain well-defined parameters. However, it's plain that Lady Selph, Eet, and other norbears I've met are *people*."

"Which is precisely why they are difficult. If they *are* people, then of course they have an agenda. Therefore, they must be *dangerous*. And how much better for everyone, to simply see them as amusing . . . pets."

They turned a corner, and Lina stopped before a door with a blue light glowing above it.

"Here is where we part. The master trader is before you, but you must not mind that. You are precisely on time."

She bowed, nuance apparent, if opaque, to her companion.

"It has been a pleasure to come to know you, Tekelia. If you have time before you return home, I would welcome another opportunity to talk."

"Thank you. I would enjoy that," Tekelia said, returning her bow with one in the Colemeno style.

"To enter the room, merely put your palm against the plate."

She turned and walked away.

Tekelia took a deep, centering, breath, and put a palm against the plate.

✳   ✳   ✳

"Tekelia!"

Padi came forward, hands outstretched, her smile warm, her pattern brilliant. Tekelia stepped toward her, smiling as their hands met, filled with a strong, and surely absurd, sense of relief.

"Lina took good care of you?"

"Yes. I was introduced to Lady Selph's cuddle. Later, we went to the observation deck, so that I could see—home."

Tears rose again, at the remembered glory. Tekelia took a breath, and blinked them away in favor of another smile.

"Master Frodo...strongly suggests that you come with me to visit, so that I may hold him—and possibly the others."

Padi laughed.

"Master Frodo is not a *little* bossy," she said, and tugged on Tekelia's hands, moving them both toward the round table at the center of the room. The master trader rose from his chair and bowed, gently, in the Colemeno style. He was today dressed in trade clothes, and the big purple ring was on his finger.

"Tekelia, welcome."

Tekelia returned the courtesy.

"Master Trader, thank you, for your welcome and your aid."

Thin brows rose.

"Have I given aid?"

"You allowed me to come aboard ship, which has already been—enlightening. I hope to learn more, before I return home."

"Perhaps you and I can make time to speak together regarding such opportunities as might be found on ships, with the Haosa in mind," the master trader said. "For now, we have other business before us. I therefore ask: Tekelia vesterGranz, are you confident in your resources, and are you able to enter into binding negotiations at this meeting?"

Tekelia looked into faintly amused silver eyes.

"Is that a ritual question?"

"It is, but I beg you consider it sincere. Remember that we may put this off until a more equitable meeting place and, perhaps, a more advantageous time, can be arranged."

Tekelia held up a hand, and *stepped aside*, to take inventory. All was well: energy high; pattern firm and centered. Padi's ribbon was glowing; its warmth made Tekelia smile.

Stepping fully back into the room, Tekelia bowed again.

"Master Trader, I am whole, calm, and confident. I see no

impediment to entering into, or refusing, binding negotiations at this meeting. It must be understood, however, that I speak with my own voice, and neither for the Haosa nor for Padi."

"I thank you for that clarity. The parties to this negotiation are Shan yos'Galan, representing Line yos'Galan and Clan Korval; Padi yos'Galan, and Tekelia vesterGranz, representing themselves."

"That is correct," Padi said, from Tekelia's side.

"That is correct," Tekelia repeated, in the service of clarity.

"As we are all fully capable, we may begin. Please sit."

The master trader folded his hands on the table and looked at each of their faces in turn.

"Our discussions here will be recorded, in order that we all may have a fair record for comparison against the final document. Are there objections to this?"

Padi said nothing, nor did Tekelia.

The master trader inclined his head.

"Now we begin. I regret that there are more questions, some of them quite impertinent. Understand that they are necessary to Thodelm yos'Galan's peace."

He paused.

"Understood," Tekelia said. Padi merely inclined her head.

"So, the first question—Is this attachment between you durable and firm?"

Tekelia blinked. Padi sighed.

"The thodelm only wishes to know if you have found a way to gain profit from pleasure," she said to Tekelia. "It is a *very* impertinent question."

"I did say that would be the case," the master trader murmured.

"Yes, you did. Still, one might be *a little* annoyed at the thodelm."

"Easily so," agreed the master trader and looked to Tekelia, eyebrow raised, waiting.

"Padi and I dance together," Tekelia said. "We share a heart-link. It can be undone, but the only reason I would agree to such a thing is if our link in some way prevents Padi from pursuing her goals and her life."

The master trader had tipped his head slightly, face arrested. One hand rose—and fell back to the table.

"I have information regarding heart-links, which I have already discussed with Padi. In short—yes, a heart-link may be cut. But, absent a death, it will grow back. At least, this is how they operate in the wide universe. I grant that Colemeno may vary in this, as it does in so many other things."

Tekelia turned to look at Padi, dismayed.

"I didn't know that. Padi—"

She put a hand on Tekelia's shoulder.

"We dance together. That is the center of our negotiations; it cannot be moved."

"Yes, but if you are denied trade—"

"Even if I *must* remain on Colemeno, which has not been proven, trade will come to me," Padi said, though Tekelia read the regret in her, for the loss of travel, and of piloting. She squeezed Tekelia's shoulder and took her hand away.

"We will find the path, my friend. Allow the master trader to work."

"As it happens," the master trader said, "I have more information regarding heart-links, which is that they neither constrain nor limit, but—enhance, support, even expand available potential. The link you share should not, of its own essence, nail Padi to Colemeno, though she may of course choose to stay."

"The link may not," Tekelia said, hotly, "but she is tied to the Ribbons, the ambient—to chaos—*through me*. And that might well constrain her."

"Then it will be Padi's decision, if and how she wishes to test that theory. Is that correct?"

Tekelia sighed.

"That is correct, Master Trader. Only—"

Tekelia looked to Padi.

"Haosa love danger."

"And Korval courts the Luck," she answered. "Together, we are a force to be reckoned with."

Tekelia laughed.

"The thodelm has one last impertinent question," Master Trader yos'Galan said. "Given your assertion that the connection between you is lasting, firm, and deep, will you cry lifemates?"

"No," Tekelia said.

"No," Padi said, adding, "Tekelia dances with others. To have one link declared more binding within a company of equals is not an accurate description of reality."

Tekelia waited for a protest, but the master trader merely inclined his head.

"Tekelia, have you something to say on this point?"

"Padi fairly represents the case. I value her, but I value—am valued by—others, in...many different ways."

"Understood. The thodelm's questions are satisfied, which doubtless relieves us all. I will now put forth a proposal that I hope may satisfy yos'Galan and Korval, while honoring your bond."

He looked to Tekelia.

"Understand that this, too, is ritual. Clan Korval is not accustomed to leaving its allies vulnerable. Padi may have told you that we are well-supplied with enemies."

"She has mentioned that, yes, sir."

"Then you are informed. Before I make my case, may I offer tea? Cake?"

· · · ❄ · · ·

Refreshments had been accepted, and Shan sat back in his chair, sipping tea and reviewing his proposal. The compromise he had found was proved, though old, and the thodelm had been able to accommodate it as a reasonable answer to Padi's connection; respectful of the Line—and of Korval's honor. If the children could be made to see it in the same light...

The bond between Padi and Tekelia was brilliant, strong; beautiful to his Healer's Sight. No doubt that they had a partnership—a working, affectionate, and accepting partnership, that supported both. Almost, it seemed disrespectful to attempt to contain it within a contract.

Almost.

Padi rose and cleared the table, carrying the tray to the buffet, and returning to her seat. She spared a tender look for Tekelia, who smiled and put a hand over hers.

Shan felt—a qualm, which was quite ridiculous.

Both sides benefit equally, Master Trader, he told himself sternly. *It is a good deal, if only you will oblige everyone by sealing it.*

He leaned slightly forward and caught two pairs of eyes—lavender and brown.

"Our purpose here is to secure a valuable alliance for Line yos'Galan, and through us for Clan Korval. We seek to extend protection to our ally, as is correct and honorable, as we expect to find joy and mutual profit in our alliance. Since both principals agree that signing lifemate lines is inappropriate to the case, I propose that we enter into *Parankaro Affidare*."

He saw Padi frown; could almost taste her reviewing her Code on the topic of alliances, and becoming even more befuddled.

"The *Parankaro* is trade-based," he said, taking pity on her. "It dates from the time when traders might be sent to live their lives on outworlds, returning to the homeworld only upon retirement, if then."

Padi blinked.

"That would be—very old," she said slowly.

Shan inclined his head. "But never deprecated."

She sat still, and Shan marked how Tekelia watched her, waiting patiently for the outcome of her thought.

"The Code states that trade contracts shall be binding upon the clan," she murmured, and met Tekelia's eyes.

"Is that important?" Tekelia asked.

"For Korval and also for you—yes. The clan will enforce a properly made contract against frivolous attack."

Tekelia glanced at Shan.

"And that is the first protection."

Shan smiled. No, there was nothing *at all* wrong with Tekelia's wits.

"Exactly."

"It seems bearable," Tekelia said, "and Padi is pleased. Are there more?"

"Alas, there are. This agreement will establish you as *kin*, as different from *clan*. As such, you will have more flexibility under the terms than would be possible in a formal lifemating, which I understand is desirable."

They exchanged glances again, and it was Padi who said, "Yes, that is correct."

"Very good. It will perhaps be most efficient if I first list out the terms. We can then discuss and adjust as necessary. I don't think it is useful or needful to contrast the terms of the *Parankaro* with those of a lifemate contract, as that is specifically off the table. May I proceed?"

"Yes, please, Master Trader," Tekelia said with a smile.

"Very well. Under this agreement, there is no requirement that the unaffiliated partner join Clan Korval. The partner will receive a quarterly stipend from Korval—" Tekelia shifted. Shan held up a hand.

"Discussion after, if you will indulge me."

"Of course."

"Very good. Continuing: the partner will have free passage on Korval ships; they will have the right—indeed, the duty!—to call upon Korval for aid. The partner keeps their own *melant'i*; they may pursue their own business, and are not required to tithe the Clan. While it is not specifically necessary for the partner to work *for* Korval's benefit, it is understood that they will not work *against* Korval's interests."

Padi leaned toward Tekelia.

"You may have to recuse yourself from certain votes that arise, when you are on the Council."

Tekelia considered her.

"Will I be? On the Council?"

Padi raised her eyebrows.

"Won't you?"

Tekelia frowned, then laughed.

"Aunt Asta said you have Foresight."

Padi turned to Shan. "Thank you, sir. Is there anything else?"

"A few more points. Children of the partnership, if any, are kin, with all responsibilities and benefits appertaining. They may remain kin for the length of their lives, or they may petition the delm to join the clan when they reach their majority. There is no penalty for making such a petition, regardless of outcome.

"And, lastly, as this relationship is defined and enclosed by contract, it may also be dissolved by contract."

He looked at them, first Padi, then Tekelia, and turned his hands palm up.

"That is the awful whole. Questions?"

"Why must I accept money?" Tekelia asked. "My family is well-enough, and I receive my birthright. My needs are modest. I can easily cover my expenses, even if Padi decides to make my house hers."

"A number of *my* living expenses will be covered by the contract attaching me to Colemeno," Padi said, and looked to Shan. "That negotiation will be between the master trader and myself, in my *melant'i* as a Tree-and-Dragon trader. The stipend from Korval would be yours." A smile glimmered. "Think of it as a reward for your patience."

Tekelia laughed—then frowned.

"This contract speaks to the...unaffiliated partner. There is nothing here regarding the...Korval partner. What is Padi required to give? I will not have her come out poorer in any way through this arrangement."

Shan smiled.

"Thank you, Tekelia," he said softly. "Padi retains her *melant'i* as a member of Clan Korval—her quartershare, her properties, her duties, and her responsibilities. Her benefit is that she has achieved her goals of protecting you from our enemies, as well as formalizing the relationship you share, gaining a new set of options, and a measure of ease."

Tekelia looked to Padi.

"Does this satisfy you?"

"Very much," she said. "Entirely. Tekelia, I could *not* leave you exposed to Korval's enemies."

There came a long pause, fraught with a sense of searching, as if Tekelia sought to See and measure Padi's intentions. Shan waited. Korval would be fortunate in gaining Tekelia vesterGranz as an ally and as kin. Padi had already benefited from the relationship. It was well.

"I See that you are satisfied," Tekelia said. "I could quibble, but it would only be that."

Tekelia turned to Shan. "I agree to the terms as outlined."

"Thank you," Shan said. "The contract will be ready for review this evening."

Colemenoport
Guard House

. . . .

THEY WERE SEATED IN A CONFERENCE ROOM—BLAYS BETWEEN Majel and Bentamin, Chief Valorian bennaFalm on Bentamin's other side, and Security Guard nimOlad on *his* other side, as far from Blays as it was possible to have him, given the table's dimensions.

Tea and cake had been brought, and at Majel's insistence, a blanket, which he wrapped around Blays's shoulders, a gesture she would have found ridiculous, had she not been so very...cold.

Blanket disposed to his satisfaction, Majel refreshed her cup, and put another slice of cake on her plate before resuming his place beside her.

"The Truthseer is on her way," Chief bennaFalm said. He leaned back in his chair, eyes narrowed, as he considered Blays.

"Why *murderer*?" he asked.

Blays felt the flicker of Majel's anger as he stirred beside her. She put her hand on his arm, and met bennaFalm's eyes.

"I have a small Gift of Foresight," she said. "When I was brought into the corridor, I couldn't breathe, and I heard—discord. My Gift rose, and I Saw myself lying dead on the floor as a door was opened."

Chief bennaFalm frowned and might have asked something more, but Bentamin put his cup aside, murmuring. "And the rest can wait for the arrival of the Truthseer."

He had scarcely finished speaking when the door opened, admitting the Truthseer in her robes of office, cowl pulled up to hide her face, and her hands tucked into her sleeves. She walked to the back of the room and positioned herself in one corner.

"We'll begin with the standard questions, so the Truthseer may find her range," Chief bennaFalm said, and nodded at Blays.

"State your name and condition."

"Blays essWorthi, Haosa. Counsel to Chaos, and Acting Speaker for the Haosa," she said, the words out of her mouth before she could wonder why she chose to give her rank.

The Truthseer inclined her head.

"Majel ziaGorn, Chair of the Citizen's Coalition; proprietor of Cardfall Casino in Haven City."

"That is incomplete," the Truthseer said.

Majel inclined his head. "I also sit on the Council of the Civilized."

"Yes," said the Truthseer.

There was a moment of silence before bennaFalm cleared his throat.

"Warden, if you would oblige the Truthseer?"

"Certainly. Bentamin chastaMeir, Warden of Civilization."

"And you, Officer."

"Port Security Patrol Officer Timin nimOlad."

"Thank you," the Truthseer said. "I have my range."

bennaFalm nodded, glanced at Blays, but spoke to nimOlad.

"Officer, why did you arrest Blays essWorthi?"

"Sir. She is a Haosa on-port. By law, Haosa are not allowed on-port."

"Haosa are allowed on-port if they're invited," Majel said, his voice cool and his pattern hot. "Counselor essWorthi was on-port at my invitation. We were going to lunch at the Skywise Provianto. I informed Officer nimOlad of this circumstance."

bennaFalm looked at him with interest.

"And what was the officer's response?"

"That I am Deaf and Counselor essWorthi is an Influencer."

bennaFalm's eyebrows rose. He glanced at Officer nimOlad, who met his eyes frankly, the portrait of a man entirely sure in himself.

"He's been Influenced," Blays said, quietly, addressing Tekelia's cousin. "Him and the back-door intake guard. They both have a script planted—I could almost See it then, but I *can* See it, now—"

"And so can I," the Warden of Civilization said sharply.

nimOlad leapt to his feet—and sat down again, heavily, as the Warden slapped restraints around him. "Get this man a Healer, Chief bennaFalm," he said tightly.

"Yes," said the chief, and, "on the way."

Her smallest Gift flickered, and Blays shuddered, suddenly much, *much* colder, though she'd Seen nothing.

Tekelia's cousin looked at her, brows drawn, then turned to address Chief bennaFalm.

"Neither Counselor essWorthi nor Councilor ziaGorn needs to be here for this examination, which I believe is the more pressing."

"Agreed," said the chief.

"I suggest they be allowed to leave and recuperate from a trying few hours."

A shadow fell across the doorway, resolving into a startlingly young man, wearing the uniform of port security, with the green sash that marked him a Healer across his chest.

"You wanted me, Chief?"

"Yes. Please assist nimOlad."

The Healer went 'round the table, calmness warming the air around him.

Chief bennaFalm looked first to Majel and then to Blays. "Give me assurance that you'll return for questioning, when called."

"I will," Majel said, calmly.

"I will," Blays said, perhaps not as calmly, holding the blanket closed at her throat.

bennaFalm waved a hand in a vague shooing gesture.

"You can go." He shoved his chair back and stood. Blays Looked at the bound lunk—*Officer nimOlad*, she corrected herself. At this distance, the tug-of-war between the script and his own good sense was achingly obvious. Blays bit her lip and hoped that the Healer was skilled.

"My official car has just arrived at the front door," the Warden was saying to Majel. "It is entirely at your disposal."

"Thank you," Majel said, rising. "Blays?"

"Yes," she murmured, and added, more or less to Tekelia's cousin, "thank you."

"This is within my mandate," he said, with a glimmer of smile that increased his resemblance to Tekelia. "Please, go and recover yourself."

"Yes," she said again. She pulled the blanket off her shoulders, folded it onto the table, and rose, Majel's hand under her elbow.

Just short of the door, her Sight flashed again, and she spun back. "Warden!"

He looked at her. "Yes."

"They were going to put me in high-risk room *three*. Who's in the other two?"

Chief bennaFalm swore, and headed for the door. Blays and Majel dropped back to allow him, and the Warden, to pass.

"I need to know," Blays said, hurrying after them.

"Of course you do," Majel said.

High-risk room one was empty. Blays stepped inside, trusting Tekelia's cousin to keep the door open. A bench built into the wall, a commode, a sink. Despite the disruptive racket where the ambient ought to be, she cast herself wide, but detected no hint of previous occupancy.

She stepped back into the hall.

"High-risk room two," said Chief bennaFalm, and thrust that door open. Lights came up—Blays held her breath—but it, too was empty.

Once again, she stepped inside, inspected, and stepped back into the hallway.

"Open the third one, please," she said, and Chief bennaFalm did so.

Malevolence rolled out of the room into the corridor, and Blays felt her throat close. Chief bennaFalm slammed the door shut.

"We'll get a team in here," he said, his face pale. "If they were going to put you in here, we know it was empty."

"No," Blays said faintly; "we *don't* know that. I am Acting Speaker for the Haosa. It's my duty to be sure that none of ours is in that—place."

"With all respect, Counselor, *no one* can go into that room as it—"

"I don't think that anyone here will stand between the Speaker for the Haosa and her duty," the Warden said. "Open the door, Chief."

Chief bennaFalm turned to him. "She's not going to be able to—"

"I can inspect the room," Majel said quietly.

Chief bennaFalm stared.

"*You?*"

Majel spread his hands.

"I'm Deaf," he said, and turned to her. "Blays? Will you accept my report?"

Bold heart, Blays thought, feeling tears rise. *Of course* she would accept his report, only he lacked the ability to See—

A thought struck her. Breathless, she Looked at his pattern, so beautiful, orderly, and dense, with the indigo ribbon shimmering new and true.

It was the ribbon that showed her what she must do, even as she reached out to take his hand.

"Bring me with you," she said, softly.

He raised his eyebrows, and she sent—*Trust me.*

"Of course," he murmured, and nodded to Chief bennaFalm. "If you would open the door, please?"

He did so, stepping rapidly back into the hallway. Majel brought them across the threshold, and for a moment Blays thought she would faint, beaten into darkness by the discord and the din, but then she found Majel, found the brilliant new ribbon, and sank into his pattern, allowing it to inform her with strength and order, as the hideous discord faded into something nasty but bearable, and she dared Look around this terrible room, and find—

"Nothing," she murmured, suddenly aware that she was trembling. "There's been no one here."

"All right. May I take you away, now?"

"Yes," she said, and he turned them to the door.

"Here."

Majel pressed a bottle of cold tea into her hands. Blays drank thirstily.

"Where do you want to go?" he asked. "There are guest suites at the Cardfall—my casino. The kitchen will be pleased to—"

"No!" Blays said, more loudly than she had intended. Her eyes stung with sudden tears and she took a deep, ragged breath.

"No, thank you," she said more moderately. "I—I *can't* spend another hour under this damned—" She waved an arm over her head.

"I have to go home," she finished, feeling equal parts desperate and foolish, but Ribbons! She *needed* the ambient *right now,* unfettered and giving...

Majel inclined his head, and reached to the call switch.

"If you please," he said, "drive us to Peck's Market."

"Yes, sir." The voice that answered was light and pleasant. "You just relax and leave that to me. Plenty of time to take a nap, if you're inclined in that direction."

"Thank you," Majel said. He pressed the switch again.

"Do you need something to eat, or something else to drink?" he asked. "The cooler is well-supplied."

"Yes, please," Blays said, trying to act somewhat less like a Wild Haosa. "I'd like some cake."

He opened the cooler, produced a fresh-box bearing the legend "cake," and offered it to her.

"Thank you."

"You're welcome," he murmured, extracting a second fresh-box, this one labeled "cheese and crackers."

Majel gave her a half-smile.

"We never did have lunch."

"No, we didn't," Blays said. "I regret that."

She had another bite of cake—and it came to her that there was something else she needed to do.

"Am I allowed to use the comm?" she asked.

Majel blinked. "The Warden made no conditions on the use of his car," he said. "And I'll need to use the comm myself, after you."

"All right." She punched in the number, cuddling the receiver between her shoulder and her ear.

"Warden?" Firgus sounded shocked.

"Blays," she corrected. "Calling from the Warden's car."

There was a delay, a little longer than she expected, before Firgus said, carefully, "Are you well, Cousin?"

"I'm—yes," she said, and took a deep breath. This was formal, after all. She had to do it right. "Speaker for the Haosa needs to talk to all who will listen tonight at Visalee Ribbon-rise. Set that up, please, Counselor."

There was a pause, as if Firgus was wondering if this was a joke.

"What happened?" he asked finally.

"I'll tell you tonight. Right now, I have to rest."

"*Are you all right?*" Raw worry there, and that wouldn't do. She needed Firgus's hard head and good sense.

She glanced at Majel, who was pretending that he was deaf in truth.

"I'm all right, thanks to a kind and clever friend. Are you setting up the meeting?"

"Yes. Give me something to interest them."

"I was arrested on Colemenoport for being Haosa, though

I was properly invited. There are high-risk rooms in the guard station that are tuned to crush Haosa."

Firgus said something soft and obscene.

"Sorry, Cousin."

"You *are* all right?"

"I'm fine—tired. Sleeping, now."

"I'll connect you an hour before the meeting opens, so you can fill me and Howe in. You'll be using Tekelia's screen?"

"Yes," Blays said. "Thank you, Firgus." She disconnected.

She returned the receiver to its hook, tucked the empty cake box into the receptacle, and curled into the seat. Smiling at the side of Majel's face, she closed her eyes.

Dutiful Passage
Colemeno Orbit

. . . .

"WELL, TRADER PADI?"

"Very well, Master Trader," she answered calmly, and gave him a smile. "Shall we finish?"

"Your schedule has been full. I suggest, with utmost respect, that you may wish to rest before continuing."

"On the contrary, I find myself energized, and eager to put the last details into place." She tipped her head. "Your schedule has been every bit as full as mine. May one suggest, with respect—"

Shan laughed and flung a hand out.

"No—there's no need to complete that! Let us admit that we're both filled with the energy of a new adventure, and eager to discuss the future."

"I agree. May I bring you something to drink, Master Trader?"

"A glass of cold tea would be welcome, thank you, Trader."

She brought two glasses to the table, and sat across from him. He smiled, and raised his glass.

"To clarity, goodwill, and growth."

Padi touched her glass to his.

"To all of those, and good trading, too!"

They drank and set the glasses aside.

"So, tell me, Trader Padi, what do you see in your future?"

"I see a tour of *Ember* with Trader Isfelm, Mr. dea'Gauss, and Dil Nem, if he'll accommodate me. I will want to bring Trader ven'Deelin current on my notes and contacts. Primarily, I anticipate holding myself at the master trader's word until he departs Colemeno. Then, of course, I will be auditing the Iverson Loop."

"Ah. In regard to that—I am remiss. Your final test was exemplary. I have made the necessary notation in your file and informed the Guild of your mastery of the material."

"Thank you. I look forward to finding how theory matches reality."

"Surely you've learned by now that theory melts in the face of reality?"

"My experience has been that theory provides useful guidelines," Padi said slowly. "At least one knows the limits beyond which one ought not step."

"Ought..." Shan murmured, and smiled when she laughed.

"Unless provoked beyond reason, of course."

"A useful emendation." He sipped tea and set the glass aside. "I hear you say, Trader Padi, that you are for the route audit."

"That is correct."

"Do you discount Speaker vesterGranz's concern that you may be tied to Colemeno?"

"I do not. I merely feel that it is a proposition which has not been proved. And the only way to prove or disprove is—to test."

"I would agree, stipulating that the test not return fatal results."

"On that head, I think we may look to Speaker vesterGranz's experience here on the *Passage*," Padi said. "Certainly, the conditions are strange, and even uncomfortable, but so far we see no sign of affliction. Though we both received a strong lesson on imprudence."

Shan raised his eyebrows.

"Imprudence?"

Padi sighed. "I'm told that teleporting is very straightforward, which is why it was chosen for the test. Had I not been appointed as watcher, it might have gone badly, indeed. As it was, we both had a very stern scare." She leaned forward.

"But that *was* imprudence, and a failure to understand just how much energy might be available only within one's self."

She produced a wry smile.

"Since teleportation has only recently entered my skill set, it's not at all the sort of mistake I might make."

"Very true. Let us accept that you know how to govern yourself. I wonder what your plan might be if you find yourself—how to say this?—entering a decline in health?"

"There are protocols in place for just such emergencies," Padi said. "If a trader is incapacitated, another trader is found to continue. The master trader has provided for this contingency."

Shan sipped tea, and Padi did.

"I accept your plan as prudent without being alarmist," he

said. "Have you reviewed the proposed contract and compensation package?"

"Master Trader, I have."

"And do you find everything to your satisfaction?"

"I do," Padi said, "with the exception of one thing."

"You astound me. Expose, I pray, the contract's deficiency."

"I found no deficiency. Merely, I wish to amend the initial period to three Standards, rather than six."

"Six Standards is our usual term," Shan said, sternly.

Padi opened her eyes wide.

"Is it, indeed?" she asked wonderingly.

Shan laughed. "I taught you that," he said.

"Of course you did. Now, shall we amend the term so the contract can be signed, and we may share a glass of wine?"

"Indulge my curiosity—why do you wish to shorten the term?"

"The route audit will have been completed, decisions will have been made based on the outcome, and a protocol adopted inside of three Standards. I wish to remain flexible."

"Flexibility has much to commend it," Shan said. "I agree to the change in term. Is there anything else?"

"No, sir."

"Then grant me one moment, please, Trader."

He had brief recourse to his screen, and turned it to her, the change highlighted.

"If that is correct, please initial, Trader."

She used the stylus, briefly.

He turned the screen back, added his initials to the change, wrote at more length, and turned the screen again to face her.

"Append your signature, and we may have that glass of wine."

She smiled and signed her name, unable to resist a small flourish, and turned the screen back.

The master trader tapped half-a-dozen keys, and leaned back in his chair with a grin.

"Done, done, done, and done! A copy has been sent to you, to the Guild, to the ship's *qe'andra*, and to my own files. Congratulations, Trader yos'Galan, and may profit attend you."

"Thank you, Master Trader," Padi said, and rose. "May I bring you a glass of the red?"

"By all means," Shan said. "Provide for yourself, as well. We have both done good work this day."

Colemeno
Off-Grid

. . . .

BLAYS WAS ASLEEP, WHICH MAJEL COULD ONLY THINK WAS A good thing.

He used the car's comm to call the Cardfall, keeping his voice low as he told the night manager that he would not be on the floor that evening, and that any emergencies should be brought to Head of Casino Security Seylin atBuro. He then spoke to that same head of security, giving her a summary of the afternoon's events, and asking her to talk to her contacts in city and port security.

These tasks taken care of, he leaned back into his seat, closed his eyes, and reviewed the events of the day.

It came to him that the petition introduced to the Council in an attempt to bypass the portmaster might in some way be related to their adventure on the port. Surely, Portmaster krogerSlyte would not have sanctioned any training, no matter how modern, that would produce the situation that had overtaken them today.

And, yet, if the training were already being given, why bother to present a petition at all? It made no sense.

Or did it? Blays had said that Officer nimOlad and the intake officer had been Influenced. The Warden had Seen it, as well. What if the training had been intended to cover a widespread Influencing of security officers?

He snorted lightly. Yes, *there* was a plot worthy of an *empato*.

Unless . . . could there be *two* groups, working for the same end, but approaching by different roads? No, that was even *more* like an *empato*. All it lacked were Ribbon-crossed lovers.

He needed more information, and someone less prone to fantasy than he appeared to be, to discuss it with him.

Best, he thought, to set the matter aside until he could lay it out for Seylin, who possessed the hardest and most practical mind of his acquaintance.

Unfortunately, putting that matter aside only left him free to think about what had happened—with what *he thought* had happened—in the hallway at the guard house. *Had* Blays heard his silent message? More! Had *he* heard Blays's answer?

That *Blays* had heard *him*—there was the evidence of his own eyes. She had returned the bench to the floor after he had—*admit it*, he told himself, between amusement and frustration—*thought at her*, begging her to trust him. Blays was Haosa; she had Gifts. Yes, *she* had heard *him*; and that was perfectly within the realm of possibility.

Had he, in turn, heard *her*?

That was impossible. He was Deaf. The Gifts of the many were not—had never been, *could never be*—for him. That he *thought* he had heard her, he supposed was possible, though he had never considered himself particularly imaginative. Perhaps his mind had manufactured a kind illusion in response to desperation, that had allowed him to move forward and do what was needful to rescue them both.

Which, he thought, with an inner sigh, would do very well, if he had not heard her *twice*. The first instance might be handily explained away by overwrought nerves and adrenaline, but the second...

He had been entirely composed, untouched by whatever forces that had all but incapacitated his companions. He had offered his service to Blays quite coolly, and she had taken his hand, saying aloud, "Take me with you."

And at the same instant, he had heard her again, whispering inside his ear: *Trust me.*

Was this Influence?

His understanding of Influence was that it was... pernicious. An Influencer used force or trickery to suborn another to perform certain actions.

The... communication from Blays had felt—honest, warm; intimate in a way that he had never experienced, but which he could not find *wrong*. He had the sense that they had surveyed the room together, each using those senses which were naturally available to them. His Deafness—he thought that his lack of sensitivity to whatever informed high-risk room three had acted as a shield for her, allowing her to calmly examine the room for any evidence of a recent prisoner.

He was pleased that he had been able to help her, even as he failed to understand how. Truly, he found much to admire in Blays, and hoped that there would be opportunity to come to know her better.

Yes, he said to himself tiredly, *after you put her into mortal peril. Lunch at the port, indeed!*

"Hush," Blays said from beside him. "Neither one of us could have known."

He opened his eyes to find her propped on an elbow against the back of the seat, facing him. Her hair had come out of its knot, tendrils wisping about a face still more pale than rosy.

"Can you read minds?" he asked.

"No," she said simply, and he knew it for truth.

"Coming in to Peck's Market in about five minutes," the driver said cheerfully.

"Thank you," Majel said automatically, and looked to Blays.

"Will you call your cousins?" he asked, nodding at the comm. "I'll wait with you until they come."

"Someone should be meeting us. I sent a whisper on the ambient."

Majel frowned.

"So there are some who can read minds?"

"There must be, mustn't there?" Her tone was careless, though he received the impression that she was somewhat anxious. "But, no—a whisper on the ambient is just that. I thought about arriving at Peck's Market, and needing transport home. Someone at Ribbon Dance Village will have been Listening. They'll have heard my thought and passed the message along."

Majel laughed.

"An explanation that explains nothing!"

Blays grinned. "It's easier done than told, truthfully."

"Fair enough." He extended a hand to touch her knee. "Blays. I hope you'll be able to forgive me."

"There's nothing to forgive," she said firmly. "We both knew that the port was possible. Tekelia drilled us all in the proper protocol—" She closed her eyes and recited in a voice remarkably like that of Tekelia vesterGranz: "A Haosa alone on Colemenoport is a Haosa in violation of the law. A Haosa *invited* by someone who has the right to be there—is merely a guest." She opened her eyes. "The precedent is well-established."

He smiled slightly.

"So it is."

"Peck's Market," the driver said. "Back doors opening."

Blays turned. Majel remained where he was, already feeling bereft. She turned back.

"Do you have a moment? I'd like you to meet my cousins."

His spirits lifted at the prospect spending of another few minutes in her company.

"Certainly," he said.

There were two people waiting with a pair of hover-wagons at the side of the drive. Blays had already been folded into one embrace by the time Majel emerged from the car. The person standing by the second wagon gave him a grin and a nod.

"Councilor ziaGorn," he said. "I'm Yferen."

"I remember you," Majel said. "We met at Pacazahno. How does Ander go on?"

"Blooming like a rose garden," Yferen said with evident fondness. "It's a privilege to watch him."

"I'm pleased to hear he's doing so well," Majel said truthfully.

"Arbour, this is Majel ziaGorn," Blays said, pulling a woman over to him.

To Majel, she said, "Arbour poginGeist is Ribbon Dance Village's administrator."

Majel inclined his head. "Administrator."

"Arbour will do, Councilor."

"Then Majel will also do," he said, and looked to Blays. "Now that you are safe with your cousins, I—"

"I think you should come back with us," Arbour interrupted. "If you have time, that is. There's a potluck tonight—and Blays said you missed your lunch."

"Aunt Asta will never forgive us if we don't bring you to meet her," Yferen added.

Majel smiled, but turned to Blays.

"If you want me, I'll come," he said, softly. "I told my staff that I won't be on the floor tonight. If you don't want me—there's the Warden's car to take me back to the city."

Blays looked from his face to the car; the driver leaning against the side, bottle of tea in her hand, face turned to the sky.

"I want you," she said quietly, and he felt something... shiver inside him.

"A moment, then." He stepped over to the driver.

"I'll be staying in Ribbon Dance Village this evening," he told her. "My own car will come for me, tomorrow. Thank you for your care."

"No," the driver told him, "*I* thank *you*. I like to drive off-Grid—not just the challenge of the road, but—" She swept a hand over her head, drawing his attention to the colors dancing above. "Look at that! We've got nothing like it in the city."

"No," said Majel. "We haven't. Drive carefully, going back."

Blays caught his hand when he returned to her side, and pulled him toward one of the wagons.

"You'll ride with Arbour," she said. "I won't risk you with Yferen."

"But you'll risk yourself?"

"Lifters never fall," Yferen called, swinging up into his wagon. "C'mon, Arbour; I'll race you."

Dutiful Passage
Colemeno Orbit

. . . .

TEKELIA HAD JUST COME OUT OF THE 'FRESHER WHEN THE DOOR chime sounded. Simultaneously, Padi whispered along their bond, *May I come in?*

By all means, Tekelia answered, crossing the room and pressing palm to plate. The door opened and Padi all but fell across the threshold, her arms around Tekelia's neck, and her mouth hungry on Tekelia's mouth.

This was a mood Tekelia was willing to nurture. Slipping an arm around her waist, Tekelia pivoted on one heel, so they were both safely inside the room, before triggering the door with an elbow.

Padi tightened her hold as Tekelia deepened the kiss, and so they were agreeably occupied for the next few minutes, until she sighed, and broke the embrace.

"I don't mean to tempt you out of turn," she said. "We are wanted at Prime with the master trader, the captain, and the *qe'andras*." She stepped back, her face aglow. "Now, that reminds me to ask if you have read the contract."

"I have, and it seems to accurately reflect everything we spoke of."

"Yes, it does," Padi said, her brows knit. "Though, you know, we *do* have two very experienced *qe'andras* at hand. I wonder—"

She broke off and raised a hand. "I haven't told you! Mr. dea'Gauss *himself* has come to assist me on the route audit!"

"Is that a surprise?" Tekelia asked, since it was clearly a welcome development.

"Well—the master trader had said he would request Mr. dea'Gauss particularly, only he is very old, and one had hardly dared hope that he would rouse himself out of a comfortable retirement to gallivant at the edge of the Dust. I had quite reconciled myself to another *qe'andra*."

"Perhaps Mr. dea'Gauss was not as comfortable in retirement as you supposed," Tekelia said. "Was he adventuresome, in his youth?"

Padi looked doubtful. "Not to my knowledge, but, you know, he may well have been, before taking the assignment as Korval's primary *qe'andra*." She gave a wry smile. "Perhaps there will be a chance to find out, this evening."

"Or later," said Tekelia, moving toward the closet, opening it to find clothes fresh and pressed. "You will be spending some time together, after all."

"So we will," Padi murmured. There was a pause as Tekelia pulled the soft shirt on and began to fasten it.

"Oh, this is too familiar," Padi said from across the room. "Never tell me that Lina has set you to lifting styli."

"No, only the one," Tekelia said, reaching for pants. "You must allow me to admire you."

Padi turned, eyebrows up. "Ordinarily, I would encourage that, but I wonder what I've done to deserve it."

"You only need to be yourself," Tekelia assured her, "but as it happens, I admire the energy that produced the second stylus on the table."

Padi frowned and turned back, "I—is that *Lina's stylus*? No, I see that it is! One of my more embarrassing errors. How came you to have it?"

Tekelia shrugged into the vest and came to stand beside her.

"Lina gave it to me; she thought I might know how to value it. While I was happy to receive the gift, I have to say that I didn't understand its full value until I tried to make the other stylus rise on my command."

"Surely, you had no trouble accomplishing that."

Tekelia laughed. "Eventually, I was successful—emphasis on *eventually*. And I assure you that I came nowhere near the energy you were apparently able to muster."

Padi began to say something; hesitated, and sighed. "As I said, I was over-zealous in the matter of Lina's stylus. I had been... triggered by a recent unpleasant event. I did finally master a gentler technique, though I don't say I quite learned the lesson Lina had hoped to teach."

"If that lesson involved tool-making, I understand," Tekelia said. "Would you be willing to show me your gentler method?"

"Willing, though I warn you that I don't know that it will be any more useful to you than Lina's tool."

"Let's try."

"Very well," Padi said, and turned to the table. She focused on the stylus—green—in the center of the table, felt warmth kindle at the base of her spine, and said, calmly, "Rise, do."

There was a small, quiet moment when nothing happened, save perhaps the warmth increasing slightly. Then, the stylus rose, gently. When it was about fifteen centimeters above the table, Padi said, "Thank you. Stop there."

The stylus stopped.

She tipped her head, waiting, then looked at Tekelia.

"Are you informed?"

"Actually, I am. You're using your core energy."

"And you're horrified," Padi said, having felt that thrill through their bond. She glanced at the stylus, still floating patiently.

"Thank you, please descend."

The stylus did so, striking the tabletop with a tiny *click*.

"It does seem risky," Tekelia said. "What were you waiting for, after you had asked the stylus to stop?"

"Sometimes, they spin," Padi said. "It's as if they're bored, and who can blame them?"

Tekelia laughed. "I see. Do you need cake?"

Padi frowned. "Not for that, certainly. If I had done something . . . energetic, then there might be need. Priscilla is prone to large workings, thus, the kitchen has 'Healer Mendoza's tray' always available. But I made no such exertion."

Tekelia nodded, looked to the green stylus, reached *inward*, rather than out, touched center, and said, "Please rise."

The stylus shivered—and rose, sweetly, easily, steadily.

"Please stop," Tekelia said. The stylus did so.

"Very good," Padi said, approvingly. "I believe you have acquired the knack. I don't mean to hurry you, but Prime is coming upon us—"

"And I need to put on boots," Tekelia finished, moving across the room.

They were on their way to the door when Tekelia checked, turning to look toward the table, and the patient, hovering stylus.

"Please descend."

After a moment, there came a tiny *click*.

"Thank you," Tekelia said, and opened the door.

"Tekelia, allow me to make you known to Mr. dea'Gauss, who will be my partner in the audit of the Iverson Loop."

The gentleman thus brought to Tekelia's attention was venerable; his sparse hair grey; his face bearing the marks of long experience. His pattern was dense; easily the most intricate weaving Tekelia had yet been honored to observe. He radiated an air of efficient tranquility nearly as pervasive as Geritsi's wafting peace, though there was no Gift apparent.

Tekelia bowed.

"Mr. dea'Gauss, I'm honored."

"Mr. dea'Gauss," Padi continued, "please allow me to present you to Tekelia vesterGranz, Speaker for the Haosa, and friend of my heart."

"Speaker vesterGranz, I am pleased to know you."

Mr. dea'Gauss inclined from the waist, not perhaps a full bow, but to be acknowledged at all by so distinguished a person must be counted an honor.

"I wonder, sir, if I might approach a personal topic with you," Padi continued. "Personal to Tekelia and myself, that is. If I am impertinent, please do not hesitate to set me back on my heels."

A glimmer of amusement illuminated the density of the elder's pattern.

"Surely nothing so dramatic as that," he murmured.

Padi laughed. "No, certainly not; I had only meant to remind you that I was until recently the master trader's 'prentice, and I fear that some of his forthrightness may have been included in my polish."

"Korval has always favored forthrightness," Mr. dea'Gauss said. "And of course *qe'andra* are trained to value clarity."

"Put that way, I am emboldened. The case is this: The master trader, Tekelia, and I have written between us a *Parankaro Affidare*, which is, as you know, a very old form. We have all done the best we were able, and the master trader twice that much, but I wonder if you might consent to read it over, to be certain that all is as it should be?"

"It would ordinarily be my very great pleasure to perform this service for you, Trader, but I fear I must decline."

Tekelia Felt Padi's disappointment, and very nearly missed the old gentleman's next sentence.

"The master trader has already engaged me to this task. Nothing else would have prompted me to withhold myself."

"The master trader?" Padi repeated.

"Am I wanted?" asked that person, stepping over to their small group. "Tekelia, well-met. Trader Padi—service?"

"Thank you, sir, but no. I'm to understand that you have already performed a service for me."

"A service for all of us, surely?" Tekelia murmured, and did not miss the elder gentleman's sharp glance.

"I only mean to say," Tekelia said to those interested eyes, "that it's to everyone's benefit that the contract be correct. Padi said that the clan—Clan Korval—will defend a proper trade contract. Since we intend to see our connection both honored and protected, an expert review would be an advantage."

"That is precisely correct, Speaker vesterGranz," Mr. dea'Gauss said, with a nod of approval. "Properly crafted contracts benefit all."

"It seems that we stand in agreement," the master trader said, "in which case I am now free to dispatch my errand. Tekelia, Captain Mendoza requests the honor of your escort to, and company at, the meal. I offered myself, but she will not have me."

Tekelia smiled. "I'll be happy to keep Captain Mendoza company."

"Stout heart. Trader Padi, will you escort Mr. dea'Gauss?"

"It will be my very great pleasure," Padi said, with a smile.

Off-Grid
Ribbon Dance Village

. . . .

THE RIDE HAD BEEN EXHILARATING, A RUSH JUST ABOVE A ROAD that was barely more than a dirt track, and sometimes not apparent to Majel's eye at all.

Yferen was in the lead before they ever left Peck's Market, but if it was meant to be a race, it was tame, indeed. Arbour maintained a steady pace, brisk without being alarming to passengers unaccustomed to wagon-travel, and while Yferen and Blays were ahead, they were never out of sight.

In a remarkably short time, the track thinned—then vanished entirely, replaced by a grassy oval where several other wagons were parked.

Yferen brought his neatly to the grass; a moment later Arbour placed theirs beside it.

"I win!" Yferen announced, as he hopped down, Blays in his wake.

"Of course you did," Arbour said, dismounting. She turned and held a hand up. "Majel? I hope that wasn't too unnerving."

"Not at all," he said, "though I will admit to exciting."

She laughed, and he accepted her hand, though he hardly felt he needed help dismounting.

"Are you hungry?" Blays asked, coming to his side. "It's a small walk to the village from here, but there will be food, I promise you."

"I'm not especially hungry," he said, "though I am a little chilly."

"Best cure for that is moving," Yferen said stoutly, and without further ado strode out diagonally across the park, disappearing around a stand of shrubbery.

"There's a sweater in the wagon, if you're very chilled," Blays said.

"No, I think Yferen has the right of it," Majel said. "A walk will warm me."

"Yferen," Arbour said as they began to walk, "is often right. Though of course it won't do to let him know that."

It was not, in fact, so long a walk. They had barely rounded the shrubberies beyond which Yferen had vanished when the sound of music and voices reached them. Arbour, who was walking ahead, danced a few steps, humming lightly.

"Early start tonight," Blays said.

"There was a meeting," Arbour countered. "I'll fill you in later."

The music was louder now, and Majel could hear not only singing, but the rhythm of animated conversation.

Arbour threw a glance aside, then looked back to Blays.

"I need to talk to Emit. Take care of Majel, will you?"

"Of course," Blays said, and Arbour was gone, striding toward a knot of people at the edge of the path.

Blays flashed him a grin, her hair swirling around her head like a nimbus. She pointed forward.

"Let's get you warm and fed."

The path curved, and suddenly they were in a village square. Musicians were clustered at the opposite side, and the space between was filled with people, dancing, talking, sitting on benches and eating...

"To the right," Blays said, and it surprised him that he heard her so clearly in the din, even as he followed her through a doorway into a large room not *quite* overfull with people.

"Principal ziaGorn?" A very familiar voice was in his ear before he was three steps into the room.

He turned to find Ander, eyes sparkling, face flushed.

Blooming like a rose garden, Majel thought, remembering Yferen's phrase, and smiled to see the truth of that assertion before him.

"Hello, Ander—it's good to see you." He turned, meaning to make him known to Blays, but she had vanished into the crowded room.

"I didn't expect to see you here," Ander said. "I—I'm not wanted...at home, am I, sir?"

There were, Majel thought, many threads to that question.

Ander was his employee, a low-level Sensitive as Civilization counted such things. His self-esteem had suffered for it, though he had been proving a natural aptitude for security before he had discovered that his Talent was...different, as Majel understood it, out from under the Grid. He had allowed himself to be convinced to take a leave of absence among his new-found cousins, the Haosa, rather than quitting his old life and his job wholesale. If he thought that his employer had come to *check up* on him, or—worse!—bear him back under-Grid, that would undo all the good Majel had hoped to do them both.

"Not that I'm aware," Majel said, answering the boy's question. "I'm here almost by chance, my—"

"There you are!" Yferen arrived at Ander's side with a cup in each hand. He handed one to Majel and kept the other for himself.

"Mulled cider," he said, "warm you right up."

"Yferen, Principal ziaGorn is here," Ander said, voice stringently even.

"I see him," Yferen said carelessly. "Didn't he ride in with me and Arbour just now? He brought Blays back to us, and the least we owe him is a cup of cider and a good supper. A kind word wouldn't go amiss, either."

"Oh," Ander said, the tension leaching from his face. He smiled, somewhat abashed. "I didn't expect it, but it's good to see you, Principal ziaGorn. Blays is staying in the village as temporary Speaker, until Tekelia comes home from traveling. I didn't know you were acquainted."

"She had come into the city to see the Council in session, as my guest," Majel said, and stopped to sip his cider.

"I don't know about you two," Yferen said, "but *I'm* starving. Majel, let me show the buffet. Ander, where's Challi, do you know?"

"The last I saw, she was playing stand-in while Binlee got something to eat."

"Let her know I'm back, will you?"

"Yes!" Ander said, and veered to the right, while Yferen bore Majel to the left.

Dutiful Passage
Colemeno Orbit

. . . .

"THE MEAL IS TO BE ENJOYED AND NOT MARRED BY BUSINESS," Captain Mendoza murmured.

"Thank you," Tekelia said. "I will make the master trader my model."

She laughed. "You've been listening to Padi."

"How else would I learn?"

"Indeed," she said, and paused by a particular chair. "You on my right, if you please."

"Of course."

Tekelia pulled out the chair and saw her seated before taking the chair to her right.

Plates were brought by Kolin, who had delivered the cart to the master trader's office, and a companion. Both of them kept their faces smooth, and their eyes specifically away from the faces of the guests, quite unlike the attitude found at a village potluck.

When everyone at the table had their plate, and the wine had been poured, the second server fell back to the door, and Kolin bowed to the table.

"Will there be anything else, Master Trader?"

"Thank you, Kolin, I believe we may safely be left to ourselves."

"Yes, sir."

Another bow. Kolin turned, and both servers left the room.

The food was tasted, praised, and tasted again. The master trader wondered gently how the homeworld fared, and *Qe'andra* dea'Fein laughed.

"The homeworld still resides in a state of self-justification," she said. "For a relumma, I was pleased to be home among kin. My brother took me to Chonselta, to see a play."

She glanced at Mr. dea'Gauss. "I believe the title was *Flight of the Dragon*. Have you seen it, sir?"

"I regret," the old gentleman murmured, "I have quite given up on plays."

"A wise move, given what we have been presented with lately. I had dared hope that the urge to rewrite history had faded while I was off-planet, but I was quickly shown my error. Liad must be seen in all things as honorable and correct. It is the Purge of the Small Talents, all over again."

Tekelia looked at her. "Are there still plays being written about that?"

She smiled. "Every so often someone will try their hand at recasting a classic—to bring it up to date, you know. But none of the classics Balance with history. Liad—by which I mean the Council of Clans and those who supported their policy—was in error and no amount of overwritten prose can alter that fact."

"So the play you saw," Master Trader yos'Galan murmured, "cast Korval as the villain?"

"No, indeed! That was why my brother thought I might enjoy it. The story hung on the facts—that the Council had been corrupted, leaving Korval to rescue Liad and its people—only to be banished by the same corrupt council."

She lifted a shoulder.

"I found it affecting. The playwright doubtless took liberties by choosing to show the personal distress experienced by Korval and by Pat Rin yos'Phelium, when they realized what they had to do, in order to perform the necessary rescue. They knew that their action would cost lives, but fewer—far fewer—than if they did not act. I found that very true to the nature of difficult decisions. Sometimes, there is no good decision, only a less-bad one." She paused to sip wine.

"In any case, the play was closed two days after we saw it, which is a great pity. In my opinion, it should have gone on to Solcintra." She lifted a shoulder. "Perhaps it will be played at Festival."

"*Flight of the Dragon*?" the master trader asked. "Is it available as a recording?"

Qe'andra dea'Fein laughed. "Perhaps it is. Allow me to send the precise title and the name of the playwright to you after I have made certain of my memory."

"Certainly," the master trader said. "I thank you."

"Do you know?" Padi said from her position next to Mr. dea'Gauss. "I wonder if the serials Tima and Karna have been watching might be available?"

That came rather close to business, Tekelia thought, though the master trader had danced only a hair less near the line.

"A worthy thought," said the master trader, "which may likewise be checked on—later."

"Of course," Padi said, and turned to Mr. dea'Gauss. "I was fortunate enough to work with Rik Ard dea'Chune on *Pale Wing*, a few Standards ago. At that point, he was hoping for a position at the Guild level. How does he go on?"

"I had reason to work with *Qe'andra* dea'Chune not too many relumma ago," Mr. dea'Gauss replied. "Indeed, he did not land at the Guild, but found himself—"

Tekelia sighed, lost in the web of connection and place that followed.

"I wonder," Captain Mendoza said, so softly that it seemed they were speaking mind-to-mind, "if I may make an observation, regarding the Gift you share with Padi."

Tekelia looked at her in surprise.

"Padi and I don't share a Gift."

"Don't you?" she murmured. "It seems to me that your description is of the two sides of one action. The half you hold is destruction; the half held by Padi is mitigation."

Tekelia frowned.

"Put that way, it's . . . intriguing. Is it common, among the Talents you know, for two to share one Gift?"

"Not *common*, but Gifts—and bonds—are as varied as the individuals who hold them. Heart-links often allow a kind of sharing. For instance, I've reached to my lifemate through our link to borrow energy."

"We do something similar, if a cousin or a comrade is in need," Tekelia said slowly. "Even if we don't share a link."

"Healers are able to do that, though the act creates a link between Healer and Healed." Captain Mendoza paused.

"Heart-links aren't static. Surely you've noticed that there are tides that flow between you and those with whom you dance—emotion, energy, thoughts?"

"I have, yes," Tekelia said carefully, and then, more carefully still, "But each of us are our own person, with our own Gifts."

"Oh, definitely. Just as people continue to grow, so do their bonds. Heart-links have a tendency to—deepen over time. It's not uncommon to see an . . . accretion of smaller links around the original; or for the primary links to braid themselves together, creating a bank from which both partners may draw resources."

Tekelia frowned. "Surely, Padi and I haven't been bonded long enough for that to be the case."

"Which is why I suggested a shared Gift." She smiled. "It will sort itself out."

She turned her attention to her plate.

After a moment, Tekelia murmured, "Thank you for your care, and your information."

She looked up, amused, so Tekelia read.

"Even if I'm obscure and mysterious? You're welcome, Tekelia. For what it's worth, I find the bond you share with Padi a thing of strength and beauty."

"Thank you," Tekelia said, glad to find something that was neither obscure nor a mystery. "The Ribbons danced us true."

Captain Mendoza's attention was then claimed by *Qe'andra* dea'Gauss, and Tekelia addressed the meal until engaged in turn by *Qe'andra* dea'Fein.

The dessert plates had been removed, and the after-wine was being poured, when Captain Mendoza again spoke to Tekelia.

"Speaking of deep links and sharing," she murmured. "Padi's father gave her a present crafted from his Gift, specifically for her. She has access to it, and can use it at need. You and she might find it an interesting study."

"Thank you," Tekelia said. "I'll mention it to Padi."

"Good. Now, tell me, did you visit the norbears? How does Master Frodo go on?"

Off-Grid
Ribbon Dance Village

. . . .

"COUNCILOR ZIAGORN, HOW HAPPY I AM TO SEE YOU!"

The person who delivered herself of this sentiment was an ample lady with an abundance of untidy silver-shot dark hair.

Majel bowed, taking care not to lose either plate or cup. Yferen had been as good as his word. He had not only shown Majel the buffet, but filled a plate for him before disappearing into the crowd, presumably in search of Challi, leaving Majel to find someplace to put either cup or plate down so he could do justice to both.

"You have the advantage of me, ma'am," he murmured. There *was* something familiar about the tilt of the eyebrows and the set of the chin, yet—

The lady half-smiled, and he had it.

"Have I the pleasure of greeting the Oracle to the Civilized?"

She laughed. "You do not, and well you know it! I am Asta vesterGranz. You may call me Aunt Asta. And it is you whom I have to thank for my pension."

"A pension is usual, when someone retires," Majel murmured.

"Yes! And that is another thing that I must thank you for."

Majel blinked. "I don't understand."

"You accepted the fact of my retirement as something quite unexceptionable," Aunt Asta said. "Bentamin swears to me that you carried all before you."

He laughed.

"The Warden exaggerates," he said.

Asta vesterGranz tipped her head, her eyes wide and dark. "But, do you know?" she murmured. "That's not at all like him."

"Oh! You found Majel!" Blays arrived, and slid the cup out of his hand. "I'll hold that," she said. "Eat something!"

"Indeed, I did find Majel," the former Oracle said, turning her attention to Blays, "and having said my thank-yous for his assistance in the matter of my retirement, I may now congratulate you both on a strong and beautiful connection. May you dance together for many years."

Majel felt Blays stiffen beside him, as he was wracked by a sudden, chill feeling of dismay. He turned toward her.

"Blays? What's wrong?"

She only stared at him, lips half-parted. The chilliness intensified, and he shivered.

"Weren't you going to tell him?" Asta vesterGranz asked, softly.

Blays swallowed. "No. No, I wasn't."

"And what do you suppose would have been the outcome of that ill-considered action?" Aunt Asta's voice was still soft, though Blays visibly wilted.

"If there's something I ought to know," Majel began—and stopped, voice catching with fear. *She had heard him—*

He leaned forward to look into her eyes.

"Did I hurt you?"

Blays blinked. *"Hurt me?* How could you have *hurt* me?"

"When I—when I *thought at you,* there in the high-risk hall. I scarcely know why—"

Blays put a light hand on his wrist.

"Majel. You didn't hurt me. You were exactly what I needed: The voice of a reasonable friend, with a plan to get us out."

He half-laughed.

"Yes, but I *didn't* have a plan. Aside from calling the Warden."

"Which worked a treat," Blays said. "Nothing good ever comes from throwing furniture. I know that, but I was out of options. I couldn't let them lock me into—"

"No, certainly not," Majel said. "Blays, I need to ask you—"

"Indeed you do!" Aunt Asta said, slipping his plate from his hand, and taking the cup from Blays. "I'll take care of these."

She stepped back and bent a meaningful glance on Blays. "It really is better to tell him, love."

"But it's impossible!" Blays wailed.

"Is it? He's such a clever young man. Perhaps if he knew, he could contrive to make it possible."

"Blays—" Majel took her hand. "Let's go outside. I'd like to see the Ribbons."

"A delightful idea!" Asta vesterGranz said gaily, and turned away. "The Ribbons are lovely tonight."

"Blays?" Majel said, when she simply stood there, her fingers tight around his.

She visibly shook herself.

"Yes," she said firmly. "Let's go outside."

Blays led him to a bench, and they sat, still holding hands. He had expected the square to be dark, but he had reckoned without the Ribbons, which were brilliant overhead, and illuminated everything below with swirling color.

"They are wonderful," Majel said, looking up into the dancing sky. "We don't see them in the city."

"That's the Grid," Blays murmured. "It was built to hide the Ribbons and to filter the ambient, so the Civilized can tell themselves comfortable lies."

"My understanding is that the Civilized need the Grid in order to build tools," Majel said, and moved his shoulders. "Of course, I have no idea what that means."

Blays laughed. "No, you don't, and you're quite admirable, sitting out here with me."

"Truly, I can take no credit for the feat, if it is one."

Blays made no answer, except to squeeze his hand. Her hair was all in disarray, floating high around her head. Majel was charmed.

It came to him eventually, that Blays had been uncharacteristically quiet and for some time.

He cleared his throat.

"What is it that Aunt Asta thinks you must tell me?"

Oh, love, she murmured inside his head, even as she stirred beside him, and spoke aloud. "Aunt Asta thinks you should know that we have an...affinity for each other."

He tipped his head. "An...affinity," he repeated.

Blays swallowed. "Actually, we share a heart-link."

"I am," he said apologetically, "very ignorant. I know that I feel—warmly—toward you, and would like to know you better. If you share these feelings, then—"

He stopped there, for surely it was ludicrous, to posit anything greater than warmth, though the words trembled on the edge of his tongue. He may have lost all sense of proportion since this afternoon, but surely Blays—

"A heart-link is what forms between two people who match each other on many levels," Blays said, sounding quiet and centered now, her hand warming in his. "Emotionally, intellectually, spiritually. I can Show you our link, if you'd like to See it."

"Blays, I'm Deaf."

"Our link let me See through your eyes in that terrible room," she said. "It can also let you See through mine."

Majel took a breath. Another.

"I have a question," he said.

"Ask me anything."

"The security guard said that you were an Influencer. Are you Influencing me?"

He felt a jolt of horror, even as Blays caught him by his shoulders and turned him to fully face her.

"I would *never* Influence you!"

It was true; he knew it as surely he knew the sound of his own heartbeat. He dared raise a hand to her cheek, while he formed the words in his head, very carefully and deliberately.

I believe you.

Blays gasped, burst into tears, and collapsed against his chest.

On-Grid
Haven City
Offices of maiLanst and alKemi

. . . .

THE HEADACHE WAS GONE.

Night Shift Supervisor Binny ardMather allowed herself to be cautiously optimistic. After all, she had thought twice in the last three weeks that the headache was gone, only to have it return, sullen and gritty, like there was sand between her eyes and her brain.

However, the headache had been gone before she went to bed. It still hadn't shown up by the time she got to work and logged into her station.

And that was a longer reprieve than any of the others.

The prompt came up on the screen; she entered her information, picked up the mug, and sipped hot tea, carefully.

The task list loaded—a meeting with senOrth was the first thing, followed by a reminder to initial the syndication agreement.

She frowned at that entry, and felt the tiniest twinge of headache.

Don't you dare *come back*, she thought ferociously, but it had already faded.

Another sip of tea, and she tapped up her messages. senOrth was due in minutes; time enough for a quick sort to retire the less-important correspondence.

She was in the middle of a detailed reply on a shared contract with her opposite number in Receivables when it occurred to her that senOrth was—late.

That—was unusual. The under-clerk had his faults, certainly, but he was always punctual.

Frowning, Binny pressed the button that activated the comm at senOrth's station.

She heard the buzz—once, twice, three times, then the click that meant she was being connected with the messaging system.

Frowning in the general direction of her screen, ardMather canceled the call. She picked up her mug, finished what was left of her tea, and rose.

"I have no record of a request for time off from Luzant senOrth," said the resource specialist.

"I think it might not be time off, so much as a resignation," ardMather said, recalling the state of senOrth's work area.

"A resignation? There's no paperwork."

"Well, he's *not here*," ardMather said sharply. "The files he was working on are in his drawer, but his screen is off, and all of his personal items are gone."

"How extraordinary," said the specialist. "I'll try to contact him, Manager. As soon as I have an explanation, I'll get back to you."

ardMather returned to her office, sat down at the desk, frowned at the screen. *Extraordinary*, the resource specialist had said. Yet ardMather had never met anyone *less* extraordinary than senOrth. He was competent at his work, and except for their quarterly meetings regarding the—the—

The headache spiked; her vision greyed, the office spun—and she heard a sharp *snap*, as a glass breaking.

The headache was gone.

She opened her eyes to contemplate the message on the screen before her. *Initial Syndication Agreement.*

She tapped the screen to access the agreement.

The renewal clause came up: *maiLanst and alKemi agrees to pass four percent of all income to the kezlBlythe Syndicate in return for considerations.*

"Considerations?" she repeated. "*What* considerations?"

She couldn't remember, despite, according to the log, having initialed this document six times.

ardMather took a careful breath—and scrolled to the top of the file.

Off-Grid
Ribbon Dance Village

· · · · · · · · · · · · · · · · · · · ·

"SURELY," MAJEL SAID SOFTLY, WHEN IT SEEMED THAT BLAYS HAD spent her tears, "if a thing has happened, it's not impossible?"

He had his cheek against her head, her hair a softly scented cloud around his face; and his arms about her waist, which he found agreeable, and hoped she found it so, as well.

"Very agreeable," she murmured, her cheek against his shoulder. "And, yes—or possibly, no—the heart-link formed, so clearly *that's* not impossible."

That was comforting, Majel thought, only—

"What *is* impossible, if not the... heart-link?"

A sigh shuddered through her and she stirred in his arms. He released her at once, regretting the lost warmth and weight, as well as the scent of her hair.

Blays looked into his face.

"The details of our lives would seem to make... fullness impossible," she said. "I live in Visalee, at the edge of the Wild. Your life is under the Grid, in the city. Your business, the council, your—family?" She blinked. "Do you have a family?"

"My father died a dozen years ago. The nearest I have to family is Seylin. We grew up together, and she cares for me as closely as a sister. I'm her daughter's sponsor."

"Good. I'm glad you have them," Blays said fiercely.

"And your family?"

"My father lives Wild; I see him from time to time. My mother died six years ago. She was the village baker. I—oh!" She leapt to her feet. "The time!"

She flung a searching look into the sky, shoulders tightening.

"Majel—I have to go to Tekelia's house. Firgus will be calling soon, and then the meeting—"

"Yes, of course." He stood. "Do you want me with you?"

She frowned, clearly puzzled.

Majel turned his palms up. "It might be inappropriate—after all, I'm not Haosa. But I was with you this afternoon, and—"

"And you're a Council member!" Blays said suddenly, and grabbed his hand. "Yes, I want you with me! More, I want you to advise me! Will you?"

"It will be my pleasure," he said.

"We'll have to make you known to Firgus," she said. Another glance at the sky.

"We need to leave now. Tekelia's house is a little distant—shall I Lift us?"

"That will tire you," Majel said. "Perhaps if we left now and walked quickly?"

Blays laughed. "Too sensible, Councilor ziaGorn! This way, then—quickly!"

She tugged on his hand, and Majel willingly went with her.

Dutiful Passage
Colemeno Orbit

. . . .

"A GIFT OF TECHNIQUE FROM FATHER, MADE THROUGH OUR heart-link?" Padi frowned. "What does that mean?"

Tekelia sat beside her on the bed.

"Captain Mendoza seems to think it means that your father gave you something that's specific to his Talent. She thought we'd find it interesting to study."

Padi's frown grew fiercer. "I hope you know that doesn't explain anything," she said.

"I can," Tekelia said contritely, "only repeat what I'm told."

"There's no arguing with that. This might be simpler, if Priscilla had cared to let you know what Father's technique wa—"

She stopped, eyes wide, one hand going out to grip Tekelia's wrist.

"He gave me a—a sweet. Sweet sleep. At the time, I thought it was . . . a balm for the occasion. Then, sometime later, when I recalled it and wished to have it again—there it was, like a taste of chocolate on the tongue." Her fingers tightened around Tekelia's wrist.

"Come with me," she said.

"This is delightful," Tekelia said, looking around at the disreputable ribbons sporting in the lavender mist.

Padi looked dubious.

"I think that may not be quite the right word," she said. "Father's Healspace is so—calm."

"But then," Tekelia said, "you're not your father."

"Now *that's* a truth."

"Is this Healspace?" Tekelia asked, and lifted hand. "Is this *your* Healspace?"

230

"If we accept the wisdom of Dyoli's teachers as a working theory, then—yes. This is my Healspace."

"It becomes you," Tekelia said firmly. "Thank you for bringing me here. Did you have a purpose other than demonstrating that it can be done?"

"Well—yes, though now that we're here I confess that I don't quite know how to go about what seemed so obvious..."

She sighed, closed her eyes, and took several deep, slow breaths. Tekelia noted with interest that the ribbons faded somewhat, and the lavender mist swirled more closely around her.

Padi opened her eyes.

"What I thought to do," she said calmly, "was to bring Father's gift to me here where we could both See it. Since Priscilla thinks we're clever enough to figure out how the thing was done. Only—I don't know how to find it."

"Is this your first time here?" Tekelia asked.

"No, I was here once before, and brought Father to me."

"How did you do that?"

"Well, I only called him, and he answered by—joining me. But to call a—technique?"

"Perhaps among your Gifts?"

"My Gifts live at the base of my spine," Padi said.

"Now, Lina told me that my *energy* lives at the base of my spine," Tekelia countered. "Which I'll grant is upsetting. But *my Gifts* are part of *me*."

Padi stared. "And, being part of you, they manifest in your pattern. Which is why Healers can See and Sort one's Gifts." She sighed. "I fear I am the least apt student in the room."

"It's a small room," Tekelia said.

"Yes, very good. A moment. I need a—mirror—so that I may see myself."

The lavender mists roiled somewhat, colors and patterns coalescing until a tapestry hung before them, bold and colorful, a little uncertain as to its boundaries; several heart-links joyously apparent, including one broad crimson ribbon, shot with random flecks of gold.

"Well," Padi said. "Not what I was expecting, but it will do. Now. How will I know where my Gifts—ah."

The tapestry grew larger, apparently in response to her wish to inspect a certain bright section more closely.

"There are my Gifts," she murmured, "that were too bright for my teachers to Sort." She looked to Tekelia. "I understand their difficulty. It's quite a jumble, isn't it?"

"Less now than when we first met," Tekelia said. "You're settling, which is what your teachers hoped for. I can See teleportation clearly now—and Healing." There was a pause, then a head shake. "I know Aunt Asta said Foresight, and I bow to her greater skill. I don't See it."

"She did say it was minor," Padi reminded. "But surely a *technique* isn't going to—"

"A gift," Tekelia said, "given along your heart-link."

Padi blinked, and concentrated. The mists tightened, as another section of her pattern began to glow.

Tekelia thought about moving closer, and was abruptly at Padi's shoulder, Seeing what she was Seeing, though hopefully she was not quite as baffled.

In fact, it seemed that she was not.

"Here," she murmured. "This is my link with Father."

It was to Tekelia's Sight a braid of hundreds of threads, most bright, some dark, the whole singing with shared joy, commitment, history, and love. Nothing, Tekelia thought, could cut that connection, not even a death.

"Well, and what have we here?" Padi murmured, leaning close. Tekelia followed the line of her concentration, and Saw it, nestled sweetly among the strands; a soft thing, much like a piece of taffy.

Tekelia extended a line of empathy, gently, as Dyoli had been careful to teach them, and invited the soft thing to explain itself.

Nothing happened.

"But," Padi murmured, "it wasn't made for you."

"And I don't share a heart-link with your father." Tekelia withdrew, taking care to be as gentle in retreat as in advance.

"Not that it does me any more good," Padi said, with a sigh. "I can See it; I can Touch it—" She yawned. "I can access it. But I can't for my life understand how it was made."

"How was it placed?"

"Oh, that, I expect, was the easiest part," Padi said. "He merely asked if he could give me something, and when I agreed, and made myself receptive, he only let it go. Knowing, you see, as I do not, what he was doing."

She yawned again. "And that was Priscilla's point, wasn't it? That the gift travels our link. Whatever that means."

She paused and glanced around them.

"The mist is thinning," she said. "That means we've been here long enough, and ought to withdraw."

"For cake?" Tekelia wondered.

"I think that would be prudent."

Off-Grid
The Tree House

. . . .

BLAYS DID HER BEST, BUT IT HAD TAKEN SOME TIME TO TELL out even a condensed version of the day. To his credit, Firgus made no interruptions, listening in complete silence. When she reached the end, he closed his eyes.

Blays took the opportunity to drink some water and to look at Majel, his face calm, and his pattern sparking. Through their link, she got a sense of . . . *weighing*—which reminded her of something else Firgus needed to know.

"There's another thing, Cousin."

Firgus opened his eyes and raised one strong grey eyebrow.

"Speak," he said.

"The Council of the Civilized voted to give the Haosa a full chair at the table. The Warden is supposed to contact the—" She frowned suddenly and threw a look to Majel.

"The Warden is to contact the Speaker for the Haosa with this news," he said calmly. "There will be an official letter sent."

"So, *that's* why he didn't call me down from the gallery. I had a bad moment, there, thinking he would." Blays looked back to the screen.

Firgus had his eyes closed again.

"You know," he said, "I promised Tekelia that I'd do something to focus our cousins on this matter of a seat at the table, and who should sit in it. Had I known you were going to outdo me by twelve . . ."

"If it comes to that, I would rather have left it all to you, eaten lunch at the port, and come home again," Blays told him.

"I understand. However, that's not what happened, and—" He glanced off-screen. "The time. Blays, listen to me. This is how we're going to run this: When we open the meeting you'll remind our cousins that you're standing as Speaker for the Haosa while Tekelia visits the tradeship in orbit. You'll say that you've called this meeting as the best way to inform all Haosa of a peril specific to us. Then you'll tell the story you just told me—keep it brief, *just* like you told me." He looked past her.

"Councilor, you're here as backup; you'll answer questions?"

"Happily," Majel said, adding, "my name is Majel."

"And you're colleagues!" Blays said emphatically.

"So we are," Firgus said with a crooked grin. "I'm Firgus, Colleague. Blays."

"Yes."

"After you've told your story, and our cousins have exclaimed and asked their questions of yourself and Majel, *then* tell them the chair has been confirmed, and call for a vote."

"A vote?" Blays stared at him.

"Up or down," Majel murmured. "Will it be Tekelia vester-Granz, current Speaker, or will the question go to a committee, to choose someone else?"

Firgus laughed. "That'll scare them!" he said.

"Yes, but Tekelia—" Blays started.

"Once the Haosa are warned, and the matter of the chair resolved, you'll make your report to Tekelia," Majel said.

"Right," Firgus said, and nodded at Majel. "You've done this before."

He grinned. "I have, yes."

"Glad you're on our side. Blays, we're coming up on time. You good?"

She took a deep breath, reached within to touch the link she shared with Majel. She breathed in his calmness, met Firgus's eyes, and said, steadily. "I'm good."

Dutiful Passage
Colemeno Orbit

. . . .

"OH," PADI SAID, LEANING OVER THE SCREEN. "WE HAVE A CHANGE in our schedule." She looked over her shoulder to Tekelia. "We're to sign contract in the Treaty Room."

Tekelia lifted a brow. "That sounds—formal."

"It does, yes." She looked back at the screen. "I wonder if Thodelm yos'Galan will be joining us."

"Is that likely?"

"It's—possible. The master trader was given leave to negotiate a solution, and the contract is a trade contract. However, it establishes you as *kin*, and care of kin falls into the thodelm's honor." She sighed and straightened. "I suppose we'll find out."

She took Tekelia's hand. "I ask—are you still satisfied with the contract and its terms?"

"I am. Are you?"

"Yes."

"Then I think you need to show me this Treaty Room. I warn you that I expect something *quite* overawing."

The Treaty Room was reached by going through the reception hall, and entering a discreet door to the right of the large Tree and under the heroic arc of the Dragon's wing.

"Is this symbolic?" Tekelia wondered, and Padi breathed a laugh.

"In fact, it is. I will have you know that to be under the Dragon's wing is no small thing."

"I'll try to bear up," Tekelia assured her, and her laugh this time was less discreet, as she put her hand against the plate. The door slid aside, and she waved Tekelia ahead of her, into a cozy, curved room, the walls all cream and ivory, subtly aglow.

It was, Tekelia thought, rather like being inside of an egg.

At the center of the room, directly beneath a creamy glowing oval, was a round table enameled in dark blue, and showing the same glittering pattern of dots as the ceiling of the reception hall.

On the table were four green folios, in a precise line, the Tree-and-Dragon symbol stamped in silver on each cover. Before them was a green-and-silver tube that, after a moment of consideration, Tekelia supposed must be a pen.

Behind the table stood Mr. dea'Gauss in a black vest and wide-sleeved white shirt. On his left was the master trader, wearing his trade clothes, down to the purple ring on his finger, and on his right sat Captain Mendoza, her face framed by the flaring collar of a rose-colored shirt. Her hands were folded before her on the table, bringing the wide enameled band Tekelia had last seen on Thodelm yos'Galan's hand into prominence.

Which meant, Tekelia thought carefully, that this was *not* Captain Mendoza, but—

"Thodelm yos'Galan," Padi murmured from behind Tekelia's shoulder. "Allow me to be . . . surprised."

The seated lady inclined her head. "I not only allow it, I share it," she said, calmly. "The clan might support trade contracts, but the thodelm's signature makes that specific."

"I suppose it does," Padi said. "Certainly, clarity is our goal."

"Exactly."

Padi came to Tekelia's side.

"Master Trader, a triumph."

"Nothing higher than expedience, I fear."

Tekelia felt the ripple of her amusement along their link before she turned to the old gentleman.

"Mr. dea'Gauss. Has the contract fallen short?"

The old gentleman inclined from the waist.

"The contract exceeds itself on every level, Lady Padi. It equally benefits each interest, and so succeeds as a document of trade. I have no hesitation in recommending that all parties sign."

"Thank you, Mr. dea'Gauss," Padi said, and paused, clearly at a loss. Tekelia, no less so, concentrated on maintaining an attitude of quiet respect.

"Mr. dea'Gauss has kindly consented to officiate," Thodelm yos'Galan said.

Officiate? Tekelia sent to Padi, and received the equivalent of a baffled shrug in return.

"It is," Mr. dea'Gauss stated in measured tones, "an honor to be called upon." He looked at Padi, then Tekelia.

"Has anyone questions about the contract?"

"No, sir," Tekelia assured him, Padi echoing.

"Has anyone discovered a reason to step aside from the contract?"

"No!" Padi said sharply. Tekelia felt the warmth of her embarrassment at being quite so adamant, and reached to take her hand.

"No, sir," Tekelia said, again.

"I am content," the master trader said.

"yos'Galan has no reason to step aside, and every reason to go forward," Thodelm yos'Galan stated.

"Then I will commence."

Mr. dea'Gauss lowered his head, as if he were taking counsel of the four folios with their guardian dragons, then looked up, face solemn.

"The contract before us has its roots in trade, and is therefore a powerful reminder that fair trade cannot exist without commitment between honorable persons of goodwill and determination.

"The *Parankaro Affidare* was created to ensure that the heart of commerce—the trader—is fully supported, and nurtured. It is a document of hope and commitment, that establishes and affirms the ties of kinship, which can only increase the worth, and the worthiness, of Line yos'Galan, and, through it, Clan Korval."

He bowed gently, and straightened to look at each of them in turn.

"I am honored to facilitate this new connection of trade, kin, and clan."

He picked up the pen, and offered it to Thodelm yos'Galan across both palms.

"Your Ladyship?"

Thodelm yos'Galan took the offered instrument. Mr. dea'Gauss opened the first folio, and placed it before her. She wrote, Tekelia thought, watching her pattern, with a seriousness that might almost have been an Intention. When she had signed all four, Mr. dea'Gauss presented the folios to Master Trader yos'Galan, who signed with a mindful gravity that struck a thrill from Padi, and, through their link, from Tekelia.

Next was Padi. She took the pen with something like rever-
ence, and bent to sign, her pattern reflecting gratitude, love, and
a tender joy that brought tears to Tekelia's eyes.

Then it was Tekelia's turn.

Receiving the pen warm from Padi's hand, Tekelia wrote with
deliberation and care, mind and heart open. Joy resonated along
the link with Padi, until it seemed they were dancing in truth,
their bond taking fire as if the ambient was braided into every
stroke of the pen.

Tekelia capped the pen, put it on the table, and stepped back
to Padi's side.

Thodelm yos'Galan leaned slightly forward in her chair.

"There is one more matter—of ritual, and of acknowledgment."

She brought her hand up, showing a gleam of silver against
long fingers.

"Tekelia vesterGranz," she said. "Welcome. As kin, you reside
under the Dragon's Wing, and are entitled to wear this."

Tekelia hesitated, and Padi stepped forward, taking the glittering thing, holding it so Tekelia could see the Tree-and-Dragon
cast in silver.

"I claim the honor of affixing it," Padi said. She took Tekelia's
collar in one hand. There was a tug. Tekelia *felt* the moment the
closure was made, and leaned to look into Padi's dazzled eyes.

"Done and done well," Mr. dea'Gauss murmured. "May your
mutual commitment bring fulfillment and joy."

"Thank you, Mr. dea'Gauss," Padi whispered, much moved.

"Yes, Mr. dea'Gauss," said Thodelm yos'Galan. "Thank you.
Beautifully done."

"Thodelm." The old gentleman bowed, then picked up the first
of the folios, which he offered to her. "Line yos'Galan's record."

She took it with an inclination of the head.

Mr. dea'Gauss picked up the second folio, and offered it, balanced neatly on the tips of his fingers.

"House vesterGranz's record."

Breath-caught, Tekelia did a rapid calculation, leaned and swept
careful fingers between the old gentleman's, catching the folio,
and bringing it, two-handed, against their heart as they bowed.

"Thank you, sir."

"It is my honor."

The third folio went to the master trader; the fourth to Padi, who took it in both hands, and bowed profoundly, straightening with her shoulder against Tekelia's shoulder.

"Lady Padi," Mr. dea'Gauss said, "the pen goes to you."

Padi smiled, and slanted a glance at Tekelia. "The first treasure of our house," she murmured.

Tekelia raised an eyebrow, and reached into a pocket, displaying the charred stylus across one palm.

"Surely, the second?"

Padi blinked, then laughed.

"Yes, very good! We will display them together! It is perfectly fitting!"

Off-Grid
Peck's Market

. . . .

"STAY SAFE," MAJEL'S VOICE IN HER EAR WAS FIERCE, HIS EMBRACE fiercer. His pattern was . . . nothing so violent as *disturbed*, but noticeably less calm than usual.

Blays snuggled closer, pushing her head against his shoulder.

By the time they had closed last night's meeting, leaving only the four of them on the screen, it had been late at the Fallow and early at Ribbon Dance. Blays had been about to say her good-night when Howe asked a question.

"Will it be safe for Tekelia to go into Haven City to sit in this damned chair Civilization offers?"

Blays had looked at Majel, who was looking at Howe.

"That's an interesting question. Haven City isn't the port, but I confess I don't have the law by heart."

"I don't, either," Firgus said, when Howe looked to him. "We'll have to check into it—tomorrow. For now—it's late even at the Fallow, Cousins. I want my bed—and I *know* Howe wants his."

"It has been a long day," Blays said ruefully. "But, it's a good question. We don't want Tekelia arrested. That—would be bad."

"First," Majel said, "we need to find what the law actually says. If Haosa are forbidden the city, as they are the port, then the matter must be brought to the Council." He looked to the screen, where Firgus and Howe were watching him closely, and turned back to Blays.

"I'm a seated councilor, and able to act for the Haosa in this matter, if the Speaker Pro Tem formally requests that I do so."

"Yes," Blays said. "Do that, as formally as you like. And—please keep me informed."

Majel's smile flickered. "Of course."

Blays turned back to the screen.

"Any more questions?" she asked, her tone suggesting that there had better not be.

Howe looked slightly shamefaced and raised his hand, fingers curled into a soft fist. "I'm done, Cousin."

"Let's we three plan on talking together again tomorrow afternoon, Fallow time," Firgus said. "That will give Blays time to bring Tekelia up to date, and find if there are more questions we ought to be asking."

"Agreed," Howe said. "Good dreaming, Cousins. Majel." His image vanished from the screen.

Firgus laughed. "Well, there's ambition. Good dreaming, both. Blays—tomorrow."

"Tomorrow," she promised, but he was already gone. She turned off the screen.

"My car will be early at Peck's Market," Majel said.

Blays reached to the comm.

"Let me call Arbour."

It was a brief call, but Majel had fallen asleep where he sat on Tekelia's couch by the time she was done. Blays smiled and curled against him, her head on his shoulder.

Arbour had arrived before the Ribbons had set, and hustled them down to the wagon park. Being the most awake of the three, Arbour steered, while Blays and Majel sat close together, sharing morning wake-up from the same mug—and, there—the car was coming.

"You have my comm codes," Majel said. "Call if you need me. Call me for—*anything*. Blays—"

"You can call me, too," she murmured, and then, "I know. I'm sorry."

"No," he said, pulling sharply back. She looked up, blinking, seeing his face and pattern equally stern.

"I," he said very clearly, "am *not* sorry."

Blays shivered as his truth reverberated along their link, and raised her hand to his cheek.

"I should have said—I'm sorry you have to go."

His face softened into a smile. "Yes, well—I can allow that."

The air hummed, and Blays sighed.

"Your car's here," she murmured.

His arms tightened once more, and she leaned against him gratefully.

I love you, he said inside her ear, and she shivered again with the weight of his truth.

I love you, too, she answered; he shivered in turn.

They ended the embrace, then, and stood apart as the car pulled up beside them.

The back door opened, and he stepped away, not looking at her again. The door closed; the car moved, slipping 'round the drive and back the way it had come.

Gone, Blays thought—and shook herself. *Not* gone. She felt him, bright, constant, and beautiful, twined around the core of her—and smiled.

Then, she turned toward the wagon waiting at the edge of the trees.

Blays Lifted into the wagon, settled onto the bench and reached into the hamper for the second hot-bottle.

She filled one cup, raised her head and saw Arbour sprinting toward her from Peck's Market, where she'd gone to make a call. Blays pulled another cup out of the hamper, and filled it, too.

Arbour swung onto the driver's bench, and accepted the second cup with a grin. "Life saver," she said, and took a careful sip. "Had a wager with myself that you'd go with him," she said.

"Weren't you listening?" Blays asked. "It's not safe. Besides, the Grid *itches*."

Arbour laughed. Blays stowed the bottle and sipped her drink.

"I'd like to update you on the reason for the village meeting yesterday." Arbour gave an apologetic shrug. "I'm afraid it's Speaker business."

Blays breathed a laugh.

"Why not?" she said. "I'll be calling Tekelia after we get back. I'll add it to my list." She sighed. "My *long* list."

"Well, since you've already started a list—" Arbour touched the controls; the wagon rose and began to move, following the trail at a decorous pace.

"You know of our twins?"

"Torin and Vaiza," Blays said promptly. "They were to be evaluated by the Healer attached to the Tree-and-Dragon trade team—" She blinked. "Did something go wrong?"

Arbour laughed. "That cuts to the heart of it! No, nothing went wrong—and yes, *everything* went wrong."

"Oh," Blays said, and reached under the bench for the snack bag. "Maybe you should begin at the beginning."

· · · ✳ · · ·

Majel exchanged greetings with Atsu, his driver, settled into the back compartment, and gave a pleased sigh. Not only was his portable screen on the pull-down, but also a sealed mug that he strongly suspected held morning wake-up, and a thermal box. He opened the mug first, taking a careful sip of hot beverage before unsealing the box. They'd had nothing to eat before walking down to the wagons. On the way to Peck's Market, they had shared a mug of wake-up, and Blays had eaten a square of cake, but surely, Majel thought with sudden, sharp concern, that was hardly enough? He would have to be more careful of her.

I'm fine, love, he heard her whisper. *Eat.*

Smiling softly, he took up one of the cheese rolls his chef had packed, and made short work of it.

Resealing the box, he drank some more wake-up, eyes narrowed as he considered his best approach to the task he had agreed to undertake for the Speaker for the Haosa Pro Tem.

He would have to invoke an emergency meeting—that was unavoidable. The question of best approach remained. As the councilor calling the meeting, it fell to him not only to state the problem, but to offer a solution that would be binding until the matter could be placed on the agenda at a full meeting of the Council.

It was, Majel thought, sipping his drink, tempting to simply suggest that the Council remind port security *officially* that Right of Invitation carried the weight of law. However, it *wasn't* law; it was a clumsy path around an existing law that, once implemented, had been found to deliver unwanted results.

Laws that were inconvenient, outmoded, or wrong, ought not to be *worked around*; they ought to be *fixed*. Whatever else had occurred yesterday, it was a fact that Port Security Officer nimOlad had been enforcing *the law*. Haosa *were* forbidden the port. It was the business of port security to enforce the law. Invitation Right was, at best, custom, and therefore fell outside the proper duty of port security.

Haosa were not explicitly banned from Haven City, as they

were from the port. However, Majel's recollection was that there was no language in the law as written that specifically stated the port ban *could not* be invoked in the city.

Which meant that the law was not only ill-considered and wrong, it was *subject to interpretation.* And it could result in the Haosa Councilor being forcibly removed from the Sakuriji. Which might, Majel thought suddenly, be the outcome that was sought here.

Blays's description of the three stern persons with their brief-cases leapt forcefully to mind. Had they been, as Blays supposed, the sponsors of the "Plan to Insure a Safe Port and Civilization"? What had been the purpose of their petition? To serve warning? To somehow use the supposition that the Haosa were a danger to Civilization to their own benefit?

Majel sighed, and finished his drink.

He would need to read the law as written. If there was *any* ambiguity, it would have to be dealt with before the Haosa Councilor took their chair. Three solutions came to mind: strike the existing law, which they could not do in an emergency meeting; amend it, which also called for a formal meeting of the Council and proper committee oversight; or move the business of Civilization from the Sakuriji to some place untainted by doubt until the matter was properly addressed and a new law crafted to replace the old.

Majel allowed himself a moment of whimsy. Perhaps Pacazahno Village could be persuaded to provide meeting space. Certainly, it would be a coup for the Deaf community.

So. Refresh himself on the law. He reached to his screen.

But before he could open the Law Register, a tone sounded—the particular tone he had associated with the members of the Tree-and-Dragon Trade Mission. As liaison, it was vital that he give trade mission matters his immediate attention.

A tap opened a letter from Master Trader yos'Galan.

Councilor ziaGorn, I extend felicitations, and my hope that all of your endeavors are profitable.

I write to you in your capacity as Liaison to the Tree-and-Dragon Trade Mission.

The facilities assessments and inventories of services required by the Trade Guild have been completed. I am

delighted to inform you that Colemenoport qualifies in
every way to stand as a Trade Hub, anchoring new and
expanding routes.

The final item necessary to complete our application for
Guild Certification is agreement from the Port of Colemeno
and the planetary governing body.

Appended to this communication is the Whole Port
Inventory, as well as Tree-and-Dragon Family's formal
proposal to open Colemeno as an affiliated trade center,
and also the pertinent sections of the Guild's regulations
regarding the establishment and maintenance of a Trade Hub.

I hope that you may secure for me the necessary hearing with the appropriate port authorities and also with
the Council of the Civilized. Regretfully, the Guild does
impose a deadline on the fulfillment of the final phase. If
the deadline is missed, then the request must be refiled.
Secondary filings are not given the immediate attention
that a new application warrants.

I leave all and everything in your hands, expecting that
you will not hesitate to notify me of any requirements that
must be met prior to the mandated hearings.

I expect to return to Colemeno within two planetary
days. My party will include Trader yos'Galan; Dil Nem
Tiazan, Qe'andra dea'Gauss; and Speaker for the Haosa
vesterGranz. Trader Namid ven'Deelin, who will stand as
Tree-and-Dragon's Hub Administrator, has arrived on-planet.
You may contact her through our portside offices.

I look forward to seeing you soon, and to a speedy
and successful conclusion of our joint endeavor to open
Colemeno fully to trade.

With sincere regards, I am

> Shan yos'Galan Clan Korval, Master of
> Trade, Tree-and-Dragon Trade Family

Majel blinked, one phrase seeming to leap from the screen
and seize his whole attention: *Speaker for the Haosa vesterGranz*.

Tekelia vesterGranz, the Speaker for the Haosa, was going to
be arriving on Colemenoport within two days.

Onto the port. Where Haosa were specifically forbidden, and
port security of a mind to enforce the law.

It came to him that calling an emergency meeting of the Council wasn't going to be sufficient to the case.

He reached for the comm, and tapped in Seylin's code.

"Majel? Are you well?"

"Perfectly. I wonder—have you learned anything useful from your contacts in port security?"

"Not yet. Why?"

"Master Trader yos'Galan expects to return to Colemeno—soon. In his party will be the Speaker for the Haosa."

There was a moment of silence, then—

"Should I make another call?"

Majel sighed. "No. Let's not seem too particular. In the meanwhile—" He paused, already making mental lists of who—

"I have some errands to run," he said to Seylin.

"Do you need security?"

Majel smiled. "No; I'll be calling on respectable people."

"Yesterday, you were only going down to the port for lunch."

"Surely my luck can't hold two days in a row."

Seylin laughed. "Be careful."

"And you."

· · · ❈ · · ·

"But that sounds like the Healer achieved everything that was hoped for!" Blays said. "The children and the norbear are free of an entanglement gone awry, and Torin's built a filter that lets her access the ambient on her own terms, which means she can live in Ribbon Dance Village without becoming exhausted." She threw a grin at Arbour. "Which is a very Haosa solution."

"Well—yes," Arbour said, guiding the wagon along a sweeping curve. "But I don't think we can escape the fact that the filter is a *tool*. Torin is definitely Civilized."

"Civilized have chosen to live off-Grid before," Blays pointed out. "Not many, but it's been done."

"It's been done *by adults*," Arbour said. "We read the law at the meeting, and it's rather explicit. Children who are deemed Civilized must remain under-Grid until they reach their majority." She paused. "There was a footnote."

"Of course there was," Blays said. "Let me guess—something along the lines that contact with the unfiltered ambient might adversely affect the proper maturing of Civilized Gifts."

"Close enough," Arbour said, as they came into the park. She eased the hover-wagon down into the empty spot, coming to rest without a bump, powered off, and jumped to the grass.

"Civilization threw them away," Blays said, rummaging in the hamper. "Cake?"

"Yes," said Arbour, and caught the wrapped square Blays tossed to her.

Blays closed the hamper, picked it up, and gently descended to the ground, the last wrapped piece of cake in hand.

"Civilization threw them away because their kin swore them Haosa—or, at least, abominations," Arbour said, as they headed down the trail that led to the village square.

Blays took a bite of cake, frowning.

"The point remains—Civilization cast both of them to the Haosa, who adopted and cared for them, as is our way. If, in the course of our care, we find that Civilization failed to do its"—the phrase slid so neatly onto her tongue she didn't, for a moment, question how she knew it—"*due diligence*, then that's for Civilization to correct."

"Yes, but now that Torin's wholly Civilized, they'll want her back."

"Who's to know?" asked Blays.

Arbour laughed. "That was the sense of the meeting. Vaiza belongs with us, and even if Civilization is cruel enough to separate them, the Haosa are not. And they're *our children*."

Blays sighed. "I'll mention it to Tekelia when I call," she said. "In the short-term, I advise—" She turned an owlish gaze on Arbour—"as Speaker for the Haosa Pro Tem—that Ribbon Dance Village continue to care for its children. Both are healthy, and separating them isn't in their best interest."

"And the law?" Arbour asked.

Blays shrugged. "Might be that Civilization will have to change *their law*."

Arbour laughed again. "Yes, *that* will happen!"

"Well, it might. After all, Cousin, the Haosa will soon be represented at the Council's table. Who knows what might happen?"

Wildege
Kelim Station

· · · · · · · · · · · · · ·

THE RIBBONS WERE DANCING. HE COULD FEEL THEM THROUGH the walls of the domi, through his shields.

His *crumbling* shields.

Perhaps, he thought, standing in the center of the parlor, this was what he had been waiting for, the moment when the Ribbons rose inside his core, and burned out everything he had ever been.

That would be, in its way, entirely fitting, for what had he done with his life that it should be preserved?

Only, not here. Kel's domi was her refuge and her peace. He would not destroy that peace. Best she simply came home to find him gone.

Vyr closed the book he had been reading, and put it tidily away. He went into his sleeping room to be certain that all was orderly, passed through the kitchen to make sure everything was clean and put away.

He left then, closing the door firmly behind him. It surprised him, faintly, that it was just past midday, even as his feet found the path across the clearing. The path that led to the pond.

He stopped, and looked at the sky reflected in the still surface, seeing the shadow of dancing colors that meant the Ribbons were on the rise.

"What are you waiting for, Vyr?"

He asked the question aloud, his voice strong enough to start a ripple across the quiet waters. There was no other answer.

Kel had once advised him to "open himself to the Ribbons," but Kel loved the Ribbons, and trusted the ambient.

Vyr feared the Ribbons, and the environment in which they

danced. It came to him just then, standing at the edge of the pond, that fear was the basis of everything that had happened to him, from that fateful meeting of the club, to his being thrown from the belly of a long-distance raft down into the devouring wilderness.

It was time—past time—to step away from fear. After all, if what he was waiting for was death, or dissolution, it was coming as surely as the Ribbons rose, whether he tried to hide, or stepped forward of his own free will.

He looked at the reflected colors dancing in the silver water. They were beautiful, really. And he ought to have been dead months ago. What did a few hours more or less matter?

Vyr dropped what was left of his shields.

Dutiful Passage
Colemeno Orbit

. . . .

"HELLO, MASTER FRODO," PADI SAID, LOOKING INTO THE NORBEAR enclosure. "Delm Briat, good day to you. Tiny, I am pleased to see you looking so stout."

The result of these expressions of gentle courtesy was a flurry of excited queries involving Lady Selph, Eet, the twins, Jes dea'Tolin, and Mar Tyn pai'Fortana.

Padi laughed and held her hands before her.

"Gently! You overwhelm me, and we all know that I am the least skilled of Lady Selph's students."

That, surprisingly, produced a pause. Tekelia exchanged a glance with Padi as the norbears dropped into what seemed to be a discussion among themselves.

It was Delm Briat who finally came forward with a face that Padi recognized with a shout of laughter.

"Oh, no! Poor Gordy! He tries so hard."

Delm Briat let it be known that Gordy did, indeed, try very hard. He had, in the opinion of the gathered norbears, simply been naturally inept.

Tekelia sputtered a laugh. "Poor Gordy, indeed. Tell me—who *is* Gordy?"

"Gordon Arbuthnot, my cousin. *Trader* Gordon Arbuthnot, and, if I'm perfectly truthful, his powers of empathy are less acute than his trade sense."

"Isn't that empathy? Or do I misunderstand the master trader?"

"The master trader," Padi said, "is a Healer. While he doesn't intrude, or, I believe, use his Gift to gain advantage—that would be unethical, on both sides of the equation—still it gives him a depth Gordy cannot aspire to."

251

"I see."

Padi turned back to the norbears.

"I have a message from Lady Selph," she said. "Who will receive it?"

Stout Tiny came forward, and stretched a paw upward.

Padi bent to pick him up, and was very quickly involved in sharing Lady Selph's regard for her cuddle, and also the substance of the call made upon her by one in need.

Tiny produced an image of Eet, and Padi responded with images of the twins.

Tekelia glanced down into the enclosure. Master Frodo was standing on his hind legs. When he saw he had Tekelia's attention, he stretched a paw upward.

"You know the answer to that, my friend," Tekelia said.

Master Frodo produced an image of Padi. Loudly.

"The question is," Padi said, her dialogue with Tiny interrupted, "do you want to indulge him? I am willing to stand, thus—" She leaned in, her hip against Tekelia's. "Or," she said, her voice lower, "I can remove myself."

Tekelia took a breath and sighed it out, looking down at Master Frodo, his fur so soft, and warm, the weight of him so satisfying, and—

"You may be jeopardizing your case," Padi said, and Tekelia laughed.

"Influencing me, are you, scamp? That's a questionable course. My excuse is that I'd like to see if your description is accurate. Padi..."

"I'm right here," she murmured, and Tekelia felt her settle closer, even as their link seemed to grow...warm.

Bending over the enclosure, Tekelia took Master Frodo up, not without a thrill of terror, which was softly smoothed away as the portly creature nestled against a shoulder.

Indeed, Master Frodo *was* a pleasant weight, in both hand and mind, and Tekelia felt a...loosening in the chest, and a tiny, wistful, spark of pleasure.

Master Frodo wriggled, and allowed it to be known that he would like to sit on Tekelia's shoulder.

This was arranged, the norbear anchoring himself by holding on to Tekelia's braid, emitting satisfaction on all levels.

All right? Padi asked along their link.

Better than all right, Tekelia answered. *Though I think I had best put him down, if we're—*

"Trader yos'Galan to comm," a man's voice said from a speaker overhead. "Speaker vesterGranz to comm."

Off-Grid
Pacazahno

. . . .

THE VIEW FROM THE WINDOW WAS OF THE VILLAGE SQUARE. THE lights had just come on in the community kitchen, directly across from the guest cottage they'd been granted. The twins, and Eet, were still asleep, as Maradel had been until the comm on her bedside table chimed, and she snatched it up to hear Arbour's voice.

Arbour's *cheerful* voice.

"Good morning, Cousin! Did I wake you?"

"Of course you woke me," Maradel said, crankily. "Why are *you* awake?"

"I brought Blays and her beau to Peck's to meet his car back to the city."

That had been enough to wake Maradel fully.

"*Blays* has a Civilized beau?"

"No, he's Deaf. I'll tell you all about it—or she will—when you come home, which is why I called you."

"Somebody hurt?"

"No, nothing like that. You'll be astonished to learn that the village voted to keep both of its children and their furry pet, too, *if* there's no harm done to any or all. How *are* the twins?"

"Asleep," Maradel said. "Like I was."

"As you noticed, I'm awake. Blays is awake. Her beau is awake. I'm at Peck's, and I can hear people banging around in the kitchen, so arguably, they're awake, too. You're not alone, Cousin. Be brave."

Maradel snorted.

"The twins are well. Yesterday was full—the whole village wanted to meet them, and they sat in on several classes, which they haven't been used to. Last night they were tired. Torin's pattern was still showing a bit of bruising, but the tool was working well. I'll examine them when they wake up. Should I call when I have a reading?"

"Yes. Did you talk with Konsit?"

"I had a meeting with her, a school administrator, and two teachers. As far as Pacazahno's concerned, the Traveling School, as they're calling it, is going to happen—and soon. A class of students has been assembled, and the teachers have a preliminary curriculum. I told Konsit to talk to you to finish the final details."

"Good," Arbour said. "I'll call her later."

"When she's awake," Maradel said. "Good idea."

"Going back home, now," Arbour said. "I'll wait for your news, Mari."

The comm clicked off. Maradel sighed and thought about going back to bed. Then, she went down the hall to make herself a mug of morning wake-up.

A shop down-square had its lights on now, and a few people had gone into the kitchen, emerging with hampers. Maradel finished the last of her wake-up—and felt a presence behind her.

"Good morning, Maradel."

"Torin," she said, turning her head with a smile. "And Eet. Good morning to you both. I hope you slept well?"

"We did!" Torin said, coming forward with a bounce in her step to rival her brother's, Eet sitting tall on her shoulder. She paused by Maradel's side and looked out the window.

"Everybody's waking up," she said. "Will we be going back to school today?"

"Arbour called and said she'd like us to come home, if we can," Maradel said. "School will be coming to you, remember?"

"Yes, but not for *weeks*," Torin said, sounding decidedly put out.

"Maybe not. The teachers have a full class, and a plan of lessons. Arbour needs to talk with Surda joiMore, but that won't take long. What *we* need to do is go home and start opening cottages, and the school, so everything's ready—in a few *days*."

"Oh." Torin turned to look at her, eyes bright. "*That* quick? I didn't think about needing to open *our* school. Vaiza and I will help."

"Everybody will help," Maradel said, and didn't add, *try and stop them.*

"Will we be going home today, then?" Torin asked.

"That depends in part on how you're feeling," Maradel said, "and in part when your brother wakes up."

"I can wake him up now," Torin said, looking over her shoulder. "Should I?"

"Why not let him sleep a little longer, while we talk?" Maradel suggested.

Torin sighed.

"You have to examine me," she said. "*Again*."

Maradel hesitated. It had been agreed, among the concerned adults, that there was no reason to make much of the life-saving and innovative work that had been done on her behalf, or to allow Torin to know how very close she had come to dying. Maradel therefore gave a careless shrug, and produced a grin.

"It's what Healers and medics do, you know."

"And teachers," Torin said, which was possibly a comment on yesterday. "Will you examine Eet, too?"

Maradel considered the norbear, who gazed back at her, the picture of saucy norbear health.

"What I will need from Eet," Maradel said, firmly, having seen this technique work for both Tekelia and Dyoli, "is *quiet*. The quieter he is, the quicker I'll be, and the sooner we can have breakfast."

An image formed just behind Maradel's eyes, of a white wall.

"That's right," Torin said approvingly. "Eet and I will think of the white wall. Do we sit at the table?"

"That would be best," Maradel said, turning away from the window. She sat down, and so did Torin, guiding Eet to the tabletop. He hunkered down onto all fours, and Maradel again received the impression of the white wall.

"In a hurry?" she murmured, and was answered with an image of a large piece of apinberry pie. Maradel laughed. "White wall, please."

It came, displacing the pie in a snap.

Maradel opened her Inner Eyes.

Two patterns leapt to her attention, the norbear's alien and oddly weighted. It seemed to Maradel that it was also more robust than it had been even last evening.

She moved her attention to Torin, and nearly gasped at the strong and ordered tapestry that opened to her Sight.

The heart-link Torin shared with her brother was broad and bright; the hazy bit of lace connecting her to Eet smooth and stable. There were in addition growing attachments—to Geritsi, Dosent, Tanin, Tekelia, Aunt Asta—and Dyoli ven'Deelin. The links truncated by loss had dimmed somewhat, while remaining integral.

Torin's pattern was bordered, as were the patterns of all Civilized persons, but there was no sense of confinement or stress. Maradel brought her attention more closely to the area Dyoli had particularly shown to her, where the tightest knots had begun to warp the whole. The bruising that had been visible yesterday was gone, the threads straight, no tangles or knots showing. Maradel Touched one small design; found it sturdy and resilient.

Carefully, she also Touched that well-defined border, finding it pliant. That was good; the border would grow as the pattern it defined expanded. So long as there was no more tampering done.

Maradel then Looked for the tool Torin had built, with Dyoli's guidance. For a moment, she thought it had failed—then she Saw it, melded so smoothly in the area that had to do with Torin's Gifts, that it seemed it had always been there.

Withdrawing slightly, Maradel surveyed the whole once again. Torin's pattern fairly glowed with a warm, steady, wholly rational light. It was healthy, vibrant—and beginning to become restless.

Smiling, she closed her Inner Eyes and spoke.

"Thank you, Torin and Eet. I have finished my examination. Torin, please wake your brother. While I examine him, I would like you and Eet to go over to the kitchen and get us some breakfast."

Vaiza's pattern pretended to no such well-confined order as his sister's. It was, Maradel thought, a quintessential Haosa pattern, hectic with energy and flares of sheer exuberance, its edges merging with the ambient. In the midst of all that activity, the link he shared with his sister was shockingly stable, as was the interface with Eet.

His secondary ties were numerous, embracing what seemed to be half the village; there was a strong link to Tekelia, and another broad, bright connection to Mar Tyn pai'Fortana. Maradel half-smiled. Vaiza was a warm boy, and in addition had a small Gift of empathy.

He was also bubbling with health. Satisfied, Maradel began to withdraw, catching a wistful mumble of hunger as she did.

"Thank you, Vaiza," she said, closing her Inner Eyes. "I appreciate your help."

He leapt to his feet. Rushing to the door, he threw it open to admit Torin, who was carrying a hamper. Behind her was one of the older students they had met yesterday, carrying a second, larger hamper, Eet on her shoulder.

"Breakfast!" Vaiza announced happily. "Hello, Razzi!"

"Hello, Vaiza!"

The hampers came to the table, and Maradel's stomach rumbled at the scent of warm bread, spice, and morning wake-up.

"I'll leave you to it," Razzi said, turning. "Thank you, Eet, for your help. Take him, Torin, will you?"

Torin stretched up on her toes, grabbed Eet around his middle, lifted him, and stepped back.

Razzi opened the door, and paused.

"See you in school?" she asked.

Torin turned to look at Maradel, who raised her hand and smiled.

"We're going home today," she said.

"We have to open the guest cottages and the school," Torin added, "so everything's ready when you come."

"Oh, good idea!" Razzi said. "I'll let the others know."

She closed the door gently behind her.

"Torin, we're going home!" Vaiza said, fairly dancing 'round the table.

"Good," she said. "But, first—breakfast."

On-Grid
The Wardian

. . . .

BENTAMIN OPENED THE DOCUMENT MARLIN HAD FORWARDED with anticipation. At last, Pel's deep notes! Surely, the kezlBlythe were now within reach of justice! He vowed to write a letter to Neeoni and Osha, with copies to their files, praising their work.

Then, he opened the document.

When he had read it twice, he got up to pour a cup of tea, came back to the desk, sat, sipped, put the cup down, shook his head, and went back to the top of the file.

After the third pass, he called Marlin, on visual.

She answered immediately. Apparently, his face betrayed him; her mouth twisted into a shape that wasn't *quite* humorous.

"You've read it?"

"Three times. Pel was playing a deep game."

"Pel was playing a *long* game," Marlin corrected.

"Long and deep don't cancel each other out." Bentamin waved a hand at his screen, which was beyond Marlin's range of vision. "Only read his notes."

"True." Marlin sighed. "I understand that he wanted to make as clean a sweep as possible, and not to warn the big players by picking off the small ones. My office of course is in the process of picking up the small players.

"If we'd had Pel's information earlier, children wouldn't have been put in peril of their lives, the Tree-and-Dragon *qe'andra* wouldn't have suffered a violation of her will, Pel himself might still be alive—and half the accounting firms in the city wouldn't be compromised."

"Is that an official number?" Bentamin asked.

Marlin threw her hands up in frustration. "The investigation isn't complete, but some of those small players I mentioned have been in place for years, Influencing one or two people in one or two key departments. It may well turn out to be closer to three-quarters. We picked up five at maiLanst and alKemi alone!"

Bentamin blinked.

"I don't mean to hold the kezlBlythe cheap, but surely they can't have—"

"Oh, some of it can be traced to Zandir and her syndicate," Marlin said, frowning. "But there's something else going on, Bentamin. We're catching just a bit of it, around the edges of the kezlBlythe investigation."

"Fellow travelers?"

"Possibly. The Protectors are mentioned far more often than I like, though not often enough to make Forensics jumpy."

Bentamin considered that. Marlin's instincts were good; in addition, she had completed the first level forensics course, in order to gain a better understanding of the work done in the field.

"It may be," Bentamin heard himself say, "that Pel had . . . other files."

His voice may have sounded odd; certainly, he was rather surprised to hear himself speak, and the look Marlin cast him was speculative.

"Maybe he did," she said. "Thank you, Bentamin; that's an interesting suggestion."

"You're welcome," Bentamin said. "Let me know, will you?"

"Among the first," she promised, and signed off.

Bentamin picked up his cup and drank of what was left of his now cold tea. Pel's file was still open on his screen. He closed it with a tap that was perhaps a little firmer than necessary.

The intercom on his desk buzzed.

"Yes?"

"Councilor ziaGorn is here to see you, Warden. He has no appointment."

"It happens that I, too, have no appointment," Bentamin said. "Please, Luzant macNamara, allow Councilor ziaGorn to enter."

"Yes, Warden."

Bentamin rose as the door opened and Majel ziaGorn stepped into the room.

There was something . . . different about the Deaf Councilor; that was Bentamin's first impression, though Majel had straightened from his bow before he had identified the change.

Since Bentamin had seen him last, Majel ziaGorn had accepted a life-bond.

That was interesting, Bentamin thought, and did not probe more deeply, which would have been a breach of both etiquette and friendship. He came around his desk with a smile.

"Majel. I hope you're recovered from yesterday's adventures?"

"I think so," Majel said. "And yourself?"

"I face frustration on all sides," Bentamin told him. "Which is my usual state, so I think we might consider that I'm operating normally. Will you have tea? Cookies? Something else?"

"Tea would be welcome," Majel said.

"As it happens, there's a fresh pot. Sit, please; I'll pour."

Majel took one of the comfortable chairs, and accepted a teacup with a murmur of thanks.

"To what do I owe the honor?" Bentamin asked. "Forensics is still investigating the situation at the guard house. As soon as—"

Majel raised a hand.

"I thought you would want to know that Speaker for the Haosa Pro Tem Blays essWorthi called a vote last night from the body of the whole."

Bentamin blinked and put his cup down.

"Did she, now?"

Majel inclined his head. "She did. The Haosa have decided that Tekelia vesterGranz will represent them. The Council of the Civilized will be receiving an official notification from the Speaker's Office."

"Of course," Bentamin said, declining to wonder how Blays essWorthi had conjured a *Speaker's Office.* The formalities were being properly attended—for which he strongly suspected he had Majel ziaGorn to thank. Tedious as they were, formalities and procedure kept the government running smoothly.

Majel put his cup on the table.

"I have—a suggestion to put forth," he said, carefully. "I can make an appointment, if I'm keeping you—"

"You're interrupting *nothing*," Bentamin assured him. "I spent the last two hours beating my head against a particularly dense and ultimately unsatisfactory document. I crave a change of topic."

Majel laughed.

"In that case—Speaker vesterGranz, as I'm sure you recall, is currently aboard *Dutiful Passage*, meeting with Master Trader yos'Galan regarding opportunity for the Haosa among the trade ships."

Bentamin waited.

"Speaker vesterGranz will shortly be returning, accompanied by Master Trader yos'Galan, Trader yos'Galan, and others. The Whole Port Inventory has revealed that Colemeno will do very well as a hub for the new routes the master trader will be building, and he arrives to make his formal proposal to port and council." He waved a hand.

"I received this information this morning, in my role as liaison to the trade team."

"I understand."

Majel paused, his eyes on his teacup, though he did not pick it up. Instead, he looked back to Bentamin, copper brows pulled over dark brown eyes.

"The Oracle's Seeing of the end of Civilization. Is that a—*true Seeing*?"

Bentamin laughed.

"Foresight is—let's say that it's *subject to interpretation*. Also, Foreseen events are vulnerable to interference from events that occur between the time of the prophecy and the prophesied moment."

He waved a hand, as if sweeping the air clean of probability.

"All prophecies are *true*, on their own terms. The question to ask, on receiving a prophecy, is *How likely is this to occur?* Applying that measuring stick, I would say that the Oracle's Seeing regarding the end of Civilization and the Haosa is—likely. Even *very* likely. We can't go on, divided as we are, especially now that the universe has found us again. Even if the trade mission leaves tomorrow and never returns, their arrival, their work, the questions they asked, and the information they shared, has already unsettled us. A collapse isn't out of the question. Will it happen?"

Bentamin extended his hands, turned them palm up, and palm down.

"Maybe. Maybe not."

"I see. Thank you."

Majel took a breath.

"Returning to my original topic—I propose that there be a committee formed to welcome our party of luminaries when they return to Colemenoport."

Bentamin looked at him, much struck.

"Tekelia vesterGranz is Haosa," he said.

"Indeed. And while it may be assumed that the Speaker will arrive on the port in answer to invitation—even several invitations—we have yesterday to inform us."

"I understand. Who do you think ought to be on this welcoming committee?"

"Myself—as liaison—Portmaster krogerSlyte, Warden of Civilization chastaMeir, Chair of Council gorminAstir, Speaker Pro Tem essWorthi." He paused to take a breath. "And a reporting team from the *Haven City Tattler*."

Bentamin considered him. Majel met his eyes calmly.

"These are heavy weapons, Councilor."

"I think they're not unreasonable, given the stakes, but I'm willing to take advice."

"I'm interested in what you see as the stakes," Bentamin countered.

"The Oracle has Seen the end of Civilization and of the Haosa, and the Seeing is plausible. The Council has determined that the best way to make this Seeing less likely to occur is to acknowledge that the Haosa are citizens of Colemeno, as well as the Civilized"—he quirked an eyebrow—"and the Deaf."

Bentamin inclined his head.

"Yes," Majel murmured. "In the meantime, there suddenly appears an action specifically targeting the Haosa—an action complete with a method to crush the Haosa bond with the ambient." He paused. "That is at the moment a hypothesis put forth by Counselor to Chaos dinOlin. We will know more once Forensics has finished its investigation."

"I understand," Bentamin assured him.

"Yes. The existence of this method argues for thought, intent, and planning," Majel continued. "Another working hypothesis—this one my own—is that some group has as its long-range goal the . . . subjugation of the Haosa. Which, if you'll permit me, Warden, would have the effect of destroying—or at least dangerously destabilizing—Civilization."

"How so?"

"Civilization needs the Haosa, not merely because they willingly receive Civilization's cast-off children, but because of the Haosa's unique relationship with the ambient conditions of our planet." He paused, and added, "This is as told to me by Blays, Howe, and Firgus, after the meeting of the whole, and the vote. Civilization called upon the Haosa to assist with the Reaver invasion exactly because of that unique relationship. Apparently there have been other such instances in history, though none so dire as the Reavers, in which the Haosa, as Howe would have it, 'saved Civilization's cake, and its cookies, too.'"

Bentamin laughed. "I don't think I've met Howe—?"

"Howe cleeMunt, Counsel to Chaos, representing The Vinery. Firgus dinOlin represents Deen's Fallow, with Visalee and Wildege under the representation of Blays essWorthi." Majel smiled. "You deal at your own level—Warden to Speaker. I, a Councilor, deal at mine."

"A kind interpretation to cover my lack of diligence," Bentamin murmured.

"If you like," Majel said. "What's your opinion of the welcoming committee?"

"I think, with the stakes as you've described them, the weapons are appropriate to the circumstances. What's your next step?"

"In my capacity as liaison to the Tree-and-Dragon Trade Mission, I will contact the individuals I mentioned, seeking their agreement. Once I have that, I'll find exactly when the master trader intends to raise port, and finalize details with the welcoming committee. May I count on your presence, Warden?"

"I wouldn't miss it," Bentamin assured him. "And not only because I can't wait to see the expression on Tekelia's face."

Dutiful Passage
Colemeno Orbit

. . . .

TEKELIA'S PATTERN WAS STERNER THAN PADI HAD EVER SEEN IT, informed by a mixture of anger and relief potent enough to make her stomach ache. A terrible tragedy had been averted, that was the understanding she received from some source she scarcely understood, yet which resonated with truth. She also gathered that the overarching danger had not been retired, and that Tekelia was *angry*.

She had keyed in the code that brought the call to Booth Three in the Library, then stepped outside, rather than intrude on Tekelia's private business.

Almost, she wished she had not been so nice. She had never before seen Tekelia overset, and this—

The door slid back, and Tekelia stepped out of the booth, face tight, mouth straight. The mouth curved very slightly, as Tekelia saw Padi, and stepped into her embrace.

"Is Blays all right?" That was her first question. Tekelia huffed, and a shiver of humor warmed their bond.

"Blays is herself, and we have Majel ziaGorn to thank for it," Tekelia said. "The short form is that Haosa are being targeted on-port—and Invitation Right ignored. Blays called a meeting of all our cousins, and word has gone out that Haosa are to avoid all locations under the grid, particularly the port. In the meanwhile—"

The humor this time was laced with resignation.

"Since she had all of our cousins together and paying attention, Speaker for the Haosa Pro Tem essWorthi called a vote, and I am chosen to sit in the chair the Council of Civilization created for the Haosa at yesterday's meeting."

"That's wonderful," Padi said, and Tekelia outright laughed, stepping back and putting her at arm's length.

"You'll be pleased to know that Dyoli was able to separate Torin, Vaiza, and Eet with no harm done, save that Torin is now wholly Civilized, and has built a tool to prove herself."

Padi frowned. "Is she to be sent back to Civilization? Will Vaiza go, too? Who—"

Tekelia placed a finger across her lips. "For the moment, she'll stay with us. As Blays put it, Civilization gave them to the Haosa. She also remarked that it was not the fault of the Haosa, if Civilization failed to perform *due diligence*, in which I believe I hear Majel ziaGorn's voice."

Padi laughed, then sobered.

"But won't it harm Torin? To be wholly under the ambient?"

"As to that—the tool Torin built, with Dyoli's help, filters the ambient—rather like a personal Grid. They've been at Peck's Market and Pacazahno these last two days, with Maradel, who reports no difficulties. I've given my support to Arbour's suggestion that they be allowed to come home."

"Where Geritsi and Dosent—not to say the village entire—will be vigilant for them."

"Not to mention her brother and Eet, with whom she shares heart-links." Tekelia smiled, tightly. "I think that Torin's danger from the ambient is small, compared to, let's say, her danger from her Civilized cousins."

Tekelia fell silent. Padi waited for a beat of three, then said, carefully, "There's more."

"There is, yes. Blays and Majel have bonded. It's a true life-bond, as certified by none other than my Aunt Asta."

"I wish them very happy," Padi said, frowning into Tekelia's face. "But, there's something *bad* that you haven't told me," she murmured, knowing it for truth—and suddenly gasped. "Is *Majel* hurt? You said Blays was well because of—"

"Far too good at this," Tekelia murmured, extending a hand to touch her cheek. "Majel is perfectly well. Blays is herself, only more so. Firgus and Howe are reportedly also well. The *bad* thing—"

Tekelia paused, gazing into her eyes; their bond warmed, and she felt something—expand—at the core of her being.

"I regret our timing, love. Had I known about this—even heard a whisper—I would have resisted Thodelm yos'Galan more vigorously."

"That sounds dire, indeed," Padi murmured. "But, you know, resisting him would only have made the process less pleasant, and for the same outcome."

Tekelia's brows rose.

"Because Thodelm yos'Galan always gets what he wants?"

"Well, no. If you'll recall the case in point, he *didn't* get what he wanted, that being a tidy lifemating. Instead, he got kin-ties—rather, the master trader did—which was less desirable, but perfectly workable, as tending kin-ties is at the core of the thodelm's honor. What I mean to say is that Thodelm yos'Galan could not *afford* to lose the point, and it really would have been too bad—not to say uncomfortable for all of us—to have forced him into taking a fuller part in the negotiations."

She put her hands on Tekelia's shoulders.

"Now. *Tell me.*"

Tekelia half-laughed. "Since you ask so nicely . . . It appears that someone has fashioned an . . . *environment*, let's call it, that's inimical to Haosa."

"Inimical," Padi repeated. "An absence of the ambient?"

"Arguably I am standing here with you in the absence of the ambient," Tekelia pointed out. "No, Blays would have it be an—*anti-ambient*, designed to suffocate."

"Who made such a thing?" Padi whispered.

Tekelia shrugged. "Forensics is seeking the answer to that question, and is also, I'm told, examining the . . . installations."

"More than one?"

"One room at least, in the port guard house," Tekelia said. "As to why—apparently someone has taken the Haosa in stronger dislike than usual."

Tekelia turned both hands palm up.

"We'll have to wait until Forensics finishes its work. Word has gone out, as I said, warning our cousins away from any location under-Grid."

"That's in hand, then," Padi said, and suddenly grinned. "You know, it's just as well this had not happened before we created our household! Only think how lowering for me, to be forced to side with the thodelm against you."

Tekelia frowned—then laughed.

"Because you would have me protected?"

"That was," Padi said primly, "my goal."

"I thought your goal was to protect me from *Korval's* enemies," Tekelia said.

This time Padi laughed, and slid her arm companionably through Tekelia's, turning them toward the exit.

"These people have announced that they are Korval's enemies, have they not? Come, let us get something to eat. I'm starving."

On-Grid
The Wardian
Department of Accountability and Justice

· ·

MARLIN GLARED AT THE SCREEN.

"Honestly, Pel," she muttered. "Would it have hurt to ask for some help?"

She sighed, then. She'd known Pel chastaMeir fairly well—brilliant, implacable, idealistic Pel chastaMeir. Quite possibly, it *would* have hurt—something—for him to have asked for help.

He'd been investigating the kezlBlythe Syndicate for years, as seemingly isolated cases of fraud and malfeasance began to show a disturbing pattern. He'd met Zatorvia xinRood in the course of investigating those preyed upon by the kezlBlythe, and fallen in love. That, Marlin thought, had been the point at which Pel's investigation became an obsession, driven by his need to protect Zatorvia and her children.

Pel hadn't been accustomed to failure. That he had failed in what had become the driving mission of his life—Well, but he hadn't lived to know that, had he?

Bentamin was of the opinion that the kezlBlythe had pushed Pel under that train, but without witnesses—*evidence*—an opinion it remained.

Zatorvia... Bentamin had spoken with a witness to Zatorvia's murder, and was convinced that the account given was accurate, and would have been damning—if the witness had not happened to be a norbear.

And here, these notes. Marlin sighed at her screen.

The notes made the case that the kezlBlythe Syndicate was not acting alone. That, in fact, the kezlBlythe Syndicate—pernicious and damaging—was the lesser problem.

She had herself been distressed by the number of times the Protectors of Civilization had been mentioned by those smaller players her office had been busily gathering up. But it was widely agreed among the *qe'andra*, Forensics, and security that the Protectors, while staunch in their belief of their own superiority, were sadly incompetent, not to say inept. The idea of the sneaky, effective kezlBlythe being subordinate to the Protectors was, well, laughable. Blustering amateurs were the kezlBlythe's meat.

No, if the kezlBlythe were a tool, the hand that wielded them would be subtle, with more far-ranging goals. Subverting the accounting systems that supported the economy would provide a steady flow of cash. Money was necessary to any large operation. But such a group would be spreading their Influence among the upper levels of power, among the scientific community, infrastructure, the Grid-works—

Marlin blinked.

The Grid. *There* was a worthy goal. Who controlled the Grid controlled Civilization.

She shivered, laughed—and shivered again.

The end of Civilization, and the Haosa, too.

Who, Marlin thought, carefully, would benefit from the fall of Civilization?

And how would one take the Grid hostage?

She took a breath, closed her eyes, and brought a white wall before her Inner Eyes for a long three minutes.

Calmer, she opened her eyes, and tapped up her file of experts on call.

She scrolled down until she had it. Yes.

cadBirn. Specialist in Grid Mechanics.

She reached for the comm and tapped in the code.

Dutiful Passage
Colemeno Orbit

. . . .

SHAN HAD JUST FINISHED THE FIRST DRAFT OF THE FORMAL
presentation in support of creating a Tree-and-Dragon Trade
Hub on Colemenoport when the incoming mail ping sounded.

He tapped the screen, finding a letter from Majel ziaGorn
in-queue, in reply to his of six hours prior.

That was, Shan thought, rather a quick turnaround. Even
someone as efficient as Councilor ziaGorn could hardly be expected
to have scheduled two formal presentations at the highest levels
in so short a time.

On the other hand, perhaps the council and the port had
decided that they preferred Colemeno to remain an obscure planet
in an inconvenient pocket of space. Certainly, he could see the
council deciding that, though Portmaster krogerSlyte was, in his
estimation, more ambitious. If they had decided against, then
he was saved having to polish his presentation, which could of
course be placed on the profit side of the ledger, but—

"But! There is one certain way to put all wonder and worrying
to rest," he said aloud, and tapped the letter open.

It was both brief and perplexing. Shan had recourse to his
glass and read it again.

He had just finished reading it for the third time, without
achieving much more in the way of enlightenment, when the
door chimed.

Surely, he had no appointment scheduled? Not that life was
so accommodating as to always run by appointment.

"Who is it?" he asked.

"Master Trader, it's Tekelia vesterGranz. May I have a word?"

"Certainly! Come in, please."

271

The door slid aside. Tekelia stepped over the threshold, paused and bowed in the Colemeno style, chagrin and dismay readily apparent to Shan's senses.

"I am pleased to see you, Tekelia," Shan said gently. "Please sit. May I offer refreshment? Tea? Wine?"

"Water?" Tekelia asked. "I'll fetch it. Can I get you anything?"

"A glass of water would be pleasant. Thank you for your care."

Tekelia crossed the room to the buffet, filled two glasses and brought them back to the desk. Placing one on the mottled green and blue stone disk to Shan's right, Tekelia kept the other in hand and sank into a chair.

Having arrived at all this, however, Tekelia did not seem to be on the edge of speech.

Shan sipped his water.

"I must thank you for returning my coaster," he said, by way of opening a dialogue. "I was quite bereft without it."

Tekelia laughed.

"Yes, so Padi told me." Tekelia sipped water in turn, sighed, and raised a velvet brown gaze to Shan's face.

"I'm afraid I've put the trade mission into—an embarrassing situation," Tekelia said.

"I wouldn't have thought you had sufficient opportunity. Of course, it can't be supposed that I have the full measure of your abilities on such short acquaintance. Do tell me what you've done."

"Done—nothing in particular. This comes of what *I am*—which is Haosa. There is a law on Colemeno which forbids Haosa the port. For years, the law has been softened by a custom known as Right of Invitation—which means that a Haosa *may* be on port, if invited by a Civilized person.

"Yesterday, Blays essWorthi, who is standing in my place as Speaker while I visit you here, was on Colemenoport—invited, and escorted, by Majel ziaGorn. She was arrested for being a Haosa on-port." Tekelia sipped water, and met Shan's eyes again. "There are more—and more disturbing—facts attending that one, but in the interests of brevity—Invitation Right is no longer being honored by port security."

Shan raised his glass.

"Allow me to understand this. Your concern is that you will be arrested when you hit the docks, despite having been implicitly, if not explicitly, invited to arrive among trade mission personnel—and that this indiscretion on the part of port security will cast dishonor upon the trade mission. Do I have that correctly?"

"Yes, sir." Tekelia took a breath. "I should be able to 'port from inside the shuttle, but—"

"No, no! That won't do at all!" Shan said, looking at his screen with a great deal more understanding. "Only think how disappointed the welcoming committee will be!"

Ice bloomed in Tekelia's pattern.

"What welcoming committee?" The question was calm, betraying mild interest, and not the least hint of that flowering of fear.

"Well you might ask! I have only just been perusing a fascinating letter from Councilor ziaGorn on the topic. Let me see—"

He made a show of leaning forward to consult his screen.

"Ah, here we are: The welcoming committee will include Majel ziaGorn, Trade Mission Liaison; Urta krogerSlyte, Portmaster; Zeni gorminAstir, Council Chair; Bentamin chastaMeir, Warden of Civilization; Blays essWorthi, Speaker for the Haosa Pro Tem; and Luzants pastirEbri and olCanon, representing the *Haven City Tattler*."

He leaned back, and smiled.

"Quite a stellar gathering, don't you agree?"

Tekelia's pattern had thawed somewhat. They took a careful breath, and said, levelly, "It's nothing more than the trade mission deserves."

"The trade mission is pleased to pretend that the welcoming committee has been produced in its honor," Shan said gently.

Tekelia awarded him a sharp look.

"You think this scheme has been put together *for me*."

"Natural modesty must of course cause you to shrink from such an interpretation, but—yes, I do."

Tekelia seemed about to say something, but instead drank off what was left of the water, and put the glass on the edge of the desk.

"There are late developments that may interest you," Tekelia said.

"By all means! I dote on late developments."

Tekelia's lips twitched, but the answer was sober enough.

"In that case, you'll like to know that the Council of the Civilized at their most recent meeting created a full chair for the Haosa Councilor. Last night, Blays essWorthi, in her capacity of Speaker Pro Tem, called on the Haosa to decide who of their number would sit in that chair. Tekelia vesterGranz was chosen."

Shan inclined his head.

"Not only is the trade mission honored with a welcoming committee, but so, too, is the newest councilor at the table. We really must pause for a moment to admire Councilor ziaGorn's efficiency. Two honorary welcomes *and* a shield in one group! Really, I am in awe."

"Yes, sir," Tekelia said. "You may also wish to know that Blays essWorthi and Majel ziaGorn have formed a life-bond."

"I will be certain to wish them happy, when we meet."

"As I will," Tekelia said. "May I ask a question?"

"By all means."

"I only wonder if you have any insight into how such a bond might have formed, given that Councilor ziaGorn is Deaf?" Tekelia raised a hand. "I mean no criticism. Only, the ambient and the Grid alike being invisible to him—"

Shan lifted a shoulder.

"The heart keeps its own Code. If you are asking after *method*—I would expect that there are points of congruency—I've noticed that Majel ziaGorn has, in addition to enormous amounts of common sense, a great deal of empathy. Not so much that I would call it a Gift, or claim him for a Healer, but enough, perhaps, to support a bond. Well! *Clearly* enough to support a bond. I would have to examine the patterns and the bond, in order to give a more detailed analysis. With permission of the principals, of course."

He picked up his glass, but did not drink, instead cutting a sharp look at Tekelia.

"Do you suspect Blays essWorthi of taking advantage of Majel ziaGorn?"

Tekelia raised both hands, palms out.

"No, sir, I don't. Blays is as horrified as the euphoria of a new bonding allows. She sees all the disadvantages of their situation, while accepting that the thing is done, and that nothing could induce her to undo it. Apparently Majel feels the same, only more strongly."

Shan laughed. "Then their adventure is well begun."

"Yes, sir."

When Tekelia said nothing else for a moment or two, Shan asked, "Is there anything else I need to know?"

Tekelia looked up with a wry smile.

"I'm afraid so. Someone has...constructed an anti-ambient—this is how Blays described it to me. It acts to suffocate a Haosa's link with the ambient, and possibly with their own Gifts. Forensics is still investigating."

Shan shivered, recalling his younger sister, Anthora, trapped in a box, her Gifts being drained from her.

"Sir? Are you well?"

"For values of well," Shan said, and lifted his glass to drink. When he was done, he met Tekelia's eyes. "Something similar was deployed against...*dramliz* on Liad. I don't have a copy of the report from those who examined the device, but I can get it, if you're interested."

Tekelia took a hard breath. "That would be—useful."

"Then I will undertake to find it for you," Shan said. "Is there anything else?"

"No, sir. I think that's everything."

"And perfectly sufficient unto the day. You will wish to know that we will be departing for Colemeno in twelve hours. Our party will include myself, Trader Padi, *Qe'andra* dea'Gauss, Dil Nem Tiazan, and you. May I hope that you have seen the wisdom in meeting the committee on the dock?"

Tekelia's smile was, perhaps, a little reluctant.

"Yes, sir. I'll stand with the rest."

"Very good," Shan said, and raised a hand. "I wonder if kin may ask a question of kin."

Tekelia blinked, momentarily off-balance—and made a recover.

"Of course."

"Thank you. Why did you think that I would give you to port security?"

Tekelia leaned back in the chair.

"Understand that I just received the information we discussed."

"And I honor you, that you came to me at once. But I wonder how I have taught you that I am unreliable." He offered a smile. "I wish to correct my error, you see."

"Error?" The last of the ice had melted from Tekelia's pattern; it now glowed slightly, perhaps with embarrassment.

"Master Trader—"

"Shan," he corrected. "We are speaking together as kin."

"Shan," Tekelia amended. "You made no error. To be completely fair, *I* made no error. Only trust is ... difficult. And you—the master trader—there's the success of the trade mission to consider."

"Very true," Shan said solemnly. "I advise, for future reference, that the master trader does not deal in lives. For one thing, it's against Guild law. And, simply put, he doesn't have the taste for it. Also, in the current situation, you failed to take a major factor into account." He paused. Tekelia waited.

Shan lifted an eyebrow and suggested, "Padi? Or do you think she would have nothing to say to the master trader selling you for a charter?"

Head thrown back, Tekelia laughed, and Shan Saw the link Tekelia shared with Padi, glowing bright, broad, and true.

"You're right," Tekelia said. "I hadn't thought it through. Do kin ask forgiveness of kin?"

"If necessary. In the case of new kin, misunderstandings are certain to occur. As long as there's no malice or dishonesty intended, there's no need to ask forgiveness. And, you know, we've both learned good and useful things about each other today."

"We have, yes," Tekelia said. "Thank you."

"It was my very great pleasure," Shan said and rose to accompany kin to the door.

On-Grid
Cardfall Casino

. . . .

THE LUMENBERRY TREES IN THE PARK ACROSS THE STREET WERE already glowing and the early crowd was at play in the main room when Majel walked into the Cardfall at last.

He went directly to the bar.

It would have been too much to say that he *expected* Seylin to be waiting for him, but he wasn't surprised to find that she was.

"Good evening, Principal ziaGorn," she said, raising a glass of what looked to be cold tea in his direction.

He slid onto the stool next to her. "Am I in disgrace?"

Seylin tipped her head consideringly.

"I wouldn't say *disgrace*," she said, as one being fair. "Not as such. Though I did expect you sooner. Even quite a bit sooner."

"I had people to see," Majel said, and smiled at Mardek, the barkeeper, who had placed a glass of cold tea before him. "Notably, the Warden, Council Chair gorminAstir, Portmaster krogerSlyte, the port news editor at the *Tattler*, and—" He picked up his glass and drank thirstily. "I stopped at the library on my way downtown, to talk to the History and the Geographic Librarians. I find myself...underinformed regarding Bodhar-on-the-River."

He put his glass down and looked at her.

"I did call you from the car."

"You did," Seylin said. "I see that it comes down to a failure of imagination on my part. *A few errands* didn't seem likely to require the day from sun-up to nightfall."

Majel laughed.

"You forget that I had to come in from Peck's Market," he said. "And—to be honest—I'd expected to be home somewhat earlier than this."

"But you are home," Seylin said. "Which relieves me, given the things I've been hearing from my colleagues."

Majel looked at her sharply.

"Which colleagues and what things?"

"I'll answer both of those questions," Seylin said. "After you tell me a Healer was among the people you saw today."

Majel frowned. "Why? Do I need a Healer?"

"You've been—attached." Seylin sighed. "Though of course it's wrong of me to be Looking at your pattern."

"Is it?" Majel asked. "You've known me since I was *three*. Surely, you've Looked at my pattern any number of times. In fact, I wouldn't be surprised to learn that it's so familiar to you that the heart-link with Blays leapt immediately to your attention."

"Blays. That's Blays essWorthi, of yesterday's adventure on the port?"

"Yes." Majel sipped tea, and slanted a glance at Seylin. "If it soothes you, she wasn't going to tell me that we'd bonded, only Asta vesterGranz wished us happy."

"This is an *accidental* bonding?" Seylin's eyebrows were raised.

Majel moved his hand. "Apparently, the bonding was always possible, or perhaps I mean fated. Howe's explanations are rather airy. In any case, the key is that Blays and I met, which allowed the affinities we share the opportunity to . . . intertwine."

He glanced at Seylin, who seemed neither horrified nor baffled.

"I understand that, normally, it would be a slower process. Blays and I would have gradually become aware of our growing connection, and had time to accommodate ourselves. Shared peril accelerated matters. That's Howe's theory, in any case, and Firgus seems to find it reasonable." He looked again at Seylin, and grinned at the so-very-patient expression on her face.

"Howe cleeMunt and Firgus dinOlin, like Blays, are Counsels to Chaos—assistants to Speaker vesterGranz. I don't know if either is a Healer. If you think it's important, I'll see our own Healer this evening. Right now, I'll need your help understanding how . . . prominent the link is to those who can See it, and if that will be a problem."

Seylin shrugged. "It was immediately apparent to me because, as you say, I'm very familiar with you—and your pattern. People less familiar will only see the wholeness of you, and, yes, it *is* rude to stare. Will it be a problem?" She shrugged again. "Heart-links are common, and you support several. Who's to know which is new, or to whom you're bonded?"

"Let us by all means depend on good manners," Majel murmured, and Seylin gave a startled laugh.

"Did I say that? I must be tired. Only tell me—how do you *feel*, Majel?"

He took a deep breath, and closed his eyes, the better to consider himself. After a moment, he murmured, "I've been trying to determine just that, off and on, today. 'Happy' is true, but useless, because I haven't, you know, been *un*happy, and *more happy* is simply nonsense."

He opened his eyes and met Seylin's steady gaze.

"I feel—completed," he said finally. "I feel as if there had been an empty space at my back, which has now been filled, and I'm the stronger for it."

He spread his hands, palms up.

"I'm no poet, as you know."

"No, I think you've done quite well," Seylin said, and turned her head, but not before he had seen a gleam of what might have been tears in her eyes.

She picked up her glass, drank, and looked back to him, gaze firm as ever.

"We now come to the gossip from my colleague on the city guard." She paused. "You might want a glass of Andram."

"I might," Majel agreed, "but I'll hold. There's an emergency Council meeting in an hour." He moved a hand. "You're under no obligation to model yourself on me."

"I'll stay with tea, myself," she said, and raised her glass in salute. "I called Robyr at Port Security. He didn't answer and I left a message. I'm still waiting for a return call.

"However! I did speak to Kaedys at the Riverview Guard Station. We share an interest in new theories of security and in-service workshops. It's been a while since I checked in with her, and she was pleased to tell me that there had been several workshops given on identifying tainted Gifts."

Majel frowned. "*Tainted* Gifts?"

"A new phrase for me, as well. What's meant is Gifts that have been used in commission of a crime, which will then display a particular...aura. And, no, I didn't know that was possible, and neither did Kaedys."

She drank some tea and put her glass on the bar. Mardek stepped over and refilled it, leaving the pitcher behind.

"The theory was presented in the first session, which was, according to Kaedys, as full of pseudoscientifical claptrap as an *empato* plot. She told me that she was being paid to attend, which was the only reason she went back for the second session—which was where the instructor's bias was revealed.

"It was stated as an absolute and proven fact that Gifts attached to patterns lacking a definitive border are most likely to have been used in criminal activity."

Majel lifted a finger.

"You will of course explain this."

"Of course. Most personality grids, or as we call them, patterns, are self-contained. They have a border—an outline of natural shielding that prevents the individual from melding with the ambient. The outline is the defining feature of what we know as the Civilized pattern."

Majel took a breath.

"Let me guess. Haosa patterns don't have this border, as the individual interacts directly with the ambient." He put his glass on the counter with a thump. "And *that* is how Officer nimOlad knew Blays was Haosa."

"And also how he knew you were Deaf, because, as you'll have deduced, that's another distinctive pattern, readily apparent to those who—" She paused.

"To those who are able to See such things," Majel finished for her. "*Is* there a body of research linking Haosa to urban crime? I shouldn't think there were enough Haosa in the city to account for all of it."

"Now *this*," Seylin said, waggling her fingers at him, "is *precisely* what confidence artists and careless teachers abhor— someone who uses their brain. Yes, the number of Haosa in the city is vanishingly small. Even granting that the few who remain are the core of a crime ring, they would still need Civilized—or Deaf—operatives to get the work done."

Majel reached for the pitcher and refilled their glasses.

"So. Has the local guardhouse installed new high-risk rooms?"

"Funny you should ask. The annual city-wide inspection of guardhouse facilities produced a recommendation that existing high-risk rooms be upgraded, because of *increasing threat levels*, which have somehow managed to escape the notice of the street guard throughout the city. The recommendation was passed on to the contractor responsible for the maintenance of the existing rooms, who refused to make the upgrades because they exceeded design tolerances—meaning that an entirely new system would have to be installed—and that the resulting space would be 'pernicious.'"

"Blays said that she Foresaw herself dead in the high-risk room at the port," Majel said, his voice stringently calm.

Seylin put her hand on his wrist. "You made certain that didn't happen."

"The Warden made certain that didn't happen. Has the city contractor been replaced?"

"Not that I'm aware of, but I called Sibeta—my friend in Ops. She's looking into it and will call me back." She took a sip of tea. "With your permission, I'd like to tell Kaedys what happened to you and Blays at the port."

"Yes, do that," Majel said. "And tell her to share it with her colleagues."

"I will," Seylin said. She patted his wrist once more and reached for her glass.

Majel finished his tea and slid off the stool.

"Old friend. I need to go upstairs for my meeting. I'll be down—"

"No," Seylin said and met his eyes. "Majel. You've had a full day piled atop a full and horrifying day. You have good staff. Mily's a wonderful host—which you know. You trained her. Ikat's wasted in the ops room. I've been looking for a chance to get him down on the floor with the regulars and see how he manages."

He was about to protest—then smiled and inclined his head.

"Yes, that's a good plan. Please ask Mily to host this evening— and let me know how Ikat does on the floor. Thank you for your care, Seylin."

She put her empty glass on the bar and stood up with a smile.

"What are friends—or, come to think of it, heads of security— for, after all? Tomorrow, old friend."

"Tomorrow," Majel said.

Dutiful Passage
Colemeno Orbit

. . . .

HEALSPACE OPENED AROUND HER—LAVENDER MIST SHOT WITH bright ribbons and dark, swirling energetically.

Padi breathed in. Ebullience flowed into her core, and she laughed. Her laughter made the ribbons dance, so she laughed again.

The ribbons swirled close, and the lavender mist thickened. Padi swallowed another laugh. No one had told her that Healspace could make her drunk, though she was well aware that Colemeno's Ribbons excited euphoria.

She took a deep breath, centering herself with a pilot's board exercise. Calmness flowed into Healspace, lulling the dancing ribbons into a gentle drifting.

The mist waited.

Deliberately, Padi reached for the pattern that was herself, watching it unfold like a flower, supported by the mist.

When it was wholly open, she brought her attention to the heart-link she shared with Father. She extended a gentle probe, as Dyoli had taught her, and made herself . . . receptive.

The first thing that came to her was a soft murmur, not song, but very like Father's voice, speaking calmly in another room. Breath-caught, Padi waited, but the words remained indistinct, merely a comforting background.

Not wanting to lose the sound of Father's voice, Padi carefully brought her attention to the linking thread itself—and caught her breath.

Seen thus, it was not merely a thread, nor even a bold bright ribbon such as she shared with Tekelia, but something like a tapestry itself, woven from dozens upon dozens of thin, tough strands, like hair, or wire. Each strand glowed; some showed more silver, some were almost entirely pink, others were mottled, lavender and pink, and the whole they described was unique and powerful.

There, nestled among the subtle glowing strands, was the soft, sweet packet Father had given her, lambent silver, discrete, and enticing.

She brought her attention closer to that sweet working, and extended a gentle query.

For a moment, nothing happened. Then, to her considerable dismay, the packet—melted.

"No!" she cried, reaching—and there it was, a pretty silver pinwheel, spinning care and comfort, subtly scented with chocolate.

Padi took a breath, and concentrated, bringing the pinwheel closer.

A *tool*, she thought, recalling her consistent lack of success at tool-building.

The silver wheel slowed slightly, offering a glimpse of a simple five-sided pattern, before it abruptly vanished.

"No," Padi whispered, her attention going to the place where it had nestled, sweet, among her connections to Father...

...and there it was, complete, and undisturbed.

Padi sighed.

Making a tool to share with Tekelia was, in Padi's opinion, asking for trouble. Tekelia's skill at tool-building was as poor as her own. Who knew what disaster they might create together?

A *gift*, the mists whispered in Tekelia's voice, *given along your heart-link.*

Padi froze—"Of course," she murmured.

She flung her attention to the area of her pattern where her Talents resided—and paused, stymied by the glare and glitter. Which was the Gift that centered Tekelia? She shivered, and absently reached for the mist, shrugging it about her shoulders like a stole.

There were ribbons dancing nearby, and the mist brought her the scent of lavender.

There had been lavender flowers in the courtyard when she had accepted the Dragon, and all of her nature. Taking a deep breath of lavender-scented mist, Padi thought, What if it was not a Gift, but *her nature*, that centered Tekelia?

The mists moved again, the scent of lavender filling head, heart, and lungs.

She looked down, unsurprised to find her arms full of spiky purple stalks. Almost absently, she reached to take up one of the ribbons floating nearby, and used it to tie the stalks together.

She thought about the heart-link she shared with Tekelia, and it rose before her, crimson-and-gold. Smiling, she laid the bouquet on the ribbon, sighing in satisfaction.

A breeze kissed her cheek, cold; and she looked 'round to see the mist in shreds around her, the ribbons reduced to shadow.

Padi!

Tekelia's voice was frantic inside her head.

Padi, come back, now!

On-Grid
Cardfall Casino

. . . .

"THE LAW FORBIDDING THE HAOSA THE PORT DOES NOT SPECIFI-
cally exclude *or* include Haven City," ivenAlyatta said. "It was a
law made for the port itself, framed as a security measure for
those off-worlders who might not be aware of the—" She glanced
to the right, presumably at another screen, and read, "the dan-
gers of dealing with persons whose actions are dominated by the
ambient conditions peculiar to Colemeno."

She looked back into the camera. "I've sent a copy of the law
to all of you for review. What's more interesting, given our reason
for meeting—which is to ensure the safety of all of our councilors, whatever their affiliation—is this, from the City Charter."

Again, the glance aside.

"Haven City is hereby established as a place of safety and
succor," she said, apparently reading from another screen. "A
haven in fact as well as in name for all citizens of Colemeno,
regardless of their station or condition."

"Clearly," targElmina said into the silence that followed this,
"I have neglected important reading. Chair, I don't think it would
be out of place to have that clause read at the beginning of our
next meeting of the whole."

"May I have that as a motion?" gorminAstir said.

"Certainly. I move that the Statement of Purpose from the
Haven City Charter be read aloud at the beginning of the next
meeting of the Council of the whole."

"Second," said azieEm.

"All in favor, please raise your hands."

The motion passed unanimously.

"This council meets in Haven City, which was created as a

285

safe place for all citizens of Colemeno, regardless of their station or condition," Chair gorminAstir continued. "Is there any location on Colemeno that has as its stated purpose anything higher than this?"

Silence.

"No," said the Council Chair, after it was clear that no one was going to speak. "I therefore move that the council meet in its usual chambers in the Sakuriji, where all of our members, from newest to most senior, are guaranteed safety."

"Second," Portmaster krogerSlyte said.

"All in favor, please raise your hands."

Again, the vote was unanimous.

"Have we other business that cannot wait until our next session?"

"Chair gorminAstir," said Portmaster krogerSlyte, "I would like to advise the Council that Majel ziaGorn, in his capacity as Liaison to the Tree-and-Dragon Trade Mission, made available to me the Whole Port Inventory as it has been submitted to the Trade Guild, as well as the relevant sections from the Guild manual, which outlines the requirements of a Hub Port.

"The Colemenoport administrative board has reviewed these documents, and, just prior to this meeting, voted to accept the master trader's proposal. We have no doubt that Colemenoport is able to meet the Trade Guild's requirements. I will so inform the master trader, when we are done here."

She paused, her eyes seeking Majel's.

"I would like the record to reflect the port's gratitude to Councilor ziaGorn, in his capacity as Trade Team Liaison, for facilitating this process."

"I move that the Port's acceptance of the Tree-and-Dragon Trade Mission's proposal to establish a Hub be entered into the record of our proceedings," said ivenAlyatta.

"Second," azieEm said.

"All in favor, please raise your hands."

tryaBent's hand was perhaps not the quickest raised, but, once again, the motion passed with neither abstention nor nay.

Chair gorminAstir bent her head briefly, then looked up.

"The Port's decision streamlines our agenda, Councilors. If it agrees with his schedule, the master trader may accompany the welcoming committee and our newest councilor from the docks directly to the Sakuriji, and make his presentation to this Council immediately. As I learned from our liaison when we spoke earlier today, there is a filing deadline imposed by the trade guild; therefore, it seems best to deal with the matter quickly. Does anyone find a flaw with this?"

tryaBent laughed. "Remember that we'll have representatives of the press with us. The master trader's proposal will take attention away from the induction of the Haosa Councilor," she said. "*I* think it's well-played."

"Well, then," said ivenAlyatta, "if Coracta is happy; I'm happy."

azieEm was also heard to laugh, very softly. The Council Chair inclined her head.

"Let it be done, then," she said. "Councilor ziaGorn, please advise the master trader of our proposed schedule."

"I will," Majel said.

"Have we other business?"

There was silence.

The silver bell sounded.

"This emergency meeting of the Council of the Civilized is declared closed. Councilors may depart."

Majel collapsed against the back of his chair, the weight of all the day's busyness descending at once, now that he'd reached the end.

But, no, he thought. He hadn't *quite* reached the end. He needed to speak with Blays.

Eat first, her voice murmured inside his ear. *Then pour yourself some of that liquor you favor, and call me—visual.*

Have you eaten? he asked, shaping each word carefully in thought.

Just sitting down now, she assured him, and he felt a mingling of care and amusement that made him shiver.

Until soon, she said, and he—somehow—felt that her attention was no longer on him.

Well.

He leaned to the comm, and asked the kitchen to send dinner up to his apartment.

Dutiful Passage
Colemeno Orbit

. . . .

"*EAT THIS*." SOMETHING WAS SHOVED INTO HER HAND, HER FIN-
gers closed, but she was so *cold*...

"Padi!" A hand gripped her free hand, hard enough to bruise.
Energy sparked and flared at her core, driving the cold away, and
snapping her eyes open.

Tekelia's face was ferocious, eyes wide.

"*Eat*."

"Yes," she said, and got the fruit-and-nut bar to her mouth.
She took a bite, chewed, and nodded. Tekelia was still holding
her other hand, she noted, but the flow of energy had stopped.

"What were you—no, that's for later. Finish that." Tekelia rose
and Padi heard them issuing instructions for Healer Mendoza's
tray to be delivered, immediately.

She finished the nut bar, ravenous now, and looked about her.
Tekelia returned to the bunk, and handed her a cookie iced in
blue. She ate it in one snap, and a second as well.

"I only brought a few of those," Tekelia said, returning and
handing her a cup. "Sweet tea. The tray should be here—"

The door chimed, and Tekelia was gone again. She drank the
tea in one long swallow, and sighed as Tekelia brought the tray
to the side of the bunk.

"Thank you," she said, taking the plate piled with cheese and
nuts that Tekelia put into her hand.

"Eat."

"Yes," she said, somewhat subdued, a sense of what had
happened—what could have happened—beginning to dawn. Suc-
cinctly, she was a blockhead.

"I didn't think I'd been away so long," she said, which was

merely a statement of fact, and not an excuse, because, really, there was no excuse.

"Where were you?" Tekelia asked, sitting on the end of the bunk and reaching for a muffin.

"Healspace," Padi said. "I needed to look more closely at what Father had done." She ate a piece of cheese—and another. "Then, I had a notion, and thought I'd try it out—" She looked over to the clock. "It was scarcely an hour," she said.

"I feel that I should remind you that it's not time which is the limiting factor, but effort," Tekelia said, very calmly. Too calmly, Padi thought, and leaned forward and put a hand against a warm brown cheek.

"It wasn't my intention to frighten you," she said softly. "I was inexcusably foolish. I didn't consider the risk. I should have waited for backup, or at least set an alarm."

Tekelia shivered and put a hand over hers.

"I came back and you were huddled in the middle of the bed, shivering. Your hands were *blue*—"

"I'm *sorry*," Padi said. "Truly, Tekelia; I didn't think—which we both know is my besetting sin."

Tekelia's laugh was strained. "I would have said that you think too much."

Padi finished the last nut, and reached for the glass Tekelia had put on the bedside shelf.

"I don't think that either of us would care for being a hungry ghost wandering the halls," Tekelia said.

"Certainly not! All that wailing, for one thing. So tiresome. No, I quite agree—it wouldn't answer."

She sighed and sat back, warm now, and only a little hungry.

"Would you like a muffin?" Tekelia asked.

"I suppose I might as well," Padi said. "In the interests of representing the least wraith-like front, going forward."

There followed a few minutes of silence as they each finished eating, and drank some more sweet tea.

"Now, tell me," Padi said. "How was your meeting with the master trader?"

"Surprising. Majel ziaGorn has arranged for a welcoming committee to be waiting for us when we arrive at Colemenoport."

Padi smiled. "How clever of him!"

"The master trader was inclined toward the same view," Tekelia said. "He then persuaded me to accept welcoming with the rest of our party, rather than 'porting off-Grid from inside the shuttle."

Padi blinked. "Well. I'm glad of that. Had I known that was your plan, I would have tried to do likewise. Not that I'm as persuasive as a master trader."

"No?" Tekelia smiled. "After, I had a kin-to-kin discussion with Shan, who wanted to know how he had taught me to distrust him."

"Oh, dear."

"We came out of it well enough, I think. I'd made two stupid errors in calculation, which he was kind enough to point out to me."

"Shan is quite lovely," Padi said. "I'm very fond of him."

Tekelia considered her from narrowed eyes. "It seems to me that you're fond of all the bits of him."

"Saving, perhaps, the thodelm. But even Shan can scarcely accommodate the thodelm, so at least I'm in pleasant company." She put her empty tea glass down and sighed.

"May I ask what you accomplished in Healspace?" Tekelia asked.

"I made you a gift, and placed it on our link," Padi said. "In theory, it should limit your ability to discorporate people."

Tekelia frowned at her.

"In theory."

"Well," Padi said airily, "it must remain so, mustn't it? Until we can find someone worthy of being a test subject?"

Tekelia sighed.

"That's the square I've been standing on since I came to the Haosa."

"Well, I could show it to you, and you can see if you think it will serve."

"This would require you to re-enter Healspace, with me?"

"Yes," Padi said.

"Let's put that off. The master trader told me that we'll be leaving for Colemeno in twelve hours."

"Yes, that came through on the daily advisory. Also, there is a reception—oh!" She glanced at the clock again.

"We wouldn't," Tekelia said, with only a little irony, "want to be late for the reception."

"Certainly not! Especially as it is, partly, at least, in our honor. Shall you have the 'fresher first or second?"

Wildege
Kelim Station

. . . .

IT WAS CLOSER TO RIBBON-RISE THAN MIDDAY WHEN KEL BROUGHT the wagon down in its place at the stead, and then just sat there, staring at the improbable.

With the Ribbons clearly visible overhead, Vyr was outside.

Not only was he outside, but he was *dancing*.

He was a graceful boy, and well worth watching, especially when he spun straight off the ground as if he were at a proper Ribbon Dance.

"You're home!" he called, alighting and walking toward her.

"I am at that, though I'd hoped to be sooner. I hope supper isn't ruined."

Vyr came to the side of the wagon and grinned up at her. "Not at all. The wind told me you'd drunk your share of cider and danced the Ribbons pale. I figured that meant you'd sleep in."

"Which I did," Kel admitted, "but I still wouldn't have been this late in the day if Amerdeen hadn't caught me with a three-way barter with a Visalee technician—well. It was an interesting offer, though I'm not convinced the girl—that's the tech, you understand—has any real idea of the distance involved."

"That sounds complicated," Vyr said, holding a hand up to her. "Help you down? I'll make supper and you'll tell me all the gossip."

"That," Kel said, taking his hand, and letting him help her to the ground, though she could float with the best of them, "sounds like the best bargain I've been offered in a week."

Kel was sitting at the table, cider to hand. Vyr was at the counter, assembling ingredients while the pan warmed.

"So, you'll be wanting to know what kept me so late."

"I thought you said that Amerdeen kept you." Vyr threw a glance over one shoulder. "Who's Amerdeen?"

"Administrator of Visalee Village. Turns out the communication satellites are coming back on-line, now that dust-cloud's moving out—" She cocked an eye at his back. "You know about that, do you?"

"The Redlands System has been engulfed in a traveling cloud of interstellar debris for approximately two hundred Standard Years," Vyr said, sounding like he was reading off a page. "The cloud interfered with navigation, signals, and other normal space-based actions."

"That's it," Kel said admiringly. "So the communication satellites are some of that space-based action that got interfered with, which is why we have the repeater system, which works fine, but not, I'm told, so fine as the satellite system."

"All right," Vyr said. "What's that got to do with you?"

"Well! Being as Visalee and the Wild are *neighbors*, Amerdeen thinks it would be kindly to outfit each station in the Wild with a satellite radio, so we can choose whether or not to get the newest news."

Vyr turned around, frowning. "I thought you chose that when you chose the Wild."

Kel drank off the last of her cider and thumped the mug on the table. "Spoken like a child of the forest!" she said.

"Are you taking the radio?"

"I didn't intend to, but Amerdeen can talk the bark off a tree, and I didn't want to spend another night away, so I said they can bring a radio, and they can set it up, but I'm not giving them my word I'll ever turn it on."

"That satisfied her?"

"It did."

The pan spat, and Vyr turned back to it.

"I'll hold the rest until you're through," Kel said. "Be a shame to ruin dinner."

Vyr laughed—laughed! "That's probably fair."

Kel got out of the chair and moved around the kitchen, setting the table, pouring them each a mugful, and watching Vyr as he worked.

His pattern was bright, lighter than she'd ever seen it. The hard borders that had confined him were—looser, and starting to look a little misty, like a proper pattern.

Well, there, she thought. *The boy must've finally made his peace with the Ribbons.* That couldn't be anything but good news. She sat down again, and folded her hands on the table.

"Here you go," Vyr said, turning from the stove with two plates in his hands. He put one in front of Kel. "Mushrooms on toast."

"That sounds good enough to eat," she said.

The meal was good, which Kel did remember to say. In fact, she might've said it twice.

"And I'm going to thank you for insisting I take that second basket," she told him. "I did need it. Come across Somi. His wagon'd thrown a spinner; had the Ribbons' own time doing the repair, and hungrier than a *grizurs*. He'd've eaten *me* if I hadn't had something else to offer."

Vyr was too busy with his own meal to do anything more than nod. It *was* good. Better than he'd expected. The only trouble, he thought, as he pushed his plate aside, was that he was still hungry.

Kel was almost done with her meal. Vyr got up and rummaged in the keep. He cut thick slices from the loaf, and some cheese off the block, then carried this additional snack to the table.

"Feeling a little peckish," he said to Kel's lifted eyebrows. "More cider?"

"What kind of question is that?"

He refilled the mugs and sat down, reaching for a piece of cheese. He couldn't remember when food had tasted so good. He couldn't remember when *he* had *felt* so good—full of energy, in touch—in touch with *everything.* The forest sang. He hadn't known that.

And he'd been *afraid* of this?

"So, I saved the best for last," Kel said, putting her plate to one side and reaching for a piece of cheese to put on a slice of bread.

Vyr looked at her. "Better than getting a radio?"

"Hard to believe, I know," she said, straight-faced. "But here's the news—Oracle of Civilization's retired."

That was news, Vyr thought, grabbing more bread and cheese. Oracles didn't retire every day. Still, the current—former—Oracle might be Kel's age, whatever that was.

"Is there a new one?" he asked.

"Well, that's an interesting thing," said Kel. "The answer being—no. Which didn't stop the old one from quitting the city, going to live with her cousins at Ribbon Dance Village, and refusing to foresee, anymore."

Now, that *was* unusual.

"The council allowed that?"

Kel grinned at him over the rim of her mug. "The story being told is *the council* didn't have a choice; the Deaf Councilor pushed it through."

"Did he?" The Deaf Councilor had been of particular interest to his former comrades, who had found him both an insult and an unlikely obstacle to certain business they had tried to move through the council. There had been some talk of attaching him, though how that would be made to work, Vyr had never understood.

"Not only that," Kel said, "she gave out with one final prophecy before she left, and it's a shocker."

Vyr shivered, feeling his Gift flicker and take fire. Stretching away into the future, he Saw the thick fabric of the Grid, sullen, red, and stifling.

"Vyr?" Kel sounded worried.

He took a hard breath and met her eyes.

"What was the prophecy?" he asked, his voice sounding strained in his own ears, while the weight of the Grid settled on his shoulders, crushing him into dust, and the forest—the forest was screaming.

"The Oracle says she's Seen the end of both Civilization and the Haosa," Kel said, no longer amused. "The question being discussed at the Market was whether the Seeing was True."

She paused, head tipped. Vyr said nothing, trying to see her through the sullen light.

"Market was of the opinion that the Oracle had laid one fine Haosa joke on the Council-folk before she went home at last," Kel said, and put her mug down.

"Vyr?"

"The Market's wrong," he said, his voice tighter still, like somebody had a hand around his throat. He reached for his mug and swallowed cider.

"The Market's wrong," he said again, stronger. "It's a True Seeing."

He took another swallow of cider, and met Kel's rainbow eyes.

"They're going to kill everyone."

Off-Grid
The Tree House

. . . .

BLAYS HAD EATEN THE SAVORY STEW AND WARM ROLLS STUFFED
with cheese that Vayeen brought her from the community meal,
then took a quick shower, and pulled on a long soft robe. She
poured herself a glass of wine, and curled into a corner of the
sofa in Tekelia's great room with a sigh.

She'd scarcely settled herself when the comm chimed. Smiling,
she Lifted a stylus off the table and used it to tap the "receive"
button.

The screen lit, and there was he was. It really was quite
foolish, how her heart rose to see him—and not in his business
clothes, but wearing a soft sweater, his copper curls disordered
and damp, as if he'd just had a shower, himself.

"Majel," she said, feeling as if she was smiling with her whole
body. "It's good to see you."

"It's good to see you," he answered, his smile wide, and his
eyes sparkling. "How was your day?"

"Busier than I had expected—I had no idea Tekelia did so
many things, though, of course, half the things *I'm* doing have
to do with Tekelia being *gone*—including calling the spaceship
and talking to Tekelia."

"Did that go well?"

"As well as it could, I suppose. Tekelia's horrified to learn
about the high-risk rooms, as anyone would be—and particularly
asked if you'd suffered any harm from the guards."

"Only by being dismissed as if I had less understanding than
a child, and by being powerless to help you when you were held
against your will," Majel said warmly. Blays Felt the effort he made
to cool that flicker of temper. He raised his glass, and sipped.

"What else did Tekelia say?"

"That we were right to tell the cousins to avoid the port, and everywhere under-Grid. I can't say how much pleasure the news of the Council seat—the *full* Council seat—caused, though Tekelia did seem resigned to sitting in it. I got the sense that at least it's settled, and *that* was a relief."

She paused to sip wine.

"Tekelia and Padi yos'Galan have signed a contract that makes them kin in the eyes of her clan, which sounds very odd to me, but Tekelia seems to consider it well done. We spoke of some village matters, and it was time to end the call."

She took another sip of wine and and tipped the glass toward him. "Your turn. How was your day?"

"I was able to form a committee to welcome the master trader and his party, which will include Tekelia, when they arrive at Colemenoport. We'll have the portmaster, Warden, Council Chair; myself, as Liaison; and you, as Speaker pro tem, as well as a reporting team from the *Tattler*. Portmaster krogerSlyte stated particularly that she guarantees safe passage for Speaker and Speaker pro tem. However, if you would prefer to stand aside—"

"Oh, no! That would spoil the look!" Blays protested. "And you know, if things go badly—though I'm sure the portmaster's word is good!—Tekelia can 'port all three of us out."

Majel laughed softly.

"Tekelia may 'port you out. As liaison to the trade mission, I'll need to stay."

"If it comes to that," Blays said, with a sigh, "Tekelia will need to stay, too. It wouldn't do for a new-made Councilor to run away." She raised her glass in salute. "Which means I'll need to stay, with no way out but up."

Majel tipped his head. "I'd like to see you fly."

He said it as if her Gift were something special—something *admirable*. Blays felt her cheeks heat.

"I don't fly, really—I'm just a Lifter. But I'll be happy to show you. I could even Lift you with me, if you'd like it."

"I'd like it very much," he said, and Blays hardly knew where to look.

After a moment, Majel stirred.

"After I made sure of the welcoming committee, I called a special meeting of the Council, which ended just an hour ago.

Not only does the law forbidding Haosa the port not mention
the city, but the city charter specifically states that it's to be a
safe haven for all planetary citizens."

He smiled. "Tekelia should be quite safe in the city, and in
the Council chambers. And you, as well."

Blays blinked.

"But I won't have to go to the Council, will I? Tekelia's to
sit in the chair."

"I've gotten ahead," Majel said, wryly. "The welcoming committee plans to meet the master trader's party at the dock. After
the official welcome, the entire party will depart for the Sakuriji.
Tekelia will be seated, and the master trader will give his presentation to the Council. I thought—"

He paused, and Blays noted with interest that color had risen
in his cheeks.

"I'd *hoped* that you might wish to stand witness to the seating of the first Haosa Councilor, in your capacity as Counsel to
Chaos. Also, the master trader's proposal will be historic, and of
possible interest to your cousins. After—"

He took a breath.

"I *hoped* that you might come with me here—to my casino.
You might meet Seylin, we could have dinner, and . . ."

His voice faded off, and he reached for his glass.

Blays took a careful breath.

"Yes," she said. "I'd like that. I really ought to meet your
Seylin. She was annoyed with me, I think."

He laughed slightly. "She was concerned, which manifests as
annoyance. And she was startled that our bond had formed so
quickly."

"She's not alone," Blays said. "I do need to meet her—she
means so much to you, and you to her. So, yes. I'll be pleased
to go home with you after the business of the day is done. Do
we know what day, and when?"

"The master trader intends to dock mid-morning of the day
after tomorrow."

"All right. If I catch the mid-night truck out of Peck's Market,
I ought to be in plenty of time." She frowned. "Actually, I'll be
hours early. Where do you suggest I wait?"

"The Wardian," Majel said promptly. "But I propose an alternate to the mid-night truck."

"Vayeen can't bring both of us that far, even with a rest," Blays said—and stopped as Majel raised his hand.

"Let me send my car to pick you up at Peck's Market or at Pacazahno Village. You can leave at a reasonable hour, travel in comfort, with snacks available, and a comm-link, if you want to work. And, you'll be driven directly to the Wardian, instead of having to take a train in from the warehouse district."

Blays looked at him with something like awe.

"That does sound a deal more comfortable."

"May I take that for 'yes'?"

"Yes! Thank you, Majel."

"It's no trouble, and I'm pleased to be able to make this easier for you." He paused, raised his glass, and put it down.

"A man came by my office some weeks ago to talk about a bus route between Pacazahno Village and Haven City Center," he said slowly. "I was on my way to a meeting, and asked him to call again—but he hasn't come back."

"Did he leave a card?" Blays asked.

"Not with me; I was in a rush. I'll ask Bevin—my aide. In the meantime, I'll call the village administrator, to see if there's any interest. Would such a route benefit Ribbon Dance Village?"

Blays turned one hand palm up. "I don't know, but I'll ask Arbour and tell you what she says. Speaking of cards, though! Marlin kelbiMyst—do you know her? She works at the Wardian, in the Department of Accountability and Justice."

"I know of her."

"I met her when Tekelia's cousin gave me a tour of the Wardian," Blays said. "I like her very much. She said that 'Counsel to Chaos' deserved a card, and that she'd have one made for me. The proof arrived this evening. I'll have to show Tekelia—" She frowned suddenly. "I suppose Tekelia will have to have a card?"

"A council card will be provided," Majel said. "Whether another card for Tekelia's office as Speaker for the Haosa is needed—"

"Do you have another card? As the chair of the citizen's coalition?"

"Yes, I do."

"So Tekelia will need a card as Speaker for the Haosa."

"Will you leave out Howe and Firgus?" Majel asked, amusement flickering along their link. Blays sat for a moment, struck. He was *playing*. How very—Haosa-like.

"Never!" she asserted, matching him in play. "Here, quickly, look, then we'll say our good-nights, love."

She extended a hand; the card came to her from its place on the table, flashing a little in the light. She held it up to the screen so that Majel could see.

"Is that meant to be the Ribbons?" he asked, and this time Blays *did* laugh.

"You got that quicker than I did, and I see them every night! It's a good idea, I think." She put the card down, and leaned slightly forward.

"You've had a long day. I can Feel how tired you are," she said softly. "Please sleep well, Majel ziaGorn. I love you."

"I love you, Blays essWorthi," he said, and she shivered with the truth of it even as she Lifted the stylus to tap the comm off.

Wildege
Kelim Station

. . . .

THE SCREAMING WOKE HIM, TEARING AT HIS MIND, AND HIS GIFT was on fire. He rushed outside, gasping, thinking the pond—the pond! The peaceful water closing over his head, the screaming silenced, and the fear.

But he was barely two steps out the door when he was pierced by light, nailed to the ground while he Saw—he Saw! People falling where they stood, the glory of their Gifts extinguished, patterns crisped to ash.

He Saw children reaching for the Ribbons—the Ribbons that were fading, imprisoned by the ropy, pink malevolence of the Grid.

He Saw medics rushing down the streets of Haven City falling to their knees, while their teammates ran on to assist afflicted civilians, until they, too, fell.

He Saw a tidy village square faced by brightly colored cottages, and the bodies of dozens in the shade of the guardian tree. He Saw a child—a child holding a norbear, standing among the fallen, her face turned toward the sky.

This is your future, a voice whispered inside his ear. *This is what your cowardice will bring. You*—You *can stop it.*

No, that was ridiculous, Vyr thought from the small dark corner of his mind where he stood, observing the death of a planet. He couldn't stop this. They were going to finish the work. He'd protested—hadn't he? And they had savaged him, bound him, threw him out at the end of the world, where the fall or the ambient would surely kill him.

But you didn't die, the voice said. *You can—you must!—stop them.*

The vision rolled before him—three figures on a rooftop, lights dancing below them, and above, a terrible weaving of dark energies, laced into the Grid, making it not a grid, but a shield, solid, and unyielding.

People would die—Civilization would fall. And yes, he *could* stop it. He knew their names. Their real names.

From the dancing Ribbons above, from the trees all around him, he felt the rise of—not fear. Perhaps it was courage.

Perhaps it was madness.

Vyr ran across the clearing, and threw himself into Kel's wagon.

On-Grid
Haven City School of
Technology and Mechanics

. . . .

"MASTER XINERDIN, THANK YOU FOR AGREEING TO SEE ME SO quickly," Marlin said, bowing in greeting and respect.

"How could I refuse, when you're kind enough to come to me?" he returned with an answering bow from his chair. "Please *Qe'andra*, sit and be comfortable. Would you care for refreshment? I can have my 'prentice fetch whatever you—"

"Thank you, no; I'm not in need. Nor do I wish to take up too much of your time," Marlin said. "Only, I'm hoping that you will be able to tell me to whom I might most profitably put a question regarding Grid mechanics."

"I will do whatever is in my power," the old man assured her. "But I must tell you that Grid specialists are not very numerous. cadBirn was our brightest, and very often our best. It was certainly our loss when he left. We have no one near his level of attainment, nor audacity of thought, if I'm honest." He smiled. "Mechanics tend toward a utilitarian view, and a conservative approach."

"Why did he leave, sir?" Marlin asked, wide-eyed.

"Well, that's a bitter tale, for I have to admit to you that I don't know." Master xinErdin sighed. "We had our falling outs, he and I—" He smiled briefly. "That will happen when audacity and conservatism meet over a project. As well as when youth and old age meet. I must say that he did produce some . . . outlandish notions, that even our younger members were hard put to accommodate. Brilliant people often have unorthodox notions, so I've noticed. It falls to the less-brilliant to moderate such ideas, even as they're taking fire from new possibilities. In a perfect world, boldness and conservatism ought to balance each other, so that all may equally benefit from progress." He sighed. "We do not live in a perfect world. I've noticed that, as well.

"As to cadBirn—I could have seen him going to a start-up firm—or founding a new school. He *was* a member of a thinker's salon, and I'll confess to you, *Qe'andra* kelbiMyst, that I had hoped that the friction of audacity against audacity would smooth his edges a bit and make him a *little* more patient with the slow and the sure."

He sighed.

"Instead, he—left. Cleaned out his office and simply left. Had I known that he had come to such a point, I would have talked with him, to find what accommodations we might have made— for he *was* brilliant, *Qe'andra*, and a credit to this institution. We valued him. *I* valued him, personally, and professionally. Despite our frequent differences, I thought that we respected one another. But—"

He threw up his hands. "Well. Young people."

"Does no one know where Specialist cadBirn has gone?" Marlin asked. "His family? His apprentice?"

"He had no family that I'm aware of. He had students, naturally, but no apprentice. There was this group he was involved in—the Exalted Philosophers Club—I tried to contact them, to see if they would perhaps pass a message. I left word, but no one has ever called me back. And, to be honest, I took that as my final answer. cadBirn does not wish to have anything more to do with us."

"Has he been gone a long time?" Marlin asked softly.

"Very nearly a year," said Master xinErdin.

Marlin said nothing; after a moment the master shook himself.

"What in particular did you wish to know about Grid mechanics?" he asked.

"I was wondering if there was a mechanism that might . . . block the Grid, or make it—inaccessible."

Master xinErdin stared at her, and gave a rueful laugh.

"Now, do you see—that is *precisely* the sort of question cadBirn asked. Vulnerabilities in the existing structure, techniques for increasing or decreasing coverage. The Grid is stable, and to be truthful, no one really knows how the ancestors produced such a working. The records say that the makers 'collaborated' with the ambient, but surely that's mere—poetry. Even the Haosa don't believe that the Grid is...sentient. It's a tool. The greatest tool of Civilization. But it exists precisely to control the flow of the ambient."

He took a hard breath.

"I'll tell you, *Qe'andra* kelbiMyst—I've told this to no one else, but an old man has his regrets, not to say his fancies. It's been in my mind for some time that cadBirn fell afoul of his own audacity. That he attempted to interface with the Grid, and, well—and it went badly for him. Is that foolish?"

"It's never foolish to worry about those we care about," Marlin said. She leaned forward and patted the old man's hand.

"Could I trouble you for the contact information for the Exalted Philosophers Club? Perhaps they'll answer *my* call."

The old man's face lit. "Certainly, certainly! Here—"

He reached to his notebook.

"And you will tell me, won't you? Whatever you find out?"

"Yes," Marlin promised. "I will."

On-Grid
Ganelets on the Quiet

. . . .

"WELL. TECHNICIAN DIMALEE." IMBYVALT PAUSED JUST INSIDE the doorway. "How good of you to join us."

dimaLee turned from the bar, glass in hand—not, if balWerz were any judge, his first, or even his third brandy. His face was flushed and there was fire in his eye. "*I* was working for the Preferred Outcome," he stated, his enunciation very precise.

"As do we all, every day," imbyValt said, moving toward the bar. balWerz went to his usual chair, nodding to ramKushin, who was in hers, drink on the table at her side.

At the bar, imbyValt poured wine, turning slightly as the door opened again, admitting trolBoi and kirshLightir.

"Gentles, welcome!" dimaLee called. "We're all present, at last. Therefore, I will put the question—have you all heard of the fiasco that took place at the Colemenoport Guard House two days ago?"

trolBoi tipped his head, standing with a hand on the back of ramKushin's chair. "I heard that security arrested a Haosa, then lost her."

dimaLee turned to him, sneering.

"If that's what you heard, you need to pay your informant more—or attach someone with more wits."

trolBoi's eyebrows lifted, but he said nothing as he moved on to the bar.

"I," said kirshLightir, "heard that the Warden has closed the security rooms at Colemenoport Central, and set Forensics to doing an analysis."

dimaLee's smile, balWerz thought, was more vicious than his sneer.

"Your informant is cut from better cloth," he said, as one making a concession. "But you still don't have all of it."

"Since you apparently believe that you are in possession of all the facts," said imbyValt, leaning one hip against the bar and raising her glass slightly, "why don't you share them, so that everyone is equally informed."

dimaLee turned toward her and produced a bow that managed to be both insolent and, marginally, respectful.

"Madame Cell Leader," he murmured.

He walked a few steps forward, taking charge of the center of the room. balWerz entertained a moment's regret, that he had not provided himself with a drink before sitting down, and settled more deeply into his chair.

"Briefly—two days ago, in the afternoon, a Haosa woman and a Deaf man arrived on the port via the train from the Sakuriji. Security Officer nimOlad, whom I trained myself, arrested the Haosa, in accordance with the law. The Deaf man insisted on accompanying the woman to the station, and this was allowed.

"The Haosa was brought to the high security entrance, and cleared for Room Three, which was awaiting just such a field test. The Haosa's incarceration in this chamber should have provided much valuable information for the tuning of more chambers.

"Unfortunately, the Deaf companion chose to call the Warden of Civilization before the Haosa was properly incarcerated." dimaLee inclined his head to kirshLightir. "The Warden set Forensics to study *all* the security rooms at the central station. A Healer was called to Officer nimOlad, and also eventually to the sergeant on-desk at the security wing."

dimaLee paused to throw brandy down his throat, and glared around the room.

"The upshot of this being that we have lost two operatives, an upgraded holding room, and brought suspicion on the holding rooms at all security stations—including those in Haven City— which are being inspected at this moment by the contractor of record, who is an ass, but well-trusted at the higher levels."

"I heard," trolBoi said, "that the Deaf person was none other than Councilor ziaGorn."

dimaLee turned to regard him with interest.

"That," he said, "is *very* good."

trolBoi inclined his head and sipped brandy.

"balWerz had an especial interest in the Deaf Councilor," imbyValt said. "Sadly, it appears he's now quite useless."

"Useless!" exclaimed dimaLee. "Far from useless, Madame, I protest! The Deaf Councilor has the Warden's ear, *and* he has a Haosa connection. He will be an asset in our work, given proper guidance."

He turned to balWerz. "Have you succeeded in attaching him, Natin?"

"Not as yet. I made an attempt, but he was rushing to a meeting, and I didn't wish to disrupt his usual behavior. I'd thought to try again, later."

"You must try again immediately!" dimaLee cried. "We will need his cooperation for the next phase!"

"The *next* phase?" imbyValt asked gently.

dimaLee spun toward her. "Yes! *You* see it, don't you, Madame? The most recent census of Gifts lays the whole tale out for anyone of vision to read. Our approach has been too gentle, too gradual; the poison continues to work its harm. We must grasp the nettle, and make the decision to place the good of the many over the lives of the few. Also!"

He looked around the room.

"Also, I have it from no more clandestine an informant than the newswire, that the Haosa have been given full membership in the Council of the Civilized."

"That's correct," imbyValt said, looking at dimaLee with a certain thoughtfulness. "I had particularly wished to address that point this evening."

"That is because you are a woman of vision!" dimaLee assured her.

"I think of myself as a pragmatist," imbyValt said, and stepped forward. dimaLee hurriedly stepped back to allow her the center of the room.

"We have been given an opportunity, my friends." imbyValt looked at each of them in turn. "How popular do you think this Haosa seat is going to be? Couple it with the Oracle's Seeing—that Civilization and the Haosa will end. We have in our hands, as Technician dimaLee has said, the means to preserve Civilization. If the Haosa should fall in the doing of it—"

She moved her shoulders in an elegant shrug. "We have no loyalty to the Haosa, and surely they would reverse the outcome, if they could."

There was silence in the room. balWerz cleared his throat.

"I'll call on the Deaf Councilor again tomorrow," he said.

"If I may give advice," dimaLee said, turning toward him. "Be forceful. Make the tie strong. He is far too important a piece to throw away."

Dutiful Passage
Colemeno Orbit

. . . .

PADI WAS TO PILOT THE SHUTTLE, THE MASTER TRADER SITTING as her second, which meant that she had gone on ahead, in order to do her "board checks."

Tekelia breakfasted alone, did a final sweep of the cabin, and, it still being somewhat ahead of departure time, went to the library.

A person who was not Lina Faaldom was at the counter. He looked up with a smile. "Service?"

"I'd like a word with the norbears," Tekelia said.

"They're popular this shift. I'll make a note to give them extra greens. You know the way?"

"I do, thank you." Tekelia moved off, wondering who else had felt a need to visit the norbears.

The answer, at least in part, was revealed to be Dil Nem Tiazan, who was leaning casually against the wall, eyes closed, face soft, pattern echoing a fondness that, in Tekelia's experience, Dil Nem very rarely allowed himself. Delm Briat was cuddled and purring in the crook of his arm.

Loath to disturb this moment of peace, Tekelia hesitated until a norbear welcome tickled inside their head. Stepping over to the enclosure, Tekelia looked down at Tiny and Master Frodo.

"I'm away in a few minutes. I have your messages for Lady Selph and for Eet. Is there anything you'd like to add?"

A moment of confusion followed this, as the norbears produced simultaneous images.

Tekelia laughed softly and extended both hands.

"Gently! I hear that Lady Selph is missed, and the cuddle will welcome her gladly when she returns."

This was met with agreement. Master Frodo, then Tiny, were pleased to have met Tekelia; Master Frodo added a recommendation that Tekelia wanted to be bolder, but not foolhardy.

Tekelia laughed again. "My life in one observation!"

"Are they giving advice again?" Dil Nem asked.

Tekelia stepped aside, to allow him to return Delm Briat to the enclosure.

There was another flurry of farewells before the norbears bumbled off toward the fountain.

"I expect I gave them something to dream on," Dil Nem said quietly. "You're bound for the shuttle?"

"Yes," Tekelia said. "Will you walk with me?"

Dil Nem smiled. "Afraid you'll get lost?"

"What if I only wanted the pleasure of your company?"

Dil Nem laughed softly, his pattern still soft, and raised a hand as they passed the library counter.

"Percy—be well."

"And you! Come back to us soon."

"Are you leaving the ship?" Tekelia asked.

Dil Nem raised an eyebrow. "I thought Padi would have told you. I'm on-contract with Colemenoport Yard until the upgrades are finished."

"She might have thought you'd like to deliver your own news," Tekelia said.

"That's not much like her," Dil Nem said, dryly. "If you still want that facilities tour, only tell me when."

Tekelia sighed. "Unfortunately, the port's closed to me."

Dil Nem shot Tekelia a sharp glance. "This is new?"

"Yes and no. The law has long stated that Haosa may not come onto the port, though it was...largely ignored. Port security has just decided to enforce it."

Dil Nem was silent for a few steps, then gave a decisive nod. "I was wondering about that welcoming committee. Not that the master trader doesn't deserve as many welcomes as can be carried in a pail."

"He said something like that," Tekelia agreed, and Dil Nem laughed.

"I wager he did."

✻ ✻ ✻

This shuttle being larger than the craft they had ascended in, the passengers were seated in a cabin separate from the pilots. Tekelia sat next to Dil Nem, Mr. dea'Gauss opposite.

"So, tell me about this law," Dil Nem said.

Tekelia raised an eyebrow. "You're not Haosa."

"If you say so. But we'll be hiring at the Yard. If the best fabricator on-planet *is* Haosa—"

"It's not likely, but I take your point. Well, then, the law. The law forbids Haosa to be on-port. The reason given for making the law was to safeguard the crews of ships from the harm they might take from interfacing with Wild Talents."

It was here that Mr. dea'Gauss entered the conversation. "One wonders if there were not already laws forbidding malicious acts committed on the port."

Tekelia smiled. "There were, yes, sir."

"Are those laws still in force?"

"Yes, sir."

"So this law regarding the Haosa is redundant and exists only to specifically deny the port to one set of persons?"

"Yes, sir."

"That is very interesting," said Mr. dea'Gauss.

"I would have said disquieting," Dil Nem said, and turned in his seat to study Tekelia with such exaggerated care that it must have been meant to be comical.

Tekelia waited.

"We have some knowledge of each other," Dil Nem said finally. "At the risk of giving insult, I have to say that you don't strike me as particularly savage."

"I'm savage enough at need," Tekelia said gently.

Dil Nem waved a hand. "As are we all. Only, I wonder what harm these naive and fragile crews might take from you, as you walk on the port."

Tekelia sighed.

"As you noticed, I've been well-brought-up. I'm in control of my Gifts, and, absent provocation, not at all violent. In this, I'm typical of my cousins. We're largely a peaceable lot. However..."

Tekelia hesitated, and glanced between Dil Nem and Mr. dea'Gauss.

"This might become convoluted."

"I," Mr. dea'Gauss said, with a small smile, "have nowhere to be until the shuttle docks."

"Nor do I," said Dil Nem. "Also, I need to understand this."

Tekelia took a deep breath. "The first thing you need understand, then, is that Haosa and Civilized differ at core. Civilized persons have very strict boundaries. They access their Gifts through a process known as tool-building. Colemeno's ambient conditions interfere with that process, therefore most Civilized live under-Grid, where the ambient is filtered."

"While Haosa run mad through the forests," Dil Nem murmured after a moment.

"There are some who'd have it so," Tekelia answered. "Haosa have an affinity for the conditions the Grid exists to mitigate. We interact with the ambient without needing to build tools. As a result of this very different relationship with Colemeno's environment, our boundaries are...fluid. Which Civilized people find—disturbing."

"After all," Mr. dea'Gauss murmured, "boundaries mean safety."

"Yes! Haosa have a personal rapport with the ambient. Our Civilized cousins believe that this means our every thought creates an action." Tekelia turned to Dil Nem. "And that's the basis for the law. After all, I might think that it would suit me very well for you to hand over your money; the ambient would immediately act on that thought, and you would give me your purse."

"I take it that this is an oversimplification?"

"It's completely inaccurate," Tekelia said, rather sharply.

"Might this...influence be exerted without either party being aware?" Mr. dea'Gauss asked.

Tekelia took a breath.

"No, sir. Influence is a Civilized Gift. It requires the building of a conduit between Influencer and Influenced. It *can't* be done by accident, and it's limited. A strong and motivated Influencer *may* be able to maintain a working conduit with three, or even four, individuals, but the risk and the effort don't make that sort of thing attractive. Not to mention that it's hard to hold for very long."

"Convincing a series of crewmen they want to give you the money in their pocket could still be a very good living," Dil Nem said, and Tekelia looked at him in approval.

"That it would be, but the effort is still considerable, and the danger of discovery non-trivial."

"Is there a comparable Gift in which Haosa rejoice?" Mr. dea'Gauss asked.

"Roughly. It's called Persuasion, and it's especially useful in crowd control. A Persuader can make everyone in a crowded room leave. It's a broad Talent, but it's not... deep. To make everyone in that same room give their money to the Persuader—it's too specific; the suggestion would shatter under its own weight."

"You said the law had been ignored," Dil Nem said. "Why did security begin to enforce it?"

"Briefly, when the law went into effect every business on-port found themselves short-handed, as their Haosa employees withdrew." Tekelia lifted a shoulder; let it fall. "Haosa rarely take employment in Haven City, because the Grid annoys. The port's still under-Grid, but the air is—lighter, let's say. The framers of the law hadn't taken into account that there would be so *many* Haosa employed on the port, and so few Civilized who cared to work where they might encounter those same vulnerable crews the new law was meant to protect."

Dil Nem outright laughed.

Tekelia grinned.

"Yes, exactly. Invitation Right was born of the need to staff vital port businesses. It stated that a Haosa invited by a Civilized person could be on the port. Security agreed to the exception, with the condition that they were allowed to make spot-checks. People returned to their jobs, and that's where matters stood until yesterday, when one of my cousins was arrested for being a Haosa on-port, though she was there with the citizen who had invited her to go with him to lunch. Her friend asserted several times that he had invited her, and the security officer ignored him." Tekelia shrugged again.

"I don't know why they decided to enforce the law now. I'm told that the Warden is trying to find the answer to that."

"This vessel," Mr. dea'Gauss murmured, "will very shortly be docking at Colemenoport."

"Yes, sir," Tekelia said.

"One had heard," Mr. dea'Gauss pursued, "that there was to be a welcoming committee."

"The portmaster has guaranteed safe passage for the trade mission and its guests," Tekelia said.

"Ah." Mr. dea'Gauss smiled slightly. "Is this the master trader at work?"

"I believe the trade mission's liaison is responsible."

"Is it so?" Mr. dea'Gauss murmured. "I will be pleased to meet this enterprising person."

"Attention, all passengers! This is Co-pilot Shan yos'Galan. The pilot has asked me to inform you that we will be making dock in twelve minutes. Please do strap in. The pilots will join you in the passenger compartment once the ship is locked down, and we will exit together."

Colemenoport

· · · · · · · · · · · · · · ·

BLAYS HAD SPENT AN ENJOYABLE FEW HOURS IN THE WARDIAN'S Reading Room before Tekelia's cousin came to fetch her to the omnibus.

Their first stop was the Sakuriji, to collect Majel and a woman Blays recognized as Council Chair gorminAstir.

"Council Chair, allow me to present Blays essWorthi, Speaker for the Haosa Pro Tem," Tekelia's cousin Bentamin said as the bus pulled out into traffic. "Speaker essWorthi, here is Zeni gorminAstir, Chair of the Council of the Civilized."

"I'm very glad to meet you, Chair gorminAstir," Blays said politely.

"Speaker essWorthi, an honor."

The Warden made an offer of refreshment, and served out little bottles of tea and small round cakes.

"Councilor ziaGorn," Zeni gorminAstir said. "Will you please review our schedule?"

"Yes, ma'am," Majel said, putting his tea bottle aside.

"We're proceeding to the port administration building, where Portmaster krogerSlyte will join us. A car bearing the reporting team, and security guards, will follow. Once at the dock, we will disembark, and send word to the trade team that we are in place. I will make introductions. Portmaster krogerSlyte will speak briefly on behalf of the port, followed by Chair gorminAstir, for Civilization. Speaker Pro Tem essWorthi will speak a few words, and return her charge to Speaker vesterGranz.

"The reporting team will be recording the event, and will wish to ask questions. I've asked them to honor a limit of three at the dock.

"When the greetings are complete, the master trader, his team, Speaker vesterGranz, and the welcoming committee will board the bus, returning to the Sakuriji in time for today's Council meeting."

"Why," Blays said, when Majel had stopped speaking, "will there be security guards?" She thought she sounded calm, though of course Majel felt her panic, and turned worried eyes toward her.

But it was Zeni gorminAstir who leaned forward and placed her hand over Blays's, where it was fisted on her knee.

"I understand that you had a harrowing experience with port security just recently," she said, and Blays felt warmth and calmness waft gently from her. "The officers we will have with us today understand that they are providing security for a diplomatic mission. The Portmaster and the Council take full responsibility, and I personally guarantee that you will not be threatened in any way."

Blays took a hard breath.

"There's precedent," Tekelia's cousin said. "This security pair have been carefully screened, and they do know the mission. If they should forget, you will be surrounded by allies."

Blays took a breath, and *stepped aside*, to center herself. She was the representative of the Haosa—at least until Tekelia was back. It was up to her to demonstrate to these Civilized people that Haosa were neither childish nor craven; that they could not only govern themselves, but were fit to govern others.

Yes, she Felt more than heard Majel's approval, and warmed to the core.

"Thank you," she said. "Of course, the master trader and his team should be treated with diplomacy."

Tekelia's cousin smiled and inclined his head.

"Allow me to apologize. The requirement that security be present came from my office, and I should have informed you immediately."

Blays gave him a smile.

"No harm done," she said, kindly, "and now I do know."

"I appreciate your understanding," he assured her gravely, though Blays Saw amusement ripple through his pattern. More like Tekelia than he cared to let on, she thought, and had a sip of tea.

· · · ⁙ · · ·

"We are currently awaiting word that the welcoming committee is in place," the master trader was saying. "As soon as we have that, we will disembark. As our intent is to be both awe-inspiring and dignified, I suggest that we proceed in the following manner.

"I will lead our little parade, Trader yos'Galan and Speaker vesterGranz will follow, shoulder-to-shoulder, then Mr. dea'Gauss, and our rear guard, Ser Tiazan. Does anyone find fault with this order of precedence?"

No one said anything.

The master trader inclined his head.

"There will of course be speeches. I will do my best to keep them under control. Liaison ziaGorn, who has been nothing short of masterly in producing these arrangements, allows me to know that, directly greetings are done, the master trader and Speaker vesterGranz will be invited onto a secure vehicle which will bring us, with the rest of the welcoming committee, to the Sakuriji. Once there, Speaker vesterGranz will be inducted, and the master trader will present his proposal for making Colemeno a trade hub."

He paused, gazing upon them benevolently. "Since I did not care to leave Mr. dea'Gauss and Cousin Dil Nem to fend for themselves on the dock, I asked the trade team to send a car. You, gentles, will be met by Trader ven'Deelin, and taken to the temporary Tree-and-Dragon residence."

Another gaze around. "Does anyone find fault with these arrangements?"

"It's going to be a rather busy day by the end of it," Padi commented.

The master trader beamed at her. "Indeed. I suspect we will savor our wine this evening, Trader Padi. What do you say?"

"I say you are likely correct, Master Trader," she replied gravely.

Something buzzed, short and sharp. The master trader took a comm from his pocket, and said, "This is Shan yos'Galan."

He listened briefly, and smiled.

"Yes, we are assembled and will come out now to meet you."

He flipped the comm closed, transferring the smile to them. "We are called! Please, take your places, and follow me."

• • • ❈ • • •

They had exited the bus, and arranged themselves in an arc somewhat back from the end of the ramp, the security guards standing one on each end. Majel stood six steps forward of the arc, the journalists four paces to his left and two paces behind. Blays was in the arc, between Chair gorminAstir and Tekelia's cousin, the Warden.

The ship, up at the other end of the ramp, was an odd thing, ovoid, with neither window nor door. Blays had somehow thought the shuttle would be shiny and clean. Rather, it was pitted and dirty. But, Blays thought, there was dust in Colemeno's space, though not as much as there had been. If the shuttle had come down through that—

Something hissed, startling Blays out of her thoughts. She looked up as a section of the skin slid back, creating a doorway through which a slim, elegant person emerged, and came down the ramp toward them.

Following him was Padi, and at her side, Tekelia; following them an elder, moving with deliberate dignity, and behind him a wiry man with greying red hair. All except Tekelia, who was wearing City clothes, were dressed alike, in dark green trousers and jackets displaying the Tree-and-Dragon symbol in gold.

The hissing came again; Blays looked past the people on the ramp, in time to see the door close, leaving the ship's skin smooth once more.

The elegant white-haired man had reached the end of the ramp. Majel stepped forward and bowed.

"Master Trader yos'Galan," he said in a clear, carrying voice. "It's a pleasure to see you again, sir."

"Councilor ziaGorn!" The master trader also bowed, straightening with a smile. "You must allow me to likewise be pleased to see you, and in such festive circumstances."

He turned slightly, moving his hand to indicate those who had stopped behind him.

"You are of course acquainted with Trader yos'Galan and Speaker vesterGranz. May I have the considerable pleasure of introducing to you *Qe'andra* dea'Gauss, newly arrived from Liad? I also bring to your attention Dil Nem Tiazan, who will be assisting in the refitting of Colemeno Yard."

Majel bowed again, though not as deeply as he had to the master trader.

"*Qe'andra* dea'Gauss, allow me to be the first to welcome you to Colemeno. Luzant Tiazan—I look forward to learning more about the refitting of the shipyard."

That was well-said, Blays thought, though Dil Nem Tiazan wasn't Civilized; he was Deaf. Of course, Majel wouldn't have been able to See that.

The two had barely straightened from their bows when a car pulled up behind their arc. Blays went rigid.

"Ah, perfectly on time!" The master trader turned a beaming

smile directly on her. "Trader ven'Deelin is here at my request. After we have been welcomed, she will take *Qe'andra* dea'Gauss and Surda Tiazan to the trade mission's residence, so that they may recover from their exertions, while the rest of us labor on."

Blays smiled at him as she would a cousin; certainly, he *sounded* like a cousin, talking casual nonsense, easy and at one with the ambient, though his pattern was everything that was Civilized.

"Thank you, sir," she said, willing tense muscles to relax.

"Not at all. I should perhaps have shared my arrangements before we came to this point. Indeed, I am persuaded that I have made an error. Allow me to attempt a recover." He turned slightly, and bowed.

"Portmaster krogerSlyte. I trust I find you well?"

"Master Trader, you find me more well than I have been for many a year." She stepped forward, bowing in her turn. "On behalf of Colemenoport, allow me to welcome you back. I must tell you that the port administrative board has reviewed your information, your plans, and the pertinent requirements set forth by the trade guild. The administrators voted unanimously to accept your proposal, and I'm charged with expressing to you their confidence that Colemenoport Hub will become a jewel in Tree-and-Dragon's network."

"The confidence of the port humbles me," the master trader murmured. "I will do everything in my power to be worthy of it."

"Master Trader, we know it. It was a fortunate day indeed when your eye lighted on the Redlands. We look forward to the future with eagerness."

She bowed and stepped back into the arc. The council chair moved forward, and bowed.

"Master Trader yos'Galan, I am Zeni gorminAstir. I have the honor to chair the Council of the Civilized. I wish to thank you, personally, for taking Colemeno under your consideration and I am looking forward to hearing your presentation."

It occurred to Blays then to wonder where Majel had gone. His pattern was perfectly calm, emitting the purring effect she had come to understand as Majel at work.

She turned her head slightly, and caught sight of him out of the corner of her eye, at the side of the car that had just pulled up, speaking with a woman in Tree-and-Dragon trade clothes.

"Chair gorminAstir," the master trader was saying, "I am

pleased to meet you, and look forward to delivering my presentation to the Council of the Civilized."

There was a slight pause after the chair stepped back into her place. The master trader looked past Blays, and inclined his head.

"Warden. It is good to see you looking so well."

"Master Trader," the Warden said with a smile. "It's good to be feeling so well."

Right. It was her turn, now. Blays stepped forward, and looked straight into amused silver eyes before she bowed. "Master Trader, I'm Blays essWorthi, Speaker for the Haosa Pro Tem. I'm here to return the Speakership to Tekelia vesterGranz."

"Of course." He stepped back, and Tekelia came down the ramp, pattern so sharp and bright that Blays nearly shouted before she remembered that this was formal, for the news.

She covered her gasp with a bow.

"Speaker vesterGranz, I return your duty to you."

Of course, Tekelia didn't bow, but only tipped their head, as if considering what Blays had said.

"What if I don't want it?" The tone was teasing, cousin-to-cousin. *So*, Blays thought, *we're to be Haosa for the camera, are we?*

She laughed. "You never did. That's why everyone thought you were the best choice."

"Yes, I remember that, too." And here at last was the bow, spare, in the Haosa style. "Thank you, Counselor essWorthi, for having held firm and true. I accept the return of my duty."

Blays looked at Tekelia and Tekelia looked at Blays, neither certain what should happen next, so it was fortunate that Majel returned just then, with the trader who had arrived in the car.

"In my capacity as Liaison to the Tree-and-Dragon Trade Mission, I introduce Trader Namid ven'Deelin Clan Ixin."

Trader ven'Deelin bowed to the group, and straightening, inclined her head toward the portmaster. "Portmaster krogerSlyte and I are known to each other," she said.

"Indeed we are!" the portmaster agreed heartily. "I look forward to many conversations like our last, Trader."

"As I do," she murmured, and turned to attend Majel, who was showing her, "Zeni gorminAstir, Chair of the Council of the Civilized; Bentamin chastaMeir, Warden of Civilization; Blays essWorthi, Counsel to Chaos; Tekelia vesterGranz, Speaker for the Haosa."

"Gentles, I am honored," Trader ven'Deelin said firmly, and turned slightly aside, with another bow, this one ornate and measured.

"Master Trader."

"Trader ven'Deelin, well met! Would you do me the very great favor of conveying Mr. dea'Gauss and Dil Nem to our residence, and seeing them made comfortable?"

Blays thought she saw the trader's straight mouth twitch, though her pattern and her voice were solemn.

"I will be very pleased to do so. Do you also require transportation? Or Trader yos'Galan?"

"These gentles and I have some matters to occupy us for the next while," the master trader told her, and glanced around. "Trader Padi, will you support me?"

"Of course, Master Trader."

"Very good." He turned back to Trader ven'Deelin. "We will find our own way home, after business has been done."

"Sir." She inclined slightly from the waist. "Trader."

She turned then, and went two steps up the ramp, offering her arm to the elder.

"Mr. dea'Gauss. How good it is to see you again."

"Trader ven'Deelin," he replied, taking the offered support, "how do you go on?"

"Pretty well, sir, though you see I became bored with retirement very quickly."

They moved past the welcoming committee, Dil Nem Tiazan walking behind, heading for the car.

"Master Trader yos'Galan," said an unfamiliar voice. Blays turned, to see one of the journalists step forward. "pastirEbri of the *Haven City Tattler*. What will you be telling the Council?"

The master trader tipped his head. "Are you permitted to observe the council while it meets, Luzant?"

"Yes, sir."

The master trader beamed. "I am pleased to hear it! Why don't you come along to the meeting, and observe everything as it unfolds?" He leaned forward slightly, and lowered his voice just a little. "That way, you know, we won't spoil the surprise."

The reporter laughed. Blays caught the taste of his embarrassment before he bowed.

"Thank you, Master Trader; we'll see you at the Sakuriji."

"I look forward to renewing our acquaintance," the master trader told him solemnly, and turned toward Majel.

"Liaison ziaGorn, Trader yos'Galan and I are in your hands. What shall we do?"

"I would be honored if you would come with me onto the bus," Majel said, nodding toward that vehicle. "There are comfortable chairs, and refreshments awaiting you."

"That sounds very pleasant," the master trader said. "Please, lead on."

· · · ✷ · · ·

The master trader and Tekelia were of course seated with the portmaster, the council chair, and Majel ziaGorn. The Warden had taken a semi-private chair at the back, pleading a need to call his office.

That left Blays and Padi to sit together slightly removed from everyone else, which suited Padi very well.

"I hear that I'm to wish you happy," she said quietly. Blays looked up, her cheeks rosier than usual, and her eyes sparkling.

"Thank you," she murmured.

This was unexpectedly subdued, given the source. Padi tipped her head. "Have I been inept?"

Blays blinked, and extended a hand to touch Padi's sleeve.

"No, you're not inept—and I thank you very much for your good wishes! I'm very happy, and so is Majel, only—it's difficult."

Padi laughed.

"Oh, this sounds too familiar!"

Blays grinned. "Now, turnabout. I wish *you* happy. Tekelia had said that you signed a paper to become kin, but the two of you are glowing like you've drunk ambient from a glass!"

Padi smiled. "Or from a pitcher. It's been put to me that the—ritual—attending the signing of the paper may have deepened our heart-bond."

"May? Have you *Looked* at yourselves?"

Padi felt her cheeks heat. "Not yet on Colemeno."

"Oh," Blays said, then, "*Oh.*"

Padi raised an eyebrow.

"No, it's nothing dire," Blays said hurriedly. "Only, maybe be private first."

"Thank you for your advice."

"No thanks needed. You do understand that there will be a party to celebrate your pairing?"

"No, will there?" Padi said. "I'm astonished. Have you and Majel already had your party?"

"Not—yet."

"We might plan both together, unless that's not done. Advise me."

Blays tipped her head. "It would have to be a *big* party," she said, cousin-to-cousin, "to make up for there only being one, you see."

"Of course," Padi said.

Blays grabbed her bottle of tea and had a sip.

"The master trader is very attractive," she said. "Is he really your father?"

Padi laughed. "Yes, he really is, and I dote upon him, so we will have no Haosa tricks, if you please."

"Haosa tricks? What can you mean?"

"No, that will not do. Besides, you know, after he and the council come to a satisfactory understanding he will be leaving."

"Where will he go?"

"Well, directly—Tinsori Light Station. After—who can tell? He is a master trader, after all. As a species, they do quite a bit of moving around."

"But—will you be going with him?"

"No, I'm to audit the Iverson Loop."

"So, you're not leaving with your—with the master trader, but you will be leaving for something else?"

"Yes, but I'll be back very soon," Padi said. "The Iverson Loop is a *loop*, you see. Colemeno is one port. I will go 'round to the others and eventually return to Colemeno."

Blays drank some more tea.

"Will your father come to your—to *our*—bonding parties?"

"Perhaps, if we arrange it very quickly. I know he wishes to speak with Aunt Asta."

"That's it, then! We'll have a shared party, and *everybody* will dance!"

Padi raised her tea bottle, and Blays raised hers. They touched with a small, but decisive *clink*.

"Done!" said Padi, and Blays echoed, "Done!"

Off-Grid
Ribbon Dance Village

. . . .

IN FACT, THE WHOLE VILLAGE *HAD* THROWN ITSELF INTO READY-
ing cottages for the incoming students, while Stiletta, Banedra,
and Emit undertook to open the school, which had been put to
rest when their own children had gone to The Vinery for their
apprenticeships.

Those who weren't actively involved in those tasks worked
with Tanin the baker, to make certain that those laboring had
sufficient food and drink, and that there would be enough to
feed their guests when they arrived.

By Ribbon-rise everything was done, and they all gathered
together in the village square to dance.

Torin was sitting with Feyance, watching him play the mandola. Vaiza was dancing with Kencia, who had just spun them
a few inches above the ground.

"Higher!" Vaiza cried. "Take us higher, Kenny!"

"What! As heavy as you are, it's a wonder we can get this
high!"

Vaiza laughed. "Only a *little* higher?"

"Wheedling will get you nothing—in fact, here comes Arbour,
looking like business. I'd best set us both down."

"Gather 'round, cousins!" Arbour called, her voice cutting
through music and chatter alike. "I have word from our friends
at Pacazahno!"

Kencia brought them to ground without a bump. Vaiza spun
away, heading for Torin, then spun back, and waved. "Thank
you, Kenny!"

Kencia grinned and waved back. Everyone moved closer to
where Arbour stood in the center of the square, still talking here

and there, because they were, after all, Haosa. That stopped the moment that Arbour raised her hands.

"I just talked with Konsit joiMore at Pacazahno. Students and teachers will be coming to us tomorrow, and expect to arrive in plenty of time to share the mid-day meal."

This was greeted with a cheer, even as Tanin raised his hand.

"How many will that be, Arbour? I'll want to be certain there are enough pies."

"Ten students, three teachers, and two wagon drivers."

"Hope they're up to a regular potluck," Stiletta said.

Arbour grinned. "We'll hold the cider. The wagon drivers are going back after, and the teachers have expressed their intention to have a class meeting."

Vaiza was standing on his toes, waving his hand.

"Yes?" Arbour said.

"Do we know who's coming—their names, I mean?"

Arbour grinned. "I think they wanted that to be a surprise." She looked around. "Other questions?"

There were none.

"Then somebody fetch me a glass of cider and let's hear some music!"

Colemenoport
Wayfarer

. . . .

"I DID SAY WE WOULD SAVOR OUR WINE TONIGHT, DID I NOT, Trader?" The master trader approached the sofa, and handed a glass of the white to Padi.

She received it with a smile.

"You did, and you were nothing short of prescient."

He sighed, and settled onto the sofa opposite her. They were alone in the common room for the moment. There had been a message on the group list inviting all who were free at the dinner hour to a picnic in the roof garden. It being somewhat past the dinner hour, Padi supposed that was where most of the team could be found.

Across from her, the master trader raised his glass.

"To the Council's successful deliberations!"

Padi laughed. "If success means that they will finish their deliberations, then I wish them nothing but speed and clear sight."

"Yes, well." He sipped his wine, sighed, and sipped again.

"Two days," Padi murmured, that being the time the Council had given themselves for deliberation.

"Well within our time-frame," the master trader said. "Though of course one had hoped to have produced an immediate and resounding *yes* from those assembled. I see I shall have to work on my presentation skills."

In Padi's mind, the master trader's presentation had been nothing short of brilliant—accessible, succinct, with a minimum of graphics. It had been backed by an information packet that was as detailed and complete as possible. Indeed, Portmaster krogerSlyte had praised it in her comments to the council and commended it to her colleagues.

She sipped her wine, and closed her eyes, letting her head fall back onto the cushion.

"Asleep, Trader Padi?"

She opened her eyes and raised her head. "Certainly not, only considering the shape of these next few days. I should tell you that Blays essWorthi has formed a tendre for my father. Nothing will do for her but that he attend the bonding party for herself and Majel, and also for myself and Tekelia. It will be held at Ribbon Dance Village, and I am assured that Asta vesterGranz will be present."

He laughed. "Blays essWorthi is not a woman to leave matters to chance, I see! Of course I'll be pleased to attend, if the timing can be made to work."

"I believe she means it to be within the next day or two," Padi said. "She tells me that she will be wanted back at Visalee Village, which I take to be some distance away, as it took Tekelia an entire day to 'port there and back."

"I see. Will Majel be accompanying her?"

Padi frowned. "I think not. She seemed somewhat cast down, that they would not be meeting often, given the requirements of their separate duties."

Shan sipped his wine, considering.

"The lack of rail and roads does make travel awkward, but I confess to you, Trader Padi, that I have failed to be a keen observer. I assumed—mark that sin!—that there would certainly be aircraft—even personal lifters—to serve the far reaches."

"Not that I'm aware of," Padi said, and covered what she had been about to say next with a sip of wine.

"Now that you are refreshed," the master trader said, "I hope you will share your observation with me."

Padi laughed.

"The people who live at Visalee and Wildege are Haosa, and, as Blays would put it, Wild Haosa at that. Civilization certainly has rail, roads, and aircraft, but there's nothing Civilization wants at Wildege."

"Of course." The master trader sipped his wine, his eyes pointed at something across the room, possibly near the window overlooking the street.

"Remind me, Daughter, to commend Tekelia for their forbearance, when next I see them."

Padi raised her eyebrows. "I don't know that it's forbearance more than a disinclination to have such things disrupting what is actually a very pleasant lifestyle."

"Yes, but change is coming," Father said. "Tekelia does realize that?"

"I believe so. Tekelia tells me that Ribbon Dance Village has always been the buffer between Civilization and the greater number of Haosa." She sighed. "And you know, change may not happen so very quickly. Look how long it has taken to convince Haven City that a rail line out to its nearest neighbor might benefit both."

"There's that. Not to mention that the Haosa have a certain amount of prejudice to overcome." He smiled and drank what was left of the wine.

"Obviously, this is work for those who are younger and more ambitious than I."

"Obviously," Padi said gravely. "I assume that the master trader will want me by him until the Council has made its decision."

"I do, yes. In for a half-bit—"

She laughed, and stretched.

"I believe that I will go to the roof and socialize for a few minutes before I fall entirely asleep."

"A very good plan. One ought to make certain that Mr. dea'Gauss is not misleading the youth. Do you care if I come with you?"

"I would be delighted to have your escort," Padi assured him, and he rose with a smile.

On-Grid
Cardfall Casino

· · · · · · · · · · · · · · ·

THE CAR DROPPED THEM AT WHAT SEEMED TO BE THE ENTRANCE to a park, and drove away.

The Council meeting had gone late, and the sky was dark, giving off the pinkish fog that was the Grid at work. Blays was tired, and hungry, but more than either, she was anxious, because now—*now*—she was going to meet Majel's Seylin.

"What do you think?" Majel murmured.

"Think?" she repeated, blinking. He inclined his head, and she looked across the street, up a broad ramp, to a facade ablaze with gold, emerald, and crimson lights. There were three doors beneath the facade, one each of gold, emerald, and crimson. People were on the move, up the ramp and down, in and out the doors. There was music, very faint, as if the building were singing.

"I think that I've never seen a casino before," Blays said, looking back to Majel. "I didn't expect anything so—large. Or bright. All this to play cards?"

He laughed, and drew her hand through his arm, bringing them across the street and up the ramp.

"We offer many ways for people to wager their money," he said. "In fact, cards are only open to elite players. I'll give you a tour—perhaps tomorrow. First, let's find Seylin, and dinner."

"Principal ziaGorn, welcome home, sir!" A woman in dark blue shirt and pants, with a gold vest over all, smiled and came around the ornate desk in the center of the lobby.

"Irtha, good evening," Majel answered. "How is tonight's crowd?"

"It's been thicker more than thin," Irtha said. "I s'pose a new shipment of luck was delivered."

Majel laughed gently, and brought Blays forward.

"Irtha, here is Blays essWorthi, Counsel to Chaos, and my very dear friend."

Irtha bowed slightly. "I'm pleased to meet you, Counselor essWorthi. I saw you on the news during my meal break."

"Quick work," Majel murmured, and Irtha turned to him.

"It was just the preview segment I saw. They were promising a full report in an hour." She glanced aside. Blays, following her gaze, saw a clock discreetly hanging on the wall.

"That'll be right about now, sir, if you want to catch it."

"Perhaps I'll content myself with tomorrow's review," Majel said, and shifted as voices sounded behind them. "I yield to our guests."

"Yes, sir," the guard said and moved off to greet the new arrivals.

"Come," Majel said softly, as they passed through the inner door, "let's find Seylin."

"You won't have to search very far, Principal ziaGorn," came a contralto drawl from the left.

Majel laughed and turned to the tall woman leaning against the wall opposite the door.

"Before you scold me—yes, I do know that it's been another absurdly long day. For whatever good it might do, this one wasn't of my making—or only partially of my making. I suppose I could have made it shorter by leaving the master trader to fend for himself at the port."

"It looked like he would have done very well. Fair took over the process, didn't he?"

"Yes, but I expect he was only trying to shorten the near end, having some idea of how far away was the far end. If you like, I'll try to bring him here within the next day or two so you may scold him as he deserves."

"I'm not firm in my own mind that he needs a scolding," the woman said. "Best to let it rest, though if you do bring him here, introduce me."

"Of course."

She came out of her lean, then, and took one step forward, her gaze on Blays's face. She bowed gently, her pattern calm.

"I'm Seylin atBuro, chief of security. I assume you're Blays essWorthi."

"I am, yes," Blays said, looking up at this formidable person.

In addition to being tall, Seylin atBuro was wide in the shoulder and slim in the hip. Her hair was dark brown, cut very short; her eyes grey; and her face austere. She was dressed in black shirt and long pants, with a red vest over all.

A smile appeared on that austere face and she stepped back. "Majel, your friend wants a glass of wine."

"If it comes to that, so do I," he answered. "Will you join us?"

"Yes, thank you."

They walked together through another door, and into a small bar.

"Four of the green, please, Mardek," Majel said.

The barman slid glasses from the overhead holder to the bar, reached beneath, pulled out a bottle and poured pale green wine. "Thank you."

Majel took one glass and handed it to Blays, the next to Seylin, the third to Mardek, and kept the fourth for himself.

"Mardek—here is Blays essWorthi. She and I have life-bonded. Blays, this is Mardek gaeDona. He raised me as much as my father did. You may depend on him for anything."

Mardek's smile was warm; his face kind. "Blays essWorthi, I'm glad to meet you," he said, and she felt the truth warming her core.

"I'm *very* glad to meet you, Mardek gaeDona," she returned fervently.

Majel touched her shoulder, moving her attention to the other member of their party.

"You've already met her informally; I now make it formal. Please meet Seylin atBuro, my oldest friend. She's also chief of security here. I trust her completely, and I hope you will also learn to do so."

"Seylin atBuro, I'm pleased to meet you, and—*thank you* for taking such good care of Majel."

Seylin laughed, and glanced at Majel.

"Satisfied, old friend?" he murmured.

"Absolutely," she answered and the truth of *that* was a gong reverberating through the ambient.

"A toast!" Mardek said, raising his glass. They turned to face him.

"To Blays and Majel—may their dance be long and joyous."

"Long and joyous," Seylin repeated, and they drank.

The empty glasses were replaced on the bar. Mardek reached for the bottle, but Majel raised his hand and turned to Blays.

"It's been a long day. I feel that I should either take you to the dining room, or upstairs to my apartment, but in either case, I want to feed you."

"And I want to be fed," Blays told him. "Your apartment, please."

"So be it." He reached for her hand, then raised his head to look at Seylin.

"Blays ought to be put into all systems," he said.

"I'll take care of it," Seylin assured him.

"Thank you." He turned to Blays, and she Read a complicated froth of weariness, excitement, and exhaustion in him.

"The lift is just back here," he said.

Off-Grid
Bodhar-on-the-River

· ·

KONCH WILBENIT RESEATED THE RAFT'S COWLING AND SEALED it, then walked to the door of the repair shed, wiping his hands on a rag, and taking a deep breath of fresh air.

Him and Zel had a bit of a falling out, early morning, which wasn't her best time of day, and rather than make it worse, Konch had announced his intention to do maintenance on the air raft, and got himself out of the kitchen.

It had gotten on to midday while he tinkered, and he was just at the point of examining the proposition that Zel had cooled down enough to hear him when the madman walked out of the wood.

Konch knew him for a madman, not by his unkemptness, which, face it, there were regular village inhabitants who preferred a certain... naturalness in their appearance. But there was nobody in Bodhar Village whose pattern was an unraveling, fiery horror, twisted up with too much energy, and feral Ribbons reweaving their core.

The thought flashed through Konch's mind that he hadn't been noticed; that he could just step back into the shed and let trouble pass by.

Only—he was headman, and letting trouble reach the village wasn't an option.

Konch stepped forward, and planted himself square in the madman's path.

"Hello, stranger," he said easily, shoving the rag into his belt, and showing both his hands palms up and empty.

"There is a flying craft at this location," the madman said, and Konch blinked.

"That's a fact," he said. "I just finished working on it. Want to see?"

"I will fly to Haven City," the stranger told him. "Before they kill us all."

The air raft was Konch's particular project, he having gotten it into his head that Bodhar-on-the-River ought not to be completely cut off from the rest of the world only because their single teleporter had decided to retire to the Wild. There were more answers than one to life's inconveniences. Civilization had some of those answers, and there were those who didn't care who they sold a kit to, or manuals, either.

So, Village Headman wilBenit had built himself an air raft and learned how to fly it, and if everyone but his wife thought he was wasting his time, still, he felt more peaceful knowing the machine was there, and ready at need.

"Who's going to kill us, friend?" he asked the madman, by way of stalling him while he worked out what would be best to do. Konch was Haosa. Near half the village was Deaf, and their best defense, once it came clear they weren't dealing with rational thinking. But there were elders, and children—Haosa, yes, but vulnerable. The madman wanted to fly to Haven City? Well, why not let him? Konch had built one raft; be easier to build a second, now he knew what he was doing.

"They're going to strangle Civilization and slaughter the Haosa," the madman told him, earnestly. "I have to stop them."

Whether that was a delusion born of the aberrant connection with the ambient, or a True Seeing—Konch shivered, and turned slightly on the path, his decision made.

"Absolutely, you need to stop them. Can't argue with that," he said, waving toward the shed. "Raft's right in here. Let's get you in the air."

"Yes," said the madman, and strode past Konch into the shed.

"You will pilot," said the madman, whose name, so he said, was Vyr.

Konch froze.

"No, y'know, friend? This is yours. I can see the Ribbons chose you special to finish this out and save everybody."

"Yes!" Vyr agreed, green eyes over-bright. He leaned forward and grabbed Konch by the wrist—*tight* grip. Konch threw up his shields to get some relief from the battering energies sparking out of Vyr's pattern. "I *will* stop them from killing us! That's my task! That's why—that's why I waited. Why I'm still alive. My task is clear—and I accept it! But I'm not a pilot! *You're* a pilot. *You* must fly me to Haven City!"

That was when Konch thought about giving friend Vyr a businesslike rap on the head and putting him out. Trouble with that was that it wouldn't solve the basic problem, which was that Vyr was being filled up—replaced—by the ambient, his pattern scorched and unraveling before Konch's eyes. When he came to, he'd be just as dangerous—maybe more.

The other option—well. Konch wasn't a life-taker. Call it a failing. He thought of Zel, the village—Ribbons! The kids. And even so, shivering with horror over the damage that would be wreaked if this man got to the village—*even then*, he didn't think he had it in him, not to kill.

That left one solution: Get the madman away from his village and everything he loved. Which was exactly what the madman himself wanted, so—

Dinner's almost ready, his wife whispered in his ear. *You coming?*

Konch closed his eyes. Zel was Deaf. Their bond let them whisper to each other—commonplaces; love-talk—but complex things, like madmen needing to fly to Haven City to stop the end of the world, wouldn't come through to her with anything like sense.

So, Konch thought—simple. *Got something to take care of,* he sent back. And, more gently: *Love you, Zelly.*

Konch?

There was worry, right there, but he couldn't mind it. The important thing was to get Vyr away from Bodhar-on-the-River; away from Zel; away—*away*—

"Time is important!" the madman said sharply, his grip on Konch's wrist tight enough to leave bruises.

"Couldn't agree more," he said, looking straight into crazy green eyes. "You want me to pilot, though, friend—you have to let me go."

On-Grid
Cardfall Casino

. . . .

"IS THE COUNCIL GOING TO ACCEPT THE MASTER TRADER'S PRO-posal?" Blays asked, once the plate of cheeses and small breads had been dealt with, and while they awaited the arrival of the entree.

Majel tipped his head. "What do you think?"

Blays sighed. "I don't know what to think. The irritable councilor—"

"Coracta tryaBent," Majel murmured.

"Yes, her. She made it seem as if the master trader was going to be taking the planet over by armed force."

"Councilor tryaBent has a particular style. She believes that forthrightness will produce interesting information."

Blays blinked. "Does it?"

Amusement glimmered through Majel's pattern. "Sometimes," he said.

"But—in this case?"

"In this case, Councilor tryaBent was outmaneuvered," Majel said. "Which also sometimes happens. If I were to hazard a guess, I would say that she had mounted an exceptionally aggressive attack in order to provoke the master trader into an indiscre-tion. Which would have been interesting, and even informative."

"But the master trader didn't get angry."

"No, he didn't. Neither did he resort to ridicule, or become visibly bored. He answered each accusation clearly and calmly, referencing the data gathered for the port inventory, as well as the pertinent Guild requirements, as appropriate."

"He must have had a lot of practice," Blays said, consideringly. "A master trader—his purpose is to sell things."

Majel smiled. "That's very true."

"Was Padi meant to lose her temper, when Councilor tryaBent asked if she thought Colemeno was the equal of her ambitions as a trader?"

Majel laughed.

"I think the councilor had lost *her* temper, a little, by then. And, again, the trader's answer was calm and informative. I hadn't myself thought much beyond receiving and considering the proposal. While the council's approval is necessary, it's only one more brick in the road the traders are building. The trade hub will not magically appear with a positive vote."

Blays smiled.

"So! Is the council going to accept the master trader's proposal?"

Majel laughed.

"I think there's a better-than-good chance of a positive outcome. Remember, the port administrators have already given their approval, and their assurance that the port can meet increased traffic."

"That will weigh with the councilors," Blays said wisely. "After all, it's the port that will have to do the work."

"Very true."

"Do you think the master trader knows he'll succeed?"

"None of us knows that," Majel said. "Any gambler can tell you that even a better-than-good chance isn't a sure thing."

Blays sighed. "Two days of suspense, then."

"Well, the analysts have to have time to do their work," Majel said apologetically. "And the councilors time to read the reports."

"Of course. Well! Since we can't do anything to hurry the council's pace, I have something to tell you! Padi and I have agreed that she and Tekelia, and you and I, will host a party at Ribbon Dance Village, to celebrate our bondings. It will have to be very soon, before the master trader leaves Colemeno."

Majel tipped his head. "Will that be—acceptable—to Ribbon Dance Village?"

"Why wouldn't it be?" Blays asked. "I did say *party*."

He smiled. "So you did."

A bell sounded from the kitchen and he rose.

"That will be the meal. I suggest that we sit at the table."

"All right." Blays rose and followed him into the kitchen, standing back as he slipped the tray from the food lift. It seemed to her that the load was not perfectly balanced, and in fact when he turned, one covered dish skittered toward the edge.

Majel took a breath. Blays extended herself, caught the dish, Lifted it, and brought it gently to the table.

"Thank you," Majel said, carefully.

"It's no trouble," she told him, equally careful. "It's what Lifters do, you know."

"Yes," he said, arriving at the table. "I do know. But there's a difference between knowing and seeing."

Blays laughed. "Yes, there is!" she said. "I remember Tekelia telling me about the effect of Padi's Gift, and I also remember the first time I saw them join hands! I was horrified—and, of course, nothing happened. Except that Tekelia laughed at me, which I'd surely earned."

She stepped closer to help him unload the rest of the dishes onto the table.

"I thought Tekelia's Gift was teleportation."

"That's one. Tekelia's a Child of Chaos," Blays said.

"And that means—?"

"It means that Tekelia can discorporate with a touch. Watch carefully and you'll see that Tekelia does not make skin contact. They're very deft, and very careful."

Majel frowned. "Is such a Gift possible?"

"It's not a Gift, exactly; it's a particular relationship with the ambient. There aren't many Children of Chaos."

"I should hope not. But Padi—"

"Among Padi's Gifts is a new one, that makes her impervious to the touch of Chaos," Blays said. She lifted a shoulder and let it fall. "Or maybe all Talents born under Ribbonless skies have the same ability. You understand that Tekelia is unwilling to experiment."

"Of course they are."

Majel took the tray to the counter, and came back to the table with a bottle of wine. "Please sit," he said, "I'll pour."

But Blays remained standing, head tipped, studying him.

"You're not afraid of Tekelia," she said.

He looked up. "Should I be?"

"Tekelia can discorporate you with a touch," Blays said.

"Yes, but *will* they? Tekelia strikes me as remarkably level-headed, and very canny. Our interests align, politically. And you just assured me that Tekelia is deft and very careful. Today alone they were in several crowded and volatile situations, and no one was discorporated, which lends credence to your assurance."

Blays felt such a thrill run through her that, had they been off-grid, it might have propelled her into the air.

"Blays?" His voice was quiet, some amount of worry showing in his pattern.

"Ribbons, I love you," she said, and kissed him.

Off-Grid
The Tree House

. . . .

THE AMBIENT *SHOUTED*, AND TEKELIA, TOO, AS THE PORCH SNAPPED into existence. One step, to grab the rail and to turn a parched face into the breeze, sweet and damp with the river's essence. Energy poured into Tekelia's core, and for a long moment they were breathless, ready to take flight, to join the ambient, to dance as a single mote of light within the Ribbons.

"Forgive me if I hope you will reconsider," a beloved voice said from very close at hand.

Tekelia turned, hands held out.

"Padi."

She stepped closer, ignoring the offered hands, and wrapped Tekelia into a tight embrace.

"I think you may have your answer regarding Haosa and ships, if even so short a time away depletes you so much."

Face buried in Padi's hair, Tekelia breathed in the scent of lavender, feeling tight muscles relax, and the dangerous exuberance cool.

"I don't think it was the ship. Or, not only the ship."

"Then you will tell me what you think it was," Padi answered, stepping slightly back, though keeping firm hands on Tekelia's shoulders. "*After* you eat something. Now. You will tell me if I ought to find something in your pantry, or 'port us both to the Wayfarer, where the trade team is having a lovely picnic on the roof."

"I think that between the coldbox and the pantry, I, and even we, are well-supplied. You should eat something, before you go back to the picnic."

Padi tipped her head.

"I seek clarity," she said.

340

"Yes, of course."

"Do you prefer that I leave?"

"No!" Tekelia said, sharply, and then laughed. "You see how it is with me."

"I do," Padi agreed gravely. "You may think that I have a duty to the picnic. I let it be known that my bond-mate had returned to our village house, and that I would be joining them there. This was met with approval by all gathered, including my father *and* the master trader. Sit. I'll bring a tray."

"First, if you would bring the tin from the counter? I think a few of Entilly's cookies would do us both some good."

"Cookies first, then the tray," Padi said. "I can manage these things. Now—*sit*."

The tray had been dealt with appropriately and the second glass of wine poured. Tekelia was being boneless in the chair, legs stretched out, crossed at the ankle, face tipped up to the sky, where the Ribbons, Padi thought, were dancing with unusual abandon.

"So," she said softly, "you believe it a long Grid-bound day *after* several days of relying on your inner resources alone."

"If I'm honest, the Council meeting was particularly grueling."

Padi looked amused. "The master trader told me he had worked very hard to make his presentation not only short, but sweet."

"It was a marvel of succinctness," Tekelia assured her.

"I'll remember to tell him so," Padi said.

"Do. There are particular committees and offices that will be working late tonight, analyzing that proposal. In the meanwhile, the Council has its regular work to do, including a discussion of the most recent Census of Gifts, which seems to support Aunt Asta's Foretelling of the end of Civilization."

"She foretold the end of the Haosa, too," Padi murmured.

"Yes, she did, but that's only reality—we're interdependent— Civilized, Deaf, and Haosa—which is something that Civilization has been trying to ignore for many years."

Tekelia sighed.

"The Haosa are not blameless. We withdrew to our villages, and into the Wild. We said we didn't care for the toys—and most especially the tools—of Civilization."

"Even though it would be convenient to have access to an aircraft to fetch, let us say, Blays, into the city."

"Even though," Tekelia acknowledged, and drank wine.

"Which reminds me that I haven't told you!" Padi said, sitting up straight in her chair.

"Told me what?"

"Blays thinks we should have a party!"

Tekelia laughed.

"Of course she does. When?"

"Before the master trader quits Colemeno, which will be in three days' time, no matter the answer he is given."

"I should tell you," Tekelia said, and stopped.

"As bad as that?" Padi murmured, and Tekelia laughed again, softly.

"I should tell you that I revealed to my siblings 'round the Council table that you and I are bonded. I then asked what should be my part, when the master trader's proposal comes to a vote."

"And your colleagues advised you to recuse yourself," Padi said composedly.

"They did. Which means that the proposal will be lacking one vote in favor."

She sipped her wine, and said nothing, though Tekelia caught a ripple of amusement through their link.

"Tell me."

"You really must learn to have faith in the master trader," Padi said gently.

"Has he Foreseen a positive outcome?"

Padi frowned thoughtfully. "I don't believe he has Sight, and I don't think he would have asked Priscilla for a Foretelling, because the matter doesn't warrant that much output of energy. No. He merely accepts the reality of the trade. He will either win his point or lose it. Portmaster krogerSlyte's approval tips us toward a fortunate outcome. But, Tekelia, think. The master trader could have easily advised the thodelm to hold off signing the *Affidare* until after the council acted, if he thought the matter hung by one vote."

She sipped wine, eyes narrowed. "In fact, victory by a single vote would not suit him at all. A large majority in favor will signal ongoing commitment to the necessities of the Hub."

"Will he withdraw if he only has a narrow victory?"

"I don't think he'll withdraw, but he may adjust the timeline for Hub development before he leaves."

"I'm sorry he's leaving," Tekelia said with feeling. "I think I could learn much from the master trader."

"As might we all," Padi murmured, and looked across to Tekelia with a smile.

"I confess that the day also weighs heavily on me. May I suggest we go early to bed?"

"That," Tekelia said, rising and holding down a hand, "is a *brilliant* idea."

On-Grid
Cardfall Casino

. . . .

BLAYS WAS DROWSING ON THE PILLOW NEXT TO HIM, HER FACE smooth and chaste with the ironical amber gaze shuttered. Her hair was spread out on the pillow, and Majel lazily extended a hand, running his fingers through the pale strands, lifting and releasing them.

Somewhat to his disappointment, they fell gently to the pillow. *Don't you like my hair?* Blays whispered inside his ear.

Majel looked down into her face, seeing a gleam of amber from beneath pale lashes.

"I like your hair very much," he said. "I only wonder what the rules are, that sometimes it floats and other times—not."

She opened her eyes, and leaned closer to kiss his nose.

"It floats best out from under the Grid," she said. "Tekelia told me to wear it in a knot, so I didn't call attention to myself when I was in the city." She looked solemn. "Apparently Civilized hair behaves itself, and unruly hair is a sign that a Wild Haosa is afoot."

"I like that it's unruly," Majel murmured.

"Well, you know, so do I. And I think Tekelia was being over-cautious. Even unconfined, my hair can't be said to be anything but ruly, under-Grid."

"Is the Grid so heavy?"

Slanted brows pulled together.

"Heavy? I guess that's as good a way as any to describe it. The Haosa don't come to the city much, because the Grid is annoying. It's less noticeable at the port, which is why you'll find more Haosa visiting there."

A thought—a *connection*—flickered in his brain, and—*no*, he would *not* think of politics now. He would—

"I love how your pattern sparkles when you figure something out," Blays said, putting her hand along the curve of his cheek. "What was it?"

"Politics in bed—" he protested.

"I'm comfortable—are you?"

He laughed.

"Yes, I'm comfortable. And it just occurred to me that the makers of the law forbidding the port to Haosa—"

"The law that was to protect innocent outworlders," Blays said encouragingly. "I remember."

"Yes, I expect you do. It just occurred to me that the real reason the law was introduced was exactly to deprive Haosa jobs at the port, with the naive outworlders a convenient cover. Who, after all, would not wish to protect innocents?"

Blays was silent for a long moment, her eyes narrowed.

"That law has been in force for twenty years."

"Yes, and Invitation Right nearly as—ah. If depriving the Haosa of economic benefit were the motivating force, it may mean that the current impetus behind enforcing it is coming from the same place."

"And this time, they're prepared to inflict real pain on anyone breaking the law," Blays said, and sighed. "That's unsettling."

"It is. I suggest that it's too unsettling to pursue in current circumstances."

Blays smiled. "All right. What would you like to do, instead?"

Majel traced the line of her cheekbone with one fingertip. "Maybe we can think of something, if we put our heads together," he murmured.

Blays wriggled closer until her forehead touched his.

"Like this?"

He laughed softly, warming Blays to the tips of her toes.

I thought more like this, he said inside her ear, and moved his head on the pillow until he had captured her lips.

Wildege
Kelim Station

· · · · · · · · · · · · · ·

THE TREES HAD WARNED HER, SO KEL WAS WAITING OUTSIDE when the tech arrived.

Nervy as she was, she tried not to rush the woman, who might get the wrong notion regarding Kel's particular brand of Wildness. Still, she walked over to the wagon right brisk, calling out, "How soon can you get that radio up and working?"

The tech looked down at her from the driver's bench.

"Last we talked, you were humoring Amerdeen and never likely even to turn it on," she said. "What changed?"

"My—boy," Kel said, and threw her hands out. "Boy in trouble, the trees led him here just before the cold came in. Night before last, he took the wagon, went off by himself. I'm afraid he's heading for harm."

The tech stared for a long couple breaths, like she was Scanning Kel's pattern. She broke it off just before Kel could ask *was it pretty*, and reached into the bag on the seat beside her. She pulled something out and jumped down from the wagon.

"Since you have is what we in Visalee call *an emergency*," she said, holding up a device about the size of her hand. "We'll call Amerdeen. You'll talk. But first, you got anything I can eat?"

"Sweet rolls in the kitchen," Kel said, turning to lead the way. "Kettle's on for tea."

Off-Grid
The Tree House

. . . .

TEKELIA WOKE, AND LAY STILL FOR A LONG MOMENT, WONDERING why.

Possibly to be aware of and grateful for the lean length of Padi's body pressed against their own? Or to consciously breathe in the scent of lavender that surrounded her? Or to stroke the light hair, and run a teasing hand over a—

Ah.

Quietly, Tekelia sighed, recalling the reason for this early awakening.

"What is it?" Padi murmured.

"I need to leave," Tekelia answered, not quite grumpy, but not pleased either.

Padi rolled away. Before Tekelia could protest the loss of her warmth, she was back, face facing face on the pillows.

"This is rather sudden," she said. "Was it something I said?"

Tekelia stared—then laughed aloud.

"I meant that I need to leave for the city. The Council meets today."

Padi rose slightly on an elbow, looking past Tekelia to the window, beyond which the Ribbons still danced.

"Surely, the Council doesn't meet this early."

"No, but I was assigned an office, which I was too . . . disordered to examine yesterday. I should go in, familiarize myself, and find if there's anything I need to do in order to get—" Here Tekelia floundered.

"Comm," Padi murmured. The ambient flickered, as if that single word had been a Foretelling—and steadied as she leaned to kiss Tekelia's nose. "Must you leave at once, or might we share a moment—even, possibly, breakfast?"

Tekelia smiled and lifted a hand to cup her cheek. "A moment *and* breakfast, I think. You know what Haosa are."

"Slaves to their own pleasures," Padi said wisely. "And always at play."

"Exactly," Tekelia said, and gasped as she rose up, and pressed Tekelia firmly down onto the mattress.

"When does today's Council session end?" Padi asked. They were sitting on the porch overlooking the trees, breakfast all but finished.

"Early afternoon," Tekelia said. "There aren't any hearings today. So I'm told."

"Blays and I will be making arrangements for the dual bonding party tomorrow evening," Padi said. "Unless Arbour forbids it, of course."

"Which she's very likely to do," Tekelia said seriously. "Disliking parties as she does."

"Yes, well. I am hoping that Blays will be able to persuade her otherwise, my own powers being so poor in that arena. Will you like to be part of these arrangements?"

"You're asking if I will come directly home after the Council meeting, and help plan a party?"

Padi smiled brightly. "Yes, exactly that."

"I'll be delighted."

"I believe Blays means to include Majel, as well. If he wishes, might you bring him with you?"

"Of course," Tekelia said, and stood. Padi rose as well, and Tekelia kissed her cheek.

"I really *do* need to go now."

Mist swirled, and Padi was alone on the porch overlooking the trees.

She sighed, very softly, and turned to clear the table.

Off-Grid
Peck's Market

. . . .

"THANK YOU, ATSU!" BLAYS CALLED, SLIPPING OUT OF THE BACK seat of Majel's car.

"That's all right," the driver answered through the open window. "You remember what Principal ziaGorn told us, right? This car's on-call for you. It might not always be me driving, but we'll come for you, whenever and wherever, no matter the time, either."

"Yes, I remember." Blays smiled and leaned into the window. Atsu was Deaf, and Majel had told her that he took great comfort in details. "I have the car's comm-code, and it will be you or Terah, or, sometimes, Dan, who will be driving."

"That's a good remembering." Atsu grinned. "You enjoy your day."

"And you, yours," Blays returned politely. She stepped to the side of the drive and waited until the car got back on the road before walking up the hill to where Vayeen waited beneath the pavilion.

"Bond-mate not with you?"

Vayeen held out a steaming cup, and Blays took it gratefully. She closed her eyes and held the warmth between both palms while the ambient sang a song of welcome-home.

"The Council meets in Haven City," she said.

"Even I know that," he said, and gave her a sharp look. "Are you going to live in the city?"

Blays very nearly choked on her swallow of wake-up.

"*No*, I am *not* going to live in the city! For one thing, the Grid itches. For another, who do you have in mind to represent Visalee to Chaos?"

Vayeen held his hands up, palms out.

"I'm just wondering, then, Cousin, how this is going to work."

Blays sighed. "That's a very good question, to which I don't at present have a very good answer. Aunt Asta said that Majel's clever—which he is—and that he'll figure it out, given time."

Vayeen reached inside the basket, setting a half pie, a box of cookies, and another, of nuts, on the table.

"So we're giving the man time to work," he said.

"That's it."

"Fair enough." Vayeen sat down and waved at her. "Eat. Then let's go home."

On-Grid
The Sakuriji

. . . .

IT WAS A PLEASANT OFFICE, TEKELIA THOUGHT, ROOMY AND bright, with a window overlooking the Sakuriji's public garden. Two comfortable chairs sat in the window, with a low table between. There was a buffet along the right wall, furnished with a teapot, a few canisters of tea, and a workaday set of mugs. The drawers yielded condiments, individually packaged fruit and nut bars, and a sealed packet of six little cakes iced in bright pink.

In the center of the room was a desk, arranged so that the diligent worker might still see out the window. Tekelia sat in the chair, finding that whoever had sat in it last had not been long in the leg, and spent a few moments adjusting it for comfort.

The desk drawers were empty—unless one counted dust—except for the bottom drawer, which yielded a duster.

Tekelia deployed that useful item, and in short order had empty, dust-free, drawers. Replacing the duster, Tekelia closed the drawers and looked at the clock that hung on the wall over the comm unit—and recalled that early morning tickle of Foreseeing from Padi.

Smiling, Tekelia crossed the room, meaning to call and tell her the comm was in place, but pressing the call button did not produce a light. Tekelia bent, checking wires and reseating connections. Straightening, Tekelia pressed the call button again—and laughed when the light remained obstinately dark.

"A True Seeing after all! I suppose I'll need to find someone to fix this."

Another glance at the clock told Tekelia that there was still some time to fill before the Council convened for its morning session.

More than enough time, in fact, to find the cafeteria, and a snack.

"Good morning, Councilor vesterGranz," a soft voice said.

"Councilor azieEm," Tekelia answered, looking up with a smile, "Good morning."

"May I join you?" she asked. She had a cup in one hand and plate holding a pretty iced square of cake in the other.

"By all means."

She took the seat across, put the plate down, and sipped from her cup with a sigh of pleasure.

"I," she said, ruefully, "have never been one to rise early in the day. This new schedule amuses my younger brother, who admires the power of ambition, as he puts it."

"Are you?" Tekelia asked. "Ambitious, I mean."

She raised her eyebrows. "Well, I must be, mustn't I? What other reason would there be to become a councilor?"

"A desire to serve others? To preserve the world?"

"Preserving the world is new on the table, and I admit that my interest is engaged. Before...I don't think it was so much a desire to *serve* as a desire to see necessary work done properly."

Tekelia sipped wake-up. "I wouldn't make a difference between those two desires. Of course, I may be unsubtle."

"Or I may be splitting hairs," azieEm said with a smile. "It's a known fault, as my elder brother will attest."

She broke a corner off of her cake.

"I wanted to let you know how pleased I am that the Haosa have accepted Civilization's invitation to the table." She raised her head to meet Tekelia's eyes. "Civilization having taken that prerogative for itself."

Tekelia smiled. "And rescinded its privilege by doing so."

azieEm tipped her head. "What an interesting viewpoint," she murmured, and Tekelia thought there was a note of doubt in her voice. "In my case, seating the Haosa as full members furthers my goal of seeing work done properly, and gives me a reason to continue to rise early."

She paused to sip before continuing.

"I also wanted to let you know that I am willing to share my experience regarding setting up one's office and other details that are—not explained very well to the newcomer. I learned by trial and error, which was frustrating and time-consuming. You arrive among us as we face an emergency, and it would benefit the council to see you settled quickly."

"I'm willing to learn. For instance, the comm in my office isn't working. To whom would I speak in order to see it repaired?"

azieEm broke off another piece of cake.

"You would speak to building maintenance. In fact, since you *don't* have a working comm, let me do that for you."

"I'd appreciate it," Tekelia told her, truthfully. "Thank you."

"It's no trouble at all. I don't like to make predictions, but it's possible that you'll have a working comm by the time the council finishes its business today. Where did they put you?"

"Hanilure Three."

"Oh, that's a *very* nice office," azieEm said, with perhaps a trace of envy.

"It has a good window," Tekelia agreed.

azieEm laughed. "Yes, that too. I'll make the call to maintenance. Further on my topic—you should know that a person will be sent to you, to be your aide. The purpose of an aide is to assist you in navigating the Sakuriji systems. It would, for instance, fall to your aide to see that your office is properly outfitted for work, that the comm is operational, that your mail is delivered speedily, and that inappropriate persons don't importune you. Your aide will also assist you in hiring anyone else you may find necessary to accomplish your work. An able, experienced aide is a treasure."

"I understand," Tekelia said.

"But you may not understand, as I didn't, that you are under no obligation to accept the first, or even the third, person sent to you. The people who arrive are in fact *candidates*, and you are expected to interview them. If you find that they will not do, you may decline their services—kindly, of course—and ask that someone else be sent."

"Thank you; I *didn't* know that. Who sends these candidates? Would it be useful if I gave them a list of my requirements?"

"Oh, that's very good! Proactive. You would call the Chief Clerk."

"Is it allowed that I call *upon* the Chief Clerk?" Tekelia asked. "Lacking a comm, as I do."

"Calling upon the Chief Clerk without an appointment may find them too busy to speak with you."

"But then I will be in a position to make an appointment," Tekelia pointed out.

"Very true. You'll find the Chief Clerk on the second floor of Evoree Tower. That whole floor is operations and support."

"Would I also bespeak a screen there?" Tekelia asked.

azieEm frowned, a ferocious expression that sat ill on her soft features.

"You really should not be wasting your time requesting a screen, and ordering repair for your comm," she said. "But, yes— the support office will be able to install a screen in your office."

azieEm finished her cake, lifted her cup—and sighed in what sounded like real regret.

"I'm glad we met each other this morning," she said. "I look forward to seeing you at the council table. I have some things to check in my office—and I'll make that call for you."

She rose and Tekelia with her.

"Thank you. I believe I'll go over to Evoree Tower, request a screen, and see if the Chief Clerk might have time to see me."

"Good luck," azieEm said. She gave a brief, cordial bow, and left.

Colemenoport
Wayfarer

. . . .

"GOOD MORNING, FATHER."

Shan looked up from his screen. He had left his door open, an indication that he was available to any of the trade team who might wish to speak with him, but he had not looked to find his heir among them.

"Padi—well-met. I confess I hadn't expected to see you this morning."

"I *had* thought I would laze about at home, communing with the trees," she said, smiling down at him. "Then I remembered I had some correspondence to take care of, and once that was done, I recalled that Blays and I are to speak with Arbour, the village administrator, today, regarding our shared bonding party. After *that* it was a very small step to recalling that Asta vesterGranz wished to speak with you, and you to her. So, I thought I should see what your plans were, and offer you a 'port to Ribbon Dance Village, if you wish one."

Shan leaned back in his chair and considered her, his tall, strong daughter, her inner tapestry afire with competence and joy. A woman grown; a trader about to embark on her first solo tour; established in her own household—and when had all that happened?

"Father?"

"Your pardon, Daughter. I was trying to make sense of this *lazing about*, as you have it. However, you had asked after my plans! My plans include not thinking about the council's deliberations regarding Tree-and-Dragon's proposal, while answering my correspondence." He leaned forward and tapped a key, sending the last letter into the queue. "And my correspondence is now complete."

"May I, then, offer you that 'port? There will be pleasant company, not confined to Aunt Asta, and I believe you will find the village interesting of itself."

"You make a strong case," Shan said. He turned off his screen, stood, and went around the desk. Holding his hand out, he felt Padi's fingers close firmly around his.

"I accept your offer of transport."

Off-Grid
Between the Ribbons and the Ground

· ·

THE VINERY WAS AN HOUR BEHIND THEM AND KONCH WAS START-
ing to worry. In theory the air raft could fly all the way from
Bodhar to the sea without a maintenance stop. That *was* theory,
and Konch couldn't argue with it, having never flown so far.
Only—he was starting to feel a tremor in the flight stick, which
he hoped was wind resistance, and not something mechanical.

If he'd been alone, he'd have found a nice flat spot and
brought her down for a look-see. Given that he not only *wasn't*
alone, but the condition of his companion, Konch was thinking
he'd rather not, even if Vyr was sensible enough to take in why
they were landing so far short of Haven City.

Konch had his shields closed as tight as they'd ever been, and
he could still feel the energy coming off of Vyr. It was like the
man was a repeater, taking in the ambient, and blasting it back
out. Unnerving, at least, and if it was bothering Konch, separate
and shielded as he was, the Ribbons alone knew what it was like
inside Vyr's head. So, that was two worries.

The third was the nav-system. There were beacons at Visalee,
Bodhar, The Vinery, and Ribbon Dance, originally set up to guide
the wagons, perfectly visible to the raft's sensors. Between beacons,
you flew with one eye on the navigation screen—which was good
for general direction, altitude, speed—and trusted in the ambient.

And here it was again, that shiver in the stick, like they
were running over gravel, except there wasn't any gravel up here
between the Ribbons and the ground.

"Faster!" Vyr said, which—credit where it was due—he hadn't
been saying more than once or twice an hour since they'd cleared
the sentinel trees and left Bodhar, safe, behind them.

Konch consulted the navigation screen. The Vinery's beacon

was a shadow behind them, almost off the edge. The beacon at Ribbon Dance ought to be—there it was!—just coming into range. Konch felt a thrill. From Ribbon Dance, it was a half-hop to the edge of Haven City.

Real soon now, he was going to be able to get rid of his chancy passenger and go back home to Bodhar-on-the-River, where, if the warmth of their link was any indication, Zelly was cooking some choice words to share with him. And, Ribbons, wouldn't he treasure every one?

"We've got as much speed as we're going to get," he said to Vyr, not for the first time. "Just you sit back and breathe easy, Friend."

· · · ❄ · · ·

"Here!" Vaiza said happily. "I *knew* these would be ripe!"

"How many should we pick?" asked Kalibu, looking around at the fruit-laden branches.

Vaiza grinned. "How many pies do you want?"

Kalibu looked a little guilty.

"I only asked if there was apricot pie because it's my favorite," he said. "I didn't mean that I'd *only* eat apricot pie. Other pies are good, too." He paused, frowning. "Well. Except prikenbur pie."

"I don't think Tanin makes that kind," Vaiza said. "And apricot pie is brilliant! We should absolutely have it!" He looked around, considering the problem of *how many*, and putting that against *how far* it was back to the village and Tanin's bakery.

"I know. You half-fill your bucket and I'll half-fill mine. That way, we'll have a whole bucket, but it won't be as heavy to carry. If Tanin wants more, we can come back."

"That sounds like a good plan. Where should we start?"

Vaiza looked around, and pointed at a tree with low branches heavy with fruit.

"That one," he said. "It needs its branches lightened."

Off-Grid
Ribbon Dance Village

. . . .

THE VILLAGE SQUARE WAS FULL OF CHILDREN.

Well, no, Padi thought, looking around from their position by the News Tree. It only *seemed* so because the total number of children she had been accustomed to seeing in the village was two.

Now, there were at least ten, the vigorous game of tag taking place along the edges of the square making an accurate count challenging.

She did see Torin and Eet among a cluster of four, talking with some animation, while closer to the Tree was another group, composed of Arbour; Geritsi and Dosent; and three unfamiliar adults.

"Have we arrived at an inconvenient time?" Father murmured.

"I'm not certain what this gathering is," Padi admitted, "but I don't see Aunt Asta. Let me take you to her cottage; it's right across the square. We only need to be certain not to be tagged—"

"Padi!" Blays alighted on the grass beside them. "Master Trader yos'Galan—welcome!"

"Counselor essWorthi, I thank you for your welcome," Father said.

Blays tipped her head, frowning. "I don't suppose I can ask you to use my name, though I'd rather you would."

"In that case," Father said gravely, "it would be churlish to refuse."

Blays's frown cleared into a smile. "Thank you."

"Who are all these people?" Padi asked.

"Oh, this is the traveling school from Pacazahno," Blays said airily. "They've come so Torin and Vaiza can have regular classes, and the other children can learn how the Haosa live here at Ribbon Dance. They hadn't been expected quite this early. Apparently, neither teachers nor students could sleep last night, for being so excited. The wagons were already packed, so they started out as soon as the Ribbons set. Arbour said we're to wait for her in the meeting hall."

"Father has come to speak with Aunt Asta," Padi said. "As soon as I've introduced them, I'll join you."

"I'll be there," Blays promised and moved off.

Father tipped his head and watched her.

"I believe that Blays is not walking on the ground," he said, meeting Padi's eye.

She nodded.

"Blays is a Lifter."

"Ah. That, of course, explains all. Shall we?"

"Certainly. Just this way."

Padi charted a course along the edge of the crowd, angling toward Lilac Cottage.

"I have a question of protocol," Father said, as they went down the walk to the door.

"Yes?"

"How shall I address Asta vesterGranz?"

The door opened, framing Aunt Asta's comfortable figure.

"You should address me as Asta," she said, smiling. "I mean no offense, but you're clearly no nibling of mine."

"I agree, without offense," Father said, and bowed gently. "Asta, I am Shan yos'Galan, lifemate to Priscilla Mendoza. Circumstances are such that she cannot come to you herself. She has therefore sent me as her agent."

"Your arrival is timely," Aunt Asta said with a smile. "Please come in. Padi, dear—"

"I have a meeting with Arbour and Blays," Padi said, taking the hint. "Will you be at our bonding party, Aunt Asta?"

"Nothing could keep me away! Now, Shan, if you'll come with me, I have a lovely office overlooking the garden where you can be perfectly comfortable."

· · · ❈ · · ·

The beacon at Ribbon Dance was steady on the screen, and Konch could see the orderly lines of an orchard through the windscreen. He took a careful breath, glanced at the navigation screen—

"Here!" Vyr snapped.

Konch nearly jumped out of the pilot's chair.

"What?"

"Put down here!" Vyr shouted, looking ready to leap to his feet and over the side of the raft. "Now! *Right* here!"

There wasn't any reasoning with that kind of panic, Konch knew, and he wasn't about to risk a wreck.

"Right you are," he said, keeping his voice calm and even. "Going down now."

· · · ✳ · · ·

"Well!" Arbour said, coming into the room with a rather dazed smile on her face. "And they say the Haosa have energy!"

"We have tea and snacks," Padi said, beckoning Arbour to the table where she was sitting.

"Thank you!" Arbour poured from the kettle, and sat down. Padi picked up her own mug.

"Blays is on a comm call," she began—

"Which I've just finished," said that person, arriving at the table. "Arbour, some news for you."

The village administrator looked up. "If it's about the missing wagon at Wildege, I've heard it, and I'm thinking it won't be our problem for at least five more days."

"Maybe sooner than that," Blays said, looking serious. "They found the wagon outside Bodhar-on-the-River."

Arbour lifted her eyebrows. "And you're about to tell me why that doesn't solve the problem."

Padi reached for the teapot, poured and set the mug by Blays's hand.

"Well, yes. They didn't find the driver—Vyr, his name is. And, the headman of Bodhar's missing, with the village's air raft." She picked up the mug. "So, it's looking like Vyr found a faster way to travel—and, also—I'm impressed. *I* didn't know there was an air raft at Bodhar." She took a swallow of tea, and sighed. "Of course, they pretty much keep to themselves."

"Any reason to suspect Vyr's coming to Ribbon Dance?" Arbour asked.

"Kel—the elder who'd taken him in—thinks he's heading for Haven City, to reverse the Oracle's last prophecy. And Ribbon Dance is sort of in the way." She cleared her throat. "Kel says Vyr has personal knowledge of—some people—who are going to kill us all. That's a quote from Vyr, and Kel thinks it's a True Seeing."

"That's unsettling," Arbour admitted. "Still, there's nothing we can do about Vyr until we have him." She looked at Blays. "Are you worried about Bodhar's headman?"

Blays half-laughed. "Konch? No, I'm not worried about Konch. He's more than capable, that man." She glanced down at her mug, and back up with a determined smile. "So! Padi and I are hosting a double bonding party tomorrow night, and we've got guests coming out from under the Grid."

"Who and how many?"

"Members of the trade team would like to wish Tekelia and me happy," Padi said. "That will be twelve—perhaps one or two more. Here's a list." She put the paper on the table. "I left a message with Tekelia's cousin Bentamin, who may wish to come and to bring a guest. There may be more family who would like to celebrate with us; I need to speak with Tekelia."

"Majel's family would like to wish us happy," Blays said. "That's three—his heart-sister and her daughter, and his heart-father."

"So—twenty, or forty, factoring for Civilized family, and for people who might just want to dance. Plus our newly arrived teachers and students. *Quite* a party." Arbour grinned, warmed her mug from the pot, and waggled it inquiringly. Padi held out her mug, and Arbour poured.

"Ribbon Dance will be pleased to send wagons to pick up your guests at Peck's Market before Ribbon-rise," she said. "A return trip becomes slightly more complex."

She chose a cookie from the tray and nibbled it thoughtfully.

"I'll call for volunteer wagon drivers to take those who need coverage back to Peck's. The shielded apartment holds four—six, uncomfortably."

"Our guests will be arriving by hired car," Padi said. "I'll stipulate that they will wait to take guests back to the city." She pulled out a note-taker. "Who should I speak to at Peck's Market, to make sure the drivers have ample refreshments?"

"Grazum, the kitchen manager." Arbour reached for another cookie. "Happens we opened a couple cottages too many, not knowing what arrangements would be preferred by our friends from Pacazahno, so if any of your guests would care to spend the night in the village, they'll be welcome." She paused to chase her cookie with a swallow of tea. "Mind you, those spaces aren't shielded."

"I understand," Padi said, and made another note.

"So, our guests are settled," Blays said. "Now! What about refreshments?"

"Have you spoken to—"

A chime sounded from the comm-station. Arbour sighed and got up. "That's my ring," she said, and gave a rueful smile. "An administrator's always on-call."

At the comm, she pressed the receive button. "Arbour."

"Ribbon Dance, this is Konch wilBenit, out from Bodhar," a voice growled in her ear. "You got trouble walking toward your lower orchard. His name's Vyr, and he's Ribbon-kissed."

· · · ✳ · · ·

The trees were whispering to him, of fruit, of shade, of rest. Rest.

"Not yet," Vyr said to the trees. "Not until we're safe."

He hadn't heard the raft lift, but the raft was no longer his concern. The pilot was able, the Ribbons assured him of that; he'd find his way home. What was important was ahead of him. The child—the child he'd Seen. That child was ahead.

Just beyond the trees.

· · · ✳ · · ·

"There's a disturbance on the far side of the orchard, which we're investigating," Arbour said to Teacher fosAnda, who was the spokesperson for the group from Pacazahno. "Why don't we call people in for that introductory meeting we were talking about?"

fosAnda wasted no time. She lifted the whistle she wore on a chain around her neck and blew three sharp blasts.

Children, and teachers, erupted from shops and houses around the square, and headed for the schoolhouse.

"You *are* organized," Arbour said admiringly. The teacher grinned.

"Children are forces of chaos. The *only* way to win is to be organized."

"I'll remember that."

They walked across the square together, into the schoolhouse, turning left to the gather-room. fosAnda went to the front, while Arbour stayed in back.

The teacher at the head of the room turned worriedly to fosAnda. "Two missing," Arbour heard him say. "Kalibu and Vaiza."

Arbour felt a chill, and raised her voice. "Torin! Where's Vaiza?"

Torin looked around from a knot of students near the door.

"He went down to pick apricots with Kalibu. Should I call him back?"

"Yes!" Arbour said, and swallowed. "Yes," she repeated more moderately. "Please do."

Torin's face grew soft—then sharp.

"He says he can't," she said to Arbour, her clear voice carrying across the room. "He says he's sending Kalibu back, but there's a man. Vaiza says he's sick."

· · · ✳ · · ·

Something—a flicker of light? A tweak against his ear? A whisper from the ambient?—disturbed Vaiza's concentration. He paused as he was reaching for a fruit, and turned his head.

A man stood at the edge of the orchard, his hair snarled around his shoulders, and his pattern—his pattern was . . . on fire.

Vaiza took a careful breath. "Kalibu," he breathed.

"Yes?"

"You need to go back to the village right now," Vaiza said. "Tell them there's a stranger in the orchard."

"But—"

"Leave your bucket," Vaiza said softly, and then, sharply: "Run!"

Kalibu ran.

Vaiza picked his bucket up and walked down to the man standing just inside the shadow of the trees.

"Hello!" he called. "Would you like some apricots?"

· · · ✳ · · ·

This was, Vyr thought, the *correct* place. The Ribbons were so pleased—so loud, and so bright—that he could scarcely hold onto his thoughts.

But this *was* the place—and there was a child, coming toward him. That was both right and wrong. The Ribbons weren't *dis*-pleased, but he felt a certain hesitation.

Vyr swallowed. He needed to think. He needed to understand. Most of all, he needed to *move*, because if they got this far, the Haosa would strangle, wither, and die . . .

"Who are you?" he asked the child, who had stopped a few steps away, and put a bucket down by his feet.

"Vaiza xinRood," the boy said readily. "Are you all right? You look tired to me."

"There's a child in this village who can help me—help me stop them."

The boy tipped his head, blue eyes narrowed—and suddenly smiled. "Oh!" he said, brightly. "You want to see my sister!"

. . . ❉ . . .

"Father!"

Shan looked 'round as his daughter rushed into Asta vester-Granz's office.

"Your pardon, Aunt Asta. Vaiza met a stranger in the orchard, and he says—" She looked to Shan and spread her hands wide. "He says the stranger is sick."

Shan stood.

"Asta, forgive me; I am called."

"I understand. Thank you for a lovely chat—and so informative! Come back, if you can. Or! Surely we'll meet tomorrow night at the party."

"I look forward to continuing our acquaintance," Shan assured her, and turned.

"Well, Daughter?"

"I can 'port us to Vaiza," she said. "If you think you might help. Our information is that this person is 'Ribbon-kissed.'"

"That means he's lost his shields," Asta said from her chair in the window. "That's what he'll need first." She tipped her head. "If he's still there, that is. The Ribbon-kissed don't survive the ambient's full attention for—very long."

"Then there's no time to waste."

Shan extended his hand. Padi took it, feeling how warm and strong his fingers were. She centered herself, showed Vaiza's signature to the ambient—

And Vaiza was standing with his back to them, facing a man who was tall, and too thin, his hair a tangled mass, and his pattern—no pattern at all, Padi thought.

She heard Father draw a deep breath.

"Padi, please see to the child."

"Yes," she said, and moved to Vaiza as Father walked forward.

"Is that your sister?" the man asked, his voice as snarled as his hair.

Vaiza didn't turn his head. "No, that's Trader Padi and some-body I don't know."

"Hello, Vaiza," Padi said, stopping behind him and putting her hands on his shoulders. "I brought my father to meet you. Father, this is Vaiza xinRood."

Vaiza moved his head slightly. "Hello, sir."

"Hello, Vaiza," Shan said gently. He continued forward, put-ting himself between the child and the man with no pattern.

"Good day to you, friend," he said, and Padi felt waves of comfort crashing out from him—an ocean of comfort that scarcely touched the conflagration that was the man's pattern. "My name is Shan, and I am a Healer. I offer service."

"A Healer." The man took a ragged breath. "My shields are broken, Healer."

"I See that," Father said calmly. "Would you like to have them back?"

The man stared at him. "Can you do that?"

"I can help you build a shelter," Father said. "It will not be proper shielding, but it ought to last until we can get you to Civilization." He paused, and Padi got the sense that he was Looking very closely. "You *are* Civilized?"

"Not any more, I think," the man said, and swallowed hard. "I have to see the child. *The child* is the key." He leaned forward slightly. "They're going to kill us, Healer; the Haosa will strangle; Civilization will burn. I have to stop them."

"But you cannot stop them in your present state. I offer relief and repair, that you may grasp your necessity. Do you accept?"

Hope flared among the flames dancing inside the man's pattern. "*Yes.*"

"Thank you. What is your name?"

"Vyr."

"Very well, Vyr. As I said, my name is Shan. I am going to take us both into a safe space, so that Healing may begin. This should neither hurt you nor harm you."

Padi bent to put her arms around Vaiza.

She Felt Father step into Healspace, and the sharp tug as he pulled Vyr to him there.

"We're going to the village now, Vaiza," she whispered in his ear, and showed the ambient the News Tree.

On-Grid
The Sakuriji

. . . .

FOLLOWING THE TALK WITH AZIEEM; A BRIEF, ENLIGHTENING visit with the Chief Clerk; and a promise wrung from the support office that a screen would be delivered to Hanilure Three, connected and ready for Councilor vesterGranz's use that very morning, Tekelia had entered the council chamber feeling not only competent, but master of their fate, a delusion the subsequent council meeting quickly put to rest.

By the end of the session, Tekelia's head ached, and they departed the chamber possessed of a profound gratitude that there was no afternoon session. The various analyses of the Tree-and-Dragon proposal were promised for later in the day, but those files could be—in fact, *would be*—accessible to Tekelia's screen at the Tree House.

"I wonder if I may ask you—for a personal favor," said Majel ziaGorn, who had left the chamber at Tekelia's side.

Tekelia looked up, startled.

"Your pardon, I was lost in the contemplation of my abject ignorance."

Majel grinned, his amusement a pretty dance of color against the sullen, Grid-bound ambient. "We've all done that exercise."

"I suppose you have. Does it get better?"

"Yes and no. You'll become familiar with procedures, and people, and issues. But there will always be new people and new issues." Another grin. "I've resigned myself to an ongoing cycle of ignorance and discovery, leavened by brief moments of competence."

Tekelia laughed. "If that's what it means to be a councilor, I'm well on the road! But—you wanted to ask me a personal question. How may I assist?"

Majel looked aside, then raised his eyes to meet Tekelia's. "Blays asked me to come to her at Ribbon Dance Village to help with the arrangements for tomorrow night's party. She suggested I ask you for transport, rather than calling my car." He turned his hands up. "I do *have* a car, and I don't want to put you out of your way—"

"No, it's fine," Tekelia said, smiling. "I'm looking forward to going home. I'll be pleased to take you with me."

Majel's eyes widened. "Thank you. I'm going to point out the obvious, which is that I'll also need to be brought back to the city."

"If you find yourself in need of a 'port, I'll be delighted to provide it," Tekelia assured him. "Are you ready to leave now?"

"I have a few things to check on in my office," Majel said. "May I meet you in an hour?"

"I suppose I ought to check things in my office, too," Tekelia said. "As, for instance, if my comm has been repaired, and my screen installed."

Majel laughed. "It's a good thing for a councilor to have a screen. And a working comm better yet."

"So I've been told. Where will I find you?"

"I'll come to your office."

"I'm in Hanilure Three, which I'm told is a *very* nice office. I'll look forward to hearing your opinion."

"Done," said Majel. "Until then."

He angled across the lobby, walking briskly but somehow not seeming to hurry.

Tekelia's pace was possibly more meandering than was due the dignity of a councilor. On the other hand, there was no real reason to be either brisk or councilor-like, and the walls of the Sakuriji were hung with artwork that surely deserved attention. Even at a meander, Tekelia's office was scarcely three minutes from the lobby, and it surely wouldn't take more than a heartbeat to ascertain its current condition.

Healspace

· · · · · · · · · · ·

ROSE-COLORED FOG SWIRLED HIGH AROUND HIS SHOULDERS, unusually agitated; glittering with silver, like knives.

Shan waited. Indeed, he waited so long that he began to fear the stress of being Called into Healspace had undone what was left of Vyr's soul.

Taking a deep breath, Shan began to reach—and snatched his will back as a fireball blazed toward him through the mist, screaming.

Shan flicked a finger. The pink fog thickened; silver threads flashed and spun, netting the fiery mass in ice.

Time suspended itself; the mist ceased to roil, the fireball hung within its icy net—and abruptly collapsed, opening into a tapestry rendered in ash and char, through which flames frolicked, flashing their colors.

Shan took a breath, centering himself. The mist gathered closer, warm and watchful.

"Vyr," Shan said, "attend me, please."

In the fog before him, the ruined pattern . . . shifted, the ashy lace surrounding a center as yet unbreached, giving off a strong blue glow of determination and purpose. Vyr himself was a ghost outlined in grey against the pink mists.

Shan's relief was reflected in the fog. Vyr—the core of Vyr—was still intact.

He widened his attention to the destruction surrounding that stern center. A few isolated patches of weaving held, here and there the memory of a boundary; a very few heart-links—the most recent also the broadest and brightest.

"Who is this?" he murmured, touching that broad connection.

"Kel," Vyr said. "Kelim of Wildege. She took me in, kept me safe. Helped me build a shielded space inside her domi."

"That was very good of her," Shan said gently.

"It was," Vyr cried, and Shan clearly Saw the play of truth, gratitude, and affection spangle among the wild, devouring flames.

"What happened to your shields?"

"The ambient wore them away. That's what it does. That's why the ancestors built the Grid—to stop the erosion, and to protect the vulnerable."

"And yet the Haosa's shields do not erode," Shan murmured, extending a line of comfort and clarity into Vyr's center.

"The Haosa and the ambient interact; they need each other," Vyr said. "Are my shields—?"

"I See no shields," Shan said. "Can you explain to me these— tongues of fire? Are they natural to yourself?"

"I opened myself," Vyr said. "Kel told me, 'trust the Ribbons,' and—what choice did I have? My shields were crumbling; the ambient was going to have me sooner or later. And I had nowhere to go."

"But you found somewhere to go," Shan murmured, extending a second, and a third, line. He began to weave them into one of the surviving patches of Vyr's tapestry, anchoring the resulting cord to that admirably staunch core.

"I was a coward," Vyr whispered. "I only cared that they were going to kill *me*. But they—they're going to kill everybody! The Oracle Saw it! Kel told me."

Cord woven and anchored, Shan extended a line to a lesser, but still coherent, bit of tapestry. He had scarcely connected the line when a red flame flashed across his construct like a knife, burning. Shan drew back with a hiss.

"Healer?"

"The ambient is jealous of you," Shan said. "Can you control the flames?"

"I never tried."

"Try now," Shan said.

On-Grid
The Sakuriji

. . . .

"COUNCILOR ZIAGORN!"

Majel made sure of the lock on his door, and turned to face a person who looked, vaguely, familiar.

"Natin balWerz, Councilor ziaGorn," the man said in a rush. "We started to speak about a bus route between Pacazahno and the city, but you were wanted elsewhere."

Majel held out his hands. "And you find me again in the same situation," he said. "This time, please, leave your card. My aide will call to arrange an appointment."

"Oh, that won't be necessary," balWerz said with a smile. "Because you're going to be available to me whenever I wish it."

Surely that was a joke. Majel smiled briefly, and held out a hand. "Please, your card."

"You don't need my card, do you, Majel?" balWerz murmured, and Majel was forcefully struck by the truth of that. He *didn't* need Natin balWerz's card. Of course not. Why had he—

"From now on, you'll see me whenever I wish," the other told him, and there was a fog—was there *fog* in the hallway? Majel turned his head aside, squinting—

"Look at me!"

Startled, he looked back, meeting dark eyes, and finding himself not inclined to look away.

He took a breath. There was something he had promised—yes. He was to meet Tekelia, very soon now. Majel shifted his feet, and broke the other man's gaze. "Your pardon. I have to—"

"You have to talk with me for a little longer. You don't want to make an error, do you?"

Well, no, of course not, no one wanted to make an error. But there was his promise to Tekelia, and the time, and Blays—

371

"We have to be certain you'll accept instruction," balWerz said gently. "I'll tell you that some of my associates are of a mind to simply eliminate you, but I think you're far too valuable to throw away. Do you agree?"

"Yes, of course," he murmured, but—eliminate? Why—

"These things are beyond you, Majel. I'll handle them for you. We only need to have a few minutes together, to build a rapport, so that no errors are made. If we can't come to an accommodation, there's always the road suggested by my colleagues, though that would be a shame. Don't you agree?"

Did he agree? Majel was becoming slightly muddled, and that—

"But you've had a long day, Surda. It's normal to be a little confused when you're tired. Sometimes fresh air helps clear the brain. Why don't you take me to the roof?"

Majel squinted. "The roof? Why—"

balWerz simply stood there, waiting, and the answer slipped into Majel's mind, reasonable, persuasive.

"Yes, of course. The air will be very fresh on the roof. Follow me."

This is not regular, Majel said to himself, as he led the way down the hall to the lift. He tried to stop walking, but it was as if something—as if *someone else* were in control of his surface mind and his actions, while beneath, the Majel who could think, and strategize, and plan recognized that something was badly wrong.

"Here we are," he murmured, and tried *not* to reach into his pocket for his ID card, which would call the lift.

His hand slipped into his pocket, withdrew the card, slotted it and pulled it out.

The bell dinged and the door opened.

"After you," his visitor—his *controller*—said calmly, and Majel, all unwilling, stepped into the lift.

balWerz came after him, and Majel felt a sharp pain in his head as he observed his hand rising to touch the button that would take them, express, to the roof of the Sakuriji.

This, thought Majel, is what Blays had endured, at the port.

"How do you feel, Surda ziaGorn?" Natin balWerz asked. "Tell me the truth."

"I feel that I am being manipulated," Majel heard himself say, and at that moment knew what he needed to do.

Blays! he shouted inside his head. *Blays, help me!*

Off-Grid
Ribbon Dance Village
The News Tree

. . . .

THE NEWS TREE SNAPPED INTO BEING. PADI, HER ARMS STILL around Vaiza, had the impression of a crowd, even as the ambient showed her Arbour's signature, Geritsi, Dosent, Torin, Eet, Blays, and—

"Hello, Warden Bentamin," Vaiza said. "Torin, that man says you can help him." He wriggled slightly, and Padi let him go.

"Can I?" Torin asked, matter-of-fact as always.

"If you can or if you can't," Geritsi said sternly, "you won't do *anything* until the Healer has made what repairs he may."

"Trader yos'Galan."

Bentamin chastaMeir stepped forward, a woman Padi did not know at his side. "Administrator poginGeist called me," he said. "Your Ribbon-kissed stranger is in all likelihood Vyr cadBirn, whom my associate, *Qe'andra* kelbiMyst, very much wishes to speak with." His companion stepped forward and bowed, straightening with a smile.

"Trader yos'Galan, I'm pleased to meet you. What is your impression of Vyr?"

"He's in very bad shape," Padi said frankly. "At least it seems so to me. I can tell you that my father, who is a very experienced Healer, was . . . dismayed by what he Saw." She took a breath, remembering the ruined pattern among the flickering flames.

"Vyr said he had to stop them from killing us all," Padi continued. "I don't know who *they* are, or if his insight is a True Seeing or a delusion."

"Oh, it's very likely True," *Qe'andra* kelbiMyst said brightly. "That's why I'm so particularly wishing to speak with him."

"That may have to wait," Padi said. "My father is attempting an intervention, and I feel that he shouldn't be interrupted." She blinked, having felt something—something like a *tug* at the center of her chest. "I have to—" she began, and stopped as the wind whispered inside her ear. The News Tree, and everyone around it smeared into color, and she saw, as if from a distance, Tekelia placing a hand on a comm—

The colors smeared again, and it was the News Tree she saw, and those gathered nearby, Blays at a little distance, watching as she hovered above the ground.

The tug at her heart came again, harder, waking a feeling of urgency. Padi snatched at her belt, pulled out her comm and threw it.

"Blays!" she shouted.

She showed her father's signature to the ambient, and was gone before Blays caught the comm.

On-Grid
The Sakuriji

· · · · · · · · · · · ·

"JUST ANOTHER MINUTE OR TWO, COUNCILOR, AND THIS'LL BE ready for you to use."

Schader, of the Sakuriji maintenance staff, had been at work beneath the comm station when Tekelia returned to Hanilure Three. She had been firm in her assurance that a full repair would be achieved in only another minute, or two—for the forty minutes that had elapsed since that return.

Tekelia had looked out the window to admire a day that was fine even in the center of the city, then turned to the desk, and the screen that had been placed in its exact center.

A tap brought up a set of instructions for connecting to the network, which Tekelia spent the next while following.

Having confirmed that connections had been made and that the council's lists recognized both fingerprint and retina, Tekelia looked at the clock over the comm.

Schader was still at work, and the hour Majel had stipulated was spent.

Tekelia was weighing whether it would be bad form to go to Majel's office, when Schader backed out from under the comm and straightened slowly to her feet.

"There you are, Councilor! One working comm unit. You just remember to tap the blue key before entering the code and you can call anybody on the planet!"

"That sounds like just what I want," Tekelia said with a smile. "Thank you for making the repair."

"Comes to that, the comm should've been inspected before the room was cleared for a new occupant. Well. Work orders get lost, sometimes."

She closed her case, and gave Tekelia a nod. "You find anything else not working, you just call, now you're able."

"I will," Tekelia assured her, and saw her out into the hall.

Closing the door, Tekelia looked again at the clock, wondering after protocol. What if someone had found Majel in his office and had business to conduct? Would he thank Tekelia or not, for interrupting? Of course a comm call was much less disruptive than the arrival of an actual agent of chaos. One could, after all, ignore a comm call.

"Still, you'd best check Schader's work," Tekelia said aloud. "Not that we think her untruthful..."

Tekelia stepped to the comm, touched the blue button, and input Padi's comm code.

Off-Grid
Ribbon Dance Village
The News Tree

. . . .

BLAYS CAUGHT THE LITTLE DEVICE BY INSTINCT.

"But, what—" she began—

Blays! Blays, help me!

Someone was hurting Majel. Terror clawed at her throat as she touched their link, gasping as she beheld his wonderful, orderly pattern awash in sticky fog.

"Well," she heard a voice she didn't recognize say, "you're full of surprises aren't you, Majel? You feel as if you're being manipulated, you say? I wouldn't have expected that. Not from a Deaf man lacking both shields and sense. Are you a fool, Surda ziaGorn?"

"No," Majel gritted out, and the other one laughed.

"You had best prove it quickly, then. Do you wish to live?"

"Yes."

"Good; we share a goal. Where were you rushing off to, when we met in the hall?"

Blays felt Majel struggle. First, he tried not to speak at all, then, as the other increased pressure, Majel changed his goal to a mere desire to be non-specific.

"A friend," he said, and Blays *felt* the effort it took him to keep control of his answer. "I was going to visit a friend."

"A pity you'll have to miss such a pleasant outing, but this is far more important. Once the conduit is built and stable, you'll be able to rest and forget all about this episode. You will simply go on exactly as you have been, until I instruct you otherwise. It wouldn't do for your colleagues to notice too particular a change, too soon. All we need do here is to establish and prove a habit of obedience. You're so wonderfully open and unprotected, that shouldn't take—"

No, Blays said urgently. *No. Majel don't listen to him. Listen to me. You can resist him.* We *can resist him.*

"What's this?" she heard the voice of Majel's tormentor say, through Majel's ears. "Are you life-bonded, Councilor?"

"What makes you ask?" Majel said, and Blays felt him twisting, striving to free himself from the other's Influence.

Blays threw her support behind that effort, grasping their link and opening her shields, stretching them wide, and wider yet, trying to enclose him—

"Enough!" snapped the Influencer. "Councilor, listen to me closely. Resistance is not in your best interest. You have a simple choice. Obey or die."

"Obey what?"

"*Obey me*," the other man said, and Blays felt as if a burning blade had been thrust into her heart.

Majel screamed, agony echoing down their link, then abruptly gone.

Blays staggered and fell, her head striking the ground with a force that sent ribbons dancing in front of her eyes. She heard Arbour yelling for Maradel, and Saw the brave indigo ribbon— their heart-link—caught up and borne away by the cold wind wailing through her heart.

In her hand, the comm chimed.

· · · ⚙ · · ·

Pink fog boiled around her, obscuring everything. Padi blew out a hard breath, and sent it swirling away, so that she Saw before her two tapestries—one ash grey and fragile, the other rich, deep—and besieged.

Again, she felt the tug at her heart, and looked down, seeing a thick silver cord stretching from the center of her chest, across the foggy distance to Father's pattern, where it became lost in the complexity there.

Padi caught her breath. Fire assailed Father's pattern, and in the rolling fog she Saw the beginning of a braid, frayed end snapping.

"Father, close your shields," she said urgently, and was abruptly at his side.

"My shields are the only thing keeping Vyr alive at the moment," Father answered, his voice perfectly calm. "In hindsight,

I shouldn't have tried to enclose him, but the flames destroyed every weaving I made, and his core can't last forever."

"It's too noisy," Padi said, abruptly understanding that particular complaint.

"Indeed. I wonder if you have insight into how I might achieve quiet. My plan is to stabilize Vyr by attaching what remains of his pattern to his core. Once that's done, I will ask you for a 'port to a . . . less lively venue. It oughtn't take but a few minutes, if the flames can be persuaded to let me work."

Padi blinked, trying to understand what she was seeing. Trying to think in terms of shelter, of quiet, of—

"Those aren't flames," she said suddenly. "They're Ribbons."

"Can you reason with them?"

"Perhaps," she said, "if we went to . . . *my* Healspace. I—" She waved her hands. "I *almost* have an idea."

"Do you know the way to your Healspace?" Father asked, even as a new wave of attacking Ribbons broke over him, met and repulsed by pink fog.

Padi drew a breath, tasting ghostly chocolate, the idea that she almost had coalescing into clarity.

"Yes," she said. "We don't have to go anywhere. It's right here."

Lavender mist rose around her, bringing her own disorderly Ribbons, which cavorted along the meeting place of pink fog and lavender, blurring the boundaries, and creating something— else—until they stood in a place that was neither her Healspace nor Father's, though it partook of both.

Her Ribbons swirled and sang, drawing those that had been attackers into a dance around her, leaving Father and Vyr in a calm space of silver-shot pink fog.

"Thank you, Padi," Father said. "Vyr—attend me."

Father was a deft weaver. Padi Watched him work with an understanding she would not have had before her lessons with Dyoli.

He very quickly had the bright and less-burned segments of Vyr's pattern woven together, like an ethereal patchwork quilt. Ribbons did continue to appear within the fogs, but Padi's sense was that they were curious, and most joined the dance around her. Even the Ribbons that had been entangled in Vyr's pattern flowed away into Padi's sphere, twisting round, and in some way melding with, her own. Padi took a deep breath, tasting lavender and ozone.

"I believe that's the extent of what I may offer, here and now," Father said. "Give me your opinion, please, Vyr."

Padi Looked and in the way of Healspace, Vyr's pattern was suddenly quite clearly before her. It was still overwhelmingly ashy, though it seemed that the patches Father had woven together were growing, even as she Watched. There was the suggestion of—not shields, she thought—but a bubble, enclosing the ragged tapestry.

"I can think," Vyr said, his voice soft with wonder. "The pull of the ambient is . . . less. How long will it hold?"

"That, I don't know," Father said. "It would be best if we could get you to a shielded place."

"Maradel's clinic is shielded," Padi said.

"Then I will ask you to take us there, if you are able, Daughter. Once arrived, we will consider our strategy, going forward."

"I need to stop them!" Vyr snapped, sounding like his former disordered self.

Padi stirred.

"The Warden was at the News Tree," she said, "with *Qe'andra* kelbiMyst. You *are* Vyr cadBirn, are you not?"

Something that was neither Ribbons nor flame flared in Vyr's pattern.

"Yes. Yes, I am."

"Then the *qe'andra* wants to help you."

"I—the child—" Vyr began, and Father moved a hand, sending pink mists swirling.

"First, the shielded space. Padi, if you would be so good?"

"Yes," Padi said. She stepped forward, her Healspace fading with the first step; Father's, with the second.

By the time she had completed her third step, they were standing at the edge of the orchard. Father extended his left hand to Vyr, who took it with some care. He smiled and extended his right hand to Padi; his fingers, she noted, were cold.

She took a breath, and showed the ambient the image of Maradel's clinic.

A breeze moved branches heavy with fruit.

The orchard was empty.

· · · ※ · · ·

Half-dazed with horror, Blays brought Padi's tiny comm up to her ear.

"Hello, Padi," said a familiar voice. "I—"

"Tekelia!" Blays cried. "Someone is Influencing Majel. They're on the Sakuriji's roof!"

. . . ☀ . . .

The pain had faded, but the sense of solidity, of balance, of *knowing* that she was there—it was gone. In its place was a cutting bitter wind, as if someone had torn a hole in his heart, and allowed despair an entry.

Majel struggled to attend what was happening. balWerz was before him, speaking, but his words were indistinct. Majel stood as if behind a window, separate from his Influencer and also from some part of himself.

He could watch, he could reason, but he could not *act against* the instructions balWerz gave him.

He therefore watched as he marched in a circle, went down on one knee, and stated, calmly, "The Deaf require assistance to navigate Civilized society. The patron system must be re-instituted."

And *that* was what balWerz intended, Majel realized. To force him to betray everything he was, everything he believed in, everything and everyone he loved.

Behind the window, he tried to touch the place where he had become accustomed—so quickly!—to find Blays waiting, but there was only emptiness and ice, and the desolate howl of the wind.

It came to him then that balWerz had killed Blays. *Through him*; through the link of joy and love and commitment they had shared, and he felt his heart seize, breath stopped—but, no. He *would not* give up. Not now. *Now*, he would free himself; stop this man, and all his like—

"Now, Majel," balWerz said, "we're going to test our connection. Do you see the edge of the roof, over there? You are going to walk toward it until I tell you to—"

The rush of displaced air rattled Majel's teeth. balWerz spun, hand going inside his vest, as Tekelia vesterGranz appeared in an eruption of soot and dust, braid flying.

In that instant, as balWerz was distracted, Majel's will returned to him. He threw himself sideways, grabbed Tekelia's wrist, and shouted, "Go!"

Everything went to silver.

Off-Grid
Ribbon Dance Village

. . . .

THE NEWS TREE SNAPPED INTO EXISTENCE.

"Blays!" Tekelia shouted. Majel shuddered, and dropped to his knees, dragging Tekelia with him.

"He killed Blays—that. Natin balWerz. He *killed Blays*!" His shoulders shook as he curled in on himself.

"What? No!"

Blays flung onto her knees beside them, a plaster across her forehead and dead leaves in her hair. She reached for Majel—and froze, staring.

Tekelia followed her gaze, seeing Majel's fingers—*feeling* them—in a grip hard enough to bruise.

"He grabbed me," Tekelia said softly, and, when Blays said nothing, added, "He does seem to be alive."

"So he does."

She leaned close, sliding an arm around Majel's shoulders, putting her hand over Majel's where he held on to Tekelia, so tight, as if to a lifeline.

"It's Blays, love," she murmured in his ear. "I'm right here. No one killed me."

"I felt—your absence," Majel whispered, still curled, as if he dared not look up to find no one there.

"The Influencer cut your link," Tekelia said. "It was, I expect, a calculated cruelty, to throw you into confusion and gain advantage. Majel, I swear to you that Blays is here, and she is holding you. She needs you to see her."

Majel raised a face wet with tears, and turned his head, eyes widening.

"Blays?" He released Tekelia, and turned sharply on his knees, pulling her to him, his hand sliding into her hair. "Did he hurt you?"

Tekelia stood and stepped away, toward a familiar shadow on the ambient—and turned to confront their cousin Bentamin.

"Warden," Tekelia said. "There is an Influencer and attempted murderer on the roof of the Sakuriji. Will you take him into custody?"

"I will—or, rather, I will bring Marlin to him, so she may have the pleasure. However, I don't know the roof of the Sakuriji," Bentamin said, looking at the woman standing at his side.

Tekelia grinned, blue eye and brown eye glinting. "Catch me."

Dust swirled.

· · · ✳ · · ·

Walls formed around them, a shelf lined with canisters took shape, slowly, a fall of sparkling mists separating them from the rest of the room.

Padi took a hard breath, feeling Father's icy hand in hers, and *pushed*.

Mist evaporated in a flare like lightning, the rest of the room suddenly more vivid than life. Table and chairs—

Padi spun, caught Father 'round the waist, and fairly threw him into one of those friendly chairs, and put her hand against his shoulder. He sagged, but sat firm, his face grey.

"I may have overstretched," he murmured, and she saw the glimmer in the ambient, recognizing it as a pilot's reviving exercise.

"There are snacks in the top cupboards," she snapped at Vyr—but Vyr was kneeling on the floor, retching.

She looked again at Father, who raised his head to meet her eyes.

"I believe I will not faint just yet," he told her, and she spun toward the cupboards—and then toward the door as it crashed open to admit Maradel and Arbour.

"Healer, I have two who have overextended themselves, and require aid," she said quickly.

Maradel charged past her, opened the cupboard, and thrust a tin into Padi's hands, as Arbour reached into the coldbox for a pitcher.

"*I* see *three* fools," Maradel snapped. "Sit *down*, Padi." She dropped to her knees next to Vyr, put a hand under his chin and raised his face.

Padi sat down, opened the tin, and put it on the table.

"Father—eat."

He reached into the tin, hand shaking, as Arbour slapped three mugs on the table, and filled each from the pitcher.

"Sweet tea. It's horrible. Drink a lot."

Padi obediently took a sip, shuddered, and had another.

"How did you know we were here?" she asked.

Arbour laughed. "Do you know how much *noise* you made? They probably heard it in Haven City." She picked up a mug and held it out until Father took it from her. "That's right. Drink all of it, sir. It truly is awful, but it's the medicine you need."

"My thanks," Father murmured. He raised the mug, drank the contents in one go, and put the mug on the table.

"You are correct," he told Arbour. "That's awful."

"I don't lie about such things," she said, lifting the pitcher. "And now you'll oblige me by having another. Padi—"

"Yes," she said. She hefted her mug, drained it, and put it down. "Another, please, bartender."

"That's the spirit."

Mugs refilled, Arbour left the table, vanishing into the back room, returning a moment later with shawls draped over her arm. She handed Padi one and draped another over Father's shoulders.

"Eat a cookie, please, sir. Better fuel is coming, but you don't want to get any lower."

"Yes," Father murmured. "Thank you for your care."

"All right, my lad," Maradel said, helping Vyr to his feet, and guiding him to the table. "Sit yourself right here, and drink this—all of it. Cookies are in the tin. Tanin will be bringing something more substantial. In the meantime—"

She turned back to the cupboards, pulled out two more tins, one full with nuts, and the other with dried apricots. Arbour shook out the last shawl and draped it over Vyr's thin shoulders.

"Eat," she said. "More importantly, drink your tea."

"Yes," Vyr said, subdued, and not at all wild.

Maradel had turned to Father. "I'd like to have a Look at you, Master Trader."

Father took a deep breath and raised his head to meet her eyes. His color was better, Padi saw with relief, though he had not yet wholly recovered his manner.

"Of course, Healer," he said quietly.

Maradel frowned. "You need to understand that I'm Haosa, sir. Civilized—"

"I am not," Shan said distinctly, "Civilized. *I am a Healer,* as you are. Please make your examination, and do whatever is needful." He smiled slightly. "For I tell you plainly, I dare not show myself to my lifemate in anything like my current condition."

Maradel grinned, and patted his shoulder.

"We'll get you back in trim," she said. "You're not the first to have overreached, nor you won't be the last. We're all the ambient's fool at one time or another. Now. Think of a white— Good. I'm going to examine you. If you find my touch uncomfortable, tell me, and I'll stop."

"Yes," Father said.

Padi drank tea, ate a handful of nuts, and looked at Vyr, who had just put his mug on the table. Arbour, standing behind his chair, poured, and turned with the pitcher to the counter. "I'll ask Tanin to hurry—" she said to the room at large.

"No need."

The door opened to admit the village baker, bearing a large hamper, which he carried to the counter, and began to unpack. He was trailed by Vaiza and Torin, each carrying a large bottle. Eet was riding Torin's shoulder, as he often did, paw gripping her hair.

"What are you doing here?" Arbour demanded, taking the bottle from Torin and putting it on the counter.

"That man said that I could help him," Torin said. She stepped aside to let Vaiza hand his bottle to Arbour.

"*That man* is Ribbon-kissed," Arbour said, and Padi Saw her impulse to protect coloring the ambient around her.

"Dyoli said that one should answer when called. Geritsi said that helping each other is how the Haosa survive."

Torin tipped her head up, meeting Arbour's eyes. "He won't hurt me. He only wants to See the tool Dyoli helped me build."

"Yes," Vyr said, turning in his chair. He held his empty hands out before him, shoulder-high. "I will submit to whatever restraints you find necessary. Only—the child—*this* child—what is your name, please?"

"Torin xinRood, sir."

Vyr's eyes widened. "Pel chastaMeir's daughter."

"Zatorvia xinRood's daughter," Torin corrected gently, "though Pel took good care of us, and we loved him."

"Yes, of course. I am sorry for your losses, and I'm ashamed for what may have been my part in them. I would make rectification. More, I would prevent other losses. I will be grateful for your help and I will stand between you and your enemies until my last breath."

Torin stared at him, and Padi felt the ambient . . . tighten, as if the child was Scanning for the truth.

"I accept your condolences and your assurances," Torin said, with a gravity well beyond her eight Standards. "My brother and Eet support me in this."

"That's fine now, sir," Maradel said into the silence that followed this. "Nothing torn, nothing broken; you're only overtired. The cure for that's almost as unpalatable as my tea—rest."

"I wonder," Father said. "If I opened my shields, and drank—"

"False comfort," Maradel said briskly. "Eat, and rest."

Father sighed.

"Eat and rest it is. My thanks, Healer."

"Maradel," she said. "Tanin's brought over some savory pies, and he'll be supplying you in just a minute. In the meantime, have some more tea."

. . . ❀ . . .

Blays and Majel sat with their backs against the News Tree, shoulder-to-shoulder and holding hands. Someone had spread blankets over them; someone else brought a hamper, and a hot-bottle. These small kindnesses performed, they were left alone.

"You should eat," Majel said.

"And so should you," Blays answered. "You pour and I'll see what's in the basket."

Wrapped plates were in the basket, each holding a slice of pie, cheese, and nuts. Blays gave Majel one, took the other for herself and settled her back more comfortably against the tree.

"So," Majel said, as he unwrapped his plate, "our link has been—cut. Does that mean—"

"It means our link has been cut," Blays said, and did *not* reach for the bright connection that had become so much a part of her, so very quickly.

Majel took a breath, put the freed wrapping into the hamper, and sat holding the plate in his hands, looking down at it as if he had never seen a slice of pie before.

"I love you, Blays essWorthi," he said so quietly that he might have been whispering inside her ear. "Your presence—the fact of your existence—completes me." He raised his face to meet her eyes, and Blays didn't need to see the reflection in the ambient to know it for truth.

"Only," he said, "there's a wind, where there had been . . . a certainty." He moved his head. "I explain it badly."

"You explain it precisely," she told him. "He cut the connection as close to you as he could—I can See the wound. That's where the wind's coming in. Eventually, it will scar over. Better—we can ask one of the Healers to close it, so you won't be bothered by the cold."

She reached out, picked a piece of cheese up from his plate and held it to his lips. "Eat."

He took the bit from her fingers, and Blays felt tenderness and warmth.

"I wonder," he said after a moment, "after your feelings. I understand that the link would have made you uncomfortable, if we were too long separated, but that isn't a factor now."

Blays swallowed pie, and turned to look at him.

"I love you, Majel ziaGorn," she said, and the ambient flared with her truth. "Our link didn't constrain me, it reinforced my desire to be with you, to share—everything that it's possible for us to share." She felt her eyes filling with tears, and glanced down to take up the slice of pie. "I regret that one aspect of our sharing has been . . . taken away. But I love you no less. My heart is—" She took a hard breath and met his eyes firmly. "My heart is *fully* engaged."

Majel said nothing for a long moment, and Blays had time to fear that she had been too bold—

Just before he leaned over to kiss her.

· · · ❄ · · ·

"I See it," Vyr said reverently. "Can you teach me to build one?"

Torin frowned, and bit into a cookie. "I think it would be better if Dyoli helped you, like she helped me. I've only done it once, and I'm not a Healer."

"It is," Father said, "rather a deceptively simple little working. If you wish to build one of your own, I also recommend that you do so under a Healer's supervision." He smiled faintly. "Notice that I am not offering to provide that supervision."

"That's very conservative of you," Padi said. The dreadful tea and the abundant food had worked their cure on her. She had folded her shawl away, and helped to serve out food to the others, including Maradel and Arbour, Tanin having returned to his bakery, with a promise to bring more food when it was needed.

"How is this," she said now, to the room at large. "I will call

Dyoli and see if she is willing to assist Vyr, and when. If she can assist soon, I will take Father to the Wayfarer, refortify myself, bring Dyoli, and refortify myself before I go to the Tree House for—"

"A nap," Maradel said forcefully.

Padi inclined her head. "You drive a hard bargain."

She turned her head, to find Father looking at her with both eyebrows well up.

"Whenever you are ready, sir," she said, humbly.

The ambient glittered with the laugh he did not allow to escape.

"Thank you, Daughter. I believe that I will be ready as soon as I've finished my tea."

"Very well, then." Padi reached for her comm, and frowned, finding it gone from its usual place.

"May I use your comm, Master Trader?" she murmured.

"Certainly, Trader, though one is compelled to ask what has happened to *your* comm."

He slipped the device from his belt and held it out. Padi leaned to take it, trying to recall when last she had—

"I gave it to Blays," she said, relieved to remember that much.

"Did you? Now, why, I wonder?"

"So do I," Padi said frankly. "Perhaps Blays will know."

· · · ❄ · · ·

Tekelia sighed as the porch overlooking the trees took shape, and collapsed into one of the chairs.

Marlin kelbiMyst had been most efficient, and Natin balWerz borne off to the Wardian with admirable dispatch. Majel would be required to present himself at the Department of Accountability and Justice, and recount the incident to a Truthseer, but that, Marlin had said airily, could wait until the morrow. There was enough in Councilor ziaGorn's preliminary complaint to justify having Luzant balWerz chat with a Truthseer.

There being nothing more to do on that front, Tekelia had 'ported home.

The breeze was cool and damp against Tekelia's face; the song of the ambient was—a little subdued, Tekelia thought, listening. A query was formed, and wafted away. Tekelia breathed in the scent of the trees, and touched Padi through their link.

Is all well?

For definitions of well, came the wry answer. *I am bringing*

*Dyoli and Mar Tyn to the News Tree in a few minutes. She's to
help Torin teach Vyr how to build the tool that lets her tolerate
the ambient.*

Who's Vyr?

I will tell you—this evening.

*Agreed. I'll meet you at the News Tree, if I may. I've yet to
see this tool of Torin's, myself.*

Until soon, Padi sent.

Smiling, Tekelia levered out of the chair and went inside.

Two of Entilly's cookies and a splash of sweet tea revived
Tekelia's flagging energies. Putting the mug in the sink, Tekelia
took a breath, eyes falling on the cookie tin. The ambient whispered; Tekelia picked the tin up and thought of the News Tree.

· · · ❊ · · ·

Backs against the warm trunk, drowsy with food and relief
from terror, Blays and Majel dozed off, his head on her shoulder.
Blays waked first, and straightened in response to a flicker in the
ambient. Her motion waked Majel, who murmured, "What is it?"

"Someone incoming, is all," Blays said. "The Tree won't let
them land on us."

"That's kind of it," Majel said seriously, and Blays laughed.

"I am not making light, Councilor ziaGorn."

"Then you're now in the position of needing to tell me how
the News Tree knows where we are, and how it imparts that
information to these people who are *incoming.*"

"Well, the ambient," Blays began—and just then came a twist
of leaves, dust, and lavender mist. It cleared rapidly, leaving behind
Padi yos'Galan, with a man and a woman Blays did not know.

"Blays!" Padi came forward, and leaned down, a frown between
her fair brows. "You've been hurt," she said, brushing her fingers
above the plaster on Blays's forehead.

"I fell," Blays answered, matter-of-fact. "Majel has been hurt
far worse. And—" Tears rose. She swallowed, and managed to
say, without *much* of a quaver, "Our link's been cut."

"Oh." Padi knelt abruptly, and caught them each by a hand.
"Oh, no! That must—" Tears gleamed in lavender eyes. She swal-
lowed and took a deep breath. "I so very much regret your pain.
But—my father says that heart-links grow back."

Blays stared at her.

"They do?"

"Yes. Absent a death, he said. And you both look very much alive to me."

"How long?" Majel demanded, his grip on her hand suddenly painful. Padi shook her head.

"How old was the link?" the woman who had come in with Padi asked.

Blays lifted her head. "A few days only."

"What Padi said is true—absent a death, heart-links grow back. In general, newer links take longer than links which are older, and more established. But they *do* grow back. Do not despair."

"Thank you, Healer," Majel said.

"Padi," Blays said. "How fares Vyr—and your father?"

"Both are stout. Father's gone back to the port. Vyr is at the clinic. Dyoli is here to teach him how to make a tool like Torin built." She glanced at Majel. "Is there any service I might offer, Councilor ziaGorn?"

"Thank you," Majel said, meaning it, "I believe I'm in hand."

"If there is anything, only call me," Padi said, and took a breath. "Blays. Did I give you my comm?"

"You did! Here!" She fished it from her pocket and held it out.

"Thank you," Padi said, taking the device and slipping it into her belt. "Do you happen to know *why* I gave it to you?"

Blays blinked. "I expect you had a Seeing," she said.

"What did I See?"

"That I don't know. I can tell you, though, that Tekelia called not many minutes after you left on Vyr's business, and I was able to send them to the roof, to assist Majel."

"To rescue Majel," he said, and leaned back as Blays rounded on him, voice hot.

"That *will do*, Majel ziaGorn! I *Felt* you fighting that man, which is more than many could have done! More—you took quick advantage the moment you were free, and removed not only yourself, but Tekelia, from danger!" She took a deep breath. "Though I confess when I saw you had such a grip on Tekelia's wrist—Didn't I tell you that Tekelia can discorporate you with a touch?"

"Only, I didn't," Tekelia said from Padi's side. "As you're aware. Hello, Padi—Dyoli—Mar Tyn."

"Tekelia." Padi smiled and straightened, turning to the others waiting behind.

"Dyoli, shall I take you to Vyr and Torin?"

"Yes, please," Dyoli said. "Mar Tyn, do you come?"

"Let me rest under the tree for a moment," Mar Tyn said. "I have something to discuss with Councilor ziaGorn."

"As you will. This shouldn't take long."

Mar Tyn laughed, and after a moment she joined him. "Yes, I know! I said that exact thing the last time! But nothing is being invented today, and we have a model to guide us."

Mar Tyn smiled. "When should I come to you?" he asked and there was a hint of levity in the question.

"In two hours," Dyoli said firmly. "And I take solemn oath that I will not snatch your hair from your head. Padi?"

"Yes. This way." She turned and Tekelia fell into step beside her.

"Hello, Healer. Do you mind if I attend you? I haven't had a chance to see this tool of Torin's."

"By all means, attend us!" Dyoli said. "I would like your opinion, in fact."

They moved off toward the clinic, and Mar Tyn looked 'round at Blays and Majel.

"May I sit with you?" he asked.

Blays considered him, Seeing the ambient dancing in delight around him, and his lacy pattern, attenuating at the edges, where it was lost amid a bright flutter of ribbons.

"Your pardon, but—are you Haosa?"

"Master pai'Fortana is a Serendipitist," Majel said.

"On my home world, I am known as a Luck," Mar Tyn added, "and unfit for polite company."

Blays laughed. "So you *are* Haosa! Sit, Cousin, and tell us the news."

Mar Tyn smiled and sat on the ground facing them, legs crossed, seeming perfectly comfortable.

"I do find that I prefer being out from under the Grid," he said softly. "The air is better here."

"I think so, too," Blays said. "Do you find the Grid itches?"

Mar Tyn tipped his head to one side.

"I wouldn't have put it so," he said thoughtfully. "Merely, I find the air stale. I think I would rather live off-Grid," he said after a moment. "Only, Dyoli and I will be managing Tree-and-Dragon's affairs at the port, and transportation is so inconvenient." He smiled slightly. "One cannot always depend on having a teleporter to hand."

"No, you can't!" Blays said with feeling.

"That problem has surely moved up in the queue," Majel said. "What with the Haosa councilor based off-Grid—as they ought to be. Things may be easier when the train line is complete, but—"

"Air raft!" Blays cried.

Majel and Mar Tyn looked at her.

"Is that a Seeing?" Majel asked.

"No. It's a remembering. Konch wilBenit at Bodhar-on-the-River has an air raft. And he's going to tell me how he managed that, for one thing—and for another, he's going to help me source more!"

· · · ❄ · · ·

Maradel was alone in the clinic's kitchen, sitting in a chair, using a small hook to make a chain from the ball of string on her lap.

"Tekelia, Padi, Dyoli," she said, without looking up. "Welcome. Vyr's asleep, and the twins were sent back to school. The teachers agree that Torin—and Eet, of course—may be released when she's needed. Is she needed?"

"Not yet," said Dyoli. "First, if you please, I would like to examine Vyr. Healer yos'Galan gave me a report of the damage and what repairs he had made. Before we call Torin from class, we should find if Vyr can support the tool."

Maradel inclined her head, eyes on her chain. "One moment, while I tie this off. Please, help yourself to refreshments." She coiled the chain around her hand and looked up.

"Are those Entilly's cookies?" she asked.

"They are," Tekelia said, putting the tin on the table.

"Can't hurt to be prepared," Maradel said, and rose, leaving her work on the table. "I'll get Vyr."

She went through a door at the back of the kitchen.

"What," Dyoli asked, "are *Entilly's cookies*?"

"Cookies made by my cousin Entilly, as Civilized a baker as you'll find," Tekelia said promptly. "She makes these for family. However, if family wishes to share..."

Tekelia opened the tin and smiled at Dyoli.

"Please, help yourself. Padi, what would you like to drink?"

"Anything but cold sweet tea."

"Good choice," Tekelia said. "I'll put on the kettle."

Colemenoport
Wayfarer

· · · · · · · · · ·

"WHAT DID ASTA VESTERGRANZ WANT TO SPEAK WITH ME ABOUT?" Priscilla asked, her voice sounding not as firm as he would like. On the other hand, Shan told himself, raising his glass, it might simply be that the speaker on this particular comm was not of the best quality.

"She wished to apologize for colluding with your Moonhawk in what was nothing more nor less than a kidnapping."

Priscilla laughed. "She can hardly be blamed for bending to the will of a goddess."

"So I told her, and she did seem to find some comfort in that. She also wished to know if she might come aboard the *Passage* as a passenger. It has, so she tells me, been her life-dream, to travel."

He paused to sip his wine, and sighed.

"We then spoke of the ship's lack of ambient conditions. I suggested that she apply to Tekelia for details."

"So, we won't be having a passenger to Tinsori Light?"

"I think not, but do you know, Priscilla? It seems to me that there might be a very good business for a small ship or six to offer tours of the local system for those interested in experiencing both ship life and travel. I believe I will mention that to Trader Namid, who has become bosom friends with the portmaster. I hope I don't bring you unhappy news."

"Not at all," Priscilla said gravely. "I'm pleased to learn that the portmaster continues a habit of forming new connections."

"Well said," Shan murmured. "Your generosity does you well, Priscilla."

There was a pause, a little longer than lag could account for, before she asked, "Is there anything else?"

"Why, yes, now that you mention it. Padi and Tekelia, with Majel ziaGorn and Blays essWorthi, will be hosting a joint gather at Ribbon Dance Village tomorrow evening, to celebrate the felicity of their bondings. I am told that it will be a party to remember."

"Has Councilor ziaGorn bonded? Please wish him and his bond-mate happy for me."

"He and Blays essWorthi have life-bonded. Blays—she asked that I call her Blays—is Haosa, and a Counselor to Chaos. She is also a Lifter, which seems to mean that her relationship with gravity is optional."

"Now, there's a Gift I would welcome," Priscilla murmured, and rather more strongly, "And is there *anything else*?"

Shan sighed. "You know very well that there is, and I state upfront that I was an idiot and only quick thinking on the part of my heir preserved my life—or at least my health. Colemeno's unfiltered ambient is a glorious thing, Priscilla, but, like all glorious things, it's dangerous to deal with."

He paused to sip wine.

"That said, I was successful in providing temporary shelter from the unfiltered ambient to one Vyr, who is now under the care of native experts, and is soon to be taught how to build a tool that will keep him safe, off-Grid."

"That sounds like it ended well for Vyr," Priscilla said dryly.

"You mustn't think that I was stinted! Distasteful and effective therapies were promptly applied, my station and my years given every respect before I was returned to the safety of the Wayfarer, which I today learned is under a somewhat lesser Grid-work than the city itself. I am now enjoying a glass of wine, and speaking with my lifemate via comm."

"A satisfactory conclusion, all around," Priscilla allowed, and he felt her laughter shiver along their heart-link.

"I would concur," Shan said, and sighed, lightly. "Now, it is my turn to come the overcareful partner. How do *you* go on, Priscilla? You seem—pulled a little thin to me."

He felt, rather than heard, her sigh.

"I'm tired, and grateful for Lina, who has of course born children, and is generous in sharing her insights. She's staying close at hand. Keriana believes that our daughter will be joining us soon, and I've given her my apology for having argued quite so strongly for being allowed to return to Colemeno with you."

"Shall I come to you?" Shan asked, beginning to do the math for the lift in his head—

"Not at all. You have commitments. You will represent both of us at the bonding party, and you must be present to receive the council's decision regarding the Hub proposal. No, Lina and I have it all arranged between us, and Keriana is, as you know, more than capable."

"Yes," Shan said. "I do know that, but, love—"

"We spoke of this," Priscilla said, sounding abruptly less tired. "Shan. We're lifemates."

"We are, yes. And you will call on me at need, for *whatever* you need. The local experts are indeed expert. I am fully restored to myself."

"I See that," she said, their bond warming with love and assurance. "I'll hold you in my heart, love. Always."

Off-Grid
Ribbon Dance Village

· · · · · · · · · · · · · · · · · · · ·

VYR WAS LOOKING CONSIDERABLY BETTER, PADI THOUGHT. HE'D had a shower, combed and tied back his hair, and was wearing a clean sweater and pants. Opening her Inner Eyes to See how he did there, she very nearly gasped. Father's repairs had not only held, new threads were growing between those he had woven into Vyr's core, widening the patches, and holding the promise of a completely restored tapestry. Where there had been ash, there was pale new color, and there was a definite, though fragile, border showing at the edge of the existing patches.

"Vyr," Maradel was saying, "here's Healer ven'Deelin to examine you."

Vyr bowed, gentle and sane. "Healer, I'm honored."

Straightening, he looked to Tekelia, who was leaning against the counter, arms folded, head tipped, face interested; one eye green and the other black.

"Chaos," said Vyr, inclining his head.

"I prefer Tekelia, which is my name. Well-met, Vyr cadBirn."

"Tekelia, then. I am honored."

"I," said Dyoli, "would like to examine Vyr in a less-populated room, if one is available, and shielded."

"You can use the recovery room," Maradel said, and pointed. "Eat one—or, better, two—of those cookies, Dyoli. You, too, Vyr."

"Good advice," Tekelia said. "I've a fresh pot of tea right here, if anyone cares to have some."

· · · ✳ · · ·

"Was Seylin angry?" Blays asked, as Majel ended the comm call.

"Say horrified—which often looks the same."

"Are you going back to the city?"

Majel sighed.

"Yes. I'll need to see at least one Civilized Healer—probably two. Seylin will insist that our Healer see me, and the rules governing the council require me to see the Sakuriji's Healer. Also, I'll need to speak with the Truthseer at the Wardian."

Blays's eyes were wide.

"So much, after—so much?"

Majel laughed softly. "I would much rather stay here, with you." She sighed, then stepped past him to the comm.

"Who are you calling?" Majel asked.

"Atsu," she said. "He'll pick us up at Peck's Market."

Majel felt tears rise.

"Us? But you dislike—"

"I dislike the Grid," Blays said. "But we've already established that you have pressing business in the city. And I'm not about to leave you alone after, after—*that*."

She punched in the code with rather more force than necessary, but her voice was quite calm when she said, "Atsu? Yes, it's Blays. Would you pick me and Principal ziaGorn up at Peck's Market?" She paused. "As quick as you safely can. If we're there before you, be sure that we'll wait." Another pause. "Thank you, Atsu."

She cut the connection, sighed, and turned to slip her hand around Majel's arm.

"Now," she said. "Let's go see who can give us a wagon ride."

· · · ❊ · · ·

Cookies dutifully eaten, Dyoli and Vyr retired to the recovery room, shutting the door behind them.

Tekelia sat next to Padi and reached into the tin for a cookie.

"I confess, I had expected a more desperate case, though he will have to build proper shields. That—bubble—"

"Was expediency," Padi said, also reaching for a cookie. "His shields were entirely missing. Father's priority was to get him under shelter, then try to repair the harm that had been done."

She paused to finish her cookie.

"The repairs not only held, but there's already new growth," she said. "Maradel will tell you what he was like when we brought him here."

"He was in bad shape," Maradel agreed. "Much better now, as Padi says, and no doubt the ambient's accelerating regrowth. He'll still need shields, and Civilization, before he comes full circle, and starts to burn up again."

"Torin's tool—"

"*Might* work," said Maradel. "Torin's tool is new, remember, and it was built special for—"

The door opened, and Torin stepped in, Eet on her shoulder. She looked around.

"Arbour said that Dyoli was here and that I could help her help Vyr."

"Dyoli's examining Vyr at the moment," Tekelia said, rising. "And if you'll allow it, Torin, I would like to examine you. I've never seen anything like this tool you've built, and I'm very curious."

"I'd like to See it, too," said Padi, "though I'll contain my curiosity if Torin would rather not have me."

"I have no objection to Padi and Tekelia Looking at my filter," Torin said to Maradel. "May I have a cookie?"

"I was just going to suggest that," said Maradel, holding out the tin. "*Don't* give Eet any."

A wistful sense of hunger wafted through the kitchen, and Tekelia laughed. Maradel rose, and came back from the counter with two pieces of fruit, which she put on the table. "Here you are, rogue."

"Look, Eet," Torin said, putting him on the table, "apricot— your favorite."

There was a moment of hesitation while the norbear apparently considered whether it would be worthwhile to refuse the fruit. Maradel tapped her finger on the table.

"Those cookies are *not* for norbears," she said firmly. "Fruit or starve."

Eet picked up the apricot. Torin reached into the tin, selected a cookie iced in yellow, and bit into it.

"This is good," she said.

"I'll tell my cousin Entilly that you approve," Tekelia promised. "Maradel, may we use the surgery?"

On-Grid
Ganelets on the Quiet

. . . .

DIMALEE BURST INTO THE ROOM, LETTING THE DOOR SLAM BEHIND him.

"Well?" he demanded. "What news?"

imbyValt, who was standing at the bar, considered him for a long moment before she raised the glass and drank off her wine. The others sat quietly in their chairs about the room.

"Were you expecting news, Luzant dimaLee?" she asked.

"Of course I was!" dimaLee said. "balWerz was to have sealed his connection with the Deaf Councilor today! I hope that I am not alone in assuming that he would be here, with our new ally, so that we may get to know each other properly, and he instructed fully in his role."

"I don't think that was ever Natin's intention," said trolBoi. "He was in favor of a quieter approach. Make sure of the councilor, then let him lie fallow for a time, so as not to raise suspicion—I believe that was his plan from the first."

"Spell it out, why not?" kirshLightir muttered, and trolBoi laughed.

"What good to be closemouthed now?" he asked.

dimaLee crossed to the bar, poured brandy, and turned to face the room.

"Is trolBoi playing the fool or is it merely kirshLightir's usual pessimism?" he asked.

imbyValt raised a shoulder, and turned back to the bar to refill her glass.

"Gentles, we are on the brink of greatness!" dimaLee said. He moved his glass in an arc, marking each one of them with a tip, brandy sloshing. "The Deaf Councilor is key to our planning.

With the Deaf properly returned to the oversight of their betters, the Grid fully sealed, and the Haosa regulated, we will stand ascendant. We are Civilization's champions, and the darlings of history."

To the right of the bar, a discreet door opened, and a woman stepped out, followed by three uniformed officers of the Forensic Service.

"I am Marlin kelbiMyst, of the Department of Accountability and Justice, *qe'andra* and agent of the Warden. You, Ivert dimaLee, are under arrest for conspiracy against Civilization, and Influence with intent to harm."

dimaLee turned to face her, insolent, and raised his glass to drink.

"What about these others?" he asked.

imbyValt laughed. "Oh, we've been under restraint for an hour," she said. "We were only waiting for you before we were transported to the Wardian. balWerz is already there."

"balWerz betrayed us?"

"Natin balWerz was apprehended earlier today after a failed attempt to Influence a Councilor," *Qe'andra* kelbiMyst said. "He is under restraint in the Wardian. Officer evoFast?"

"We have them all, *Qe'andra*."

"Well done. Let's move."

Off-Grid
Ribbon Dance Village

. . . .

"HEALER YOS'GALAN HAS PRODUCED A REMARKABLE RESULT," Dyoli said, when they met again around the kitchen table. "Vyr has demonstrated to me that he is able to make what we term 'basic tools' in this environment. I am willing to assist in an attempt to replicate the filtering system designed for Torin. I make no guarantees that it will produce the same results for Vyr."

"Understood," Vyr said. "It looks promising, this individual Grid-work. If it could be taught widely, then dimaLee's argument for sealing the Grid falls apart."

Tekelia looked at him. "*Sealing* the Grid?"

"Yes! It's dimaLee's argument that the Grid *leaks*, and the continued intrusion of the ambient is causing the fall-off in Civilized children."

"The Grid was *intended* to leak," Tekelia exclaimed. "Without some connection to the ambient, even the Civilized wither. The ancestors kept a record of the Grid's construction. Their original intention had been to create a shell—a roof—but the ambient refused to lend itself to such a working."

"And that," said Vyr, "is dismissed by current scientific thinking as allegory—or, worse, poetry."

"I have read the accounts written during the Second Wave," Tekelia said. "The description of working in collaboration with the ambient is not only precise, it agrees with my own experience.

"There's something else," Tekelia continued, rather warmly. "Torin allowed me to Look at her tool, which reacts *to the ambient*. In a low ambient condition, such as the surgery, it does very little. But once we stepped out from under, it sparked and began working with a great deal of efficiency, adjusting the flow

401

of the ambient to the exact degree that Torin finds comfortable and useful."

"Then the technique must be taught in low-Grid situations," Vyr said, moving a hand in dismissal. "Mere details. Think! If everyone could build and utilize such a tool—"

"If everyone could accommodate such a tool," Tekelia said, "then the need for the Grid is obviated; Civilization and the Haosa are exempt from the Oracle's Seeing."

"No," Padi said thoughtfully, and Tekelia looked at her in surprise.

"If no one *needs* the Grid," she continued, feeling her way, "and all interact with the ambient personally, with the degree of filtering self-adjusting, then Civilization falls and the Haosa, too, leaving only the people of Colemeno."

Tekelia blinked, the ambient alight with a potent mixture of awe and amusement.

"That would make the Oracle's last Seeing True."

Padi smiled and put her hand over Tekelia's.

"That's not a bad thing, surely? And, really, what a masterwork of divination! True on both obverse and face. Aunt Asta ought to make her bow to Civilization."

"Or the whole world bow to Aunt Asta," Tekelia said. "No Grid. It sounds so—strange."

"It sounds very good to me," Dyoli said. "Especially as Mar Tyn is tending to find being out from the Grid preferable to being under it. However! All is sky-pie, until we prove the case. I note that Torin made her tool under conditions very like these. I am willing to oversee, if Torin is willing to teach."

The adults turned to look at Torin, who was sitting in the window, with Eet on her lap, looking out over the square.

"Yes," she said. "I *said* I would help. And, if you please, I would like to help *soon* so that I can go back to school."

Tekelia laughed, and rose.

"In other words, we should stop wasting time with all this speculation when the main point is still unproven. Very good. As it happens, I'm expecting the arrival of some reports to review. I should go home and check my screen. Padi?"

"I am expecting some information regarding the route audit," she said, rising. "I'll come with you, if that will suit." She looked around the table. "Unless I am wanted here?"

Maradel turned her hands palm up, and Dyoli moved her shoulders. Torin said nothing.

"Excepting Vyr, we have all done this once," Dyoli said. "We are as experienced a crew as you will find on all of Colemeno."

"Very good," Padi said. "We will leave you to your work." She reached out and took Tekelia's hand.

Crimson and lavender mist swirled thick, and faded.

Padi and Tekelia were gone.

Off-Grid
Bodhar-on-the-River

. . . .

HE'D SEEN LIGHT FROM THE AIR, AND BROUGHT THE RAFT DOWN on the dormant field, the Ribbons dancing him to the kitchen door.

He pushed it open.

"Konch wilBenit!" Zel shouted, jumping up from the rocker, spilling embroidery silks onto the floor. "I'm going to—"

He swept forward, caught her in mid-stride, and lifted her in his arms. She grabbed fistfuls of his hair and held him still as she kissed him, relief, anger, and joy pounding down their link, mixing with his own relief and gladness—*so* glad to be home and on the ground—until he was dizzy with it all, and leaned back against the wall, letting it guide him down to the floor, Zel hanging on to his shoulders now, her face buried in the side of his neck.

"What're you going to?" he mumbled, feeling a little damp around the eyes.

"I'll think of something," she said, raising her head. She wriggled, slowly settling into his lap, and releasing the hold on his shoulders.

"You couldn't have told me what you were doing?" she demanded. "'Got something to take care of Zelly'—*really*? That's all you could say?"

"I was distracted," Konch admitted. "Had a madman to get rid of."

"And where," an unfamiliar voice asked, hard and sharp, "did you get rid of him?"

Konch looked past Zel's shoulder at the elder standing in the middle of their kitchen, white braid over one shoulder, and if not murder then at least a very strong talking-to in her eye.

He looked back at Zel.

"Who's this?"

"This is Kelim from Wildege," his wife said, without turning her head. "Kelim, this is Konch wilBenit, headman of Bodhar-on-the-River. My bond-mate."

"The man with the flying machine," said Kelim.

"Air raft," Konch corrected absently. "Madman wanted me to take him to Haven City, but he changed his mind as we were coming up on Ribbon Dance. Had me put him down there. I called ahead so the village administrator would be ready to welcome him. Figured I'd done what I could, so I came home."

"*Why* did you take him?" Kelim asked.

Konch sighed, suddenly as weary as he'd ever been in his life. Zelly patted his shoulder. "Stay there," she said, and rolled off his lap.

"Sit down, Kelim," she said as she passed the elder. "He's not going anywhere; he's gotta eat."

Konch leaned his head back against the wall and looked up into Kelim's eyes. *Rainbow eyes,* he thought drowsily, *Ribbon eyes*—and then he remembered.

"Wildege," he said.

"That's right," Kelim answered, turning a chair to face him and sitting down, all nice and civilized.

"I took him because—one—I didn't want him in the village; and—two—because he was Seeing *something*, but I'm not the one can tell you was it true or was it dreaming."

"It was true," Kelim said. "Vyr is Sighted."

"Here," Zel said, pushing a mug into Konch's hand, and putting a plateful of cookies on the floor by his knee. "Kelim?"

"Tea, thank you, Zel," the elder said.

"So, if it was a True Seeing," Konch said, after he'd gulped down half his tea, "my taking him to where he wanted to go was—not a bad thing to do."

Kelim took the mug Zel brought her with a smile and a nod.

"He was going to confront people who had already tried to kill him once," she said, and sipped her tea.

Konch ate four cookies while he thought about that.

"Are they *likely* to listen to him, at Ribbon Dance Village?" Kelim asked.

Konch sighed.

"His shields were gone, Kelim. Last I saw him, his pattern was burning up."

Silence.

Zel brought the pot over and refilled Konch's mug.

"You think he's dead," Kelim said, her voice perfectly flat.

"I do," Konch said. "We can call—"

The comm pinged from its shelf across the room. Zel went to answer it.

"Bodhar-on-the-River, Zel daiLilin, headwoman. How—yes? Yes, he is. Who are—ah. One moment, please. I'll get him to the comm."

Konch was on his feet by the time she'd hit the mute button.

"Arbour gorminAstir?" he asked, walking carefully across the kitchen.

"No," Zel said, making room for him at the comm. "Blays essWorthi, Counselor to Chaos."

Off-Grid
The Tree House

. . . .

THEY MET, BY ARRANGEMENT, ON THE PORCH, TO WATCH THE Ribbons rise and to share a glass of wine.

"The news from Dyoli is good," Padi said, after they had their first sip and were standing side-by-side at the rail. "Vyr has successfully built a filtering tool, and anchored it. He's resting now in the surgery. Maradel wants to observe him. *Qe'andra* kelbiMyst has agreed to that, as she has his list of names in hand, and also his parole."

She rocked sideways, bumping Tekelia's shoulder companionably.

"Only think if this succeeds with Vyr as well as it has with Torin! Ribbon Dance may need to found a school of advanced tool-making!"

"More changes," Tekelia said, with a large sigh.

Padi grinned. "No, my friend, that is not how you fox a dragon. You *wanted* change."

"Well, I did," Tekelia admitted. "I just hoped that someone else would do it."

Padi laughed. "Leaving you to pursue a life of idle pleasure, as you were when we met."

Tekelia grinned. "Caught! And, you know, we'll need more people at the council table, or more tables—smaller councils in charge of specific items, which will then report to an over-council."

"That's not a bad idea. You should propose it."

"Possibly. First, I mean to take advice from Councilor ziaGorn. Also, I believe there are matters in the council's queue ahead of a radical restructuring of the government."

"The Tree-and-Dragon proposal," Padi murmured.

"For one thing. Also, we need to make the port safe for Haosa.

I'm starting to get letters from our cousins who want to go back to work. I believe I will make that my first order of business, once the proposal has been dealt with. Will you accompany the master trader to hear the council's decision?"

"I think it would be fair to say that nothing could keep me away."

"Good. How goes your own business?"

"Trader Isfelm sent me *Ember's* records for review. I've done that, and spoken with her. We've arranged it that Dil Nem, Mr. dea'Gauss, and I will board for an inspection tour after the council adjourns. Assuming that everything is as represented, Dil Nem will return to Colemeno, and *Ember* will embark on its Loop, which has already been somewhat delayed by Tree-and-Dragon necessities."

"Deserting me in my time of need," Tekelia said mournfully.

"Yes, very good! You're coming into the way of it," Padi said, and leaned over to kiss Tekelia's cheek. "My work is finished for the evening," she said. "Have you more to do?"

"No, I believe I'm free for the rest of the evening. Would you like to help me prepare a meal? I think there are vegetables needing to be chopped."

Padi laughed. "Just what I was wanting to do!"

"I am remiss," Padi murmured sometime later, as they lay together under the blankets. "Thank you for not discorporating Majel ziaGorn."

Tekelia huffed, disturbing the fine hairs at her temple.

"I believe *I* am remiss in failing to thank you for whatever it was you did for us in Healspace. It was the second-most terrifying moment in my life when he threw himself against me, and grabbed my wrist." Another huff. "*Go*, indeed. More heart than wit."

"No, I won't have him abused," Padi said, shifting to fit more comfortably against Tekelia's chest. "I think he was splendid—quick-thinking *and* quick-acting." She paused before adding, very softly, "And you know—you said he thought Blays had been murdered, with himself as the means. He may not have...*minded* discorporation."

Tekelia shivered, and pulled her closer.

"There is that. How did you manage this alteration in my nature?"

"Well, I put lavender across our links, but I'm coming to think that was merely a pretty gesture."

"Which begs the question," Tekelia said.

"Not quite, no. You told me that Lina saw no Gift of destruction in you, though she found you a *life-worker.*"

"That's right."

"In addition, Priscilla would have it that the Gifts of those who share heart-links are at the very least complementary, and may in certain conditions be available to both."

"Yes. But the point she made with your father's gift to you—"

"Was a red herring!" Padi said warmly, "and I mean to take her to *severe* task for it. Really, Priscilla has been spending far too much time with Liadens!"

Tekelia laughed, and in a moment, Padi joined in.

"How long," Tekelia asked eventually, "do you think it will be before their link grows back?"

"Dyoli was of the opinion that new links take longer than old, established ones, though she was careful not to offer a specific time frame. I fear it may be a case of *vot'itzen.*"

"Which means?"

"*In good time,*" Padi said. "Only, recall that Mar Tyn was going to sit with them; he had *something to discuss* with Councilor ziaGorn."

"Do you think his Gift might have acted?"

"I think the Luck is in it," Padi murmured.

On-Grid
The Sakuriji

. . . .

THE MORNING'S COUNCIL SESSION HAD BEEN LISTED AS "INFOR-mal" and "working." That, so Tekelia was informed by Councilor ivenAlyatta, meant that there would be no press coverage, though they would of course be recorded, for the council's own archives.

The meeting itself had been lively, their focus the various analyses provided of the Tree-and-Dragon proposal by in-house experts and committees. Several of those experts had been on-hand, and Tekelia had been prepared for Councilor tryaBent to provide acrimony, or at least to quibble at every point. However, the elder councilor had been cogent and even-handed, her questions not merely intelligent, but in a few notable cases, piercing.

Majel had arrived not *quite* late, and had been greeted with exclamations and queries from their colleagues.

"That such a thing should occur in the halls of the Sakuriji!" tryaBent said. "Are you well, Councilor?"

Majel bowed. "Perfectly well, ma'am. Two Healers have said so."

"Two Healers!" ivenAlyatta had cried. "No wonder the man looks worn thin. Sit, Councilor, and—ah, youth rises."

This, as azieEm left her chair for the buffet, pouring a cup of tea and taking up a packet of iced cakes. She brought them to the table, and put them at Majel's place.

"Thank you," he murmured, and smiled. "I did miss my breakfast."

"Bad practice, missing breakfast," said targElmina. "Eat, Coun-cilor. Our newest member was just about to give an opinion on the Tree-and-Dragon proposal."

Tekelia blinked, for a moment wordless, but then recalled

that there were two matters in particular that had stood out in reading over the analysis, and tapped the screen.

Lunch had been served in chamber, and an hour or two after, Council Chair gorminAstir had asked the room at large.

"Are we all informed, Councilors?"

Ayes went 'round the table.

"And are we agreed?"

More ayes, though not, Tekelia noted, from tryaBent.

"I need a motion," the council chair said.

"I move that the working session on the Tree-and-Dragon trade proposal be closed," targElmina said promptly.

"Second," said azieEm.

"All in favor?" asked the council chair.

Every hand went up.

"The motion passes. Good day to you, Councilors."

"Will you want transport?" Tekelia asked Majel, as they left the council room.

"I have a bag," Majel said.

Tekelia laughed slightly. "Does your bag triple your mass?"

Majel laughed.

"Hardly. I only thought I should be—a little more festive this evening, so I brought a change of clothes."

"I am perfectly capable of transporting you, your bag, and myself to the Ribbon Dance," Tekelia said. "When do we leave?"

"Come with me to my office," Majel said. "I'll get my bag, and we may go."

The Summerlands

. . . .

DUSTY PINK, THE SKY, A THIN SILVER CRESCENT RIDING HIGH.
Below it, a graceful land adorned with trees, among which
rainbow-colored dragons sported.

The breeze was gentle, tasting of ozone and mint.

Priscilla smiled, pleased. One could remain content in such
a place for—an eternity. Once arrived, it seemed a shame ever
to leave.

A cloud glided across the pale, peaceful sky, briefly obscuring the moon.

It was getting late.

Priscilla sighed, and smiled, and called.

"Aramis!"

The dragons settled among the trees.

"Aramis!" Priscilla called again.

The moon's light dimmed, and shadows grew beneath the trees.

Priscilla breathed in. A shooting star traversed the sky.

"Aramis!" she called, for the third time.

For a moment, all hung suspended. Leaves rustled—wings,
too—and a high, childish voice called out in the distance.

"Coming!"

Off-Grid
The Lilac Cottage

. . . .

"LET ME KNOW WHEN YOU'RE READY," AUNT ASTA SAID, OPENING the door and waving Padi and Blays inside. "I'll go across the square with you."

"It will be very early," Padi ventured.

Asta laughed.

"At my age, arriving early means finding the best seat. Also, my love," she put out a hand and cupped Padi's cheek, "you are not accustomed to Haosa parties."

"She's right," Blays said, as the door closed. "People have already been bringing food to the meeting hall, and putting out chairs and benches. Kencia and Banedra were on their way to help Emit move his harmonium out into the square, and I *know* I heard a mandola being tuned."

She pulled her sweater over her head, and sat down on the edge of the bed to take off her boots.

"They were trying to hold class, is what Arbour told me, but the teachers gave it up as impossible, and instead teachers and students are decorating the school's gather-room, and putting out tables, for a dancer's buffet."

Padi sat down on the chair near the window.

"I had no idea we would be putting the whole village to so much—trouble," she said.

Blays laughed. "Trouble? It's never any trouble to throw a party, and a double bonding party doesn't come down the road every day!"

"No, I suppose it doesn't," Padi said ruefully, and leaned down to cope with her own boots. That done, she stood to take off her trade jacket and drape it over the back of the chair.

"I'm a little relieved, if you must know," she said, unsealing her shirt. "I was afraid I was going to be overdressed. But, if people are expecting a spectacle..."

She opened the bag she had brought with her and pulled out a whisper of creamy silk, patterned with pale swirls of lavender. The neck was round, the sleeves long, belling from elbows to fingertips.

Reaching into the bag again, she brought out a darker bundle, which unrolled into chocolate-brown leggings. One more dive into the bag produced supple leather dancing slippers.

"Oh," said Blays, in admiration. "That's going to look fabulous on you." She flashed a grin. "Which you don't need a Wild Haosa to tell you. Now, look at mine."

A sleeveless bronze tunic with a deep neckline was shaken out and laid on the bed, with black leggings and ankle-high boots.

"That's exceptionally handsome," Padi said admiringly.

"It is, isn't it?" Blays grinned. "The pair of us are going to stop them dancing."

"Is that desirable?" Padi asked, and Blays laughed.

"No, nor is it possible. Come and let me see what that looks like on you."

"Well," Blays said a little time later, as they stood together before the mirror. "Maybe they'll miss a step or two."

Padi laughed. "Your hair is already dancing."

"So's yours," Blays answered.

Padi stared at her. "Mine?"

"Look in the mirror, woman! I don't just say these things, you know."

Padi looked, and, indeed her hair, that she had let loose for the dance, was rising and falling as if moved by a sporting breeze, some tendrils flying high, while others simply waved. In comparison to Blays's hair, it could scarcely be said to float at all, except—

"I don't think it's ever done that before," she said.

"This is what comes of bonding with a Child of Chaos," Blays said. "Did no one warn you?"

"When would they have had time?" Padi asked, and suddenly spun, admiring the way her tunic flared, and her sleeves floated.

"I," she announced, "am ready to dance. I suggest we get Aunt Asta, and go to a party."

"Spoken like a true Haosa!"

· · · ✳ · · ·

"You look extremely," Tekelia said to Majel, as the councilor came out onto the porch. He was wearing a long shirt, silver embroidered on white, a short, deep blue vest, soft dark trousers that clung to his legs, and low shoes.

Majel looked conscious. "I wanted to—dress for Blays," he said. "To honor our attachment."

"I understand," Tekelia assured him. "I thought the same, with regard to Padi."

It had taken only a little thought before Tekelia had chosen a wide-sleeved lavender shirt under an embroidered black vest. The lavender flowers on the vest repeated down the side of the deep black pants. Short black boots, comfortable to dance in, completed the effect.

"Then I should say that we both look extremely," Majel said.

"Are you ready to go?" Tekelia said. "Will you have something to eat, first? Wine?"

"I'm ready," Majel said. "If you need to provide for yourself—"

"I've taken care of that. And, you know, there will be no shortage of food at the party. Dancing is vigorous work."

"I suppose it is," Majel said, and smiled suddenly.

"Shall we walk?"

"Ordinarily, I would say so, but we don't want to risk our finery. If you don't mind, I'll 'port us."

"I don't mind," Majel said, and held out his hand.

Dutiful Passage
Colemeno Orbit

. . . .

"SOON," KERIANA SAID, TURNING FROM HER READOUTS.

"I agree," said Priscilla.

"Shall I call Shan, *denubia*?" Lina asked.

"No, not yet," Priscilla said. "It's soon, not now—is that so, Keriana?"

"That's so," Keriana agreed.

Off-Grid
Ribbon Dance Village

. . . .

THEY ARRIVED AT THE NEWS TREE, AND STOOD LOOKING OVER the square.

"So soon?" Majel said, eyeing the groups of people standing about the square, talking, of course; eating; some few dancing in place.

"Haosa are never late to a party," Tekelia said. "In fact, to be sure they don't miss anything, they're often early."

"I see Blays," Majel said.

"Go, by all means," Tekelia said, smiling as the other moved off, deftly weaving through the crowd until he put his hand on Blays's shoulder, and she spun to embrace him.

"Tekelia?" Geritsi sounded tentative, and that was wrong; Geritsi was never tentative.

Tekelia turned toward her. She had on her best dancing clothes; her hair tied loosely back from her face. Dosent stood quietly at her knee.

"Geritsi," Tekelia said, with genuine pleasure. "Good meeting."

"Good meeting," she answered, and stepped forward.

"Is—they say that the ship's field has made you—safe."

"Is that what they're saying?" Tekelia said, surprised. "I don't—"

"Others are saying it's your link with Padi—Blays would have it so."

"That's truer," Tekelia said. "Apparently my bond with Padi is—evolving."

Geritsi looked at the ground for a moment, thinking, then looked up, extending a hand.

"Would you?" she faltered.

They both felt Tekelia's fear ripple against the ambient. Geritsi stepped back, hand falling, even as Tekelia stepped forward and caught it between warm palms.

"As much as any of us, I've been taught to fear my touch," Tekelia said, and leaned to look more closely into her eyes. "Geritsi, my friend, well-met."

Something bright and frantic happened in the ambient. Geritsi snatched her hand free and flung forward, her arms going around Tekelia in a tight hug, cheek against cheek.

Tekelia returned the embrace, arms around Geritsi's shoulders, feeling them shake.

"No need to cry, surely?"

"I'm not crying," she said, defiantly. "I'm—happy."

She raised a face that was just a little damp, and eyes that were alight with the ambient.

"Tekelia, my dear; I'm *so very* happy."

"As you can see," Padi's voice came from quite nearby, "Tekelia's touch is no longer dire. If it ever was, which no one ever proved *to me*."

"How would you have chosen the provee?" Kencia asked in his usual manic style. "Draw straws?"

"Dice roll," Padi said promptly, and Tekelia heard Vayeen laugh. "Spoken like a partner in chaos."

Geritsi stepped back, gently ending their embrace, and they turned to face Padi, Vayeen and Kencia.

"My turn," Kencia said, and threw himself against Tekelia's chest.

Arbour had seen the growing knot of people at the News Tree and stepped forward with Teacher fosAnda. It seemed even Haosa respected the authority of the silver whistle. A line was formed in very quick order, while Arbour established the four of them, two on each side of the path.

"People can greet Blays and Majel first, or, if they're occupied with another guest, they can cross over to speak with Tekelia and Padi," Arbour said, standing in the center of the path, with her hands on her hips, and glaring down the line of—almost—quiet Haosa. "We want to make sure that everyone has a chance to wish the new bond-mates happy. Once you've said your be-happies, there's food in the hall, in the school, and on tables in front of the bakery. I believe that there might be music, and there certainly will be dancing. Are we agreed to the order of this thing, Cousins?"

A shout went up from the line. Arbour laughed, and spun, holding her hands out to Blays and Majel.

Her grip was strong, and Majel fancied he felt a warm breeze flow over him.

"Be happy in your bonding," she said. "May your dance be long and filled with joy."

One last squeeze from strong fingers, then she had spun away, holding her hands out to Padi and Tekelia.

The Haosa, unnaturally orderly in-queue, held their collective breaths.

Tekelia reached out, and took Arbour's hand. Padi took her other hand.

The gathered Haosa sighed.

"Be happy in your bonding," Arbour said, her voice carrying over the square. "May your dance be long and joyous."

A pause, then Arbour turned away and walked up the path into the meeting hall.

There was a moment of hesitation as if the first in line was not quite sure—and was thrust ahead by the one immediately behind. "Go on, then!" and Majel recognized Yferen's voice. "We all want our turn!"

The lanky figure straightened his shoulders and walked with some dignity to Majel and Blays, while the two following went to the other side.

"Principal ziaGorn," Ander said, holding out his hand. "Be happy, sir." Belatedly, he extended his other hand. "You, too, Blays. Dance forever."

"We'll do our best," Blays told him.

"Thank you, Ander," Majel said, squeezing the boy's hand firmly. "There's food in the hall."

"Yes, sir," he said, and left them, to be immediately replaced by Yferen and Chalis.

. . . and so it went, a long line—cousins, family, outworlders—overflowing with care, and joy, and sincere wishes for their happiness. It was exhilarating and, Tekelia expected, would have been wearying had the gathering not focused the ambient, informing them all with energy.

There came at last a pause. Tekelia took a deep breath, looking across, where Dyoli and Mar Tyn were speaking with Blays and Majel.

At Tekelia's side, Padi let out an odd half-gasp, half-laugh, and stepped forward, holding out her arms.

Tekelia turned, to see Master Trader—no. To see *Padi's father*, step forward. He was wearing a dark blue shirt, with ruffles at the neck and cuffs, long, soft dark trousers, and sensible boots. Tekelia, wise now in the way of such things, glanced at his hands, but there were no rings on display, his sole ornament was a blue eardrop that matched the color of his shirt.

"Father, you look splendid!" Padi cried.

"No, surely, that's my part," her father answered, coming forward with long strides, until they were embracing, close and fond, and Tekelia could See the interplay of their patterns and Feel the strength of their bonding.

"Here." Padi's father stepped back, one arm still around her waist, an arm extended. "Tekelia."

"Sir—" Tekelia began, immediately correcting to, "Shan." And stepped into the offered embrace, joining the flow of love and strength; Feeling strands knitting their tapestries together.

"Dance well. Dance long," Shan murmured, for their ears alone. "Take care of each other."

"Yes," Padi whispered.

"Yes," Tekelia said, and the ambient flared with the force of their promises.

The line had been retired; Blays and Majel had joined Tekelia and Padi in the center of the path.

"That," said Blays, "was—"

The News Tree shouted, and they all four turned, Majel somewhat behind, as he took his cue from the others.

Bentamin chastaMeir was strolling toward them, on the arm of Marlin kelbiMyst.

"I see we're in good time," she said. "We come to wish joy to the bonded dancers."

They paused at the edge of the path, as if unsure what to do next. Tekelia stepped forward and held out a hand.

"Here's a challenge!" Bentamin said.

"Will you accept?" Tekelia asked.

"Oh, more than that!" Bentamin cried, and stepped forward into an embrace that quite took Tekelia's breath.

"I would like a turn," *Qe'andra* kelbiMyst said, after a long moment had passed, and the embrace showed no signs of weakening.

Bentamin stepped back, though he still kept a grip on Tekelia's hand. "Bonding is good for you, Cousin," he said.

"I agree," Tekelia said, extending their free hand.

"None of that, if you please!" said the *qe'andra*, stepping forward. "I want the full effect!"

Bentamin grinned, dropped Tekelia's hand, and turned to Padi, holding out both hands, which she willingly took.

Tekelia held both arms slightly to the side, and waited. Marlin kelbiMyst laughed.

"I'm to make the commitment, is that it? You're very like your cousin."

She stepped forward, delivering an embrace that was both enthusiastic and gentle.

"Warden Bentamin," Padi said, with a smile.

He laughed. "Vaiza sets the style, I see! Be happy in your dancing, Padi yos'Galan. I can't help but be pleased in the changes you've brought us."

Marlin stepped back from Tekelia, smiling, and turned.

"Now your turn, Trader yos'Galan."

"Padi, please," she said, stepping into the offered embrace. "I look forward to getting to know you better."

"And I, you!" The hug sealed that bargain, and both stepped back, smiling. Marlin turned.

"Blays, how good to see you again, and in much improved circumstances! Introduce me, please, to your bond-mate."

"Yes. Marlin, this is Majel ziaGorn, the most amazing person on all of Colemeno."

Marlin gave a shout of laughter and turned to Majel.

"I can See it in you," she said, playfully, and Majel smiled.

"I am under strict orders not to denigrate my accomplishments," he said. "So I will remain modestly silent."

Marlin laughed again, embraced him, then Blays.

Standing back, she continued to hold Blays by her shoulders.

"You must tell me what you thought of your business card."

"It's beautiful," Blays exclaimed, "though I'm afraid it's wrong. I've got a new title."

"But, this is terrible!" Marlin cried. "Counselor to Chaos was so lovely! At least tell me that you're not to become a mere administrator, or an aide."

"Nothing so Civilized, I fear. I'm now a Voice of Chaos."

There was a moment of silence as Marlin kelbiMyst tipped her face up, eyes narrowed as if she was taking counsel of the Ribbons.

"Do you know? I think I like that better. Voice of Chaos. Yes. It suits you. Do you have companions in this honor?"

"There are two more. We'll each be appointing our own counsels."

"I know exactly what to do!" Marlin said, turning as Bentamin came to her shoulder. "Bentamin, Blays has risen in responsibility. She is now a Voice of Chaos."

"Congratulations," Bentamin said solemnly.

"Thank you."

"Tomorrow, or, given the potential of this gathering—the day after—I'll send you the information for my printer, who after all, has the files, and you may order cards for yourself, your fellow Voices, and those who will be assisting you."

"And Tekelia, too," said Blays. "No one has been foolish enough to stand up as Speaker."

"Yet," Majel murmured.

Blays looked at him fondly.

"I won't wager against you," she said. "Yet, it is."

"We are keeping our principals from dinner," Bentamin said, and offered Majel a hand. "As useful as both instances have been to Civilization, I hope you'll stop putting yourself in harm's way. We need you."

Majel laughed. "You ought to speak with Seylin and harmonize on the theme."

Bentamin grinned. "I'll be pleased to do so. Marlin? Can I interest you in something to eat?"

"I'm interested," the lady said, tucking her hand around Bentamin's arm. "Blays—until soon."

Off-Grid
Between the Ribbons and the Ground
. . . .

HE RUSHED THE MAINTENANCE AND HAD THEM BACK IN THE AIR quicker than even he'd expected. At least, Konch thought, this passenger was more restful than the last. Which was good, because he'd had a tussle with Zel, who'd wanted to come, and was prepared to be stubborn about it.

Konch had to show her how the raft would take him—the pilot—Kelim—the passenger—and the tool kit, in conformed seating.

"And I won't be lashing you to a wing," he said, "so, no, Zelly, there's just no room."

She'd crossed her arms over her chest and looked as mad as fire before it melted away and she grabbed him for a hug.

"You get home again, and I'm *nailing* you to the ground," she snarled in his ear, and then pushed him away. "If you're going—go. You'll get back sooner."

"I'll call," Konch said, swinging into the pilot's slot, "when we get to Ribbon Dance."

"Thank you, Zel," Kelim said from the passenger's seat. "For everything."

Konch pressed the ignition, and pulled back on the stick.

The Ribbons were well up when they caught the beacon at Ribbon Dance, and Konch reached for the comm.

"Konch wilBenit, coming in, like we arranged," he told Arbour. "Light me the landing, Ribbon Dance."

Off-Grid
Ribbon Dance Village

. . . .

THE FOUR OF THEM WERE MET AT THE DOOR TO THE MEETING hall by Torin. She showed them to a table in the center of the room. Vaiza, and fellow students Kalibu, Razzi, and Pikka set themselves to deliver drinks and numerous plates both sweet and savory, then retired, giggling only a little, to their own table set with treats. Vaiza kept looking over his shoulder until Razzi poked him.

"They'll let us know when they need more!" she hissed, and Majel laughed, throwing up a hand.

"Indeed, we will. Thank you for your care."

Blays leaned close to him. "That was—much more effort than I had anticipated," she said, and kissed his cheek. "You were magnificent."

He laughed. "I had you as a model."

"In fact, we all did well," Padi said. "And really—what a crush!"

She looked around at three puzzled faces, and laughed. "It means—this is a highly successful party! Who knew that we had so many friends?"

"And not all of them are here," Blays said. "We'll have to have another party, once we have air service from Visalee."

"Is that going to happen soon?" Padi asked.

"Sooner than you might think," said a rough voice.

"Blays," Arbour said, quick on the heels of this, "I believe you asked Headman wilBenit to bring you some information?"

Blays stood up, and put her hand on Majel's shoulder when he would have joined her.

The man on Arbour's arm was a Haosa of middle years, worn in face and pattern. Arbour was holding him close, calm bathing the ambient around them.

"Konch, you need to eat," said Blays.

"Getting to it," he said, and reached into the pocket of his jacket. Leaning forward, he put a data-key on the table.

"Catalogs, names, and costs," he said. "A few years out of date, but it'll give you an idea of what's possible. As close as Ribbon Dance is to the city, it might be easier, and cheaper, to buy pre-mades from the Haven Sky Park. There's a piloting school there, too, so I'm told."

Blays took the key, and looked down into Majel's face. "Haven City has all that—and libraries, too?"

"It's not entirely a bad idea, the city," he said softly.

"All right," Blays said, slipping the key into a pocket. "Delivery made and received. *Eat.* Rest, if you need it; otherwise, there's dancing."

Humor glimmered through Konch wilBenit's dire pattern.

"Heard the music, coming in," he said, and executed a very credible bow in the Colemeno style. "Dance joyfully and long, bond-mates," he said. Straightening, he looked to Arbour.

"I'll have a bite now, thank you, Cousin."

"This way," Arbour said, and led him toward the buffet.

Padi looked at Tekelia, and Tekelia looked at Padi, then both looked at Blays and Majel.

"Well," Blays said, sinking back into her chair. "I guess I have some research to do—" She grinned suddenly. "And Tekelia, too."

Tekelia raised an eyebrow. "I'll have my aide look into it."

"Have you an aide?" Majel asked.

"Not yet, but I'm beginning to understand the need for *several* aides."

Majel laughed. "If you like, I'll ask *my* aide who among his colleagues he thinks is up to the challenge of a brand-new councilor."

"I like," Tekelia said. "Also, I have spoken to the chief clerk, and given them a list of my requirements."

"Does anyone want more food?" Vaiza asked. "Razzi and me can get whatever you want."

"Thank you for the offer of service," Tekelia said, looking around the table. "Are any of us in want?"

"I," Blays announced, "want to dance. Majel?"

"I want to dance *with you*," he said.

She laughed, and caught his hand, bringing him with her as she rose to her feet. "Done!"

Tekelia glanced at Padi, who was already pushing her chair back.

"I'm of Majel's mind," she said, holding down her hand. "I want to dance *with you*, Tekelia."

· · · ⁂ · · ·

"Party food," Tanin said, hefting the hampers onto the kitchen table. "From the bond-party."

"Thank you," Vyr said politely. "Maradel was called away."

"She'll be back," Tanin said comfortably. "You need anything else, you know how to call me."

He left, closing the door behind him. Vyr half-laughed. He'd given his parole to *Qe'andra* kelbiMyst and the Warden of Civilization. The door was unlocked. All that kept him here was—honor.

And, strangely, he found that honor was enough.

The repairs made by Healer Shan had saved his life. Healer Dyoli had told him that he had been very lucky indeed to have so skilled a practitioner available to do an intervention.

"Your pattern will regrow itself," she said. "Perhaps not exactly as it was, because of the influences of ambient conditions. However, you will be largely yourself. The tool is integrating well, and I think it will be of some interest to those who require a filter to function."

So, he was a test case, and doing well. He'd given his information to the Wardian, therefore accomplishing his goal. All that needed to be decided now was—what was he going to do with the rest of his life?

He thought of Kel, out in the Wild, the trees and the Ribbons for company. It had been a refuge. Could it be a life? Not with Kel, of course; he'd intruded on her solitude long enough. But—Vyr Station? Was that a future?

He heard a step on the walk—that would be Maradel, coming back from wherever she'd been called. He could See her pattern. Her pattern, and—

He leapt to his feet and flung the door open.

"Kel! What are you doing here?"

She paused to look up at him. It came to him that she was tired, but her smile was wide as ever.

"Might ask the same of you. Couldn't leave a note saying you were taking my wagon to Bodhar?"

He laughed, and caught her arm, barely registering Maradel's presence.

"Sit, sit, and tell me everything!" he said, pulling a chair out. "Tanin just brought the hampers over. Eat—and tell me *everything!*"

· · · ✳ · · ·

Padi and Tekelia paused on the edge of the square, hand-in-hand, letting Majel and Blays go ahead, watching the dancers, letting the music warm their blood.

"Well, here's one pair!" Kencia called out, his voice overriding the music. Dancers stopped where they were, looking about.

"Where's the other two?" Kencia called then. "Surely, they can show us how to dance!"

Tekelia sighed. Padi laughed.

"Shall we ignore him?" she asked.

"Ignoring Kencia only makes him worse," Tekelia said. "Best we accept the challenge."

Hand-in-hand, they walked forward, and those who had been dancing moved aside to let them pass, until they came to the center of the square, where Blays and Majel stood together, four feet firm on the ground and her hair swirling like storm-clouds.

"At last, the laggards arrive!" Kencia called, and stepped back to the edge of the square. "Musicians! To your duty!"

There was a long moment in which the only movement was the Ribbons, dancing overhead; the only sound that of breathing, and the sweet singing of the ambient.

Across the square, Padi saw Father, standing a little apart from the other guests, his pattern alight with pride, and love, and, a little, sadness.

There came three soft notes from the mandola; the timpani rolling beneath like thunder. A tintringo shivered delicately.

Blays and Majel began to sway, their patterns brilliant shadows against the ambient.

Padi drew a breath.

"Are *we* that bright?" she whispered.

"Open your eyes and Look," Tekelia said, and heard her gasp as she beheld the tapestry of *them* against the ambient.

"We're beautiful," Padi said.

"Yes," Tekelia answered.

The harmonium spoke.

"*Now*," Tekelia said.

They stepped into the music, and began to dance.

· · · ✳ · · ·

Slowly, others joined the dancing, though the center remained theirs. The music swelled, growing gay, and, perhaps, a little, wild.

"Blays," Majel murmured in her ear.

"Yes?"

"Can you dance—and fly?"

She laughed.

"Of course I can! And what's more, so can you!"

She spun them and Majel felt the breeze as they rose, shoulder-high to Tekelia, who looked up at them and laughed.

Hoots and applause came from the other dancers and those watching. The music increased in tempo. This time it was Majel who spun them about, laughing, heart full; feeling complete, whole, and happy as he had never been—

"Yes!" Blays said, bending back to increase their spin, her hair in its own dance around her head. "Majel! Our bond! It's back!"

Off-Grid
Ribbon Dance Village

. . . .

THE MUSICIANS HAD ONE BY ONE LAID DOWN THEIR INSTRUMENTS and spread out to find something to eat, to drink, someone to talk to, or dance with. Some of the guests had gone home. Others were dancing to the music of the ambient. Still others were clearing away the empty trays, bottles, and pots.

The children from Pacazahno—and the teachers, too, had long since retired to their beds, or at least their cottages. Most of the guests from under-Grid had left for Peck's Market, where the fleet of hired cars waited to take them back to the city.

Father was still about—Padi had seen him talking with Aunt Asta and Mr. dea'Gauss.

Majel and Tekelia were by the News Tree, speaking with Bentamin and Marlin.

A sigh brought her attention to Blays at her side, and about six inches above the ground.

"Are you disappointed?" Padi asked.

"Oh, no!" Blays said, flashing a tired smile. "It was a lovely party, but now it's time to make an end. I'll be going back to Visalee."

Padi tipped her head. "The Council is meeting tomorrow."

"Well it is, and I'll be there, to see how it all comes out," Blays said. "Konch needs to rest, then the raft needs routine maintenance before it goes up again. I'll be leaving for Visalee the day after tomorrow. Amerdeen—Visalee's Administrator—she's going to be *interested* in that machine."

"Well." Padi sighed. "I will miss you."

"But you're leaving yourself, aren't you?"

"Yes, I leave to do a ship's inspection tomorrow evening."

Blays laughed. "Then it will be me, missing you!"

Padi laughed, then sobered.

"What about Majel?"

"He has his council work, and the coalition, and the casino."

"I see," Padi said slowly. "I—forgive me if I am impertinent, but—I was wondering about the state of your link."

"Oh, that!" Blays rose slightly in the still air, her expression soft and her pattern warm. "Our link is back. We noticed while we were dancing. I think it was how Majel was able to spin us so high." A quick grin. "He'll have it that I'm flying, when it's no such thing."

"I'm pleased to hear about your link," Padi said. "Truthfully, I hadn't expected so quick a regrowth."

"No, neither did Dyoli. I think Mar Tyn helped us along—not that he *did* anything. Just sat with us and—here come our bond-mates."

"Blays?" Majel said smiling up at her. "Shall I bring you something to eat?"

She bent to take his hands, and drew him up beside her. "It's a strong offer and I'm inclined to accept, but—you need to be in the city tomorrow. I therefore make a counteroffer."

"I'm listening."

She leaned close and whispered in his ear. "Let's retire to the cottage Arbour gave us to use."

"A much stronger offer," Majel said. "I agree."

He smiled down at Padi and Tekelia, happily world-bound and holding hands.

"It was a wonderful party, and twice the joy, for sharing it," he said. "Trader yos'Galan—"

"Padi."

"Padi. I look forward to renewing our acquaintance when you return from your tour. Tekelia—" The smile became wry. "I'll see you at the council table, tomorrow."

"And I'll see you," Tekelia answered, "with pleasure."

"Until then."

They left, skimming above the grass, Blays a little in the lead. Tekelia extended a hand. Padi took it and turned as the ambient whispered in her ear.

"Father," she said. "Did you have a pleasant evening?"

"It was very agreeable," he said easily, though she Felt the weariness in him.

"May I get you something to eat?" Padi asked.

"I think not. There's a car waiting for me at Peck's Market, if I might trouble either of you for a short 'port, though you're doubtless exhausted. I'm told there are wagons. If there is also a driver—"

"The two of us can 'port you to Peck's," Tekelia said. "If that's acceptable."

"I would find it a joy to be attended by kin," Father said, and the ambient rang with his truth.

"Then we'll take you as soon as you like," Padi said. "Is Mr. dea'Gauss—"

"Mr. dea'Gauss and Asta vesterGranz had some further discussions they wished to make," Father said. "I believe he will find his way back to the city tomorrow."

He held his hands out.

"Is now a convenient time, my children?"

Padi took Father's hand; Tekelia took the other.

"Peck's Market," Tekelia murmured. "Padi, please guide us."

Padi breathed in, and showed the ambient the pavilion at Peck's Market.

There was a feeling of lightness, a flash of Ribbons, dancing, and a flow of mist, sliced by the sharp edge of a dragon's wing.

The mist evaporated, and they manifested, all three, hand-in-hand; looking about them in consternation.

Above, a lambent pink sky supported a lustrous silver disk that cast their shadows far ahead across velvet grass, until they mingled with the shadows of the trees.

"This," Tekelia said, quite calmly, "is not Peck's Market."

"No," said Priscilla, from under the trees. "It's the Summerlands." She paused on the spot where moonlight met tree-shadow, and looked to the left and right. A dragon flew over her head, wings cocked, and caught an updraft toward the high-hanging moon.

"At least," Priscilla said ruefully, "it *ought* to be the Summerlands, though I don't recall any songs praising the dragons found there."

"That might, after all, be my input," Father said, slipping his hands free from Padi's grip and Tekelia's. "To *our* Summerland."

"Of course," Priscilla said and smiled.

"I'm glad you came—Padi and Tekelia, too! It will be very soon, now."

"What is happening?" Tekelia asked, of the sky, or the meadow, or perhaps the dragons.

"I believe my sister is about to be born," Padi said, "and Priscilla Called Father to support her."

"He answered the call, while he was linked to you. A happy accident." Priscilla stretched out a hand.

"Shan, I need you."

"I'm here, love." He took her hand, joining her at the meeting of silver and shadow.

Padi slipped her hand into Tekelia's.

"Is there anything required of us?" she asked. Priscilla shook her head.

"Witness, welcome, and share."

Leaves rustled as dragons slid from the branches, winging upward into the dusky sky.

Padi followed the line of their flight, watching as they danced before the silver orb, their shadows flashing along the ground.

"Now," Priscilla breathed, and Father called out, "Aramis! Come to us, child; we want you."

Nothing happened. Shadow-dragons flickered over the grass. Padi's chest grew tight, and she squeezed Tekelia's hand.

"Aramis!" Priscilla called, her voice strong and steady. "Moon's child! We want you. Come to us."

There was a faint rustle from the shadowy forest; Padi saw the bright gleam of eyes; heard the rustle of wings. And yet, no child appeared.

Mischief already, she sent to Tekelia. *A true child of the house. What will you do?*

I believe in such cases that I am permitted to come the elder sibling.

"Truly, sister?" she said, loudly enough to pierce the shadows. "Will you play foolish games when adventure awaits?"

There was a snap, as if of a branch breaking. A dragon burst from the highest boughs, flying for the moon. At the apex of its climb, it folded its wings—and plummeted groundward.

Father put his arm around Priscilla's waist. Priscilla stretched her arms high.

The dragon struck—

...and melted into shadow.

Priscilla brought her arms to her breast, murmuring. Father leaned his head against hers. And from that close embrace came the sound of a baby's gurgle.

Off-Grid
Peck's Market

· · · · · · · · · · · · · ·

A SINGLE CAR STILL WAITED IN THE DRIVE. THE DRIVER HERSELF was in the parlor, watching an *empato*.

Grazum had stepped outside for a breath of air, and a look at the Ribbons dancing high and lovely over the tops of the trees. It was purest chance that he happened to look toward the pavilion and saw the silver funnel that meant a teleporter arriving. Only there was something . . . not quite right about this particular funnel. For one thing, it was—unstable. And for another, it was taking too long to resolve.

Grazum dashed back into the kitchen, grabbed a plate of cookies and a hot-bottle, shouted for Cyn to bring a hamper to the hill, and set off at a dead run.

The funnel had delivered by the time he got to the pavilion— three people in rumpled party clothes. Grazum recognized Tekelia from Ribbon Dance, and the master trader from the media news. It took him a little longer to recognize the other trader, with her hair loose and swirling around her head.

"Here you are, now," he said, putting his burdens on the table. "Sweet things and wake-up. Got a hamper coming, but I thought—"

"Thank you," Tekelia said, reaching for the hot-bottle. Grazum pulled collapsible cups from his apron pocket, and snapped them into shape. Tekelia poured and pressed the first cup on the master trader.

"Shan. Drink. It's wake-up, and it'll hit like a landslide, but there are cookies right here, and better on the way."

They had each accounted for two cups of wake-up and several cookies by the time Cyn arrived with the hamper, the driver with her, carrying more bottles.

433

"Master Trader!" she said, and Grazum heard something a little more chilling than worry in her voice. "Trader—what happened?"

"Tima." The trader put her hand on the driver's arm. "We're all well. Really. Only, it was a fine party, and we just now learned that a new yos'Galan has been born."

The tension went out of the driver's shoulders.

"Oh—*oh*! That's good, then. But—"

"Tima," the master trader said, gently. "All's well. As Padi says, it was a *very* fine party. It's been a long time since I danced night into morning. We'll just have some of this delicious food provided by—" He looked around, and Grazum ducked his head.

"Grazum, sir. Kitchen manager here at the market."

"Grazum. Thank you for your care."

"No trouble at all, sir. Nobody wants an incident."

"Indeed not."

"Is there anything else we can bring you?"

The master trader glanced to Tekelia, who raised a hand with a smile.

"We're well supplied, thank you. We'll bring the leftovers in, after we see the master trader into his car."

Grazum bustled off, his helper following. Tekelia found another cup in the hamper and poured for Tima out of the hot-bottle.

"I'm going to miss this stuff," Tima said, taking the cup with a smile.

"Maybe we can arrange a trade," Tekelia said, and Padi gave a shout of laughter.

"You're learning far too quickly for my peace of mind," she said.

"Oughtn't I forward the family business?"

"Isn't it enough work, changing the world?" Padi retorted, looking into the hamper.

"Never has it been said that there's too little work to be done," the master trader murmured. "All that's needed is to pick the tasks at which you excel, and do them to the best of your ability."

"Here," Padi said, putting a plate down. "Father—eat the pie, then we'll make you up a plate to have in the car. Unless you'd like to stay here tonight."

"I would like to return to the city," he said. "Tima, you will please eat, too."

"Just finished a good bowl of stew and some cheese bread not half-an-hour past," she told him. "I'm ready to drive when the trader clears you to go."

She glanced at Padi and apparently saw something there that she did not care to engage. Throwing back the rest of her drink, she put the cup on the table, and turned to go down the hill.

"I'll just go get the car started," she said.

"Frightening my bodyguard, Daughter?"

"Only reminding her not to hover," Padi said, putting a plate of pie on the table in front of Tekelia.

"I will meet the master trader at the Sakuriji tomorrow," she said.

"He will be delighted to see you," Father replied, and Padi laughed.

There was a little silence while the master trader addressed his pie, and Tekelia gave Padi her own plate.

"No one wants an incident," she sighed. "Yes, I know."

The car was gone. They had taken the hamper and the bottles back to the kitchen, and stood outside under the fading Ribbons.

"Shall we go home?" Tekelia asked.

Padi smiled, and took Tekelia's hand in hers. "Yes," she said. "Let us by all means go home."

On-Grid
The Sakuriji
. . . .

IT WAS A FORMAL MEETING OF THE COUNCIL OF THE CIVILIZED.
The press gallery was filled to overflowing. The public gallery was
also crowded, and not only because the entire Tree-and-Dragon
Trade Team had come to witness the outcome of their efforts.

"Councilor ziaGorn, I was distressed to hear that you were
assaulted in our halls, and I am personally grieved that you have
been subjected to mistreatment."

"Thank you, Council Chair," Majel murmured, standing behind
his chair in the Council Chamber, waiting with the rest for the
bell that would call them into session.

"In addition to my own concern for your well-being, my
duty as chair of this body requires me to inquire into your current health and your fitness to participate in the business of the
council."

"I am pleased to report myself healthy, and competent to
address the council's business. I've been examined by my personal
Healer, and by the Healer on-staff here at the Sakuriji. Both
pronounce me fit and able."

"Very good. Thank you, Councilor. Again, please accept my
regrets. Don't hesitate to call on me if there is anything I may
do for you."

Majel bowed slightly, and Blays, watching from the gallery,
sighed.

The bell rang; the council sat, Majel's pattern shining like a
beacon.

"Shields," Blays muttered. "Before I leave this city, I am teaching that man to build shields."

"If you wish assistance, please apply to me," said Dyoli, who was sitting next to her. "There are techniques that have proven useful in teaching those without Gifts to protect their centers."

"Techniques?" Blays repeated. "Is there much call for that, on Liad?"

"On Liad," Dyoli said, "most people are what you term Deaf. People like you and I—are in the minority. In fact, I don't think I've ever met anyone like you."

Blays laughed. "You're not the first to say *that*," she said, then bit her lip as the bell rang again in the chamber below.

"Our first item of business is the proposal submitted by Tree-and-Dragon Family to create a trade hub at Colemenoport on the planet Colemeno of the Redlands System, submitted by Shan yos'Galan, Master Trader. Each council member has received a copy of this proposal for review, as well as the analyses provided by the appropriate departments and committees. In addition, Master Trader yos'Galan made a formal presentation at our session two days ago, and answered questions put by the councilors. Does anyone need more time for review?"

Silence.

"Does anyone feel that the council's diligence in this matter is in question?"

More silence.

Council Chair inclined her head.

"On behalf of the Council for Colemeno, I ask Master Trader yos'Galan and Trader yos'Galan to enter the chamber."

There was a slight stir, then Master Trader yos'Galan came to the front of the room, his white hair gleaming in the lights. Padi came after, and took a position at his left shoulder, one step to the rear. The master trader bowed.

"Councilors of Colemeno, greetings. As has been said, I had the honor of addressing you previously. For the record, I assert that I am Shan yos'Galan Clan Korval, Master of Trade, representing the Tree and Dragon Trade Family. Assisting me is Padi yos'Galan Clan Korval, Trader representing the Tree and Dragon Trade Family. We are pleased to answer any further questions the council may have regarding our proposal to establish Cole-menoport as a Tree-and-Dragon trade hub."

Blays had expected a storm of questions, but after a long silence, only grumpy Councilor tryaBent stood to be recognized by the Chair.

"So, Master Trader yos'Galan, you are going to change Colemeno beyond recognition."

The master trader smiled, perhaps a little sadly.

"Life is change, Councilor. I fancy that everyone in this room
is old enough to understand that truth. If Tree-and-Dragon with-
draws immediately, change will still find Colemeno."

"In fact," said the councilor to Majel's immediate left, "change
is advancing on many fronts, Coracta. The question before us
is—will we guide it to our advantage, or allow it to uproot and
confuse us?"

Councilor tryaBent laughed. "Correct as always, Remik," she
said. "I thank the Master Trader for his patience and good-nature,
and also for producing so comprehensive and easily digested a
proposal."

She bowed and sat.

"Councilor krogerSlyte," said the Council Chair. "In your
capacity as portmaster, is Colemenoport ready and able to meet
the requirements set out in the formal proposal?"

"Council Chair, we are more than ready; we are willing, and
able," the portmaster said fervently. "I stated this previously, but
in the interest of making the record of this historic meeting
complete, I again say that the Colemenoport administrators voted
unanimously to accept the Tree-and-Dragon proposal, and have
filed a letter of agreement contingent upon the council's decision."

"Thank you." Council Chair looked around the table.

"Is there anything else to discuss regarding this proposal?"

No one raised a hand.

"Very well. I call the question. All in favor of accepting the
Tree-and-Dragon proposal as written and reviewed, please stand."

Every councilor did so, with the sole exception of Tekelia, who
remained seated, hands folded on the table. Blays, heart-caught,
half rose out of her chair.

"What—" she began, and Dyoli whispered, "Shh..."

"Councilor vesterGranz," said Council Chair, "do you vote
against the proposal?"

"No, ma'am. I abstain. Trader yos'Galan and I are bonded,
and I am kin-by-contract to Line yos'Galan."

There was a long moment of silence, as every eye in the
chamber and the public gallery, and every camera in the press

gallery fixed on Tekelia. Majel's pattern, Blays noted, was calm, even cool. Blays breathed in that cool calmness, and relaxed.

At last from below came a rustle; a movement. Council Chair gorminAstir inclined her head.

"Appropriately done," she said. "Let the record show both the abstention and the reason." She smiled and glanced aside. "Already, things change, Coracta," she said.

"So they do," said the grumpy councilor, sounding almost affable. "So they do."

Colemenoport
Wayfarer

. . . .

HIS FINAL MEETING ON COLEMENO CONCLUDED, THOUGH NOT TO his best satisfaction, Shan went up to the roof to say his good-byes, and to drink a final glass with those who would be staying behind to make the Trade Hub a reality.

After the toasts, he moved around the little park, stopping for a moment with this one and that, at last finding his daughter, his heir, the registered lead Tree-and-Dragon trader on Colemeno, by the perfect tiny waterfall, fingers trailing in the water, contemplating the colorful fish populating the pool.

"Priscilla and I came to the conclusion that they were probably not very good to eat," he said, sitting on the ledge beside her.

She looked up with a smile. "Beside there needing to be so many to make a meal."

"Exactly. Entirely unsatisfactory. Best to have something from what the kitchen sent up."

"I'll do that, bye-and-bye," she said. "Did you speak with Lady Selph?"

"I did, and I found her adamant. Not even my most compelling arguments could move her. We left it that she will rejoin the ship and her cuddle at Tinsori Light. I think she and Jes will travel well together."

"I think so, too," Padi said, and put her hand on his sleeve. "Are you going now?"

He smiled and put his hand over hers.

"Well, do you know—I think it would be prudent. The delm does expect the master trader to pay a certain amount of attention to their specific orders.

"And I believe I ought to renew my acquaintance with Aramis, before she comes to believe me a wraith left in the Summerlands."

"*She* is going to be a handful," Padi said, forcefully. Shan laughed.

"I expect she will be. Fortunately, I have just recently completed an advanced course."

"Wretch."

"Yes, entirely. But you are going to be leaving yourself, are you not?"

"This evening. I hear from Trader Isfelm that she won't be going with you."

"It was her decision, though I confess I was glad it fell that way."

"She did say that there will be other opportunities, now that the port is open, and a delay will give her time to *come up to speed* with current trade practice."

"Wise of her." He sighed. "I *must* leave, Padi."

She leaned forward and kissed his cheek. "Go safely, Father. Give Priscilla—and Aramis!—my love."

"I will."

They rose and embraced.

"I love you, Padi yos'Galan. Until soon."

They stepped apart, and Padi looked up into his craggy, beloved face.

"Until soon, Father. I love you."

Off-Grid
The Tree House

. . . .

DAY'S END, AND PADI STOOD OVERLOOKING THE TREES, IMPRINT-
ing the scene on her memory. *Home*, she thought, and took a deep
breath of river-damp air, before she raised her face to the sky.

Above, the Ribbons danced, bright and joyous as ever, and
her heart danced with them.

Soon, it would be time to go.

"Your wine, Trader," Tekelia murmured.

She turned to take the glass.

"Thank you."

"It's my pleasure," Tekelia said, leaning beside her and looking up in turn.

"I'll miss this," Padi said softly, pressing her shoulder against
Tekelia's.

"The Ribbons?"

"Oh, certainly, the Ribbons!" she said. "And everything that
dances with and beneath them."

She turned to look into eyes that were both green in the
moment, and leaned to kiss a brown cheek.

"And you. Most of all, Tekelia."

"You'll be back," Tekelia said.

"Yes," Padi answered, and felt the ambient give weight to her
intention. "I will be back."

A · P · P · E · N · D · I · X

. . . .

Author's working notes
Abridged and (very slightly) organized
for General Consumption

. . . .

PEOPLE, PLACES, AND WEIRD WORDS

Language Note: Civilized persons are addressed as "Luzant" as in "Luzant carnYllum"; Deaf persons are addressed as "Surda" as in "Surda ziaGorn"; Wild Talents are addressed as "Haosa" as in "Haosa vesterGranz."

. . . .

PEOPLE

. . . .

On-Grid Characters

Talents are recorded, where known

CIVILIZATION

Arranged by affiliation, if any

Cardfall Casino
    Majel ziaGorn (m)—Deaf. Principal
    Seylin atBuro (f)—Telepath. Head of Security
    Mardek gaeDona (m)—Sensitive. Bartender
    Ander makEnontre (m)—Sensitive. Security
    Nester (f)—Seylin's second
    Erbet—chef
    Beni—eldest bouncer
    Mily (f)—night manager
    Veerin (m)—floor security
    Ikat (m)—floor security
    Atsu (m)—Deaf. Majel's driver
        Other drivers: **Terah, Dan**
    Irtha (f)—main entrance security desk

The Council of the Civilized
    Zeni gorminAstir (f)—Healer. Council Chair
    Urta krogerSlyte (f)—also portmaster
    Coracta tryaBent (f)—grumpy, has a grudge against Clan Korval
    Remik ivenAlyatta (f)—the Council's archivist
    Jenfyr azieEm (f)—newest seated Councilor

Betya seelyFaire (f)—resigned in *Ribbon Dance*
targElmina
montilSin (deceased)—azieEm took their seat
Majel ziaGorn (m)—Deaf. Also Chair of the Citizens Coalition and owner of the Cardfall Casino
Bentamin chastaMeir (m)—Teleporter; strong multi-Talent. Warden of Civilization

Offices of chastaMeir and urbinGrant

Pel chastaMeir (m) (deceased)—Multi-Talent
Peesha urbinGrant (f) (overwhelmed)—Truthseer
Osha (m)—Pel's aide

The Exalted Philosophers Club

Natin balWerz (m)—Influencer
ramKushin (f)
trolBoi (m)—Jenfyr azieEm's cousin
Neesha imbyValt (f)—club leader
Ivert dimaLee (m)
Din kirshLightir (m)

Haven City School of Technology and Mechanics

xinErdin (m)—Department Chair
Vyr cadBirn (m)—Seer. Specialist in Grid Mechanics

Haven City Tattler—the city newspaper, which includes a cop log aka "Offenses Against Civilization"
Luzant pastirEbri—reporter
Luzant olCanon—photographer/video

kezlBlythe Family (also the kezlBlythe Syndicate, the kezlBlythe Association)

Zandir kezlBlythe (f)—Influencer; head of family, currently under arrest
Avryal kezlBlythe (f)—another cousin
Jorey kezlBlythe (m)—Teleporter, currently under arrest
termaVarst—the kezlBlythe Family's legal representative

Offices of maiLanst and alKemi

Binny ardMather (f)—Night Shift Supervisor
senOrth (m)—under-clerk

Riverview Guard Station

Kaedys (f)—friend of Seylin

The Sakuriji

> **Schader** (f)—maintenance staff

The Wardian

> **Bentamin chastaMeir** (m)—Warden of Civilization, strong multi-Talent
>
> **Suzee macNamara** (f)—the Warden's secretary
>
> **Marlin kelbiMyst** (f)—head *qe'andra* of the Department of Accountability and Justice
>
> **Neeoni** (f)—Marlin's 'prentice

Others

> **Entilly** (f)—cousin to Bentamin chastaMeir and Tekelia vesterGranz. Renowned for her cookies.
>
> **Nersing carnYllum** (m)—Project Manager
>
> **Torin** (f) and **Vaiza** (m) **xinRood**, maternal twins. Mother **Zatorvia xinRood** (deceased) Healer. **Pel chastaMeir** (deceased), Zatorvia's second husband, investigator.

Colemenoport Guard House

> **Timin nimOlad** (m)—port security officer
>
> **Valorian bennaFalm** (m)—chief, Colemenoport Guard House

Colemenoport Ship Yard

> **Moji tineMena** (f)—yard master

Wayfarer Inn

> **Ysbel** (f)—Nightside front desk

Others

> **Chudith Isfelm** (f)—Natural shields. Trader and principal, Isfelm Trade Union. Lead Trader on Ember, out of Dallimere. Brother, **Jamie Isfelm**.

. . . .

Off-Grid Characters

DEAF and HAOSA

Arranged by affiliation, if any

Pacazahno Village

> **Konsit joiMore** (f)—Deaf. Village Speaker
>
> **The Traveling School**—three teachers and 10 students
>
>> Teachers: **fosAnda** (f), **brokLutin** (m), **chevRotain** (m)

Students: **Razzi** (f), **Toonen** (f), **Desmet** (f), **Kalibu** (m), **Shatha** (m), **Pikka** (m), **Mel** (f), **Basiminda** (m), **Zeelix** (f), **Cary** (m)

Peck's Market

Grazum (m)—Deaf. Kitchen manager

Cyn (f)—Deaf. Kitchen staff

Ribbon Dance Village

Arbour poginGeist (f)—Healer; Telepath. Administrator of Ribbon Dance Village

Asta vesterGranz (f)—Oracle, retired

Banedra (f)—Rememberer

Blays essWorthi (f)—Lifter. Counsel to Chaos, Visalee, and Wildege; Speaker Pro Tem for the Haosa

Chalis (Challi) (f)—Psychometric

Emit torikSelter (f)—Seer

Feyance (m)—plays the mandola

Geritsi slentAlin (Ritsi) (f)—Peaceweaver; bonded with *sokyum* **Dosent** (f)

Kencia afrinBorer (m)—has an extremely chaotic talent

Maradel arnFaelir (Mari) (f)—medic and Healer

Maybri (f)—Persuader

Stiletta (m)

Tanin karPelin (m)—Ribbon Dance Village baker

Tekelia vesterGranz (nb)—Child of Chaos, teleporter. Speaker for the Haosa

Uri (m)—Persuader

Vayeen cozaLima (m)—Teleporter

Yferen (m)—Back Sighted

Ribbon Dance children fostering at The Vinery, eldest to youngest: **Manci** (f), **Gust** (m), **Spryte** (f)

Bodhar-on-the-River

Konch wilBenit (m)—Haosa. Headman; Zel's bond-mate

Zel daiLilin (Zelly) (f)—Deaf. Headwoman; Konch's bond-mate

Deen's Fallow

Firgus dinOlin (m)—Counsel to Chaos, Deen's Fallow

The Vinery

Howe cleeMunt (m)—Counsel to Chaos, The Vinery. Howe is courting **Timit**.

Visalee

Amerdeen (f)—administrator of Visalee Village
Blays essWorthi (f)—Counsel to Chaos, Visalee, and Wildege
Ryanna (f)—of Visalee

The Wild

Kelim (Kel) (f)—has an affinity for wood
Vyr (m)—Seer. Lives with Kel
Nimbel (m)—Seer. Ryanna's uncle
Somi (m)—Kel's closest neighbor

Tree-and-Dragon

(aka Clan Korval D(oing) B(usiness) A(s)
Tree-and-Dragon Trade Family)

Trade Mission

Master Trader Shan yos'Galan (m)—Healer, Padi's father
Trader Padi yos'Galan (f)—Evolving multi-talent. Only recently graduated from apprentice to full trader; Shan's heir.
Jes dea'Tolin (f)—Deaf. *Qe'andra* with a specialty in trade.
Dyoli ven'Deelin Clan Ixin (f)—Healer. Trade administrator. Til Den's sister, Namid's daughter.
Mar Tyn pai'Fortana (m)—Serendipitist. Accountant-in-training. Dyoli's partner/lover.
Dil Nem Tiazan (m)—Deaf. Former yard master at Lytaxin.
Til Den ven'Deelin (m)—Master Trader, brother to Dyoli. Silent partner in opening Colemeno as a trade hub.
Namid ven'Deelin Clan Ixin (f)—Til Den's and Dyoli's mother, also a Trader
Mr. dea'Gauss (m)—Deaf. *Qe'andra*, called out of retirement to assist in audit of trade route
Elassa dea'Fein (f)—Deaf. *Qe'andra*, bound for Tinsori Light.
Security: Grad Elbin (m), **Karna Tivit** (f), **Tima Fagen** (f)—all Deaf.

Dutiful Passage

Priscilla Delacroix y Mendoza (f)—Strong multi-Talent. Captain; Shan's lifemate.
Danae Tiazan (f)—Deaf; First Mate
Keriana (f)—Deaf; chief medic
Lina Faaldom (f)—Healer; Chief Librarian

Percy (m)—Deaf; Librarian
Kolin (m)—Deaf; Kitchen staff
Toria Valdez (f)—on officer track, replacement third mate
Aramis (f)—Shan and Pricilla's newborn daughter

NORBEARS

Eet—companion to Torin and Vaiza xinRood

Lady Selph—with the trade team

Delm Briat, Master Frodo, Tiny—on *Dutiful Passage*

. . . .

Associated but Not Present

Clan Korval (including Line yos'Phelium, and Line yos'Galan)

Val Con yos'Phelium (Uncle Val Con) (m)—lifemate to Miri

Miri Robertson Tiazan (Aunt Miri) (f)—Val Con's lifemate

Delm Korval—Val Con and Miri; the administrator/last word of law for all members of Clan Korval

Nova yos'Galan (Aunt Nova) (f)—Rememberer. Shan's sister; Padi's aunt

Pat Rin yos'Phelium/Boss Conrad (Cousin Pat Rin) (m)—Boss of Surebleak

Quin (m)—Pat Rin's heir

Anthora yos'Galan (Aunt Anthora) (f)—Healer. Shan's sister; Padi's aunt

Gordon Arbuthnot (Gordy/Poor Gordy) (m)—Deaf. Trader; Shan's foster-son; Padi's cousin

The Carresens-Denobli Family

Janifer Carresens-Denobli (m)—senior commissioner, Terran Trade Association

Reyshel Carresens (f)—second administrator at Tradedesk

Vanz Carresens-Denobli (m)—Trader, Janifer's nephew. Padi's business partner

PLACES

··

ON-GRID

Haven City
- Cardfall Casino
- Ganelets on the Quiet
- Haven City School of Technology and Mechanics
- Offices of chastaMeir and urbinGrant
- Offices of maiLanst and alKemi
- Central Haven Public Library
- Sakuriji
- Wardian

Colemenoport
- Colemenoport Guard House
- Offices of the Tree-and-Dragon Trade Mission
- Skywise Provianto, Schoodic Street
- Wayfarer Inn

OFF-GRID
(moving out from Haven City
aka nearest to furthest)

Peck's Market

Pacazahno Village
- Community Kitchen
- Guest Cottage
- School

Ribbon Dance Village
- The News Tree
- Meeting Hall
- Village Square
- Bakery

Surgery
The Rose Cottage
The Lilac Cottage
The Tree House
School

The Vinery (sometimes Terbit's Vinery)

The News Tree

Dean's Fallow

The News Tree

Bodhar-on-the-River

Visalee

The News Tree
Market Square
Way-lodge

Wildege

Kelim Station

ELSEWHERE

The Redlands System—three planets around a red dwarf

Colemeno—agriculture, commerce, and system administration
Metlin—scientific base
Ukarn—mining

Surebleak—the home port of *Dutiful Passage*

Tinsori Light—a derelict spacestation that has recently fallen into the care of Clan Korval

RANDOM WEIRD WORDS

Colemeno

    Andram—honey whiskey

    Census of Gifts—generated annually, counting Civilized Talents under the Grid, as well as Haosa and Deaf. It does not count those who live Off-Grid.

    domi—a berm house

    empato—popular dramas known for their emotional appeal, melodramatic (and unlikely) plots, and cliffhangers.

    grizurs—bear-life, native to Colemeno

    provianto—a deli and/or caterer

    sokyum—large cat, native to Colemeno

Liaden

    denubia—darling

    dramliza—singular—a Gifted individual, Liaden-style. Plural, *dramliz*

    melant'i—who one is in the present situation, this is extremely fluid, and may change within the space of a paragraph

    Parankaro Affidare—a trade contract

    qe'andra—a master of business and law

    vot'itzen—in good time

Real-Time English

    niblings—

"Nibling is a gender-neutral term used . . . as a replacement for 'niece' or 'nephew.' The word is thought to have been coined in the early 1950s, but was relatively obscure for several decades before being revived in recent years."

—Merriam-Webster

Archaic French

    tendre—A word that found its way into the authors' vocabulary via the Regency novels written by Georgette Heyer. "Fondness" would be an apt translation.

"I did once feel a tendre, but that was when I was young, and I recovered from it so quickly that I shouldn't think I was truly in love."

—Frederica, Georgette Heyer